Julie

JULIE

by
Jane Kesner Morris

McGraw-Hill Book Company, Inc.

New York   London   Toronto

For Florence and David L. Kesner

JULIE

Library of Congress Catalog Card Number: 52-6011

Printed in the United States of America

Prelude

That was always the Christmas to remember. She had been sick and she had begged and begged for Grandpa Stodel, but he lived across the Channel in Holland; and then once she opened her eyes and there he was with his brown face that looked like tobacco and smelled like tobacco and was smooth and hard with just a tiny scratchy patch near the ear. He hugged her tight and sat down with her on his lap.

"Oh, Grandpa, I like you and I love you, both," she said. That made him laugh with his wonderful yellow teeth.

"Did Saint Nicholas come, too? Did he leave toys? For me? For Fred and Ethelyn and me?"

He searched his pockets and brought out a package thin as a stick; when the paper was ripped away, there was a white fan with soft, feathery plumes on each spoke and lovely glittery bits all over. It rushed the air in waves, and she fanned violently, tickling her nose with the soft fuzz. Just then a head poked in, quick as a bird.

"Aunt Mathilda, Aunt Mathilda, see my fan!"

"So, you're awake. Well, Merry Christmas, dear." And in hopped Aunt Mathilda with her round high breast and thin feet. She brought a mug of hot buttered milk that was boiled and hateful, but the other children were drinking theirs, she said, and Julie wanted something warm in her stomach if she was to come downstairs today.

"Emma?" asked Julie skeptically.

"Yes. Emma, too."

"I like Emma." She swallowed, carefully, so as not to breathe through her nose. "I don't like the Uncle Louis cousins so much."

Aunt Mathilda chided Grandpa Stodel for laughing. The Uncle Louis cousins would not be able to come. They'd taken chills skating and were at home sick.

Julie tried to lick off the mustache of milk on her top lip. "I'm sick," she said. "Dr. Potter says I'm puny."

Grandpa tilted the mug so she'd drink more, and Aunt Mathilda brought out the hairbrush. The comb made a hard line on the top of Julie's head. Aunt Mathilda brushed one half and started braiding it into a firm plait.

"She looks like a gypsy with it curling loose. Leave it loose, Tilly." Grandpa said it, so Aunt Mathilda did. Then Beatrice brought warm water from below and there was the washing and drying with a rough towel and her pantalets and petticoats, six of those, and the red cambric dress with lace inserts. Grandpa Stodel thought the red dress splendid. He buttoned it himself and pinched her cheeks, but not hard, saying now they matched the dress, and she must wear this very gown when she came to Holland to visit him.

"When, Grandpa, when?"

"In summer," he said. She would go out to the tobacco fields with him and soak up sun till she was a gypsy through and through.

Then there was a great commotion below which meant the rest of the company had come—her papa's parents, Grand-père and Grand-mère, and the Louis. Aunt Mathilda hurried to tie the last ribbons, and Grandpa carried her because she'd been sick, down the steps into the cinnamon and raisin smells, the chocolate, the roasting meat, the blistering smell of melted cheese, the throng of people. Everyone talked at once, and thin sun fell through the fanlight over the door, laying colored triangles of light, a blaze of blue ribbons on

Grandma Stodel's breast, a patch of ruby velvet on Aunt Dee. Spots of brilliance floated like jewels or bits of water.

Grand-père's great voice and hearty laugh boomed over the rest because he was an opera singer. He and Grandpa Stodel hugged each other, everyone chattered and kissed, Aunt Dee giggled. Julie's feet felt funny and far away. Emma took her hand and they raced. Cousin Jack showed how he could stand on his head, and Freddie tripped over the ottoman and fell flat.

"I have a fan, Mama, see, from Grandpa." Her mother murmured it was lovely, did Julie feel all right? She mustn't overdo.

They were moving to the parlor now, the whole mass of them. The aunts and Grandma Stodel, even Uncle Henry and Uncle Louis were gathering around Grand-mère to see her dress, all radiant yellow velvet with tucks and folds, the skirt rounding out like a great bell. Julie touched the soft velvet in back where no one could see, except the curved mirror. The mirror saw and reflected everything only smaller and swollen at the edges. Most curious of all about the mirror was that in it everything was better than real. The yellow velvet was yellower, Grand-mère's earrings were brighter, the polished rosewood and dangling crystals, the flowers under their glass bell, the cross-stitch on the ottoman, the fluted red silk front of the piano—everything was smaller and sharper and more alive in the glass.

"Oh, and your shoes!" gasped Aunt Mathilda. Grand-mère lifted her skirt to show the little yellow velvet boots.

"Your mother is still the belle of them all," Grand-père said, speaking to Julie's papa; and Julie's papa kept his face to the fire and tossed back one word.

"—viously," he said. "Obviously."

Beatrice tried to help with the wraps, curtsied and curtsied, fumbling everything she touched, and cook's Emil had to come. Julie ran with the children, teasing, laughing. Then round chords plunged from the piano and there was Grand-père at the keys, roaring, "God rest you merry, gentlemen."

Papa grabbed her by the wrist, took Freddie and Jack each from behind, and hurried them out to the nursery. His mouth was tight together under the black mustache, and his eyes, the narrow slits that showed, were blades of anger.

"Your mother would have obliged me by leaving you upstairs," he told Julie. "This fuss will only make you sick again. As for you two, one more misdemeanor and you'll feel my strap. Obedience knows no holidays." Then he was gone. Beatrice hurried in Emma and Ethelyn while Grand-père sang like an organ and Grandpa croaked alongside.

"Now it ain't my fault," Beatrice said when they whimpered. "Just keep still if'n you know what's good for you, or there'll be no dinner with the ladies and gentlemen." But after a while Grandpa Stodel came, bringing pinafores for her and for Emma and Ethelyn, and they went to the dining room, which was so bright the sun might have been shining in. Hundreds of candles throbbed in the chandelier, candles burned in tall candelabra, their pointed flames trembled and shook, each from its small blue eye, and light spilled over the shining cloth, over the glasses and plates and silver. The crimson curtains went waving into flames. "Grandpa, listen, I can feel my heart out loud."

"Remember your manners," Mama said softly, "as it says in the children's etiquette. You must please your papa." Her hair was like palest silk under the candles. Like Emma's and Ethelyn's and. . . .

"Why can't I have yellow hair?" she asked Grandpa. "Why can't I have yellow hair like all of them?"

"But then you wouldn't be my gypsy!"

Julie wound her arms about his big arm and sat as close to him as she could. Now Aunt Anna carried in the big tureen. She wasn't really an aunt, but better. She could jump like an imp.

"Jump like an imp, Aunt Anna. Do it now!" Julie whispered as loud as she dared.

"Ain't bewitched today," Aunt Anna whispered back. "Went to church like a good Christian and just ain't be-

8

witched." She had placed the tureen on the sideboard and she stood, hanging down her crisp, gingery head, while Papa said the prayer and everyone went to sleep. Julie and Emma almost giggled. They peeked at each other and the giggle rose, but Papa said Amen just in time, the lid was off, and the clear meaty scent of soup flew into the room.

Grandpa Stodel took a first sip and said it was good, try it; but it was more fun just to fish for floating bits of custard, catch, hold them on the spoon, and then drop them back into the spicy soup, plop. It made your mouth water to smell. So did the fish with lobster sauce. There were glistening green olives Aunt Anna said she shouldn't have; Grandpa said one wouldn't hurt if she chewed. She chewed all right, and when she'd cleaned off the pit with her teeth, she eased it down under the cloth and dropped it to her friends, the cupids who lay cradled against the massive table legs. When you first came into the dining room they looked beautiful, much nicer than Freddie or the new baby, but up close, their eyes were horrible empty holes, their fingers were pounded flat against their knees, and you couldn't tell whether they were boys or girls. Their legs were crossed, and when you tried to get your fingers in between, it was so tight it pinched.

"Are they boys or girls, Grandpa? The cupids?"

"Boys." He chuckled.

"That's what Beatrice says. She says the way they're lying with nothing to do. . . ."

He balanced the heavy platter of ham and the platter of beef and gave her a little of each because Papa was looking.

"The Queen could not set a better table," Aunt Mathilda said.

"It hardly seems fair we have so much when times are bad for others." Julie didn't see who that was. Maybe Uncle Henry.

Papa held the carving knife in mid-air and every word was cold and hard as a dot. "Times are what people make them!"

"The potato famine in Ireland and the blighted harvest here, Frederic?" That was Grand-père.

"You sound like a Chartist, Father."

"Please, Mr. Corper, the fowl is getting cold," Mother said.

"Calamity plays into *our* hands this time." Papa stabbed a slice of white meat. "The Corn Laws," he said. "The Conservatives."

Grand-père's face flooded with color. He was her papa's papa but it was hard to see how. His eyes were so blue. She wished he'd tell how, when he first sang at the opera in Paris, Napoleon came to the stage and pinned on the diamond medal. Instead, Grand-père stood and raised his glass to the table. "Let us drink to the repeal of the Corn Laws." And they did—Julie, too, out of her water goblet. "Even if it's the Tories who do it."

No one breathed. Julie held Grandpa Stodel's knee under the table. "What is it, what is it about?" she asked; but it was over. Aunt Dee giggled and the first dessert came, cheese and raw celery that cracked and apples sliced in tart gravy. Up and away went the white cloth with its knobby border, leaving wine-colored damask below. It felt like satin, like a lady's dress. Aunt Anna brought on flaming pudding, and Beatrice the lemon cream. "Both of those, Grandpa, both," Julie said, and she swallowed every bit.

Oh, there never was such a Christmas. Grandpa was all hers, every minute. She sat beside him singing carols, and when her head began to ache, he carried her off to bed. He undressed her himself, which was ever so much nicer than Beatrice; and after she was curled down, he didn't leave her alone, but sat close and told her favorite story, how he had been stolen away when he was a lad, put on a ship, and sent to America to be a servant. It was hard to hear. Even knowing the story by heart, the words made funny shapes and grew as light as air.

"Grandpa, don't go. I'm not asleep. Don't go away."

"Soon you will come to be with me the whole summer. You know what we will sing? We'll sing,

Trip a trop a traunches
De varken in de braunches
De conjes in de claver
De pardens in de harver
De enjes in de water plass
So gute mein klina joris vass."

"*Trip a trop,*" she murmured. "*Trip a trop.*" She tried to hold tight to his hand; but she lost him in her sleep and never found him again. He wasn't there in Holland when she finally went. He was gone, he was in heaven, they said.

"But why did he go without me? Why? And he left his pipe!"

No one answered that. They went to the church and sat in the gloom on stiff little chairs. They smelled like black crepe, and when you looked at them they pretended not to see, sitting to fit their chairs, straight ahead and unacquainted, like people in a hack. Maybe they'd use their Mrs. names to-day. Emma sat beside Uncle Henry and stared at the floor. What was everyone waiting for? You didn't dare to talk, you scarcely dared to breathe. The mountain of flowers was overpowering, it pushed up like a giant peony, blinding white into your face. At the very front stood a black box, polished and sleek with handles of silver. The ladies sniffed at their handkerchiefs, some like Grand-mère, holding her square just so, some like Aunt Dee, sobbing and flooded with tears. The minister talked and talked and light from the candles danced in ripples on the sleek wood of the box.

Small, blue-robed Luke watched it all from his crimson window. "This is my grandpa's funeral," she told him. "I can't find my grandpa. Once when there was a war he fed the soldiers. My mother swung the lantern so they'd know to come, back and forth, like the blade of a scythe, she swung the lantern. That jolly man is my other grandfather, Grand-père, and next to him Grand-mère. She's not like us, being French. Her waist is smaller than the other ladies' and look how she bulges on top, like a pillow. She can't walk fast.

11

Little beads of water line up above her top lip like rain blisters on a window ledge. She has to wipe them all the time. Sometimes she forgets." Music groaned and rumbled, awful music that quivered in your stomach pit. Everyone stood, the music rose like thunder. Candles blurred and waddled in their holders, licking at the walls as if to melt them. Blurred too was the voice of the minister coming back from the walls indistinct and dense as tangled thread.

Out they went, away from the music, out into the warm, fresh daylight, across the churchyard, under the trees. Soft grass, darkly leaf-dappled, moved and swam. You set your feet upon a flickering, flexible wobble of light and dark. Sharp leaf forms here, uncertain slippery shapes, holes, globules of shifting light, like stepping on a moving, living thing. They stopped before a deep ditch, moist and earth smelling.

"Now," the minister droned on, "the solemn, final moment has come, my friends. We who knew and loved Heinrich Stodel bid him a last farewell, consecrate his body to its resting place, his soul to God."

The men of the family hung over the abyss, letting the black box gently down. ". . . his body to its resting place, his body to its resting place. . . ."

"Mother! Is Grandpa in that box?"

"Yes, dear."

"But heaven?"

"He's going there."

"Grandpa won't like it in that box. How can he move?"

"He's dead, Julie."

"Ashes to ashes," chanted the minister, "dust to dust." He picked up a handful of damp earth and threw it on the glossy wood. There was a hollow sound. Two men with shovels advanced, tossing down dirt.

"Don't do that! My grandpa's in that box!"

"Hush, darling." Mother took her hand. The shovels dropped pile on pile.

"He has to get to heaven!"

"The box will melt into the earth, darling, and Grandpa

will be free." Mother was weeping now. The tears rolled on her face, leaving wet paths. She knelt on the grass beside Julie. "Rain will pat on the grave, little one, and flowers will grow."

"Out in the rain all by himself? My grandpa! Oh, Mother, don't let them do it. Don't let them. Don't let them!"

But Mother only held her close. The two of them were wrapped together in a pause. Wind swept past, brushing them, the thump of earth on earth continued steadily, leaf patterns wove around them like a nest.

This she remembered.

Part I

In her uncle's house, Julie stood with Aunt Mathilda and
Uncle Henry and Emma, welcoming the guests. Faces and
hands flowed past, streamed away into the pulsing light and
graceful, beating music. The leader of the little orchestra was
no taller than she. He stood beside the potted palms shaking
and nodding his fuzzy head, encouraging everyone, beckoning with his bowing arm, come in, come in to Emma's eight-
eenth birthday. He arched his brows, arched his great owl
eyes, and fretted the violin to a nervous tremolo, keeping
time all the while with a foot thin as a puppet's. Send them
in faster, he seemed to bid Julie. But would anyone dance
with her? She had started shaking when she and Emma stood
before the glass for the last time. There were the two dresses
just alike, the big white one with blue flowers and the small
white one with pink, but, but— Cool living blossoms shivered on her breast because no one might dance with her.
The leader of the orchestra bowed his fuzzy head and she
bowed in return. He was a magician, the little man. This
morning the room had seemed so big, so naked without
carpets or furniture, but tonight it was a castle hall. Golden
fleur-de-lis on the wallpaper quivered to the music, the mirrors shimmered; rich light echoed upon the floor until it
seemed of stretched and polished gold, and the orchestra
leader did it all with his wand.

14

"Mr. Webber, Mr. Saunders, Miss Ainsworth," murmured Aunt Mathilda, saying the names over to herself, nervous as a wren. Uncle Henry patted her waist. He shook hands with the gentlemen and bowed awkwardly to the ladies. His deep, nosy voice was full of cheer, and his face folded and bulged with smiles. Mother said that when he was a baby, Uncle Henry put a nail crosswise in his mouth and turned blue. They had to shake him upside down to get it out. But not now. He was stout now. The yellow hair had worn away at the back of his head, and Uncle Henry didn't even care. He presented the guests heartily to Aunt Mathilda, to Julie and Emma, and the hands and faces flowed past without names anyhow.

"Miss Ainsworth is Mr. Saunders's cousin," repeated Aunt Mathilda. "I swear I can't keep them in my head, I'm all a-tremble." And she trembled a little extra for them to see. Dear Aunt Mathilda, she had planned this for so long. Let Julie's papa say what he would, the joy of having children, especially girl children, was to dress them up and let them be gay. And it was beautiful to dance. On the hill behind Grandma Stodel's, wind used to shiver the long grass, send it rippling, silvering, dancing down the hill; and Aunt Mathilda would tell them over and over how she had danced at Almack's years ago. Those were the days when she had been a schoolmistress under the patronage of the Countess, the same old countess who came now twice a year, her visits occasioning a flurry of floor scrubbing, painting, polishing, and disinfecting which would have done justice to a medical ward on the Crimean front. The old Countess walked with a cane for her gouty foot, but she had been young then and gave the brilliant dancing parties at Almack's of which Aunt Mathilda loved to tell. She cherished every word about Almack's, never altered a syllable to describe the gowns and the beaux, how the Countess had praised her French accent and the to-do when they first tried to waltz. And now here was Emma's birthday ball at last and Ludwig Dekker—*Ludwig Dekker*—had come from Holland.

15

"Mr. and Miss Smithers, Mr. Rice, they've all come, haven't they?" said Aunt Mathilda. "There won't be any more, will there, Mr. Stodel, until the Corpers come from the opera? Shouldn't the girls walk about and meet their friends?"

"If you mean Ludwig Dekker, why don't you say so?" Uncle Henry chuckled. "And as for this 'Mr. Stodel,' Til, I'm still your same old Henry." Aunt Mathilda had to laugh. She put her arm through his. Emma and Julie followed, moving slowly down the room the way Aunt Anna had shown them. "Keep your heads high," she'd said. "If you're going to wear your hair in topknots, live up to 'em." She had minced up and down showing them how not to and then how to. After a few turns the crinolines balanced just so.

"Julie!" Emma touched her arm urgently; down at the far corner were the Dekkers. Emma's healthy yellow hair shone, her teeth shone, her flesh was hot with pink above the tulle, and not a single court lady, not a one in the *Illustrated News*, could hold a candle to her. Oh, Ludwig Dekker couldn't help but love Emma in this dress. She walked so proud and sure, wearing her decolletage without any embarrassment; and seeing how firm and flat and proud Emma's bare chest was, Julie blushed miserably. She was so different. The top of her, the part you couldn't mention, was so shamefully different. She tugged at the tulle and satin bodice, pulling it as high as it would go.

"Your papa is the handsomest man in London," observed Aunt Mathilda; but Julie was watching the gentleman who sat beside Papa, a young gentleman whose face grew rosier with each step Emma took. Finally, he could bear it no longer, jumped up and came toward them. Everyone crowded around, and the first dance was called.

This way to Cousin Jack, that way to Graves, Julie could feel the floor speeding beneath her because of Emma and Ludwig Dekker. His parents were old friends of Grandma Stodel's, but tonight she was seeing him closely for the first time. There they went, Ludwig bobbing up and down, not quite so tall as Emma, and Emma flying, her gold braids high as a queen. It was not quite as you thought love would be, Ludwig so soundly built, his rounded head, his rounded cheeks, his nose like a button; and yet, his smile was wide and generous, and he never took his eyes or his smile from Emma's face. He patted his moist red cheeks with his handkerchief, the quadrille ended, and as Julie's partner led her away, Ludwig led Emma, drawing her bare arm through his with tender concern as if he had saved her life.

Papa was talking with one of the junior law clerks from Uncle Henry's office. He was known as a very thorough and efficient young man, and Uncle Henry sometimes brought him home to dinner and upheld him as a model for Jack. His name was Munzell.

"Julie, dear, you didn't overtire yourself, hadn't you better rest?" Mother pulled Ethelyn's sash into a firm bow while Ethelyn craned her neck, flirting like a jay at Mr. Munzell; but that worthy gentleman stood stiff as a board to his full six feet, talking earnestly with Papa.

"Utter stupidity," he said. "Sebastopol could have been taken in three days if they'd marched from the north. It merely proves that there's one man more incompetent than Lord Raglan, and that's St. Arnaud."

Julie's papa almost smiled. Mr. Munzell articulated precisely as if he were addressing the bar. "We've no business in this war at all, sir. If you'll permit me, any time we find ourselves allied with the French, we're in the wrong war." Seeing Papa's almost-smile, the young man permitted himself similar facial relaxation. Then he turned quickly, gave Julie a short bow, and shook hands.

"Well, Miss Corper, I've had the pleasure of meeting your father, making myself known, you might say." Her hand was lost in his great smooth one, and he bent down such a look of mingled pleasure, care, and solicitude that she said how do you do more cordially than she had planned. Ethelyn ogled with rapture and swung her dance program.

Papa said, "I've enjoyed our talk, young man. You should call on us, get to know my son. Fred's in with a strange lot at

17

school. Facts are what they need, not romantic nonsense. They're wild to sail off and liberate the universe, at least the part of it under the Czar's thumb."

Mr. Munzell wet his lips carefully. "That's Palmerston's jingoism, is it not, sir?" He shifted weight from one great leg to the other, straightened his collar, and glanced toward the orchestra to see what occasioned delay. The leader was bidding his men tune up. Julie looked at her program for the first time, and—it was filled! The very next dance had *Munzell* printed across painstakingly, and the name reappeared several times farther down.

"Hm. I've engaged for as many dances as I thought you might grant me, Miss Julia."

"Julie," she said, and he led her to the floor while Papa and Ethelyn and Mama watched approvingly. From across the room, Emma smiled and nodded, and so did Aunt Mathilda. Mr. Munzell turned and paced her neatly into the music, dancing smoothly, heavily, with perfect rhythm and not one jot of relaxation. His broad shoulders, his tall handsome frame were of one piece of wood, the dance steps coming punctually, perfectly, from the knees. Now they twirled past a pier glass and she caught the picture of a man and girl, all white and black and tall and short and beautiful together; then they twirled back and it was she and Mr. Munzell! The surprise and wonder of it forbade another step. She hung lifeless against the firm support of his hand without seeming to do anything, was carried and furled about, and there were admiring glances on all the faces dancing past.

Once while they danced, it was a polka this time, Julie felt faint and had to steady herself with his sleeve. Mr. Munzell was promptly compassionate. He took her to the small room Uncle Henry used as a library, brought her water, upbraided himself for having danced too hard, and wanted to get her mother; but Julie firmly said no, she was well enough, this would pass. Besides, it was rather nice to be quiet. It caught and held the evening, kept it from racing off. Mr. Munzell applied his handkerchief to his brow, high, where the neat

18

hair was plastered; he wet his lips carefully, Now that he was seated and his face on eye level, she noticed how plump and round his lips were under the fierce little mustache. It was the only thing about his wax face that was different, not quite thorough, not quite Munzell, the plump rounded lips lying upon each other with a slight gap in the center where they didn't fit. No, they didn't!

Mr. Munzell had possessed himself of her fan, and waved the air gently at her while he said how much he admired the Stodels and the Corpers, how very feminine and decorous her mother and aunt were, how much he admired the ladylike in ladies, the delicate, even the near fainting. He picked up an end of her tulle skirt and fingered it absently in his smooth, moist hands, making a curl. He used the same hairdressing her papa used, she could smell that, and something else besides, a faint, sharp, lemony tang to Mr. Munzell's breath.

The nurses working in the Crimea, for example. How unfeminine, how unfortunate. Julie cut him short. Florence Nightingale was wonderful! And all those others, undergoing hardships, saving the wounded from certain death!

"But you, Julie, certainly you wouldn't—"

"I wish I could! I wish my health allowed me to do something."

"Bravo, bravo!"

She and Mr. Munzell turned quickly.

"Oh, Grand-père, how was *Rigoletto?* This is Mr. Munzell. Are you going to dance with me? With Aunt Anna Perry and me?" How he laughed. He kissed Julie and shook hands with the junior law clerk.

"My granddaughter talks all at once. Let me look at you, Julie. *Exquise!*" he said, turning her slowly.

"Tulle, Grand-père, look, yards and yards and yards!"

"Come," he said, "if Mr. Moonzelle will forgive me, I have brought friends from the opera, I should like to introduce you both."

Mr. "Moonzelle" looked unhappy and ill at ease. Grand-père led the way. He wasn't a tall man, but he was so lively and buoyant, his clothes were richer than anyone's, his linen more immaculate, and the diamond blazed on his chest as he bowed left and right.

"Oh, Grand-père," she said, "I'm glad for you."

In the dining room, stout dazzling ladies and gentlemen were being served by Aunt Mathilda with oysters, anchovy toast, and sherry. They laughed, talking out loud as if they were at home, and even without their spangled costumes, wigs, or stage make-up, they were different from other people.

"Monsieur Lablache, Monsieur Tamberlik. Fanny, Fanny, turn your pretty head and meet my granddaughter. Mademoiselle Persiani, Mr. Moonzelle." Mr. Munzell bowed rigidly and withdrew to one side, away from danger, away from the rich, sweet, unguent scent which clung to all of them, men and women. They made enormous gestures, stroked Julie's hair and touched her dress, and their deep, booming voices dwarfed the room. They thundered out like gods on Olympus, alluring and somehow incorrigible, a trifle naughty, so that Papa kept himself in the other room and undoubtedly expected members of his household to do the same. And they smelled so sweet, so like beef suet and hyacinth, it must be in this very essence—Julie breathed deeply—that the guilt lay, the slight corruption. Madame Grisi took her by the hand and Julie saw how deep the madame breathed, her chest moving up and down carrying with it a panoply of diamonds. Mr. Munzell blushed painfully when he was presented, moistened his lips, and stared at the floor.

Then they strolled over to the corner of the room to see Grand-mère. You could see her small foot and her skirt. Some thin young man was standing before her, waving his arms.

"This wild fellow calls himself McManus," Grand-père said, "Phillip McManus. We met only tonight but I think I like him very much."

The young man acknowledged the introduction. He shook

hands with Julie, nodded briefly to Mr. Munzell, and continued his sentence to Grand-mère in French.

"A smart young man," explained Grand-père, "he ushers at the opera to get in free." Mr. Munzell, who had been growing stiffer and more unhappy, begged to be excused, he would return to claim Julie for the polonaise; he bowed himself away, giving a wide berth to the Zeuses and Athenas.

Julie wanted to know how the opera had been. How had Grand-père sung? And Grisi?

"Magnificent!" the young man said. "The scene at the end of Act Two when she confesses her dishonor!"

Julie looked quickly, but Grand-père was nodding his head.

"You see, you do agree. Verdi is the most dramatic of all. Wait, wait, McManus!"

But McManus couldn't wait. He was strung together with excitement; he talked so fast, such strange, eloquent words, you could barely follow. Grand-père interrupted and he interrupted Grand-père and they flung the hot words back and forth about Verdi.

"I'll grant you this, monsieur, *Rigoletto* is new and virile; if the action is melodrama the music has tragedy."

"Dada de da," shouted Grand-père from the quartet. "Verdi develops all the time, strength, subtlety, a great composer."

"A great *Italian* composer," insisted the young man. Grand-mère tilted her head, laughing. It was about Wagner now, Wagner was the genius, look what he'd done with the leitmotiv. The leitmotiv, the leitmotiv. Julie definitely did not get that. The words rushed, leaving her outside. Aristotle, he said, and Wagnerian music was not just music it was something else. But what? What was it?

Mr. Munzell came and reluctantly she let herself be led away. Grand-père and Grand-mère and the young man followed to the drawing room to watch the dancing. Aunt Anna joined them and the talk went on, the mad jumble of words. Julie could see as she swung into the dance. Leitmotiv. Verdi, Wagner, structure, passion. She tried to think of operas she had seen and what in the world had there been in them to make the young man wave his thin hands and Grand-père wave his plump ones and argue so?

Mr. Munzell was trying to explain. *His* words were certainly easy enough. Yes, yes, poor Mr. Munzell was trying to excuse his earlier derogatory remarks about the French. He would never have criticized the English-French alliance had he dreamed the Corpers were. . . .

"It's quite all right," Julie smiled. "Papa feels the same way. But don't say it to Grand-père. He wants England and France to be friends. He says it's a useless war but it's almost worth it for the alliance. A very famous man, my grand-père."

She wished he would look out this way, the young man who ushered at the opera. Now, he was certainly looking now. He would think she had the blackest, most flashing eyes he'd ever seen and such long lashes she looked like a gypsy. She tossed her head, being as gypsylike as possible. She looked up coquettishly at Mr. Munzell and he gazed down amazed, more ardent than ever, drawing her closer by almost an inch. But when she ventured to see how all of this had impressed Grand-père's young man, he was standing with his back turned toward her, ruffling his hair. And when she looked again, he was gone.

2

Festivity ebbed slowly from the house. Long after the last guests said good night, lights withering in the shining white globes of the gasoliers, the family sat together in the disordered dining room having a late cup of tea and talking it over. No one was ready to sleep; they wanted to relive the night before it escaped them.

"Poor Lud Dekker, Em danced his feet off," Jack said.

But Emma didn't answer. She darted swift, inquiring

glances at her father, at Julie, and drank her tea steaming hot in a sort of trance. There was something about Emma. Julie could feel how tense she was when finally they had gone upstairs and lay side by side in Emma's big bed. Papa had granted the unusual permission that she might stay this second night, and Ethelyn, too. They were to get to sleep, not sit up gossiping, he said, and be home in time for lunch the next day.

Lying across the room on the chaise longue, Ethelyn talked a blue streak and wouldn't sleep. Mr. Munzell was the best dancer, how handsome he was!

"He didn't dance with anyone but Julie," Emma said. "Oh, Julie, I could hardly wait to see if he'd asked you for the polonaise. He's in love with you, I'll bet he is."

"Emma, don't be silly."

"How about you and Ludwig Dekker?" retorted Ethelyn.

But Emma only said, "Did you watch Aunt Anna? And Mama and Papa?"

"Did you meet the young man Grand-père brought from the opera? I wish he had danced."

"Who, Julie, who is that?"

"Oh, you remember, Ethelyn, the thin homely one who looked as though he hadn't eaten for a week." Emma laughed. "That's the Irish. Go to the opera and not a cent to keep body and soul together."

"Grand-père likes him. He's a student. He ushers at the opera so he can get in every night."

"I don't remember him."

"Ethelyn, you do. He had wispy sort of hair and spoke French with your grand-mère and has no manners."

"Emma, you didn't talk with him."

"I like the way Mr. Munzell talks," persisted Ethelyn. "Like an orator."

But suppose he had danced, had put his thin hand on her waist and spun her around and around, what would she have said to him? She tried to think of *La Traviata*, the way it was the time she had heard Grand-père; but she could only recall sound flying up; the singers' mouths made holes down on the stage, spangles blazed and hopped all over their clothes, and Grand-père wore a beard.

It had grown quiet in the room. One slice of moonlight fell across Ethelyn and the bedclothes lay quiet.

"Julie, you're not asleep? Oh, Julie," whispered Emma, and Julie could feel how straight her cousin lay. "He's going to speak to Papa. Ludwig is. Tomorrow. He wants to marry me. Oh, Julie, Julie!" Emma threw her arms about Julie and hugged her.

"So soon, so soon, Emma?"

"How do you know?" shrieked Ethelyn, leaping out of bed.

"Ethelyn, you sneak!" hissed Emma.

"Hush up, Ethelyn. Do you want to wake the whole house?"

"I heard every word," cried the culprit. "Tell us, Emma, what did he say?"

"Julie, if she wasn't your sister—" But Emma wanted to tell. She'd been afraid he wouldn't be the same, "as when we were in Holland, I mean." But after the waltz, he'd taken her to Papa's study. He told her he'd thought of nothing else since last summer, his family were pleased, and he'd speak to her father while they were in London—if she didn't mind. "If I didn't *mind!*" cried Emma, burying her face in the bedclothes, laughing and crying.

"What else?" asked Ethelyn.

"Nothing else. Go back to bed, you baby."

And no more was said until Ethelyn was really asleep.

"Julie, please fall in love," Emma whispered. "Nothing's ever been like this. I know he isn't handsome. He isn't even as tall as I'd like. The handsome one in that family's his brother, Leon, the one who's in the army, he's the handsome one. But I don't care, if Ludwig had warts, I'd love him. He's so kind and so jolly and when I'm with him— Julie, he kissed me! I don't care! I'm glad he did, I'm glad. Now close your lips and I'll show you how. There, just like that."

24

3

The young spring wind was playing tricks. It snatched a box top from cook's trash and sent it scuttling across the square. It sailed bits of crazy paper, seized a loose shutter, banged it against the house, caught another down the street. Trees shook and swung their bare arms.

"Spring's a-comin'," Aunt Anna said, sniffing the wind. She and Julie tilted their bonnets, hurrying downstairs before it could play wanton with their skirts.

"Look at the elm trees, Aunt Anna, look at the leaves!"

So long as they were on that street they hurried, but once around the corner, they breathed deep of the moist green air and strolled along gay and guilty. They were supposed to be at home resting after last night. Aunt Anna was to have explained the complexities of a new embroidery pattern. But Mother was paying calls on the sick, and how could you sit jabbing a needle when you still heard the words and the music from last night, and over at the other house Ludwig Dekker was talking to Uncle Henry?

"I'd give a plenty to be an imp in your uncle's bookcase."

"Poor Emma, imagine her with Mrs. Dekker and Aunt Mathilda," while Ludwig and Uncle Henry sat closeted in the study, the tiny room where Mr. Munzell's breath had smelled of lemon drops and now no female could intrude. One of those sacrosanct moments had come, a mysterious male matter to be settled by them alone. Did Aunt Anna think everything would be all right?

"Right as can be! Your Uncle Henry's the easiest pa in the world. He'll settle twice the dot he can afford, not that the Dekkers care. They're wholesome folks without airs, and

Ludwig's doing well enough for anybody, eight hundred pounds, I'd say."

"But will it—will she be happy, Aunt Anna?"

"Happy? With eight hundred pounds and a nice, solid Dutchman who loves her? You're lucky to do as well."

"But I didn't mean—I'd never thought of the money."

"Well, miss, when you get to marryin' you'd best think of it. Heaven knows I didn't." Then her tone softened. "Most likely wouldn't if I had it to do over again."

"Oh, I'll never marry," murmured Julie, and there was a sadness, a wistfulness and wonder, that made her voice break.

"What're you planning to do with the Mr. Munzells as they come along?"

But Julie knew she wouldn't. She wasn't handsome like Emma, she was sick so much, and something else, something far away she could not explain. Grand-père had fallen in love with his Leonie in Paris, at the Conservatoire. They'd eaten caviar in great blocks of ice when their allowances came, and sardines and cheap white wine when the money was gone, and after they'd known each other *two months*, they'd run off and been married, which was scandalous. No one had even known about it until her own papa was to be born. Then pretty Leonie had laughed as she told her family, and had been cut off without a sou. Grand-mère still laughed, telling how they had lived in the little room under the roof; she played and Gustav sang—and how could anything like that ever happen again? Even if she weren't sick half the time, how could anything like that happen?

"Mind if I walk along?" Someone strode briskly between them. Grand-père's young man from the opera! The wind had blown him in his brown suit, sent him rushing along out of breath. Oh, and how she looked! Julie tried to adjust her bonnet. She tried to smooth her disheveled hair, fix her skirt, fold her pelisse.

"Don't trouble, you look great all blown to bits!" She felt blown to bits. "Had a glimpse of you two from Gower Street and thought I'd say hello. This wind's a howler, isn't it?"

Aunt Anna wagged her bonnet. "Phillip McManus, a fine one you are, galavanting around in the middle of afternoon classes." But her voice trilled up and down as if she were talking to Grand-père, and when Julie ventured a glance, Aunt Anna had taken his arm. He did look the way she'd remembered, only he was smiling, which wrinkled his fine nose. His Adam's apple pointed out; wind ruffled the soft brown brush on his chin, on his lip.

"I saw you from the window. I *was* in class, Mrs. Perry, a class they choose to call 'The Shakespearean Theater.'" He pronounced it thee-a-tah. Julie began to smile. She wished he'd say it again.

"I should add that any relationship between the theater and what is taught in that class is illusory." The hand nearest Julie tugged at his chin whisker. "London University, and they hand out the same trash we got at Queen's. My God, you can learn more in one night watching Phelps."

"Blasphemer!" Aunt Anna said.

"There aren't words strong enough for the dullards who emasculate Shakespeare."

That's what he said, Julie heard him. She grew hot all over trying not to listen, trying to hear how Phelps went to the Folios for his text, none of the songs or other drivel that had been going on since Dryden.

"Don't you agree, Mrs. Perry, isn't Phelps the best?"

"Where does he play, Phelps?" And immediately, Julie wished she'd held her tongue.

"Of course, you West Enders are not aware of Islington. You might like to know, Miss Corper, that Sadler's Wells is the truest theater in England. The peddlers and clerks and sports who go there know more about Shakespeare than the people in Grovesnor Square." There was no stopping him. "You'd do better to make the pilgrimage, even if it does mean passing a few shabby lodgings, than to sit in style watching Charles Kean."

"But I've not seen him, either."

"You've—well, what *have* you seen?"

"The panorama, and—and the pantomimes, Lydia Thompson once in *Jack, the Giant Killer*."

The young man was standing stiff on the pavement.

"Her pa doesn't fancy the theater," Aunt Anna said.

"Take art out of this filthy, money-grubbing city and what's left?"

"You don't know her pa."

"And your grandfather. . . ."

"He's taken me to the opera," Julie said softly.

"Well, I'll take you to the theater! I'll take you everywhere, there's no place a woman can't go." He drew her hand swiftly through his arm, kept his right hand over hers to keep it warm, to keep it from shaking, for it was shaking. "We'll see something magnificent the first time. You've at least read Shakespeare? I'll bring you *Macbeth*, we'll read together."

She wanted to say something, but it was hard to catch her breath.

"The night Sadler's Wells opened—"

"I was there! You weren't, McManus. You were a sniveling brat of a schoolboy."

"Mrs. Warner's a little woman, no taller than you, Julie, but how she uses that body!" Phillip stopped in the street. "Phelps enters on top of the palace stairs and sweeps her into his arms."

"That first night," Aunt Anna said, "the whole house gasped. I tell you, in Islington, they never heard of a man kissing his wife." She laughed, and so did Phillip. Julie managed a little embarrassed cackle, too. On they went through the spring wind, Phillip's words pouring and pounding. Macbeth had the imagination of a poet, the audacity of a strong man. Aunt Anna told how good Edmund Kean had been. It was almost like seeing a play to hear Aunt Anna and Phillip.

Suddenly they stopped, Phillip was sorry but he was to go on duty at the library and he got paid by the hour.

"Julie," he said. Her hand was still on his arm, she didn't know how to take it away. "It's been such a pleasant meeting,

Julie. Remember me to your grandfather." He took the hand and shook it solemnly. His eyes were light brown. The wind brought a tint of color to his face. He would bring her *Macbeth*, and had she been to the British Museum? Then he was gone down Gower Street. She and Aunt Anna watched him sprinting along on his thin legs.

4

Julie and Aunt Anna developed an ungovernable impulse for exercise. Every day for a fortnight they stepped briskly out of the house, inhaled, remarked on the quality of the ripening spring, and retraced to within an inch the exact course of their original excursion. They tried other hours of the day, they walked on several awful occasions right up Gower Street itself, past the university, around down Russell Street before the British Museum. They never met him.

"Walks are good for what ails you, wonder we didn't think of 'em long ago," Aunt Anna said.

But he had been blown to them by magic and had disappeared the same way. Julie couldn't even remember exactly. His face had been so mobile, talking and laughing and melancholy and eager. The sound of his voice tumbled up and down and nothing was left. Some tall thin man would come hurrying up the street and Phillip's name would wear a quick path over every nerve. It was never he. The next day they would start out again. Finally Julie said Aunt Anna had been sweet to humor her but they should walk no more in the afternoons.

"Nonsense, walking's good for you. Today we'll visit the British Museum. We can go by ourselves without anyone taking us, if you please." Julie ran for her shawl and her bonnet with the new ribbons, and out they went eagerly into the pale warm day, straight to Russell Street, up the museum steps. It was dark and cool. You swam through the great lobby, the corridors, over noiseless floors to the reading room. Aunt Anna pushed the door and they walked into light and a smell like sweated saddles, and a whole world of books. First cautiously, then wildly, Julie surveyed the room, up and down, the tables, the desks, the shelves. After that, her heart still hammering, she sat quietly, fingering a book of English history.

Phillip studied here. He sat in the leather smell reading, writing notes down. She saw other students. The door opened and closed three times and each time she was sure. . . . The pages of the book turned in front of her. Her pulse ticked off. After a decent interval, Aunt Anna told her to come and see the exhibits, and they went to a big room where a person in uniform explained the importance of the Rosetta stone and the Elgin marbles from the cornice of the Parthenon, and his own importance as custodian and guard. Julie looked into several cases, trying dutifully to decipher the handwriting. Keats's letters she could follow. This one told his sister that "it may not be consumption but a gentleman called Shelley has invited me to the country and it might be good. . . ." Tears for poor Keats rushed up into poor Julie's throat. She sobbed right there where the stiff little guardsman could see her. She rushed past his wobbling, wavering blue cap, down the stairs and out into the day that had grown heavy and dull. It was going to rain, Aunt Anna said, you could tell by the festering lavender smell of the drains, and if the sky was to be counted on they were late to tea. Julie swallowed down the dark air. There were things you could not make happen, they were outside of you, beyond you. She had tried to bring Grandpa back when she was a child.

Lights had already been lit as they came down the street, but there were carriages before the house so they had company, thank heaven, and Papa couldn't ask. She and Aunt Anna slipped out of their bonnets and hurried in, greeting Emma and Uncle Henry and Jack and Ludwig Dekker and—

Mr. Munzell! Yes, Mr. Munzell standing tall and stiff beside the tea table, balancing a cup on the platter of his hand and talking for an extra moment, studiously, to his hostess. But his smooth face colored, and Emma and Mother were both radiant, as if Mr. Munzell had declared himself, coming to tea so promptly after the ball, staying and behaving in a princely fashion even though Julie was late, and turning, when she finally did come, pink as any peppermint.

She spoke quickly to Uncle Henry. What had they heard from Grandma Stodel? She talked quickly to Ludwig Dekker. He had just sent off a long letter to his brother Leon in Java, telling of the betrothal. She avoided looking at Mr. Munzell, but she could hear him and Papa talking with precision, and no one was going to emerge from this war with any glory. Certainly not Palmerston, certainly not Raglan.

"Even Aberdeen," said Mr. Munzell. "There's an appalling lack of efficiency."

"Miss Nightingale's cut the death rate twenty per cent per thousand," Uncle Henry said. "I'd call that efficient."

"Indeed," agreed his junior law clerk. "It has been most unfortunate, however, that Mr. Russell sees fit to publish statistics which give away our losses to the enemy."

Papa agreed.

"If he hadn't, we wouldn't know either," Julie heard herself say. "Miss Nightingale could have worked till doomsday. If Mr. Russell hadn't aroused public indignation, she couldn't have gone over official heads. That's what she's done, she's saved the sick and wounded in spite of the army!"

The teacups clicked. Mr. Munzell grew pinker, and Papa said, "If you don't mind, Julie."

"Let the child have her say, Frederic. She's not far from right," Uncle Henry said.

But she was frightened and wouldn't offer another word. She walked away to the window seat only to find Mr. Munzell stalking her. She detested his stiff, smug way of putting each foot down. She wished he'd unbend and smile without planning it first. She'd like to take that little mustache and muss it, muss it, muss it.

The door knocker rapped, and Ethelyn ran to see if Beatrice had heard. Mr. Munzell inquired if she believed in suffrage for women, too, and never having thought of it in her life, Julie said yes, she did. If a female was fit to be queen of England, there was no reason why other females should not elect her Parliament.

"A letter," screamed Ethelyn, "Julie, for you, a letter!"

"Ethelyn, why are you raising your voice?" asked Papa. "It is certainly not the first communication that has ever come to this house. Take the letter to the hall stand and leave it there." But Julie had snatched the packet and ran as fast as she could, up the stairs in her enormous skirt, her heart thick and slow as a mallet because the letter could only be, there was only one person. . . .

Dozens of pages he had sent, all written with a clean backhand stroke, and she gobbled them as fast as she could read, intoxicated, enraptured. He was ill with a fever, had been ill for two weeks; but he was better tonight and they had smuggled him a candle. He was sitting up the whole of this night to write to her. The fever was intolerable, it was keeping him from the one person he had ever met who filled him with the same glow, the same awe, as a great work of art. He poured onto the paper the whole of his yearning for life, for beauty, for uncompromising courage. To compromise with one's ideal was to commit spiritual suicide, one must live toward a synthesis of thought and feeling, he said, like Victor Hugo, what the Germans called *natur und geist*. And now he had found her. He wanted to be with her, read with her, see the magnificent fire and passion in her face. Thank God for the French grandparents who had saved her from the cold bourgeois type of her home. They had given her the heart, the soul with which to worship beauty and she must, they would, together. He would come—"to you, my darling"—as soon as he was able.

5

In the sitting room at Aunt Anna Perry's, Julie and Ethelyn laid the table for tea. Phillip tended the kettle over the spirit lamp and Aunt Anna tripped in from the kitchen, exhibiting jam turnovers so hot from the oven that little blobs of blackberry and apple gum still bubbled on the outside crusts. The Flying Pieman, Phillip called her, with her plates of winkles, her thin, buttered brown bread and the pot of scalding coffee with its pungent flue of steam.

"Coffee! At teatime?" said Ethelyn.

Aunt Anna handled her cups and saucers with crooked fingers, and if Phillip liked coffee, coffee was what he should have. She had a choice piece of mutton to boil for dinner and the place had been turned upside down in preparation, every muslin length of curtain so white and starched and neatly mended.

"More tea, Ethelyn? Julie? Coffee, Phillip? Come, eat hearty, I have guests so seldom." And when did she ever have time for guests? Julie had always teased Aunt Anna to stay and sleep at their house, never go "off home." But not today. Seeing Aunt Anna preside with elegance at her own tea table, seeing her hand the steaming cup to Phillip and ply him with cream, "good and thick, I got it special," urging him to more turnovers, more buttered bread and winkles, as if she were trying to feed him up at once for good and all—Julie was glad for the two small rooms in Bow Road, glad that Aunt Anna had what she called "an establishment beholden to none."

Phillip ate with relish, more than he ate at her papa's table. "God," he said, "if only you hadn't abandoned the theater, Aunt Anna, if you could still kick over your head *and* make coffee like this, I'd marry you!"

Ethelyn gasped.

"And who's sayin' I'd have you, you blaspheming Irisher?"

Julie laughed at the look on Ethelyn.

"I don't suppose you can make coffee, Gypsy?"

"She can't make anything but rum cakes and trifles," Ethelyn said. "Cook hopes Julie never has to live on her own cooking. She'd starve in a week, cook says."

Phillip tilted his chair. He laughed and gasped he laughed so hard. "Dramatic irony! We do have to eat, Gypsy. For heaven's sake, learn to make coffee."

Aunt Anna brewed more tea. She told them how they used to take their cup backstage at Drury Lane, how they'd huddle around on cold days, heating the kettle on the stove lid and shivering in their tights. She brought out a few faded illustrations, dancing girls in plumes and satins, and in the very front, one tall, wiry young lady with magnificent limbs and a long nose, and of all things, an impish expression exactly like Aunt Anna's own!

"I should have known you then," said Phillip wickedly. "Tut-tut, such legs."

"Then? Why, you weren't even a dream." She lifted up the curtain to Bow Road. "Not a mite damp. Julie, you and Phillip run along, get some exercise so's you can enjoy this good boiled mutton." She handed Julie her bonnet.

"I'll go, too," volunteered Ethelyn, reaching for hers.

"And leave me with the tea things? A fine how-de-do. Besides, miss, I've been wanting a chance to pin a pattern for your new blue mull."

So Julie and Phillip escaped into Bow Road, into the soft, late afternoon. Each house was like the next, you had to study to see where one ended, one began, all bilious yellow brick with brown maws and not a tree or blade of grass. The spear-shaped, cast-iron railings ran in a dark green file as far as one could see. Sun put a torch to the windows.

"Very poor, aren't they?"

But Phillip said he could breathe here the way he never could "up in your West End where everything is covered over and buried down and beaded and tasseled to death." He pointed out a couple walking across the road, then another couple, tough young workingmen and their girls. The girls were red-faced, like Beatrice. "They're decent and they're free," he said. "Even we are free down here."

"We're alone for the first time," murmured Julie.

"Darling, darling, I've known you six weeks, all my life."

"But how did you *know*, Phillip?"

He grinned and swung her hand. "It was easy, dear. I saw that poor well-meaning ass, Munzell, and the black-eyed witch leading him astray, and I simply saved his life."

"Phillip!"

"One untarnished barrister, my gift to posterity."

Up Hoxton Street, miserable dwarf houses huddled down into the dark. A crowd had gathered at one corner, and a workingman was talking. She couldn't understand much of it—"Owen," "Brisbane," "Engels"—but the people listened without blinking.

"Look at those faces, what magnificent strength," Phillip said, pointing out this man in a peaked cap, that one in a blue shirt. They looked rough and dirty to her. She was glad when Phillip moved on toward the park. New-cut grass breathed up here and ragged people walked about in the twilight. Children ran shrieking with sickly old faces.

"These people had the nerve, the indiscretion, to be born in rags." Phillip spoke bitterly, his mood had changed. "I've seen it in Ireland all my life, people born in the wrong nation to the wrong religion; here in England it's the crime of poverty. We'll go to America, Julie, as soon as I finish my play."

They sat under a tree. Phillip stretched out on the grass and put his head in her lap.

"Phillip, we're out of doors, anyone might pass!"

"And what of it?" he said coldly. Then the tenderness came back into his voice. "Don't be afraid, my darling. Don't deny us one beautiful minute in this bleak world."

What could she say to that, with his mouth so close?

"In America I may find my father." Darkness deepened,

blotted against the sky. "I want you to know about him, Julie, he ran away. No, listen, he was right. I believe that with all my heart."

"But he left your mother, Phillip, and you."

"He should never have married her. I love my mother, but she lives on her level. He made a mistake. He was very young."

"But no gentleman—"

"You're quoting your papa, Julie. What does your papa think of his own talented father? He thinks he should have wasted his life in business! Some men have dreams. I don't know what my father's was, but he certainly didn't want to stay in a town of two hundred dull beggars working leather. And my mother wouldn't leave. She wouldn't. I'm glad he had the courage. To me, he's twice the man my stepfather is, even if he did rescue us and leads a virtuous, stupid life."

The dark made a small, safe place for them beside the tree. She had never been out in the night like this, nor heard talk like this. People must have courage, he said, and they would have it together. They could go anywhere and life would never defeat them. Stars pricked sharp holes in the sky, tipped, spilled their light, and suddenly his mouth was in her hand. Julie bent her head, leaving the stars to themselves.

"'You turn your face but does it bring your heart?'" The soft, deep tone of his voice trembled. His hands sought her face, drew her down, down breathlessly, her parched lips quivering even before they came to touch on his.

6

Papa paced the station waiting room, found it exactly twelve feet, turned and paced back. The air hung hot, suffocating as a hood. They were alone. Even the station master had stepped out to the platform to catch the breeze and to peer up the empty tracks for the train. You could hear the gay chatter of the crowd who had come to see them off—Mama and Aunt Anna and herself—off to visit Grandma Stodel. And why didn't the train come?

"I wish to speak of Mr. McManus," Papa said dryly. "It is a subject I would choose to avoid. I still hope never to allude to it again."

"Papa!"

"But before you leave to spend the summer in Holland, let me suggest you turn the time to profit, get your emotions in hand, as it were. You've been making a public spectacle of yourself."

Let the train come, quickly, before another word.

"I have usually respected your judgment, Julie, but in this infatuation, you're acting like any common girl. My father had no business introducing that young climber. I've no liking for the Irish." He massaged his gleaming mustache. "I've certainly none for this particular specimen. Not that I'm going to act the tyrant or forbid him the house. I like to think my daughter can cope with all circumstances, and perhaps this interlude with your grandmother will improve your taste."

The hot, angry temper tears had been swelling, the wrong thing, she knew. She defended Phillip. He was gifted, he was brilliant, how unjust to be prejudiced by nationality.

"Some parents are concerned with nothing but getting their daughters married." In his cheek the two bones fenced like swords. "We are not. I doubt that your health would support a marriage or profit thereby."

"I'm all right. I'm as strong as anyone. Look at Elizabeth Barrett Browning!"

Papa turned his back on that. "If and when the time comes, there are several young men. I think of one in particular, who has already spoken in your behalf."

"Papa!"

"I am alluding to a professional man with an excellent future. Your Uncle Henry esteems him highly."

37

"You didn't say yes, Papa, you didn't!" She stamped her foot and the hot tears scalded over.

"I said neither yes nor no. Bear in mind, my dear, I detest displays." He shook out his pocket handkerchief, touched the linen against her cheeks. "I told the gentleman it would be at least a year before you could be permitted to think of marriage. If he still wishes, he might pursue the matter then."

At least he'd said a year. She took the handkerchief and blew vigorously. The train whistle blew, right with her.

"Your mother and I hope a great deal for you, Julie. Mind you don't fail us." Then he took her arm and led her out onto the platform. The train came rumbling and thundering. She shook hands with a blurred Mr. Munzell in elegant white gloves. She embraced Grand-mère, who seemed as dried and fragile as a leaf.

"I love you," Phillip whispered. He took her hand, and for one wild minute she thought he might take all of her.

"You look lovely," Mrs. Dekker said. "Now don't you go falling in love with any Dutch boys, Julie. You wait till my Leon comes home."

Crazy laughter rumbled in with the train, skidded through the handclasps, whirled and sobbed until the conductor saved her, hoisted her firmly by the elbow and into the train carriage.

"Wave your handkerchief," Mother said, waving hers.

"Good-by, good-by," shouted Aunt Anna.

There was a shudder, the wheels turned. Let them turn faster, faster, take her away from Papa and Phillip who were tearing her apart and from Mr. Munzell with his maddening way of looking and talking and eating and walking. Take her away. She closed her eyes and leaned wearily against the glass, pretending to sleep.

It was a melancholy crossing. But when they were on land again in their hired carriage and the horses strained, galloping down the swells, some irresistible happiness began to grow. Windmills swung. Time caught in the whirling spokes, shuttled back and forth. She was little Julie on her way to

38

Grandpa, she was big Julie, she couldn't help it. It was as if Grandpa were waiting and she was going to him, going home. Grandpa in his velvet cap. She could tell *him* of Phillip.

"I feel like a girl again," Mother said. She looked like a girl, too. She looked free.

"Does you good to get away from that medicine man and all his pills," Aunt Anna said. "I say hang that Dr. Potter."

On and on through the warm sweet hay and clover air, the sharp juniper-berry air. They drowsed, talked, counted windmills. It was a shame Papa couldn't come, too, Mother said, but she didn't mean it! They turned down their special road, plunging through buckthorn and bramble bushes, across the creek bridge into the yard, Bess bounding and barking alongside, Bess who must be as old as Grandma but who wore, instead of a velvet collar, a silver-studded band around her neck. She jumped like a puppy and tried to lick their faces while they stood with Grandma exclaiming over everything —the brown wood house not quite so big as it used to be, the oaken stoop worn hollow as a trough, the broken arm of the elm where the swing had hung, and the long lines of plants, hardy and green across the fields. Everything just the same, the fragrance of bread baking, the rich, hot, buttery chocolate sponge and the raisin-nut and orange bread, Julie's old room and Grandpa's with his rocker and his pipe left in place, as Grandma left everything, as if he might come back.

And *you* had come back. It almost seemed you had never been away. Julie was up and dressed quickly every morning, in the blue linen country dress, the thick boots. She'd splash cold water on her hands and face at the pump, then dry, grab up bonnet and shawl and be off. Skipping warmed her and she skipped, ran, panted to the top of the hill where the sun stood, pale as Grandma Stodel's butter. A shiny gray snake twisted in and out. That was the Ijsel River. Fine white mist rose, fumed from its coils, the sun couldn't touch it. Then down the hill, her bonnet falling back, while wind ran its fingers through her hair.

She longed for word from Phillip but he had not written

and it was no fault of the mail packets either. Letters arrived from Emma and Papa, she even received a polite, well-punctuated notation from Mr. Munzell, each letter formed as if he held one ruler above his pen, one ruler beneath. Mr. Munzell quoted from poetry in his missive:

> *Tell me not in mournful numbers,*
> *"Life is but an empty dream."*
> *. . . Life is real! Life is earnest!*

and analyze that sentiment as he would, Julie found it pedantic, hackneyed stuff. She was alive and bright with new eyes.

When a letter finally came from Phillip, she knew without tearing the seal that it would not be the Phillip who had given her the lovely Shakespeare volume, but the angry Phillip who thought she had no right to go away. She should be with him, sharing life with him, pouring out her full spiritual strength.

Julie brought some of her square white paper to the creek and wrote, describing the rain they'd had, how the young trees bent under it. She had really seen none of this before, she wrote, she was learning so much, she was growing old. She was not quite sure what he wanted, or was "wanted" the word—demanded. The important thing in life, it seemed to her, was to be simple, to do each day what was needed, make it a good day. She loved Phillip, she admitted this to him simply, in defiance of all her training and of Papa. "I love you, Phillip, I love you. Your face is in everything I see." But Papa had a point. Whatever one might do in America, in England a young lady could sully her lifetime with a false step. It said so in every book. She didn't say that to Phillip, but she made up her mind she could love him and still be demure. It wasn't necessary to sit under the trees in Victoria Park.

7

Papa made no comment on her dress. She sat at dinner with the white tulle skirt spread neatly under the table and a mantle of chiffon over her bare arms. Ethelyn and Fred and John looked at her excitedly, then at Papa, but he made no comment and why should he? She was a lady now, she had returned from Holland integrated and sure of herself. She tried to swallow down a spoonful of soup, and it made a large noise. One over the other her smooth, slippery little boots folded, white satin, lovely, gleamy white satin. In Gower Street, Phillip would be tying his cravat. When Papa started carving, Aunt Anna brought in a small puff of omelet.

"Here, you'll digest this easier."

"And where does the young lady think she's going?"

"To see Rachel, Papa, Rachel herself! She's playing *Phaedra* at the St. James!"

He dabbled a limp slice of beef in its own juice and laid it across a clean, hot dinner plate. "No one seems to have consulted me." Now he did look at her with his piercing eyes. "I was quite unaware that members of this household had taken to frequenting cheap public entertainments." Each word clean and deliberate; when he bit off "cheap," the subject was closed.

"But, Papa, everyone is going, the Duke and Duchess of Aumale, they're friends of Grand-père's. Everyone's going."

He sliced the beef relentlessly, dropped mashed potatoes hard from the spoon so they stood in leaning peaks.

"You will forgive my surprise, Mrs. Corper, that you permit the mention of that actress in your home. Or are you unaware of the exploits that have made her notorious?"

"Mr. Corper, please," murmured Mother, frightened. "We can discuss this after dinner."

Beatrice rushed around the table.

"You're mistaken, my dear." He masticated thoroughly. "I have no intention of discussing it at all."

"Papa, please, Phillip's taken a box, he's spent his wages for a month. And Grand-père says Rachel's a darling."

His eyebrows had elevated, the left a trifle higher than the right. "I think we have had quite enough theater in this family. I personally have been trying to forget it for forty years."

There. Freddie and John rattled their silver. Mother and Ethelyn chewed potatoes as Papa would wish, sadly, yes, but as if they could have told her from the first. Beatrice hurried to the kitchen and didn't come back. Emil came.

"And you will kindly partake of dinner, Julie, since it was prepared especially to your taste." Her fork rose obediently and touched the flattened omelet. What would Phillip say? Dear, darling Phillip. She sat miserably through dinner. After that, she stood in the middle of her own room and waited.

At a quarter before eight, she heard the knocker, heard him greet her mother, heard the parlor door close. Ethelyn brought information that they were talking, Phillip and Papa. Would Julie like her to stay? But she was furious with Ethelyn, who had witnessed her indignity. Phillip would despise her, he would think her no better than a child. And Rachel, and *Phaedra!* If only you could go back to before dinner, have the words altered. If you could go back to when she and Phillip first had planned. It was growing later and later, their seats would stand empty. Oh, Phillip!

"Get your shawl. Hurry, don't stand like a dummy." Aunt Anna ran in out of breath. "Your pa's stubborn, but that Irishman's stubborn, too. I'm to tag along and protect you, but you're going. Just this once, he says."

Julie snatched the shawl and skimmed down the stairs. She didn't look at Phillip or her mother or anyone; she skimmed down, hot, seething with anger and shame—out into the moist, sweet August night. The dark was filled with wet flowers, you could sense them water-heavy in every garden on the square, nodding, sodden flower heads, swollen with tears. There had been a miracle; she was out in the night. But the meeting with Phillip had been ruined; she had failed him when he'd planned so carefully, even hiring a carriage; it wouldn't hurt Papa to see that.

On the way, Aunt Anna made conversation. She imitated Charles Kean, "His dabe is Godzago, he poisod hib id the garded."

Phillip was a stranger, locked together and remote. He didn't notice her satin boots or the way she'd done her hair.

"Drop me at Charing Cross," ordered Aunt Anna. "I'm going home."

"What? Why, Aunt Anna, what would Papa—"

"Pick me up on the way back. What Pa don't know won't hurt him."

"But it might be late."

"Makes no difference. I'll have a cup of tea ready and maybe a glass of port, eh, McManus?"

Then Aunt Anna disappeared as if she'd never been. It was quiet in the carriage. The iron wheels ground out a raucous song. Phillip looked at his watch. It was very late and he was very angry; she could feel how stiff he held himself when the carriage swayed. Lights flashed, the streets were thronged, a clown and a dancing girl performed right on the walk for coins; but Phillip remained stubbornly in profile. Might he smoke?

"Yes," she said quickly. Embarrassment rushed over her chest, mounted her face. It was the sort of cheek you could expect from the Irish, Papa said. Phillip scraped the match on the sole of his boot, caught the flame and sucked until the cigarette caught. He breathed out slowly and strands of gauze laced the air. Why shouldn't he? Papa was not infallible. The feeling of insult persisted just the same.

"Grandpa smoked a pipe, Grandpa Stodel, even in the house!" She ended on a note of triumph.

And now he inhaled with real insolence. The carriage was slowing. He flung the cigarette and leaped out after it, seized her arm, and they ran across the empty foyer up the stairs. He didn't wait for an attendant, they ran, hearing the muffled music from inside. Phillip rushed her down the corridor, tore open the door to the box, and there was the radiant blue velvet curtain, waiting, quivering in the dark. Someone pushed forward their soft, thick chairs, and they sank into the waiting audience.

"We made it!" He pulled his chair so close, his knee lay along her dress. The curtain parted.

"The palace at Troezen," whispered Phillip. Then Hippolytus walked in with his tutor. They talked French. When Grand-mère and Grand-père talked, someone was always interrupting to ask what they meant. "If we wanted you to know, . . ." Grand-mère would say. The old man who played the tutor had a faint lisp; his advice to the golden-haired young man was blurred; but it was supposed to be wonderful and Julie listened as politely as she could. They walked off, leaving the stage empty. What a fine straight nose Phillip had, and the thin furry little tuft on his chin made his chin seem bigger than it was! Rachel entered. She was a delicate, graceful wraith of queen, emaciated and pale. Her eyes were hot. From her first words, you felt she was wasting away under a withering flame. All through the apostrophe to the sun, something intense pulled and tied you to the stage. Phaedra wished to die, some hidden guilt was too intolerable, her hands, her hands, would that her heart was innocent as they. Low, muffled, the voice sank into darkness and it was love destroying her, the draining, burning agony of love. Julie knew. Phillip's supple hands were on the velvet ledge, and a longing like Phaedra's rose in her. Those tenuous wrists, the fingers with their spray of fine, dark hairs.

"Oh, my darling," he said, studying her face, seeing all that had happened while she was Phaedra.

With the second act, he took her hand. The nervous flesh held her finger tips, the two hands together with a life of their own. Now at last the Queen came to Hippolytus. She grew taller, she actually did, the great eyes burned black in

44

her pallid face and the sentences of love, flexible, melodious, grew fierce against the cold courtesy of the golden man. Phillip's nails dug into Julie's palm. The play rushed headlong. After Hippolytus had died, after Phaedra had confessed her sin and died, they went out into the moist night shaken and sealed together.

The cabman drove them around and through St. James Park. For a while they were mute. Then Phillip spoke, of Racine and Euripides, of Rachel's magnificence and passion. She was not afraid of love or of life, she lived openly, to the hilt, allowing nothing to dull her pagan senses.

Julie understood. The tumult of feeling she had shared with the Greek queen opened warm and ripe into the summer night, the swollen flower heads, the compulsive savor of Phillip's skin. They rode clasped together through the molten dark. Her breasts rose into points against the tulle. Phillip's soft mustache brushed on her throat.

The trees in Kensington rusted into a blaze of color for her and Phillip and Aunt Anna. In the years before, this had seemed the least likely season, but Phillip loved the wind so she loved it, too, tied her bonnet on good and tight and let the wind blow. If night was barred to them, they had all the exhilarating days. Papa could do nothing about them. They saw Kean at the Princess and comedies at the Haymarket, went again and again to matinees at Sadler's Wells, and walked through the empty, russet park.

Phillip always carried a roll of manuscript in his pocket; he'd read, striding up and down before their bench, taking every part, reading so eloquently it was hard to say what moved one most, the sentences or how Phillip uttered them. When he finished the end of Act Two, Aunt Anna took out her handkerchief, wiped her eyes, and blew her nose frankly.

"I'm not a one for fancy talk, but I say it straight out, Phillip, you've a gift." She put her glasses back on. "Not that anyone needs to tell you." The way she snapped it made them laugh. When his writing went well, his mood *was* high. When he found a flaw he was dejected, almost sullen. Julie felt the same. It was as if the words were her own, as if she were the writer; and Phillip said, of course, she was as much a part of it as he, she had given rhythm to words and made the universe intelligible. He said that!

Often she couldn't sleep. His exuberance could so easily be followed by a drop, like waves lifting and lowering a boat over the Channel. She lay awake then, searching for the magic clew that would bring him back. It was always a chance. When you were buoyant, he sat on the park bench with his head in his hands. The times you were tuned to moodiness, he arrived transformed, a gaudy waistcoat, a yellow cravat, and a semijocose air as if he had traded in the tragic playwright for the gay young blade.

One afternoon he took them to Soho to visit Jan van Stret, the artist who had painted Grand-père.

"Papa would not approve of this neighborhood, would he?" laughed Phillip. "But the fashionable people who want to be painted feel so wicked coming."

Herr van Stret stood stiff and thin, bowing as they came in. Slowly, with wonder, Julie circled the bare, high-ceilinged room. One wall was of glass and a plane tree fluttered its branches, the other walls were lined with pictures, beautiful women with thin throats, stout jolly gentlemen, matrons in black lace. She stopped short before the head of a woman gazing at a crow, her ashen face soft, wooing, its full lips sucked to kiss.

"Like a phantom, isn't she?" Phillip said softly, and she clung to his hand. The desire of the girl was such a haunting thing, so wasted on the crow. And how had the artist made it mean so much? Just the faintest light through slanted lids and the haze which framed all this yearning made a world for it. She turned to Phillip, and he was watching not the painting but herself, avidly, solemnly, as if she were being born.

"A very sad girl," said Herr van Stret. "I do not paint her for money but for my pleasure."

"Here she is again," Aunt Anna said.

But this time it was the whole girl and without clothes!

"Julie, Julie!" Phillip said. "Open your eyes, see the skin tones and the grace."

"There's nothing nasty except in some folks' minds," Aunt Anna said dryly.

Julie let herself drift into the picture. She grew almost used to the bare skin and rose-tipped breasts. How could you love the human soul, Phillip said, without loving the flesh, the lips, and eyes that showed it forth? She thought about that after they had gone home, and the next time they visited Herr Jan, it was easier. The room became familiar. Under the table was the worn place in the carpet, here they stuffed wool back into the shabby sofa, under the round table were scars where he scraped his knives.

When he was painting, Herr Jan was young. You saw the lean, lithe line of his back. He was tied to the canvas with veins, and blood beat back and forth through his brush. When he stopped, he was an old man. A thousand lines ran on his face like cracks in a painting. There was a small wood stove in the studio, and always a dish bubbling and cooking. When they should have been taking tea, the artist would spoon out a rich stew or a pot roast cooked in wine. He would line up plates on the rough, spotted planking where his brushes lay to dry, and onto each plate a portion of meat, white onions, carrots, and the rich, winy broth. There was claret in odd glasses and strong cheese she and Aunt Anna must eat, ladies or no. Everything was so right with Phillip.

But the free autumn days couldn't last. Wind came howling across from the sea, fog surged over the world and winter settled down, the dirtiest, longest, sickest winter of all time. After weeks of isolation—she'd never seen such stubborn, thick fur snow—Julie dragged Aunt Anna through the slush to the British Museum. She must see Phillip! Down the corridors they lumbered in their draggled skirts, and how delighted he was. He rubbed her cold little feet and wrapped them in his overcoat, but she took cold just the same. Dr. Potter had to lance her abscessed ear, and after that she was allowed out no more in the winter air.

9

She rode in the gilded carriage beside Emma through an enchanted world. The city was burnished with light, every window flaunted itself to catch the morning sun. Uncle Henry had hired the handsomest of equipages, coachmen with powdered wigs, footmen in cockaded hats and gold aiguillettes, caparisoned horses so great and fierce their hoofs raised thunder. Jack and Uncle Henry joked as always, and under her floppy hat, Aunt Mathilda discussed ham and jam and hot breads for the breakfast; but if the coach turned into a pumpkin, if Emma's shoes were of glass. . . . Church bells swung, from every steeple in London their golden ringing came in waves, the far-off tinkly bells and close brazen bells sounding the chorus for Emma's wedding.

Uncle Henry leaned out the window, waving. "Your young man's carriage just fell in at the rear, Em, guess he's going to show up after all." He laughed, mopping his florid face and the spot of thin hair at the back of his head.

Jack winked at Julie. "Not me. No old girl in a birdcage is ever going to trap me!" Emma smiled, keeping her head just so in its white veil. Aunt Mathilda reached across to touch it.

"You'll wear it next, Julie. Then Ethelyn, and after that you can put it away for your girls."

Think of it—the hoofs and bells and sunlight, Papa on the seat where Uncle Henry sat, Grandma Stodel's lace veil on her head, and Phillip.

"If only Leon Dekker could have come. It would have meant so much to Ludwig, like my having you, Julie. Imagine either of us on our wedding day without each other."

"Leon was sensible," declared Aunt Mathilda, waving her floppy hat. He had written that Lud should get married at once, and Emma and Aunt Mathilda both loved him sight unseen. He would have given a good deal to come home, but there was over two years' service still before him; he wanted to get it over and then come home for good. He begged them to go ahead. He sent a magnificent silver service decorated with Sumatra filigree, some Javanese andirons, and an Oriental shawl to Emma, who, he said, had better be a good cook by the time he came. The letter had been well received by both families. Mrs. Dekker had cried over it to her heart's content.

"Julie! Julie, there's Grandpa's flower woman, there she is!" Emma had grabbed her arm and they turned, peering through the back window at the vanishing, dwindling figure with its basket of pinks and white and lavenders. It was no bigger now than people in the curved mirror at home, and still you could see every flower on the tray, the clumps of lilac, the sweet peas, the spicy carnations, just as they had been that day when Grandpa came home to London.

"Carnations, lilacs, sweet peas," Emma laughed. "Grandpa asked her the way to the Dutch consulate."

And suddenly nothing mattered except Emma, who was going far away to live in Arnheim, not the alien Emma to whom she couldn't speak of Phillip, but the old Emma, whose roots went back with hers into the past. Grandpa had belonged to them both; they had romped with him and gone to his funeral and heard over and over how it had been when after twenty years the stolen child inquired his way of the

49

flower woman on London Bridge. Nothing could change the deep roots. The old affection welled up warm and sweet. They had played and grown and shared everything. Staying the night with Emma had been the greatest boon Papa could grant, and how they had whispered, keeping warm together, their knees up like two spoons in a box. They had found out about babies, they had found the shameful secret of growing up, Emma first because Aunt Mathilda didn't believe young girls should be frightened. Aunt Mathilda had heard of a girl who took pneumonia washing out her clothes, dabbling in cold water because she didn't dare ask hot water from cook. Emma had known that first, she had known about love first, she had been kissed first. It was as if the carriage had divided and Emma's half was racing ahead with the clanging bells, fast, so she could never sit beside her again, into a world where she couldn't follow.

"You're going so far away, Emma."

"Why, it's not far. You'll come every summer, oftener if you want. The little blue room is just for you, that is, it's for you unless . . ." she laughed, baring her white teeth with their edges ridged as if she'd bitten thread. "Don't try to tell me good-by forever. You're never going to lose me, Julie, we're alike as two peas in a pod!"

The rector was standing at the side door. Even the rector seemed polished by the sun. His face was powdered and his ears stood out like two clear white shells. Julie carried Emma's prayer book, she kept close beside Emma as if she might hold her that way. Bridesmaids came fluttering in their pale blue gowns, and the musty old room was given over to the spicy blossoms in their nosegays.

A burst of music swelled through the door, and two by two the pale blue girls moved into it. All through the ceremony, Julie stood beside Emma watching her breathe, watching the minister who would look that way, say those things to *her*. Someone sobbed throatily from the front row and burst into tears. That would be Mrs. Dekker. In her explosive happiness, Aunt Mathilda tried to sniff, too. It was over.

There they all were, as the bridal party marched past, the Uncle Louis cousins with husbands and wives and a few new children, Aunt Dee with a hand to her ailing heart, skinny Mr. Dekker supporting his wife. Julie tried to keep up with Emma, but the procession broke at the door and Aunt Anna grabbed her into the vestry.

"This here came to the house just before we left. I managed to snitch it before your pa did."

Julie tore the envelope. "Phillip—he's not well, Aunt Anna, do you think—would it be all right if we dropped by for a minute on the way? They'd never miss us."

"If it's a matter of savin' a life," Aunt Anna said.

So they took one of the gilded carriages and galloped off to Gower Street. She told the coachman to wait, and he folded one stuffed calf over the other and prepared to do so. Up the steps, into the house she had passed so often in panic because Phillip might just be coming out. Blindfolded she'd have known that house, that street, by the bird wings, the familiar whir and gap of pain.

In the dark corridor, a deer head glared at them, a tall, unkempt maid appeared from behind a hanging. Julie, her face on fire, said they had come to see Mr. McManus who was ill. The girl gave an impudent smirk.

"Sick, is he, well you'll find 'im right up those stairs, third to yer left."

Right up the stairs they went, without a backward glance. Julie knocked timidly at the door, and if it hadn't opened at once, she'd have turned and fled. Phillip in a dark wool dressing gown welcomed them as if the visit was most usual.

"Hello, darling, Aunt Anna, good of you to come," and he showed them into his room which was not at all sinister or wicked. The bright sun that had fallen for Emma's wedding lay on the starched counterpane and scattered among the thousand papers on his desk. "Sit down, let me take your hat, Aunt Anna; God, how gorgeous you are, Gypsy." He hadn't shaved. The dark beard fell in hollows along his cheeks, his eyes were fevered.

"Phillip, you're ill!" She put her hand to his forehead. "Aunt Anna, he's hot."

"I just haven't slept, I'm all right, darling." He paced the narrow rug. "I can't stand living this way, Julie. You're all I ask of life, but we must be together. The play is nearly ready. Let's be married and go at once!" He raised her to her feet and kissed her simply, as if Aunt Anna understood. "Life is short, we haven't the right to waste it. Julie, say we can be married. I'll speak to your father."

"I can save you the trouble." It was Papa, there he stood, in the whirling, blackened entrance to Phillip's room.

10

Papa sat on one side of the tea table, Phillip on the other. They stood for Julie and Aunt Anna almost as usual, almost as if the hidden flood were not knocking the brick walls of the cellar into rubble. Freddie sauntered in and Ethelyn came, pouting because something was up and she didn't know.

While she brewed the tea, Mother in her gentle voice told Phillip of the wedding, keeping it polite, always playing a part and keeping it polite. Freddie ran his finger under his tight collar and muttered about a lot of fuss. Mother said pay no mind to Freddie, it had been a beautiful wedding, the minister had spoken so nicely, poor Mathilda was so happy and so sad, and the breakfast had been beyond belief. Papa sat like stone in his wedding suit, cut off as effectively by silence as if he graced a show window in Bond Street, tall, stiff Frederic Corper wearing the latest cut for gentlemen. Aunt Anna passed the bread and butter. And now, Mother said, Emma and Ludwig were on their way, traveling by special coach to Dover. Papa's broadcloth shoulders crashed through the plate glass.

"I understand, my dear, that Mr. McManus is planning a trip of his own." Julie's tea rocked. "To America, is that right, sir?"

Phillip smiled, accepting Papa's unexpectedly light tone. He was indeed planning to cross the ocean. Edmund Kean had found that country receptive to good acting, so had the Kembles and Macready and Rachel. Look what Boucicault was doing! It seemed like the best place on earth to attempt a playwright's theater.

Aunt Anna took a deep draught and settled back. Phillip talked and Papa listened, pursing his lips as if he found it tolerable. His own play was finished, Phillip said, except for one scene which he would polish en route. Several faculty men had read and thought well of it.

"We're eager to go as soon as possible. We can be married by the end of the month, catch the *Liverpool* packet or the *Isaac Webb* and reach America before the February storms."

Ethelyn almost fell off the settee. Mother watched Papa, alarmed. Papa stirred his cup.

"You've evidently been misinformed about the *Isaac Webb*. The worst type of cattle boat, McManus. I believe that aboard her as many of your unfortunate countrymen have perished of typhus as have ever reached America." He blew away the steam and sipped slowly.

"We wouldn't go steerage, they say second class on the packets isn't bad. I thought. . . ."

"A sad list of disasters on those packet boats. Hm." He daubed a napkin to his mustache as if the history of sailing ships was his sole concern. "I needn't remind you of the *John* or the *Grimshaw* or the *Europa*, and you are aware that lifeboats are provided only for cabin passengers. But let's not anticipate disaster," he finished, for Phillip's face had gone gray with anguish as if they were already hanging to a spar in a flaming sea. "Second class, you say, what is second class, sir? A partition dividing steerage to suit the imagination of the ship's broker, bad business that second class! Even were you not subject to disease and filth, the freight is usually pig iron or hides. Imagine the stench locked in the hold with hides! And pig iron shifts so, those small vessels pitch like box tops."

Phillip had jumped to his feet. He walked, hands in his pockets, staring at the carpet.

"There are a good many things to consider, Mr. McManus. You have estimated perhaps, the delicacy of my daughter's health? We barely saved her when she had pneumonia in adolescence and I regret to say it has left her permanently impaired. You'll forgive my inquiring too into matters of a rather personal . . . how much capital, for instance, do you have?"

Phillip flushed, but he answered in a voice brave as ever. "Fifty pounds. Traveling second class, we could get there with enough to keep us modestly until I find—"

"And suppose you don't *find?*" Papa interrupted, almost kindly, nothing like what one might have thought.

"There's no question of that, sir. If I don't sell the play at once, I'll do anything. I'll work as a stage hand."

"But let's just suppose—because I am a man of business and I've seen such things happen—let us suppose that nothing does appear available in your theater. I presume nothing avails in London or you would be less impatient to leave? Suppose it is the same in America. Even granting that those people are as frantic for culture as you think—and I don't pretend to agree, I hold with Mrs. Trollope that only the lowest type of European has ever gone. Still, suppose your descendants of adventurers and servants are as avid as you think for—shall we call it—art? Don't you conceive the possibility that you might not find a vacancy for several months?" He waited. "Wouldn't it be fairer to yourself to go without responsibility, free to wait and work for the type of employment of which you are specifically in search?"

"Julie and I love each other."

"I want to go." She ran and put her arm through Phillip's. "I want—"

Ethelyn coughed shrilly.

54

"Your desires are obvious. Control yourself, Julie."

"Ethelyn, Freddie," murmured Mother, and they went out, not wanting to.

"This young lady happens not to be of age, Mr. McManus. An immediate marriage is out of the question. Not that we have anything against you, nothing at all. I won't pretend that I'd have chosen a—playwright—but that is your business. What I suggest is simply that with your very limited means—I am correct in assuming that when you leave this country, you are also cutting yourself off from any further allotments from your stepfather? Well then," and he almost smiled, running his finger down the arc of his mustache, "well then, why not go alone, establish yourself, and then contemplate matrimony?"

Phillip's thin shoulders bowed under the load of it. She ran along beside him from the piano to the hall and back, the words almost choking her.

"Dear, dear Phillip. Perhaps Papa is right. I'd be a drag right now."

"Inasmuch as you are under age, I assure you, you wouldn't be anything right now." Papa advanced his cup for more tea.

"We belong together," Phillip said bitterly.

"Yes, yes, but for just a few months, Phillip."

"You wouldn't be afraid, you'd come when I sent for you?"

"Anywhere, Phillip."

"I've tried to skimp along on fifty pounds myself," Aunt Anna said gravely. "You do get panicky."

"Aunt Anna, you could come with her!" The eagerness rushed into Phillip's voice. He could go at once, steerage, on the cheapest boat, he'd get a job, maybe with Boucicault, in less than six months he'd send for both of them. That made it real, vivid and sensible. Aunt Anna said she'd always wanted to go to America, she'd come along quick as a wink. She watched Papa closely, but Papa was very fair. He hadn't mentioned the scene at Phillip's or held it against them. He sat drinking his tea, almost smiling. The two small bones moved in his cheek.

11

Once a person made up his mind to go to America, he went fast. Crowd what you would into the days, there was no holding them. Aunt Anna put up a cask of potatoes and pickled beef. They salted down eggs and bought a fine big cheese, so strong Lord help the other passengers, and a tin of tea. Julie bought something else besides, a leather writing case filled with white paper. She bought a stock of steel pens and black ink in a metal flask, all of herself she could send along.

Up in his room on Gower Street, they packed and unpacked his portmanteau. Yes, they went to Gower Street blithely now, sailed past the grinning elk's head and the grinning maid, as if the events of Emma's wedding day gave them leave. It was in the open now, Papa knew she was going to marry Phillip, even if he didn't precisely know. . . .

"Your pa's like to explode before the month's out," Aunt Anna said. "I didn't credit even him with that control."

"Now Aunt Anna!" For Papa had been generous, he was giving them all this freedom when actually he would rather have her marry, well, someone else. And she blushed because that morning's post had brought a letter in Mr. Munzell's painstaking hand, would Mrs. Corper and Miss Julie honor him on a given week end by coming down to visit his sister, in Surrey? The note was addressed, of course, to Papa and accepted by him promptly.

"Getting thick I'd call it," Aunt Anna said.

But Julie didn't mind going to Surrey or meeting Sister Munzell either, nothing would matter, Phillip would be gone. He'd be in Liverpool bargaining for passage with the crafty agents who looked like Legree in the play about slaves.

"Let's have jam tarts for tea, Aunt Anna. Phillip will love them."

What gay teas they had on the last fast afternoons. Phillip was ravenous, he'd eat a dozen tarts. He was keyed to fever pitch, the crossing would be a lark, why not one more Irishman jammed in with the rest? He'd find a snug apartment in New York, with a wood stove where Julie could cook their stews, he'd keep an eye out for work for Aunt Anna, they must need good wardrobe and costume people. He held Julie's hand, kept her near him; for underneath the gaiety and thrilling closeness was something else. Would life ever again be quite the same? They clung together, discovering every day some new tone, some new touch that must be kept alive between them.

And finally there were no more days. She didn't ask Papa if she might go to Aunt Anna's, he would have wanted to know why she couldn't bid Mr. McManus good-by in her own house. She took the precious leather writing case and wore the red dress Phillip liked best. She had insisted on coming alone. Phillip was at the university and Aunt Anna was cooking. Besides, if you were capable of traveling to America, as she was, as she *would*, you were certainly capable of going to Bow Road on the omnibus. Covertly, she watched the people, the six across and those crowded to either side of her on the dirty cushions. Perhaps they thought it strange for a lone young lady . . . but they were listening with amusement while a red-faced woman shouted to a deaf, uninterested husband the way to cook bloaters. She couldn't make the poor man hear, and finally, exasperated, turned to the whole coach, bawling, "Ain't that right, ain't he a old bloater hisself?"

Julie got down from the coach and ran along Bow Road. Often she dreamed of running this street to Aunt Anna's and in her dream she saw every house, the dull monotonous wall, bilious yellow, real as life, the skimpy iron gratings shuttled by. Past the Smithers' and their fringed red lamp, past the Riordans' who were always borrowing a pennyworth of tea, past the dirty gray curtains of the Morrows'—all true to life until she came to the little gate that turned into Aunt Anna's. *It* wasn't there. The Morrows' gray curtains swung, but tight, up next to them without a break was the Jones' house which should have been to Aunt Anna's left. That's how the dream was, Aunt Anna's house swallowed up, gone.

But tonight the gate was there and the walk, and she ran through the door into Phillip's arms. Aunt Anna had gone to the chemist's for some hippo and tartar emetic Phillip was not going without. They laughed over that but they held each other close in the crowded little room, knowing it was the last time. How, exactly, was his face, the beloved face? Not quite the same as yesterday or the day before, always strange again, some trifle new, the head at a new tilt. She put the cool ends of her little fingers in the corners of his eyes. She drew her fingers softly along the closed lids, around, tracing out the eyebrows, back to the secret cups beside the bridge of his nose. She learned the whole of his face by touch, and suddenly his hands were on her, his urgent, stroking hands.

Aunt Anna did not come but dusk came, great waving flames of it filled, fanned the room, pressed warm on them. The clock throbbed. And why couldn't it stop, just for now, for a moment while her mouth had found its home? This would be a dream she might not be able to remember, his hands, his thrusting tongue, her body shaken with some strange life of its own, desire fusing and flowing so she couldn't hold Phillip close enough.

"Darling, dearest, you're crying." He kissed her eyes, she could taste the salt on his lips. They knelt together, Phillip who worshiped science and read Malthus and Darwin's papers, knelt with her in the small room on Bow Road. He didn't pray, he just held her and put a golden wedding ring on her hand. It was his mother's, the ring his father, his real father, had given her. It was for Julie. She was to keep it near her, wear it to sleep at night and, please God, in a few months she'd wear it always.

12

Mr. Munzell sat expanding his thighs on the swaying seat of the carriage, expanding his chest with the brisk country air. He had left the Inner Temple promptly at noon, having somehow found time to don a fresh white stock and a brand, spanking new canary-colored waistcoat; at half past twelve he had settled her mother and herself and taken up his post facing them; henceforth each turn of the wheels was calculated to the dot. As they passed the lordly parks and manors, he indicated the wondrous oaks, the sleek lawns, the healthy cattle. He was an authority on the holdings of the noblemen of England, could point out property with his umbrella and estimate within a farthing of its value. This park in Deptford was once the residence of the Duke of Essex, John Evelyn had lived here; this seamen's hospital had once been the site of Greenwich House granted by Henry V to Thomas Beaufort from whom it passed to Humphrey, Duke of Gloucester. The full multifoliate course of English history rose mellifluous to Mr. Munzell's lips.

Then he paused, produced a small box of chocolate drops for their refreshment, and extracted his fat gold watch from its tight fob pocket. They should arrive, yes, in time for an early tea, then a brief turn in Addington before dark and in the morning after church a visit to the Royal Military College for the East Indian Army.

"Our friends, the Dekkers, have a son in the Indies," murmured Mother.

Mr. Munzell conceded it a worthy profession for military-minded men, of which, he hastened to add, he was not one. No, and he writhed sedately on his seat, he would like to live the whole of his life in England, he wanted some day to buy some rich historic tract of land. Business was very well in London, but live, live in the country, build a sanctuary where professional friends could be entertained far from the bustling crowd, he said. He said. . . .

But Julie was rushing on to the crowd in Liverpool. Phillip was there, his long hands were carrying her leather writing case. How good it would be when they were together, day after day, to sit in the same room conscious of his breathing. He would write his plays and there would be times when he'd withdraw, frightening times, she'd lived through some already; but she would have her own work to do, and when he was through, they'd stay up the whole night, the kettle simmering on the stove, reading what he'd written, acting the parts, changing the words. . . .

"Julie," Mother said. "Do attend. You have missed a delightful anecdote." Mother was looking at Mr. Munzell with a proud, personal look, as if it were John or Freddie home from school with his stories. Julie looked, too, trying to see what Mother saw, but there was nothing in his smooth, good-looking face except the caution habitual to it and the unbounded good humor which had to do with this excursion.

Ever since the night of Emma's ball, he had spoken of his sister who represented womanhood incarnate. She was the perfect wife, the perfect mother, and not the least interested in women's rights. Which was why it seemed strange, his wanting them to meet. Yet here they were trundling every minute closer to Croydon, while the last details of importance issued syllable on syllable from the familiar fount. The manor of Croydon had been presented by William I to Archbishop Lanfranc. Julie would want to visit the old church, they would accomplish that tomorrow after services at his brother-in-law's. Brother-in-law was, unfortunately, no gifted orator—Mr. Munzell made it clear that before the altar as before the law, a mighty delivery was well-nigh indispensable—but the man's devotion was beyond question and whatever his merits or demerits, the Almighty had evidently singled him out by uniting him in wedlock with that paragon of creatures, Sister Munzell.

Her name was, in fact, Peabody, and she turned out to be a surprisingly pleasant person, a young matron with smooth brown hair, who stood smiling and waving. You could see her a long way off in her black dress, with a brown-haired boy and girl on either side of her. They waved from the minute the carriage turned up Brighton Road, and Mr. Munzell brandished his umbrella, then his hat, from the window and finally thrust out his head, so plastered and dressed the wind could not disengage a strand. Mrs. Peabody reached up to kiss his flushed wax cheek.

"I'm so glad you've come, Herbert, and you, Mrs. Corper and Julie. We seldom have a chance to meet Herbert's friends. Herbert, you're pale, you're working too hard." She led the way through the kitchen garden while the boy and girl each tried to climb a Munzell leg. It was a charming garden with an oval pool for the boy's fish, and the way it lay half-hidden by overhanging trees, it seemed like a piece newly fallen from the sky.

"Uncle Herbert, the goldfish!" They dragged him off to the pond. The little girl cried he must fix her doll perambulator, the wheel had come off.

"Frank, Anna," Mrs. Peabody said in a firm low tone, "you promised your father to gather leaves, and you'd best be to it before tea or there'll be no trimming for the altar."

"I'll go with them, eh, Frances?"

"Uncle Herbert. Uncle Herbert!" They dragged him around the gravel walk, off toward the copse.

"We'll be right back," he called, then something more, but he was going too fast. Ethelyn should see how Mr. Munzell could run!

"I feel sorry for girls who don't have brothers," said Mrs. Peabody. "I don't know how I'd have got on without Herbert." Her cheerful face was so tender that Julie felt ashamed, as if Mrs. Peabody were alluding to someone she had pretended to know but did not. And it was true, she

61

didn't know the gentleman whose sister lived at Croydon and who had just gone galloping into the woods in his best boots.

She was to learn even more. He planned to enter politics, he confided that evening, as they strolled about the town. As soon as he was ready he would be put up as a borough representative to Commons, from Croydon, which was his official residence. There was a tract of land he had his eye on, but of first importance was the selection of a wife who would help him, a gentlewoman like Mrs. Peabody but well versed in political affairs as well, for she would have to be a charming hostess and hold sway at gatherings of her husband's peers. She would have to be—there was a great deal she would have to be—and he dwelt on it, his great thumb holding Julie's wrist steady on his arm. In the dark street, he bent slightly, protecting her from vast dangers, and the tinge of lemon breathed on the clear air. But Julie was not inclined to mock Mr. Munzell, she liked him very much here at Croydon and responded to his confidence. With all her heart, she hoped he would find a suitable lady to grace the halls of Munzell, and the halls would materialize. Wasn't it wonderful when you made up your mind what you wanted? She spoke of Phillip's adventure to America and her own adventure which was yet to come, Mr. Munzell listening attentively as no one else had, as Emma never had.

"So, Julie, you are formally betrothed then, to Mr. McManus." He said it so solemnly she had to laugh.

"Oh, not formally, not betrothed at all, I'm just going to marry him." He absorbed that, every word, then he laughed too, a not quite natural ha-ha.

13

"And the other ear, Mrs. Peabody, don't miss the other ear!" Julie leaned so far out the window that Mother clutched her skirt. The Peabodys laughed and hollered back. Mr. Munzell tried to holler, too, his voice muffled by rushing water and the towels about his neck and the racket of the boy and girl who ran deliriously around the pump.

"He'll have to be well doused, won't he?" called Julie.

"Washed clean for the Lord," said the Reverend.

"And his mustache, too," she laughed, "clean for the Lord."

Elegant Mr. Munzell knelt on a small square of carpet beside the pump, his great figure bloused out in red and white checked cambric, his perfect head bowed over a tub of soapy water as unceremoniously as if Mrs. Peabody were dressing a chicken. She sat on a stool pouring a stream of amber soap. It was her best soap, made from a recipe of old Grandmother Peabody, just three gallons a year, and she rubbed it in with her strong narrow hands, chafing and lathering until the head grew big, white, soapy curls. Then Frank was allowed to work the pump. He pumped the handle, he pumped harder, there was a gasp from underground and a flood gushed over the white hair, melted it, flung suds on the board planking and the dark Munzell head was left gleaming naked.

Then there was the drying, the penitent still on his knees being flayed, boxed, smothered, and rumpled with towels, and finally the shapeless checked cambric clambered to its feet exhibiting a pink face and a mass of brown hair which crimped and waved from the brow, adding at least another two inches to tall Mr. Munzell. Mrs. Peabody stepped back to admire her handiwork and he did look better, his mustache too, even if it did splay out; but Mr. Munzell moaned he was ruined. It would take hours to repair the damage, get himself oiled fit to be seen in church. What defenseless creatures men were, he moaned.

"Breakfast will be a while yet," Mrs. Peabody called. "Why don't you ladies walk down the road? The air is so light."

Julie and her mother strolled toward the copse into the fused, musky-sweet decay of leaves and wet bark. It was going to be a splendid day. The air was so clear that when you looked through the smoke from the Peabodys' chimney the sky danced, quivered as if it were under water. Now and again a few dry leaves came sailing, they traveled jauntily, pretending they hadn't really fallen dead off the chestnut tree. Julie and her mother sang. They walked arm in arm, without their bonnets, without shawls. A leaf landed right on Mother's head, and they kept step, singing of Laura's smile and the winter wind and *de varken*. Julie skipped a step.

"What fun that was with Mr. Munzell's hair. I wish Phillip were here, I'd wash his hair."

"Julie!"

"After we're married, I'll always wash his hair. It's soft and wispy and. . . ."

"You don't know what you're saying, dear. Certainly you've never heard your mother—"

"But I feel that way, Mama. I love every bit of Phillip, even the little brushy bit on his chin."

"I don't know what your father would say, Julie. There are some things . . . a lady doesn't allow herself to *think* some things, not even about her husband."

"But why, Mother? That's how I feel."

"You're not even *betrothed* to Mr. McManus," her mother whispered, as if the woods might hear.

"I'm going to marry him. You do believe me? I'm going to marry Phillip, I love him, I'll never stop loving him!"

"My dear child, every young girl thinks that at some time. You're very young. Mr. McManus is only a student and he's going a long way off. Heaven knows what may happen or how you'll feel in another week."

Julie withdrew her arm. She trod angrily, smashing the crisp leaves.

"Now, dear, control that quick, bitter temper. I am telling you what any mother would tell her daughter. It's a beautiful thing to marry with affection on both sides, but one finds such happiness by patience and tact and not by rash demonstrations. Mother is speaking for your own good, my sweet Julie." And she tried to link arms, but Julie would not.

"You don't believe I love Phillip."

"You were always willful, Julie, you must fling yourself all the way into anything you do. You're stubborn, dear, and you are very young."

Julie picked up a switch and as Mother spoke, she switched at her own palm.

When you looked up, the bright autumn leaves frisked and blurred, but down among the trees it was forsaken, noiseless. When Mr. Munzell came running, they could hear him a long way off. He was good humored from his scrubbing, he couldn't understand why Julie had nothing to say, nor at breakfast either. Let the others gabble and titter, she carried her sulky burden all the way to church, sat in the brown box pew and stared unseeing at her hymnbook. She didn't mean to sing, but the familiar tunes came droning from the organ, everyone sang as loud as they could, and soon she did, too. Ribbons of sun unwound and sprawled on the rough floor and how could she have been so mean?

Mrs. Peabody sat there calm and proud, even the children had settled themselves on the hard seats and gave attention to their papa, who was not their papa now but the thin voice of God. Mr. Munzell was holding the prayer book for her mother. Mother herself, her dear face in its black bonnet, how could she have spoken so to poor, frightened Mother, who was only trying to think of her good, wanting the safe and sane way, and not understanding that there had been enough sanity and safety, one wanted to break with it, throw it off, find excitement and significance and life! She'd explain to Mother, she'd beg forgiveness, she was so sorry, she almost wept with the pity of it; and at the thought of what she would say, some mighty weight lifted, slipped into the organ din, went bellowing up through the pipes.

"And as ye would that men should do to you, do ye. . . ." Mr. Munzell nudged her urgently.

Mother was swaying against Mr. Munzell, her lips white. Mother! He picked her up quickly and carried her up the aisle and out of the spinning Luke. Julie hurried after, hunting frantically for the smelling bottle. Out in the vestry, Mr.

Munzell tried to prop his limp bundle on a bench. Oh, Mother!

"Sit here, hold her, Julie."

Mrs. Peabody hurried in. Then others. Hiding their faces in their bonnets, they rushed around the vestry room whispering, hiding, trying to evade some unembodied menace. Water, camphor, blankets, ice, and Mother lay like a heavy child, hardly breathing. Some unseen, blindfolded giant was coming! And what could you do? How could you save her?

"Mrs. Peabody, Mrs. Peabody! Mother's—"

"No, she isn't, Julie. She's coming out of it." And she held the camphor bottle under the little blue nose. "There, you see." A tremor had shaken, was shaking the whole frame. "She'll be around again in a minute." One of Mother's hands felt its way out of the blanket, reached up uncertainly, and drew a line down along the smooth hair next to her cheek. Her eyes opened, looked straight into Julie's, and closed tiredly. The breathing grew more regular. By the time church was over, she was able to say she felt better; but Mr. Munzell wouldn't let her take a step, not until old Dr. Malcolm had seen her. He carried her to a carriage, then through the kitchen garden and up the stairs to their room.

"I'm quite all right," Mother kept saying. "Don't be frightened, hasn't a lady the privilege of fainting?"

But Dr. Malcolm didn't regard it as fainting. He said she must be kept quiet, at least a week. There was to be no thought of returning to London with Mr. Munzell as they had planned—Mr. Munzell had planned it all so minutely, even to the full moon—no indeed, Mrs. Corper must rest, she must sleep, she was going through a difficult period right now, he would come again tomorrow. He didn't like her heart action, either.

In all, the visit to Croydon lasted a month, a slow, steady turning of days, and she had Mother to herself for the first time. Just the two of them, close and uninterrupted, no longer mother and child but something more, for they had traded places in a way. Mother, the grownup and guardian, was the protected now, it was Julie who must be strong. And what would she not have done for Mother, anything, soothe her, serve her, make up for the awful Sunday when she had flung the dear arm off and spoken in anger. In some half-mystic way, she felt responsible for this illness, even though she knew the full physical explanation. Mrs. Peabody had explained what the doctor meant by "climacteric."

Once, while Mother rested upstairs, Mrs. Peabody explained the conclusion of that strange story which Emma had begun long ago, when they were children and Emma had learned about flux and change because Aunt Mathilda thought young girls should not be frightened. It did not go on forever, according to Mrs. Peabody, there was a beginning and an end and Julie's mother had never been too strong, she would have had ever so many more children if she had. Mrs. Peabody spoke firmly and gently. They sat in the garden and she shelled her peas, pressing each pod with narrow thumbs, popping and scooting the peas with her thumbnail, as firm and sure as if she'd grown on the kitchen stoop and was rooted there.

"You're so sure of everything, Mrs. Peabody. If I came back in a hundred years, you'd be sitting here shelling your peas, neat and quick, and the children would come from school. . . . You're so orderly!"

Mrs. Peabody laughed and patted Julie's apron. She certainly wouldn't be there in a hundred years and you had to be orderly if there was mending to be done and you were to have a clean house and dinner ready and a currant pie baked before Herbert and Mr. Corper arrived from London. She scooped up her apron with its load of pods and it seemed that, mentioning her brother's name, her glance became especially penetrating. It made Julie hide her face, take up the bowl of peas and wash them under the pump with more vigor than was needed.

Then Mother rang her little bell and Julie raced up the stairs to give herself to Mother, do whatever she wished. The patient seemed much improved. Color was coming back to her lips, her face looked rested, happy, and young, sunlight mantled her hair so you could not see one strand of gray. You forgave her for kowtowing to Papa. What else could she do?

"Mother, I feel as if I'd never known you before." Julie combed the pale hair and tied it with ribbons like a girl's. They sewed and read aloud. Autumn wind blew around the house, waved the curtains, and brushed the dried sticks on every tree. Julie closed the window against the draft. Leaves were hanging on as best they could now. A whole company of them clung to the tree outside, twirling and fluttering like thin flakes of a tambourine.

14

It took so long for a letter to come from America. Almost forever. She sat through the London winter stitching, stitching, reading aloud to Mother who must still convalesce, rose in the morning, retired at night, and at regular intervals confronted food. Phillip was somewhere, but where? He seemed lost in the universe and she yearned for him, yearned to go to him, thought of nothing else and felt deeply guilty, for Mother's illness had drawn the family close in love and fear and anonymity and she was part of it. Then finally a letter came with her name at the top, the one word telling who she was again after the weeks when she hadn't known.

"Julie:

"This is the paper you gave me, the pen and ink. I take them up eagerly to tell you I have seen my first show on Broadway." She could hear Phillip saying it. "I say again that the theater offers the most exciting experience one can find in a civilized society. But for me tonight it had a deeper significance. The theater you and I have known in

London, the theater I have studied, takes on new meaning in this free, teeming city. There is poverty, and the streets would be better for a good scouring rain, but there is completely lacking that sense of guilt," guilt, he said! "that stifled, sick sense that oppressed me so in London. Here all is color and motion, a constant rush of traffic, omnibuses, hacks, and drays, gorgeous carriages all the way from the Battery up Broadway. Don't think of this as some small borough. High buildings dovetail into each other with scarcely a foot to spare, huge signs proclaim wares of all sorts. What showmanship! The marble pillars of the Astor House, the shops glittering with displays, Barnum's Museum, the spire of Trinity. You are swept up by the gala, festive spirit of the crowd, the last-minute excitement before the curtain." How she longed to be there, to hurry with him through the lobby.

"Broadway fascinates me. I spent the first day walking, saw the Astor Place Opera House where they staged the riot over Macready, and Wallace's Lyceum, Niblo's, Burton's, and Laura Keene's. It was Burton's I attended tonight. Edward Davenport in *Hamlet*. He isn't Phelps, but his Hamlet is tender and gravely humorous and not to be discounted. Tomorrow Laura Keene's for *As You Like It*. She, incidentally, is the first woman manager here and as successful as she has been as an actress. Oh, it is quite the country for women, my darling. You should see them walking up and down in the afternoons, shopping, beautifully dressed and *unattended* which is quite proper and right here—until after dark. Once the lamps are lit, lone ladies are considered women of the town. The courtesans take over then, and some beautiful and exotic creatures there are, all elaborately gotten up to appeal to the kid-gloved and Japan-booted gentry." What would Mr. Munzell say to that?

"One moment gives way to another only to reveal some fresh sensation. The oysters are magnificent, washed down with rum or with coffee at the Brevoort. I've walked past

69

the house where Cooper, the novelist, lived, I've been to the market where we'll shop. Hunting season is on and they exhibit quail and venison.

"But in all the magnificent glamour, in the midst of thousands of people, I am overwhelmed, Julie, by our separation. I need not say how saddening it is to go alone to the theater, to walk down Broadway inspecting the lovely shops with their display of jewels and lace. Your being here would make it real, my darling, and time and again I turn to touch you by the hand." She couldn't see the page after that, the script had changed, there were blots in the ink and big welts.

"Why you are so far away is a mystery, when all that matters is that we belong together. I look back on what has gone before and find much in our relationship childishly clandestine, stupid. It never will be again. The atmosphere here is sharp and real, the people one passes in the street are men and women, free in a way utterly incompatible with what you have known, your indestructible home life. Against such a backdrop, your family, with the exception of the French Corpers, seem a trifle ludicrous. I should never have allowed them to separate us, not even for a few months. I should never have catered to that snide economic morality. I want you here in this little room, the room we have dreamed of. It is high up on the fourth floor and down below I can still hear the murmur of the crowds, the after-theater stages rumble over the cobbles, the drivers yelling, 'Wride up, Wast Broadway, Wride up.' It is a room built for you and me, its walls so close our knees would touch, and I could take you in my arms and. . . ."

She sobbed. She rocked back and forth, sobbing, memorized the words, those that flayed her and those that made up for that. Phillip had no right to speak so about her family, but then, he didn't know yet how Mother had almost died at Croydon. He didn't know how it felt to have the family intruded on by death, how soft the feeling was when you were going far off to America, out beyond their warm, solid shelter. He would never have said. . . .

That was always the way with Phillip's letters. She wrote as often as she could, but like as not these testaments crossed in mid-ocean a batch from Phillip, so only think how long since he'd heard. Sometimes after an endless space, a whole bundle would be dropped in her lap, a welter of letters, each contradictory and which to believe? To which Phillip should she send her answer? The same packet that brought the sound of sleigh bells brought a description of Central Park in spring. She loved the part telling where they would walk, the ramble glittering with streams and the mall with its line of elms. But he now said little of himself, and that was frightening. He had planned to see Boucicault, but a man like Boucicault was not easy to see, Aunt Anna said. He didn't mention going to the theater, it might mean he hadn't the price.

It was a world without walls that year, an unsteady, wobbling world. When Phillip finally wrote saying he had work in the theater, he did not say what work; Aunt Anna admitted it might be ushering which didn't pay *much*. Then toward fall, no letters.

If she had been less absorbed in her own affairs, she might have noticed sooner that there was some difficulty abroad in the world, but there was only Phillip in her world, or the gap where he should have been. The less one heard, the more need to keep busy. At the British Museum she could obliterate the emptiness, trying to make of herself the woman Phillip wanted her to be. There was still so much to learn about the theater, about art, and she'd work away in the gloomy room where he had worked, emerging at twilight, eyes heavy, head dull.

"You'll be a walking library," Aunt Anna said one day. "Phillip won't know what to make of you."

"Aunt Anna, you do think he loves me?"

"Loves you? He's all but touched. I'll warrant something's

71

happened to the mails that makes sense if we only knew it. Might even be word today."

You never knew when something might be waiting on the hall stand. Tonight there were no letters, just two umbrellas, Papa's and Mr. Munzell's, and their hats, the one band especially shiny from pomade. The gentlemen themselves were not in evidence, they were closeted together as they had been every evening, emerging with furrowed brows, just long enough to do justice to their dinners, then back behind closed doors until long after the rest had gone to bed. Even Freddie wasn't in on it. He pouted like a child, rubbing his lip where he was trying to encourage a mustache. Ethelyn pouted, too. She thought it horrid of Papa to keep Mr. Munzell to himself this way, as if he did it to spite her.

"I'm hungry," she whined. "They're not coming to tea, Mother. Let's have ours."

But Mother had pulled the bell. "Beatrice, just step to Mr. Corper's door please and say. . . ." There was no need to *say*. Papa and Mr. Munzell were coming down the stairs, jubilant, both of them stroking their mustaches. Mr. Munzell's was not really long enough, it squatted thick and stiff, but he admired Papa so he had adopted the same gesture, tracing its short length as Papa stroked his luxuriance. And Papa had never been in such fettle; he went straight to the decanter and poured a glass of port for himself and his guest, tossing it down so rapidly that Mr. Munzell had hard work to follow suit. Papa savored his lips as an aftertaste.

"We are deeply indebted to this gentleman, who has proven himself not only an astute lawyer but a good friend."

Mr. Munzell turned in deference to his hostess. "We have had a few harassed days, Mrs. Corper. I'm glad to say you are safe. Your husband's holdings, your home, everything is quite safe." He ventured an oblique, rose-colored look at Julie.

"If you'd stop talking in riddles!" Aunt Anna said; and although both gentlemen made haste to ignore her, they did get around to telling, as delicately as possible and so as not to injure the frail female feelings, the exact nature of a

72

calamity which was sweeping the world but from which the Corper security had been saved by the timely intuition, the perspicacity, of none other than Mr. Munzell. It had all started in America.

"America? What started in America?"

"A financial panic, Julie. I see no reason to burden you ladies with details."

"Papa, tell us!"

"Mr. Munzell, perhaps you would," said Ethelyn.

So Mr. Munzell, wiping his lips thoroughly, told that in August, the Ohio Life and Something or Other had failed. It was supposed to be one of the wealthiest and most trustworthy institutions in America, but it had gone under owing seven million dollars.

Julie cut in impatiently. "What happened, what does it mean?"

He was coming to that, he said. He had noted the disaster and began watching the American banking scene with care although business had been active, harvests excellent, and credit extended up to the last minute. Then several banks suspended in Philadelphia; old, established merchants began to fail; and Mr. Munzell had foreseen a possible run on Wall Street. He had suggested that Mr. Corper withdraw all moneys from American investments and from the Bank of England. He felt it unsafe to await further news from New York, and Mr. Corper had courageously trusted his judgment, unfounded though it might have seemed. "Not at all," Papa said. Today they had had the news. Men and women, young and old, had filled narrow Wall Street clamoring for their money; and before another month was over, they'd be clamoring for bread.

"The towering fabric of our mercantile credit lies in ruins," the *Tribune* said. She snatched the sheet and read it herself. Europe would be plunged in ruin, too. English businessmen who had not been quick would be snowed under.

"Luckily, we have nothing to worry us. Ethelyn, now that we have reviewed the horrors, you had best enliven us with a tune. There is absolutely nothing to worry us, Mrs. Corper." Papa took Mother's hand to confirm it. "As a matter of fact, the failure of other factories will enhance our own business, though certainly one doesn't care to dwell on that."

Ethelyn had gone obediently to the piano. She played "Home, Sweet Home," lifting her hands high over the keys.

That's why Phillip had sent no word. How could he write without even money for postage? He was destroyed like the rest, clamoring in the streets for bread. She had never doubted Phillip, that he would succeed and send for her and some day his play would be produced and they would go, she and Phillip, in full evening dress. He would wear an opera cloak and carry a silver-headed cane and there on the stage would be the lines, the words they knew so well.

"Wherever we may roam," they sang. She clenched her hands to hear them. So Papa had saved his money and whoever else starved or lost their homes, the Corpers were saved by a Munzell. Yet he was a perfectly decent man, he sensed her anguish and tried to make it up to her. She had taken her embroidery frame, and he came to bend over it solicitously. What an admirable design! Julie must describe it to his sister when she wrote, for she did not write as often as Mr. Munzell would have liked and he found indirect ways to spur her on. Yes, his sister would be delighted. He pinched his trousers carefully above each knee, sat, and almost inaudibly breathed regret at having been the purveyor of disturbing news. She was not to be upset, her father was quite safe; he watched not her face but her embroidery and she stabbed her needle, refuting the gallant gesture.

"I am not worried about Papa."

He cleared his throat. "You have heard from your friend in America, perhaps?"

She couldn't answer that. The months of loneliness rose in her throat and one great tear fell, spreading across the tight cloth.

Part II

Emma's was quite the nicest baby she had ever seen. Oh, not at first, it was just a wobbly bundle of white shawls at first, with a clenched face not unlike her own brother John's had been. But she grew and changed, almost from day to day. They called her Elsa and when you said the name, the tiny tent of her mouth trembled at one side and fell away into a grin.

"Elsa," Julie would say, "you have been dreaming. What did you dream of, Elsa-Elsa?" The little pink tent would tremble, the cheeks push up; the round button nose had no place to go. Except for the nose, she was a Stodel, with fine blond hair Julie brushed into a peak and blue eyes like Emma's. Only they were different from Emma's, there was a tinge of violet to them, and better still, they were empty— lovely, blank blue eyes that knew nothing about you. Julie loved them for that. She could minister to the baby without self-consciousness or resentment, the first human being in three long years who asked of her only what she could freely give; and from the beginning, Julie spent so much time in the nursery that Elsa was recognized as her charge and the nurse was free to care for Emma, big, healthy, handsome Emma who had had a difficult time in childbirth and did little now but lie on the chaise longue sewing, then napping because sewing tired her.

It was good having something needful to do. Julie fed and

bathed the child, took care of its clothing, and slept in the same room at night so she could hear the cry when it was hungry. Elsa screamed for her bottle and drank it down fast, pulling and sucking so her cheeks grew moist, and iridescent points glistened in the cradles of her eyes. Hateful as it was to be awakened in the cold night, the baby was warm and cuddled close, moving and squirming; there was a sheen of candlelight on its plump, restless little hands and such an intimate aroma of talcum and sweet oil. Darkness confused and changed the room, made it stretch out mysteriously, but in the core of light she and the baby were safe and warm together while it sucked rhythmically at its milk.

The only defect in this pleasure was an occasional aware-ness of observation, the family exchanging significant looks of "ah, we have found something at last to interest poor Julie." To be watched was infuriating; she had been watched for three years. Ever since that last letter from Phillip saying *come*, ever since Papa had defeated her and the cabled money had been returned and her own sad, apologetic letter had gone by post—they had been trying to amuse, divert, or interest her, take her in again. Well, let them try! She was a different Julie, she was no part of them. The old world swung below like some cosmic disk on which Corpers and Stodels revolved slowly in scenes of the past. Grandpa held her on his knee on Christmas Day, she and Phillip rode through St. James Park, Uncle Henry had been bled and in one week was dead—all on the great disk crowded and cloudy with people. She had left that, climbed the skinny staircase, and now rode another disk alone with Elsa in the dark night room. She could hear only echoes from that old world, that's how she wanted it.

The one person who did not fade was Ludwig, and during the months after Elsa's birth, Julie came to like Emma's husband very much. He kept to an even keel, coming and going as serene and genial and kind as could be, soothing Emma who was nervous, never minding anything sharp Aunt Mathilda might say, relieving Julie at night when Elsa was

76

taken with colic. He handled his baby gently and with pride, she liked him for that. His brown bead eyes twinkled; when he walked the floor he sang softly, songs left over from his boyhood and his brother's. He was an honest, jolly man, Ludwig, and—he didn't notice her broken heart. He didn't act as if she were an old maid either, the way the rest. . . . Ethelyn making no bones about it, Julie looked like an old maid, she even dressed like one, Ethelyn said. But Ludwig treated her as another human being, without intruding on that.

During the evenings while Emma dozed and the new grandma devoted herself to correcting the new great-grandma's game of Patience, he read Julie letters from brother Leon in Java and discussed plans for Leon's homecoming which should be no later than June. They were saving Elsa's christening until he came. Ludwig only hoped Leon wouldn't get himself in trouble before his enlistment was up; for the letters he read aloud were bitter against the culture system, a policy of terror and exhaustion of both the men and the soil, he said. He was a fighter, Leon. Ludwig told stories of their boyhood exploits, Leon always emerging so much bigger, braver, and more ingenious, that Julie could have kissed her cousin on both his shiny cheeks. She helped him all she could with his plans, shopped, sewed christening robes for Elsa, arranged a room at the top of the house where Leon could stay, checked supplies and menus with Emma's cook, and helped Aunt Mathilda supervise a drastic house cleaning. Aunt Mathilda was surprised the way she took hold. So was Mr. Munzell when he arrived from London to confer with the Stodels on business; for Mr. Munzell had taken over Uncle Henry's affairs after his sudden death. He was Aunt Mathilda's prop and mainstay.

The official satchel was produced promptly after dinner and papers laid out with his most official mien; but the greater part of his visit Mr. Munzell spent in the nursery. He would talk softly while the child slept, telling Julie the news from London. Aunt Anna was suffering with rheumatism, and that,

Julie knew, was her fault. If they had gone to America out of the yellow, muggy, melancholy fog. . . .

The baby cried and Julie could hurry away with her shamed face to see what was needed. She changed the child's clothes and brought her to the delighted Mr. Munzell who must dandle her energetically on his knee, bracing to keep her at suitable distance from his immaculate waistcoat. While he jounced up and down, he addressed Elsa in words abbreviated so she could understand them. Just then, owing perhaps to the unaccustomed jolting, a thick whitish yellow liquid spouted from the baby's mouth, accompanied by a whimper and then a shriek. Mr. Munzell was not to be gainsaid. He took out his own white handkerchief, shook it, and with fine avuncular disdain mopped up the curdled milk.

"She's seasick, riding your knee. Let me. . . ."

Mr. Munzell yielded. Eyes barely blinking, he watched Julie tend Elsa. He talked baby talk and shook a rattle to attract the infant; but there was a watery, glazed look in his eye and Julie led the conversation around in most animated fashion. To no avail.

"You know, Julie, you are so altogether suited. . . ." He went on at length as to her suitability for motherhood.

"Elsa must be put back to sleep, it must be quiet." She retreated to the low chair where she could rock. Mr. Munzell promptly took his place across, and so they sat on either side of the cradle, the subject not ended, much as Julie wished it might be. He was an honest man, Mr. Munzell, and she must be honest in return. So, when finally she could cease rocking, when the baby's soft breath was the only sound in the room, she leaned across—knowing at once that was wrong, for Mr. Munzell leaned toward her on the instant, and the thin citrus scent flung out like a message over wireless.

"Dear Mr. Munzell," she spoke in a whisper. "I am going to scold you, yes, take you to task severely." There, that was better. "I have begged you before. . . . I am not going to

78

marry, you know that. You are not to say things, you are not to think. . . ." He had picked up the edge of the baby's shawl and rolled the wool fringe back and forth.

"Such an attitude is not uncommon to young ladies of good breeding, Miss Corper." He tried for an expression of jocularity and mastered it. "It would certainly not deter a suitor who had been willing in the first instance to pay court to an advocate of women's rights."

"Really, Mr. Munzell! Marriage is not in my plans. I know Emma and Ethelyn are quite disgusted with me." She said "Ethelyn" purposely, watching his face for any change, but he dropped the wool fringe and put his big, hot, fervid hand right over hers.

"You are fully aware of my feelings in your regard, Julie."

"Please, Mr. Munzell, that's just the point. You are not to feel anything for me, except as a friend. You deserve a real love affair, a woman"—she said *woman*—"who will love you honestly and marry you and give you the home you want and deserve, and the children. There are several most desirable matches available to you, I know, charming ladies who love you already. You are to forget me, you hear?" But he looked so woebegone, she left her hand in his. "I envy you that love is still ahead of you, and hope, and happiness. It is only sad when it is all over."

. . . When you had written Phillip the one last letter, folded and sealed it and sent it out into the void . . . when you had lost him.

2

They stood before the altar rail, Julie holding the baby in its long gown, the minister addressing them, parents and god-parents in the name of the child, Elsa Theresa Dekker. At the first drop of baptismal water, the baby screamed, lunged, threw nerself like a demon, right out of Julie's arms. Ludwig's brother grabbed her. He was a great, strong man. He cradled Elsa against his chest, and scream as she would, the ceremony went on. He managed the child as if she were a doll, carried her home in the carriage, too. Neither Julie nor Aunt Anna was tough enough to cope with that, he said. He called her Aunt Anna and the old lady wagged her hat. She'd be switched if she couldn't handle that baby and him, too. She flirted over her spectacles, plying him with questions about the heathens, while Elsa fiddled with gold buttons and reached for the plume on his jaunty shako. Yes, Ludwig's brother had come. Lud had waited at the Hague a week with the boat overdue, and finally had brought his captain home that very morning. Mr. Munzell, helping them from the carriage, expressed his admiration.

"You manage amazingly for a bachelor," said he gallantly. "As if you'd had experience with a dozen."

"Oh, the Indies, the Indies," sang Cousin Jack, and all the gentlemen except Mr. Munzell shouted with laughter.

Captain Dekker wasn't really such a giant when you looked more closely. To be sure, he wasn't so tall as Mr. Munzell. (But could you be sure?) Certainly he was not so tall. Mr. Munzell's well-oiled head reared above his, but Mr. Munzell was white as paste and this man was so dark. His hair curled loosely, his eyes were the color of his gray-green tunic, and all the soldier gear was strapped powerfully across his broad shoulders. Mr. Munzell said something at lunch to make him laugh and he clapped Mr. Munzell on the back in a way that startled the gentleman, made him a trifle indignant, too, as if his words hadn't intended fun. And the mustache wasn't curled or pomaded or glistening like Papa's or Mr. Munzell's. It was left wild and clipped well above the lips so the dark mouth was free to laugh as wide as it liked.

"Ho-ho," he roared to a question of his mother's. "That I can't answer. It's even worse than you think, Mama." He patted her hand and Mrs. Dekker shook with a hidden motion that made the pearls roll. It was Java they spoke of, and he

80

went on to describe the Javanese women, the herbs and flowers they wore in their hair, the sarongs loosely draped.

"No stays?" gasped Aunt Mathilda. "That's barbarous."

The style was sensible, it gave women freedom, he said. His steady gray eyes looked right at Julie, and he did seem to know who she was. How could one have forgotten what the Dekkers had meant to establish long ago, that Leon was the handsome one? Not handsome as her father, to be sure—there was that phrase again, when she was not sure. Leon was different. He had an easy way of his own, which came, Aunt Anna said, from having traveled the world and knowing something more than the old family palaver.

In the afternoon, when Elsa had been put to sleep, they sat on the terrace enjoying the sweet Arnheim air. Julie worked with Emma and Ethelyn over a hooked rug of blue and white. Sun rained down, and the needles shimmered to the talk of foreign affairs. It was good to be back in civilization, Leon said, talking seriously for the first time. Something terrible happened to Europeans in their relationships to faraway peoples. Look at the lethargy of the Dutch public to Parliament's reactionary policies. Explain Thorbecke and the Liberals who loved the profits of a degraded colonial system as much as the autocrat William himself!

Papa stroked his mustache. Sun etched a spray of white in the curve of it and Papa rubbed those hairs lovingly as if he knew they were there. He did not agree with Captain Dekker. The Dutch policy was one England might well emulate in India. Native labor, indeed, native life was of small value until directed by European intelligence.

"And assisted by European capital," added Mr. Munzell quickly.

"European intelligence, on the island of Java? In our province last year they made the poor devils prepare the fields for indigo—a spot so obviously unsuited by soil and climate that no one but a squareheaded Dutch politician would dream of it—then two months later, when the fields were rank with weeds, what do you suppose arrived? The

81

indigo seeds from Batavia. Intelligence! Say stupidity and avarice."

For a moment no one spoke, then Mr. Munzell cleared his throat and offered a bit of wisdom. He had read, just before leaving London, he had perused with much profit, a book by an English barrister named Money, J. W. B. Money—*Java or How to Manage a Colony*. Mr. Money had gone to Java with an invalid wife and was more than favorably impressed. The natives were asked to donate only one-fifth of their land, a fifth of their time under benevolent Dutch rule. The colony was paying handsomely, both parties were benefiting, and Mr. Money thought. . . .

"*That* lout! He knows not a word of Dutch or any native tongue, either, saw no one but officials and planters at stag hunts and shooting parties, and what he collected was a pack of lies." He spat the words and the Dekkers edged up a little on their chairs, not agreeing with Leon, mind you, but so proud of the way he spoke out.

Mr. Dekker quivered with pride. He was a wizened little man, almost bald, with a gentle, obsequious air. On close study, his facial structure was not unlike the soldier son's, but age had exhausted it. One eye was smaller than the other from squinting at diamonds; his head seemed sunken by the weight of its big, naked ears. He'd been half dead ever since Julie'd known him, but today pride in Leon brought him to attention. He followed the conversation as if he might jump in at any second.

Mr. Munzell looked about to be sure he was noted. "In our holdings, England has found the natives inclined toward indolence. You have great admiration for the Javanese, Captain, but—"

"They're human beings, that's all, entitled to the same dignity you all have in Europe. It's a man's right, that's why the war is being fought in America."

"Weave, Julie, weave," Ethelyn nudged her.

"And they'll undermine their national economy if the Federals have their way," Mr. Munzell said.

Leon wouldn't hear it.

"You worry too much about the world, son. You'll find the world has a way of getting along pretty well by itself." Old Mr. Dekker winked for anyone to see. "It's high time you worried about yourself."

Mrs. Dekker pressed Leon's arm.

"Not that we aren't proud of you," continued the father. "But you're twenty-seven years old. . . ."

Ethelyn tittered and prodded Emma.

"High time you settled down."

"There's a lot of the world I haven't seen yet, Papa."

"If I were a man, I'd go everywhere," cried Julie. "Wouldn't you Emma, Ethelyn?"

"Those two stick-in-the-muds? Why not ask me?" Aunt Anna yanked her bodice. "Settlin' down's tomfoolery if you ask me. Settle plenty once you're in your grave."

Aunt Mathilda said aye to that, and wiped her eyes for Uncle Henry.

"We've counted on your coming into the business," Ludwig said. She'd forgotten Ludwig, how he'd planned. . . . "Papa has turned it all over, there's plenty for us both."

Leon tried to pass the subject by.

"The Captain no doubt has his plans," suggested Mr. Munzell.

"Not a plan," laughed the prodigal. "I've been hog-tied for ten years. You don't know what it's like. God knows I didn't, or I'd never have gone."

Not a stitch went into the embroidery frames. Freddie's mouth had fallen open.

"You want to know what I'm going to do? Well, first we're going to have a holiday. Lud and I have a lot of catching up to do. We've all changed, now comes the fun of meeting again. It's high time this pretty Emma got out of the house. Isn't that right, Lud? Julie? We'll have a holiday right here in Arnheim. We'll use up every gulden of my discharge pay on music and dancing and Rhine wine. You know how thirsty a man can get? Let's open a bottle now, Lud!" And seizing

Ludwig by the arm, he tore up the terrace toward the house. Mr. Dekker shook his head. Mrs. Dekker shook hers, but they smiled benignly and Freddie looked sharp at Papa to see what he thought of that.

3

"Where do we go today, Leon? What will it be?" Emma would come running in to breakfast like a child, grab up a roll, pile it with elderberry jam, and bang on the bell for cook to bring more. After the long time of lying listless, she was the Emma who first set her cap for Ludwig Dekker and turned Aunt Mathilda's house upside down.

"Do we boat or drive, or have you another surprise? You needn't go to the shop, Lud, not even for an hour, I won't let you." And around the table Emma would go to sit on her husband's knee.

"Just for an hour, Em, time for you ladies to primp." But that never settled it. Emma whispered in his ear, pouted her glistening lips until he was miserable with mirth. "Go away, there's a girl, Oh-ho-ho-ho, Em!"

The freedom, the undiluted joy, of being in Arnheim in the lovely summer caught them up. Leon had a flair for fun, a gusto such as Julie had never seen. It was altogether different from most peoples' passive enjoyment. He could tap any rock and out flowed streams of sport. Everything had a story. It was not the river on which they boated, but a string of moats that had creviced the town when it was a walled city. They rode over the magnificent boulevards, explored churches and shops, and the streets were an endless drama. Color made a fairy world of Arnheim, the terraced roofs, the verandas and gardens lustrous and blazing green. Under the staring sun foliage fell into triangles and spears of translucent, gaudy light that dazzled the eye and made the

frosted brick walls faint to chalk. They were such tender
colors, tender pastel, and every house elegant with carved
ornament. Light was a strange alloy, it coaxed color here,
sent shadows spiraling. Julie loved to walk, for the terraces
and gardens were filled with people, everyone living outdoors, and as you passed, there were unexpected, intimate
glimpses of family life.

"Look, Leon, quick, look there."

Aunt Anna said their manners could stand improving, prying on folks, but when they passed a garden dilated with
tropical flowers, she stared with the rest of them at the Indian
family lying about in exotic clothes, calling and chuckling.
Phillip could have made a play of it; she told Leon about
Phillip's play.

When the days were excessively hot, he drove them out to
the heavy, ornate clubhouse of the Buitensocieteet, high on a
hill overlooking the Rhine. It was always cool here, shaded
and stone cool, and you could see the country laid out in its
clipped, undulating hills, the neat tan squares of wheat, the
deep green squares of tobacco, the tawny stubble grazing
ground. Late in the afternoon, the breeze sprang up, carrying
soft and clear the chimes from the Groote Kerk of St.
Eusebius. Leon would whistle with the chimes. He loved
music, so much that everyone perforce loved it with him.
The manager of the public gardens saved his best table for
Mein Herr and Captain Dekker, and there they would sit at
night, sipping chilled wine, and follow the swaying rhythms
of the orchestra. Leon sang as he danced. He and Ludwig
sang all the way home.

> *Het daghet in het osten*
> *Het licht is overal.*

Moonlight paled against the walls, the air was scented,
wind ravished the flowers. The brothers were always hungry
then. They'd tiptoe down to the kitchen, trying not to wake
cook.

"Stick with us, Julie, we'll make you as fat as Emma," Leon
would say, and Emma would spring up to box his ears. After

all this, they would finally fall into their beds so happy and tired that brushing one's hair was an effort. Sometimes Julie forgot to kiss dear Phillip's gold band ring. She had it with her as always, secreted in the pocket of her portmanteau; but once in bed, stretched light against the sheets, she couldn't get up to fumble for the ring. It would have to suffice to murmur, "Good night, Phillip, wherever you are," and to remind God that Phillip needed him.

For some of their festivities, they had added guests. Mother and Ethelyn were with Grandma Stodel thirty miles away and frequently came in to Arnheim, Ethelyn angry about something, more tight lipped and peevish than ever, until at last it came blurting out that the least Julie could do, since she wouldn't let anyone else have Mr. Munzell, was to marry him herself. Poor Ethelyn, she had finally despaired of their old friend and pledged herself to another barrister named Potter, a perfectly respectable gentleman with more than ample wealth; so her future seemed assured, except for Papa's delaying the betrothal until Julie could be disposed of. Julie wrote to Papa and spoke with Mother, too, insisting that Ethelyn's engagement be announced at once. For heaven's sake, they were not to worry about her since she had obviously chosen to be an old maid.

But such a very gay old maid, dancing and singing every night, so that even Ethelyn didn't fuss when she came again to Arnheim with her dull and rather whey-faced Mr. Potter. Jack heard of the fun and came down from London for a week, Mr. Munzell tagging right along. All together, they galloped through a very gay holiday.

London was dull after that, dull and dreary. Neither Fred nor John had ever been diverting playfellows, and they were not improved. Nothing happened to them. John was an apprenticed clerk in the postal service, but question him as you would . . . and Freddie had to watch what he said, working for Papa. Once in a while, he came up with something he thought clever, but it wasn't very, and Ethelyn's chatter was so insipid one's heart went out to barrister Potter who would have to listen to it the rest of his life. Mother tried. She was so happy to have them all at home, there was not a night she didn't bid Ethelyn go to the piano that they might sing together.

The days lagged even though they had frequent guests. Mr. Munzell came often to tea, assuring Julie how responsive "London" was to her return. Mr. Potter came with him; for Mr. Munzell was fond of Mr. Potter, patronized and clove to him as to a younger brother, bringing to Mr. Potter's attention in numerous ways the delectation of acquaintance, indeed intimacy, with a family like the Corpers, whom he had known so much longer. They would sit beside the tea table, waiting seriously for the brew, Mr. Munzell compact in face and body, the great trunks of his legs rounding the trousers to full breadth, and Mr. Potter colorless and thin, his cheeks sunken under their pale, mutton-chop whiskers. It seemed to Julie that Mr. Potter's advent quite spiced these visits for Mr. Munzell, that he liked best to come when he could bring the prospective bridegroom. He sat most impressively beside his confrere then, as if to say, "See how much stouter and more robust I am. That comes from association with this incomparable family. You, too, will swell and broaden when you know them as well as I." Then he would walk over majestically to talk with Papa, leaving poor, skinny Mr. Potter sitting there simpering at Ethelyn.

For her taste, give Aunt Anna the Dekkers. The Dekkers knew how to live, how to eat and drink and have some fun out of it. Some folks were dead from the start and didn't have gumption to order up a hearse. Personally, she didn't fancy these tea parties with "prissy Potter, he and Munzell both coming, your ma says, and I says I can take one of 'em or leave both of 'em alone, but I can't take both at once."

But she did take them at once in more ways than one. There stood the carriage. Mr. Potter was paying the driver while Mr. Munzell insisted it was his turn and happily fingered the rejected florin. The gentlemen were in excellent spirits. Mr. Munzell had brought Julie a bouquet of carnations and Mr. Potter clutched a paper of white roses for his bride.

"How do you do, darling," sighed Mr. Potter and sank into a parlor chair seeming grieved, although Ethelyn had greeted him most cordially for Mr. Munzell's benefit. Then they both rose again, like pallbearers, to honor Mother. Julie rang for Beatrice, but Mr. Munzell waylaid her at the bell pull. He craved Julie's own attention to the flowers, he admired her handiwork, she arranged them so. . . . So Beatrice brought the vase and she did arrange them, prolonging the task since there was nothing to talk about anyhow. Ethelyn diverted Mr. Potter. She had found a piece of watered silk for draperies, an innocuous piece it was, Julie'd seen it. Just then, another carriage rattled to the door, Emil was shouting at the horses; at least Papa and the boys were coming and let them make conversation limp along. They seemed to make more than the usual noise coming in, their voices seemed—Julie jumped to her feet, she dropped the last of the carnations.

"Leon, oh, Leon, Leon!" she cried, running into his arms. For he hugged her heartily, of course, just as Ludwig would. "When did you come, how long do you stay, how are Elsa and Ludwig and Emma?"

Aunt Anna came hurrying. "Well, you renegade soldier, where've you been? It took you long enough!"

Leon kissed the old lady cordially.

"Away with you, your mustache tickles." She was laughing, they all three laughed just to be sure they could.

"Good evening, Papa, yes, we're quite ready for tea." They turned to the parlor where Papa and the boys had preceded them, Leon with one arm about Aunt Anna, the other good and tight around Julie. The gentlemen were standing, Mr.

Potter sad eyed and gaunt, Mr. Munzell somewhat florid, to greet Captain Dekker and welcome him to London.

"Hang that 'captain,' " declared Leon. "Believe me, the first thing I did when my back pay came was toss regimentals away forever. Lord, I can move!" He flexed his shoulders to show how free he was in his new clothes. "And the collars," running his finger under the soft neckcloth. "You civilians have no notion what it means to be choked to death." He bade Mother touch the spot on his throat, feel where the uniform had rubbed a callus.

He made himself quite at home. When Mother passed his tea he whispered he'd enjoy it even more, dear, if he could have a dash of rum; and Beatrice was sent red-faced and panting to the cellar. It was the sort of talk Beatrice fancied in gentlemen, she made it to the cellar and back faster than ever she had in her life. Papa declined the liquor, but since the precedent had been set, Mr. Potter agreed to a drop; Freddie and John clamored for some. Leon even converted Mr. Munzell. A sure preventive for colds, he told him.

How different it became from the usual lachrymose tea. Julie chattered with Mr. Munzell, she joked with John; Mr. Potter smiled wanly and told her a riddle. There was scant opportunity to talk with Leon, but it was all right, he was here and he had already appointed to take her and Aunt Anna next afternoon to see the sights.

"I see you took my advice about coming to London," said Mr. Munzell significantly. "The advice I so presumptuously offered the night of Mrs. Dekker's party for the visiting London belles." He looked at Leon with meaning.

"Well, not exactly, Munzell, not exactly."

"On business then?"

"On most important business." Leon's eyes twinkled, but the assembly accepted his news with gravity and pleasure; it indicated that the young man was emerging from his period of wildness, he was settling *down*. Did it mean he had decided upon London as his place of business rather than Arnheim? "Let us say I've decided against Arnheim. It's gay but it's decadent. Besides," he smiled as genially as if they all agreed with him, "besides, the best of Arnheim vanished when Aunt Anna and the gypsy came back home."

"My father called Julie that," Mother said. "She doesn't look the least like a gypsy to me. Have another cup, gentlemen, I'm brewing fresh."

Such a good tea you hated to have it over; and even when it was, when the guests had gone, the house was warm with the sounds of it. Papa was unusually bland. He sat in Mother's room after dinner, reading aloud.

"They missed an item in the *Times*," he said, peering up and down the pages as if hunting it. "Hm. They missed one item I'm sure you ladies could supply."

What had got into Papa?

"In the matter of our friend, Leon Dekker. I imagine you are well aware what business brings Mr. Dekker to London."

"No, I'm not, Papa. Tell us."

"Such innocence is barely in accord with the warmth of your greeting for that gentleman today, Julie. But since he particularly asked me to convey his information, he has come to London—yes, my dear," and he smiled at Mother, for it was to her he was speaking, "to ask us for our daughter's hand in marriage."

5

"Julie, you look glum as an owl. Sure you aren't taking seasick?"

"I'm all right, Aunt Anna, quite all right, Leon." She sat between them as straight as she could on the slatted wooden bench that vibrated and trembled. Flurries of wind scooped up from the river and she held her great skirt primly. No, she wasn't seasick. It was another kind of sickness, a quavering

90

sort, so she gave all her attention to the awkward skirt. Gusts sailed up underneath, and the wire frame wobbled indelicately from the gasping, jerky motion of the small steamboat.

"We've passed Carlyle's house. Over there, toward King's Road." She lifted one hand, brought it back fast to her skirt.

"Let go," teased Leon. "I dare you. Take both hands off and you'll sail right over our heads, maybe drop down on deck again about Vauxhall."

"We were better off in the old days, with petticoats and bonnets. At least a body had something to hang onto." Aunt Anna caught at her own rusty hat. "Someday I'm going to take off for those islands of yours and prance around without stays or steel cages in a what-do-you-call-it—sarong."

Leon advised against that. Javanese clothes were all right, but you got sick for civilization after a while, you got sick for freedom, to be able to go anywhere, out on a boat like this without accounting. He liked chugging along down the gray Thames, past coal barges and freighters. This was the way to go sightseeing, get the lay of the land. They were lucky to have a day without rain, and Julie and Aunt Anna were good sports and good sailors to come when the river was choppy. He looked as if he were enjoying himself mightily, as if nothing had happened. Wind whipped his brown face, his eyes glistened as the water glistened in the pale autumn light. It was oily light, filtered through smoke and grit.

If there was any thanks to be given, Aunt Anna said, she and Julie'd be giving it to him for coming last night and saving them from another tea with those two poor excuses who might do well enough in courts of law but were limp fish on the social shore, if you asked her. Didn't even know how to shake a body's hand, either one of them, and she made Leon grasp the lifeless hand she held out.

"Why, Aunt Anna, Mr. Potter is often very pleasant, and Mr. Munzell—Mr. Munzell long ago proved himself—"

"A jackass," quipped Aunt Anna. Julie's moral and reproving tone broke into laughter. Then she caught Leon's eye, and he had come to London, because. . . .

"Right up ahead, the river bends," she said quickly. "We'll turn straight so you can see Parliament, then right again. They're building a new bridge at Westminster."

But when they headed into the north breeze, Aunt Anna gasped. She was done in, she couldn't hold her hat, if they were so crazy for air, they could just go right ahead and breathe it and pray God they didn't sniff the cholera along. For herself, she was going inside like other Christians and get to rights. No, she needed no help from Leon, she wasn't too old to walk around a river boat, thank you, besides, she'd caught sight of an honest, merry-looking old gent inside; if she needed help, she'd be bound she could find some to her liking.

"Here, take this scarf, tie it around. Your pa should catch you out here with your bad ear. Leon, see to it she doesn't blow away."

Aunt Anna staggered off, lurching up the deck and into the cabin where other passengers sat huddled over their papers, not interested in the sights at all. It was too late to join Aunt Anna, Leon had taken the scarf, swung it over her hat and hair, and knotted it firmly beneath her chin. There, she was snug now, wasn't she, she even had color in her cheeks —Julie felt sure of that—and they had the whole deck to themselves. He drew her arm through his and started briskly.

The wind was easier on the embankment side and you couldn't blow away with your arm in Leon's. He was sturdy balking the breeze and there was a resilience, the same as in dancing, as if he had hidden springs. He was humming; wind stole snatches of his song and blew them away; they turned and the melody came spinning into Aunt Anna's scarf. There was no reason why they should go home for tea, he said. They could take tea at a little inn he'd heard of, just off from the customs. How would she like a drop of brandy in hers, that'd warm her, and some scones and perhaps. . . .

Julie's eyes had gone hot and fluid. "Leon, why did you do it? Why did you speak to Papa?"

92

"Well," he said lightly, "that's gratitude. Most young ladies take offense if you don't speak to their papas."

"Leon, Leon!" For a moment she stood half turned from him, the streaming wind splashed tears across her face and wiped them dry with one stroke. Then Leon put her hand back on his arm and they continued to walk, without springs this time.

"Forget it, dear, forget the whole thing. It was only a few words altogether, and I said them to your father because I thought you knew the words as well as I." He smiled down at her in his easy way, "We're as we've always been, happy and good together, you see?"

"But we can't be the same, Leon. It's spoiled because you feel differently. We were such friends before."

He wheeled her around and started back down the deck. "Come now, Julie, if that's troubling you, I don't feel any different, not a whit different, than last week or last month, all the while we were having such a good time in Holland."

"You were . . . ?"

"The very same, dear, I knew from the minute you walked in the first day."

"But you never said."

"I wanted to give you a chance to know me. You can't just walk up to a young lady and say, 'How do, will you marry me, miss?'"

Julie had to smile. She pressed her fingers a little on his arm. You couldn't stay strange or angry with Leon.

"Well, look what we have here."

They had come around aft now and at the very stern, set in the wall of the cabin, was a space where ropes and buckets were piled. Leon set her in, out of the wind. She had a fine seat on a coil of rope and he stood before her, leaning with one arm braced against the wall so she was shut off from the breeze.

"I've seen Jack-in-the-box, but this is my first Julie-in-the-box. You look very sweet and funny. We'll tie your hat on

93

this way when we go skating, when the pond freezes. Even your Mr. Munzell's going to skate."

"But, Leon, you didn't know me, either. How could you make up your mind the first day? I thought you planned not to marry, Ludwig said."

"I certainly did not intend to." He pulled off his hat and let the wind toss his hair. "Believe me, sweating out my time in the islands, I was not thinking of coming home to some cozy marital hearth. Far from it. I dreamed of being free, ranging about wherever I liked, working hard and eating hearty and none of the staid, steady family business Lud likes so well. I never will be a pillar of stability, Miss Corper, and you're undoubtedly saving me from making a very bad husband." He looked out without seeing. "I came home to Arnheim big and free as the universe. And then in you walked in that saucy yellow dress, crisp and curly with your black eyes snapping."

"You didn't know me."

"I knew you, all right. I knew you had spirit and a good stubborn will of your own."

"You didn't even speak to me," cried Julie. "I didn't think you knew I was there!"

"You don't suppose I was going to yield up my precious freedom without a struggle?" But he looked down gravely, fathomed her with his gray, resolute eyes. "Then I did get to know you, Julie. I know you very well, dear, and everything you've said or done brought you closer. No, don't be afraid," for Julie had looked away and her mouth quivered. "It's simple and can't hurt you, Julie. I've never cared for marriage, but I'd never had you before, either; and we're good together, you know that. I've been so happy, I thought perhaps. . . ."

"I've been happy, too," she breathed, so warm and sheltered in the little box, with Leon's clean, healthy face and tousled hair. "But I tried to tell you, Leon, I did tell you about Phillip."

"What of that? I certainly didn't think you'd been waiting for me like some Dresden shepherdess on a shelf in the cupboard. I haven't been on a shelf, either. But the world goes on, dear, the happy loves and the sad loves. We can't live in the past or in the future, either, like your young Phillip. We live in a present that is all we have." He stood aside for a moment and cool air rushed in.

"But I loved Phillip. That can only happen once."

"Oh, Julie!" laughed Leon, he actually laughed. "Of course you loved him and you'll love other people, men and women and children; that is, you will if you don't stay a little girl in your box of the past. Many people in many ways, little Julie. I think you care for me, I know you do."

She did, she cared a great deal, hadn't his coming yesterday been most delightful? But love must have suffering in it, she knew that, she had suffered so for Phillip, and there was nothing in this but pleasure, not even a bit of pain. There couldn't be, since in a lifetime, you could only once. . . .

Leon smiled as if she were no bigger than Elsa. That was the end of it, he said, unless someday she wished to renew the subject, it was settled, they were friends, and she was not to neglect his introduction to London. This bridge up ahead, he pulled her out into the cold air, the bridge that was throwing its purple shadow, was that Southwark already and if so, was the cathedral to right or left?

"But what am I to tell Papa, Leon?"

He put his arm about her waist. She was to tell her father she had not made up her mind, that she didn't know him well enough. He stopped abruptly and held her at arm's length while her skirts flapped.

"Look at me, Gypsy, and let us get this straight here and now. This decision is something your father has nothing to do with, or your mother. It's a choice for only one Corper and you know which one. You have a stubborn will, learn to use it. You don't ever have to marry if you don't want to. There are other valid ways to use your life, don't let them frighten you. If you should come to want me, that is our concern— yours and mine. And either way, nothing can keep us from having fun together, eh, Julie?"

6

" 'Hark the herald angels sing, glory to the new-born—' Aunt Anna, is this basted right?" But the raucous noise of the sewing machine swallowed the words whole. Aunt Anna drove the thing without mercy; she sat straight as if she were riding sidesaddle, her long pearl earrings swung, her wispy hair trembled, one foot plied relentless on the treadle. Shapeless pink silk moved, swirled under the needle as if it were alive.

"Aunt Anna!"

"Land sakes, Julie," bringing her beast to a halt, "you're a noisy one with your singing and shouting. Scare a body to death. Yes, I see. The basting's good enough if you hadn't seen fit to do it hind foremost." She flashed out her scissors and ripped the offending sleeve. "There, this way and the ruffles here. My, it's pretty."

"Elsa will look like a doll."

"She'll look plumb naked if folks keep interruptin'. Don't know how we'll get it all done anyhow. Me with only one pair of hands."

"By Christmas Eve, Aunt Anna. He wants it all in the little trunk by Christmas Eve."

"He wants so high and mighty, he'd best learn to wiggle a needle!" But she threw her weight against the treadle and rode away. Leon didn't give her a minute's peace, Elsa's first Christmas this and Elsa's first Christmas that. She'd be switched if she'd make such a fool of herself for a baby, but it was *his* first Christmas, too, whether he said that or not. Ten years in barracks not fit for a cat. Did Julie know how those Christmases had been? Playing cards and watching the rain swill down, no better'n a heathen!

Not since the days of the grandfathers had holiday preparations been so exciting, as if they all believed in it again. Down
in the cellar at night John and Freddie pounded and hammered making something for Elsa, drowning out Papa's harp-
ing about the war which he thought should be declared
against America. Ethelyn drew threads in a tiny coverlet and
Mother crocheted, as she did, morning, noon, and night,
making the dainty edges for Elsa's clothes, because, as they
all kept saying, this *was* Elsa's first Christmas. Emma and
Ludwig were bringing her from Holland, and the Dekkers
and Grandma. Aunt Mathilda had returned to London to put
her house in order. The festivities were to be there; she'd
insisted on it.

And then it was almost spoiled. While the cookies baked
and the puddings ripened and needles rippled through the
silk—the Prince Consort died, suddenly, right on the heels
of the royal bulletin that said he was only slightly ill, just a
touch of influenza which would be over in a week. Dead! Why
only the other day Prince Albert had reworded Lord Russell's
ultimatum to America! Papa came home stunned. He had
always distrusted and disliked foreigners meddling in British
affairs, and that included Albert. Still, at this solemn moment,
the Prince's attitude toward industrial progress had been all
one could wish, he had tempered Palmerston and supported
Peel, and who was to deny the importance of the Great Ex-
position? Papa sat with bowed head and Mother wept into
her handkerchief for the Queen. They were joined immediately by Messrs. Munzell and Potter. The Inns of Court
had closed down and they had hastened hence with correct
funereal visage, as dour as if the corpse were in the room.
There they sat, trying to feel whatever it was they should feel,
when Leon and Aunt Mathilda arrived, their arms so filled
with packages that Beatrice ran down the front steps to help.
They were all to be stowed in her clothespress until Christmas
Eve, and Beatrice trundled them off importantly, although
the Lord knew where she was going to put them. Julie had
been in the girl's quarters and the clothespress was bulging,

the table, chair, and dresser piled so high with Leon's bounty that there was almost no room for the original occupant. Beatrice ambled off, grinning to crack her red china cheeks, and Leon and Aunt Mathilda went to the fire to rub their hands. To subdue their high spirits, too. Julie had seen them glance from Papa to Munzell to Potter. Papa told the sad news. Yes, Leon said, they had heard.

"I'm sorry, Mathilda, after your holiday plans," murmured Mother. But Aunt Mathilda's eyes flashed quick and sharp from the fire. There was nothing to be sorry about, she said, except the poor man's death. People lived and died and it was tragic when it was your own, but this had nothing to do with Christmas, the family had been in mourning too long as it was. Aunt Anna was glad someone had sense, all of 'em fit for a wake when they'd only seen the man once in their lives, and that so far off in the parade you only knew you were saying hurrah for something under a beaver hat.

"Good for you, Anna," said Aunt Mathilda.

Mr. Munzell fidgeted on his chair. Albert had been one of the mighty men of England. He took out his notebook, balanced it on his round thigh, and meticulously identified the day of the Prince Consort's death. But no, he had no argument as to whether or not sorrow should be courted, and he permitted himself a tea cake as if a period of fasting were óver. He availed himself of a clean pocket handkerchief, too, pressed it neatly against his head, and sighed. Mr. Potter watched this from squinted eyes, looking dolorous and relieved at the same time so he could be right either way.

"Why *make* yourselves unhappy?" Leon said.

And for just an instant, there was Phillip, dear Phillip who thought you had to be unhappy, that love could grow only through suffering, could be achieved only through loss and grief. Maybe that was why Phillip at times had flung the scathing words which made you think love was over.

Well, Aunt Anna said, she'd found out long ago you didn't have to go looking for trouble, more than a plenty came your way; and the Prince had gone off to a better world where he wouldn't have those mule-headed court dandies to contend with. No, sir, she'd go and stand in the funeral procession out of respect to the Queen, and that was that.

Leon and Julie went with her. They stood in Hyde Park while the band slow-footed past, sounding deep notes. The cortege barely moved. People about them sniffled and blew their noses and whispered about Albert, using a different voice than they'd used when, for instance, Palmerston resigned. It was a clear, gray day. White winter light, sharper than moonlight, speared through the wadded clouds. One oblique tendril then another fumed out long to undermine the sky. Aunt Anna grew tired and went to find a bench, leaving Julie and Leon jammed in with the rest. Horsemen came clanking at death's pace, muffled and monotone, the horses straining against the tight reins. Suddenly one black horse reared and bucked toward the edge of the crowd. He was just opposite and they could see his whole glistening black back, the rider hanging head down in his fur shako. The wild beast reared, flung his rider, wheeled, plunged into the crowd, right at them! Everyone screamed. There was a riot of screaming and shoving, some great cloth back smashed against Julie's face, and she was blocked off, drowned, the hot wet breath of the horse coming to her as she reeled.

Suddenly she was up. She didn't open her eyes, she just clutched both arms tight around Leon's neck, flinching against the awful noise. Slowly she was jolted along. He had to push a way. Then it was freer, there was air about.

"Hello, up there."

"Hello." She was afraid to open her eyes.

But they were free, she could feel the air moving. Leon stopped walking and sat down.

"My heart's beating."

"That's fine. It's supposed to. My, you're a brazen hussy sitting on my knee in broad daylight."

She jumped up at once, shook out her skirts and sat primly beside him. Leon's hat was gone, his coat was torn.

"I love to save young ladies' lives. They're always so grateful."

"Don't laugh, Leon, we were almost killed."

He looked at her very steadily and kept both her hands in his. "But we weren't killed, dear. It was just a close shave, something to tell your grandchildren."

The way he said it made her laugh. Some impudent joy came shooting through Hyde Park, and she loved every twig trembling and quaking in the wind. Nothing could stop Christmas now!

7

She ran into the merry music and down the stairs, her skirts held high above her purple boots. That was Leon's voice, she was sure. She sang, too, down the stairs and across the hall, into the dazzling light and warmth, the air spiced with pine boughs and warmed wine. But at the archway someone seized her, someone grabbed both her bare shoulders, her future brother-in-law, Mr. Potter, kissed her hard with his stiff little wooden lips. It was so surprising, so funny, so like kissing Elsa's wooden duck! Sad, sallow Mr. Potter earnestly begged her pardon and explained himself. It was mistletoe. If Julie would look up, there was mistletoe making it right and proper. Across the crowded, shimmering room, Leon watched with wicked satisfaction. So it was he who had placed the dangerous twigs! Mr. Potter was carried away, he could think of nothing he would so like to do as start Christmas Eve with a dance, and before she could say yes or no, he was romping her down the hall.

"Mr. Potter, Mr. Potter! This isn't dance music. What will they think? We haven't paid our respects to Aunt Mathilda's guests!" The guests were gathered about the blazing tree drinking hot wassail. Julie made haste to disengage herself, to

100

welcome the Peabodys, and to wish them a merry Christmas. The Reverend was merry already. He had traded Christmas pulpits with an old schoolfellow, and here he was in this fine company. His good, spare face shone with happiness, you could see how he loved the Christmas spirit and felt it truly as Leon did, and was friends with all men. His wife's greeting seemed a shade less cordial, tinged with chill, as if she had changed in some way and was not the same Mrs. Peabody who had shelled the peas. Certainly Mrs. Peabody spoke warmly and admired Julie's dress, but there was the hot, miserable sense she might not mean it, that actually she was observing with disapproval the low, plunging, purple velvet neckline, the long-headed yellow roses Leon had sent. The Reverend Mr. Peabody made a special point of her looking well, much healthier and happier than at Croydon. Mrs. Dekker thought she looked well, too.

"Younger than your sister, like a little girl, Julie," and linking arms, she walked Julie off a pace inquiring what she had done to bewitch Leon. No sooner had he come home, than off again to London and they hadn't seen him since.

And soon the clock chimed, it was midnight and time to distribute the gifts. They, like the mistletoe, had appeared out of nowhere. There had certainly been nothing under the tree this afternoon when they trundled out the empty wheelbarrows and hammered the last holly bough; but there were stacks of packages now and Leon waded in under the tree on his knees, handing them up to Aunt Mathilda who read off the names. There were dainty handkerchiefs with crocheted edges for all the ladies, rough, nubbly red or pink or blue borders that could have only been worked by Grandma Stodel, and handsome linens for the gentlemen. Grandma shook her head, they had come like everything else from Saint Nicholas, but she was so pleased that they *knew*. Her white head nodded, nodded, and couldn't stop.

"Here's one for you, Ethelyn. Something for you, Ludwig." Quick the papers were torn off, while everyone crowded around to see. Gifts galore. Aunt Mathilda's trinkets were chosen with a lavishness to have astonished poor Uncle Henry. Julie thought she had seen all of Leon's purchases, but there was a burnished copper kettle for her mother, that must be from him, for with it was a package of the Chinese tea Mother especially liked; and an embroidery hook for Ethelyn who was always mislaying hers, and a set of tools for Freddie and John who had complained bitterly of their inadequacies while building Elsa's wagon. Aunt Anna's present came in a long box. When she managed to get it open, her hands trembling over the twine, there, packed elegantly in tissue, were two lengths of dress goods, one of pure black silk, the other gray with a dim burnt-orange stripe, just the rusty color of Aunt Anna's hair. She touched the goods, her glasses glistening with light. Then she stood bolt upright, marched over to Leon, and said she'd like a word with him. Her tone was angry, but while they all watched, she led him to the archway, threw both long arms about his neck, and kissed him soundly under the mistletoe. There was some mistake, Leon insisted, but if everyone wanted to thank him for Saint Nick's bounty it was all right with him, come ahead. For he'd bought something for everyone, a red woolen tasseled skating cap for Mr. Munzell, and a gold bangle for Julie's wrist. It was a gypsy bracelet with emeralds in the band, not at all appropriate, but then he had given a silver bangle to Emma, too, so what could anyone, what could Papa say? Emma shook her flashing silver links and helped Julie clasp on hers; before Papa could say anything, the little band struck up a quadrille. Julie was employed in a dignified romp on the hand of Mr. Munzell. Through all the figures, parted and rejoined, they kept their perfect step and when the dance was over and the music swung into a waltz, he took her around and around in excellent rhythm, out past the dangerous arch, and then stopped short in the hallway, holding her, just a handful of velvet he said, swaying back and forth to the music. She wasn't at all sure why they had stopped, for she had looked around earlier trying to spot the sprigs of white berries.

"A-ha-ha, a-ha-ha," sang Mr. Munzell. Now he had caught

her, now she was trapped. So she had steered him away, had she, been on her guard, well, right over their heads was mistletoe she hadn't seen and they were right beneath it where he could take full advantage, kiss her without any explanation, what did she think of that, Miss Julie Corper? He swung her from side to side, bending his own body rigidly backward from the waist, an awkward vantage point from which he could see her the better. What did she say to that, she was in his power, what did she say? Julie only laughed, swaying against his big hands. What could she possibly say? Wasn't this Christmas Eve and wasn't the mistletoe a license to dallying? And she swayed there, her head tilted enticingly, her almost bare breast with its heap of flowers offered up wickedly, naughtily, to tantalize good Mr. Munzell, who grew warmer and pinker and pinker and warmer. Well, it served him right, wanting to kiss her for years and years and never having the courage or the sense. She let him draw her closer, her flowers brushing his coat so there was nothing else for him to do. Slowly, he bent his head, thinking—she was sure he thought that at any second she might safely stop him —until his lips were resting against her own. And he *had* wanted to for a long time. Once there, the lips pressed hot and plump and lemony, avidly pressed and pressed, until. . . .

"There, you see," she said brightly, releasing herself. "There's nothing to it at all, Mr. Munzell, nothing at all." And she ran away to join the others who were disappearing toward the dining room to partake of cold buffet. It was an enchanted forest through which she ran. The Christmas tree, the yule logs, and the holly branches made the great drawing room an outdoors which was indoors, a forest of pine and living holly, blurred floor shadows and the fleur-de-lis rippling on the walls like liquid gold. There were the magic white berries, too. That imp, Leon, he was the only one who had taken no advantage.

In the dining room the Reverend Mr. Peabody offered his glass to Mr. Munzell who was going to run for Parliament next election and help bring Britain back to the traditions of

Canning and Peel. Leon did not drink, nor did Julie. She wasn't so sure the past *was* desirable, and if Leon wasn't going to drink, she'd not have to, either. Old Mr. Dekker proposed long life to the next happy couple, Ethelyn and Mr. Potter—and Ethelyn'd better marry him this very night if she was ever going to, he'd never again be one-quarter so alive. "To this happy day," Leon said, for they were all together, and when would they be again? It sounded almost right, and yet. . . . He wasn't thinking of kiting off to the ends of the earth, was he? Aunt Anna asked the question. Julie could not.

Yes, he said lightly, yes, with the new year he'd be off. Even holidays couldn't last forever and as friend Munzell had suggested, the time had come for serious and sober thought. Mr. Munzell, glassy-eyed and florid with kissing, inclined his head benignly. Besides, laughed Leon, there was a slight matter of money. Everyone talked at once. The Dekkers, father, mother, Ludwig, and Emma, tried to wheedle him back to Arnheim, there were a thousand suggestions as to what might be done, Papa said he had hoped Leon would stay in London, he had offered him a place in his business, even if he knew nothing of cigar manufacture, there was no reason why he couldn't learn. Jack said, and Grandma said, and Freddie said. . . . Leon just joked with them, and Aunt Anna kept her mouth straight together.

Julie knew how they felt. She felt alarmed herself. Leon had changed. He hadn't said a word about going, so it meant he had ceased to love her. Or did it? As soon as she could, as soon as the group in the dining room began to disperse, she tried to catch Leon. Mr. Munzell detained her. Most intimate now, he stood fingering her velvet sleeve. She had to fling away from Mr. Munzell, hurry to the drawing room. Leon wasn't there. Aunt Anna hadn't seen him. Upstairs to the old card room, down again, a plague take that fool Munzell, back to the drawing room, short of breath and tremulous as if he were gone already. He didn't have to run away on her account. If he had stopped loving her, they could be friends all their lives. She flew down the hall, her bracelet chinking

and chiming, spilling a thin golden rivulet of music. He might
have gone, sneaked off already in the middle of Christmas.
She burst wildly into Uncle Henry's old study, she didn't even
knock, and there stood Leon smoking calmly.

"I've something to say, Leon." He had changed. He didn't
love her any more, but that was no reason to go away. That
was all the more reason. . . .

"Now, little woman, what is it? What do you want to say,
dear?" He took her in his arms, without any mistletoe. He
moved his warm mouth against her temple to help her think,
against her mouth to help her speak; but the little oration had
fallen apart. She could only stand there with her trembling,
crushed roses, and whisper, "Take me with you, Leon. Take
me with you."

Papa greeted the announcement by bringing forth his fine old
stone bottles of brandy, his choice wine. He bid the family
to the house on New Year's Day, allowed Mother to order
pork pies and guava jelly, woodcocks and partridges, handed
about his best Havanas with a largesse scarcely credible. And
if they had sense, they'd drink the brandy and smoke the
cigars and cram the truffles while they could, Aunt Anna
said, they'd not see Frederic Corper making such a show of it
again, sly enough he was, marrying off two daughters for the
price of one. Marrying off one of them almost at once! for
Leon said they should be married soon, with no betrothal
fuss. If Papa objected to speed, he would not object perhaps
to the fact that marrying quickly gave small chance to lay out
for an elaborate wedding. "Amen," said Aunt Anna. Amen,
said Papa, too, in his own way—he promptly offered Leon the
position as foreman in his factory; in time, the Lord willing,
there'd be a partnership.

Papa also suggested that they stay on at home. Leon's starting wage would not be unduly handsome, although it would increase as the young man showed his worth. Meanwhile, living at home would leave Julie where her health could best be looked after and would give him a chance to get on his feet, save his salary, and acquire a substantial and most essential nest egg. Even Mother urged Leon; she, too, warned him of Julie's health; but he just laughed, he liked her slender as she was and she'd probably outlive them all, he said, that was the way with tantalizing little frails. And they must live alone, didn't Julie agree? To build the new life with their own hands, a life no one from outside could add one whit to. "Yes, Leon, oh, yes!" But did she realize what it meant, moving from the richly appointed house with its plush and gilt and ormolu to something very modest at first, not much above what Aunt Anna had in Bow Road, with Britannia metal and lucky for that?

He discussed it all in frank details she was to weigh against the "take me with you." His knowledge of language could best be put to a luxury business with traffic in exports and imports, but what appetite had he for spices or silks, tinctures, perfumes, and rare dyes he'd seen men sweating out their lives for? Lud could have his diamonds, too. Tobacco was certainly a lesser evil, even the poor man liked his smoke; so Papa's offer appealed to him. He wasn't going to quibble over salary, either. No need for a million bank notes to stash away, why stash anything? If you had a good bottle of wine, drink it; if you had a new suit of clothes, wear it! All he and Julie needed was enough to enjoy life and help others do the same.

It was a trifle bewildering, she hoped he wouldn't try explaining it to Mr. Munzell or to Papa, who would think him mad and stop the marriage. Leon's views were not new to her. He and Ludwig had laughed and joked about such things in Holland and neither then nor now could she see a difference between having no surplus money and having lots of it which was untouched. Never fear about Leon. When you walked down the street on his arm you felt steadied and free, you felt his strength as undeviating as that of a railroad carriage when the wheels began their exciting promise of speed and destination. He would do anything he put his mind to. Papa said it, too; there was a fine future for Leon, he said. The business was growing, it would grow by leaps and bounds had he a man he could trust to help him. His eyes kindled with a hard, bright light. Tobacco consumption had increased eighteen per cent in ten years; the race for markets was wide open. Leon would learn from the ground up, but the actual cigar making was nothing, hands could be hired sixpence a dozen. What he needed was a helpmeet who'd not shy from responsibility. And why wouldn't Papa want Leon when all he had was Freddie, the stupidest boy you'd ever seen. *Corper and Dekker.* That's how it would be on the side of the building some day. She could almost see it the afternoon she went with Leon, the afternoon he was to look the place over and settle the matter.

Papa frowned to see her. He did not approve of family visitations. So far as lady Corpers were concerned, he was to disappear into a void every morning and spring out of it every night. So this was where Papa lived—a small, brownish office, filled wall to wall with the compressed, condensed scent of cigars; furniture, floor, the thin filter of dust on the windows, all partook of the gloomy color of dried leaf. Papa took a box from his desk, flipped the lid, and there lay the neat brown tubes, solemn, spare, and silent under the graven word *Corper's.* Leon took one; so did Papa.

"You'll excuse us, Julie, if you must go invading premises where you've no business, you bear the brunt." Papa cut the tip carefully with his silver knife. "We're trying out some new molds at table three. Might be a place for you to start, get your hand in," he told Leon. "I've an old fellow named Becke can look after you the first weeks." He twirled the cigar between his thumb and first finger, showed Leon where it had been gummed. Then he threw open the door to the workroom and stood aside that they might enjoy the magnitude of the spectacle, the long work tables, the dozens of men busy before their piles of tobacco leaf. She'd had no idea Papa employed so many. The scent burst full, a great bulbous vacuum filled with stale molasses; she stepped inside, the balloon swaying and sailing.

"Quite a jump from the days when cigar makers went from factory to factory begging for work like journeymen, eh?" Papa said.

Leon looked eagerly. Knives flashed on the wooden cutting blocks, scissors flashed, the workers' hands sped over their piles of moistened leaves. One after another would lift a limp web, strip the stalk, feel, form the dry shreds, and secrete them in the moist elastic wrappers. At the far end, thick, dreamy white vapor rose from the drying pans. For some reason, it frightened her, the men seemed drugged by it; they floated mute in the balloon drugged by the sweet, white smoke Papa had put to snare them. She'd had dealings with Papa before, she wanted to hurry Leon, run, get him out of here! Papa led the way down the aisle between the tables, his head sharp left, then right. He stopped to pick up a newly finished cigar and held it to the light, his mustache curling. Leon steered her on. At one table, filler was being pressed into smooth wooden molds. The man chewed as he worked, the mound in his cheek moved rhythmically. He didn't look up when they stopped, but he opened a mold to show the smooth, dead cigars.

"Allus somethin' new," he said shifting his wad. "Seen the new Prentiss machine? Ten cigars a minute. Not up to the ones by hand. I'll match 'em any day." Then he saw Papa coming.

As fast as cigars accumulated on each table, they were passed to the end baskets and carted forward to where Freddie and another chap sat in a high cage. Freddie scrutinized the baskets vaguely, passed them on to the sorter. He didn't smile.

"It's all right to be friendly with the men," murmured Papa, "but keep your distance."

"They seem a good lot," countered Leon.

"You won't be sitting at a table forever, mind."

Steam hissed from the drying pans. Now and then a glint of light cut the thick vapor, the browned fingers sped against the bitter air. Papa told Leon how many cigars were produced a day, a week, a month; the output needed to be doubled. He had the customers, but the workers wouldn't sweat it out. They were no good since they'd organized. He introduced Leon to Becke, a dried shred of a man with eyes clear as spring water.

"My son-in-law to be," said Papa. "He's joining us."

Leon shook hands with the old man. "And this is Mr. Corper's daughter, sir, who is going to be Mrs. Dekker."

Becke peered over his glasses, considering what he might say. "Dekker, ya, Hollander?"

"Ya," laughed Leon. He rattled off a string of talk so fast Julie couldn't catch it all. Heads raised. The look of Papa's face was funny. He wheeled away, since there was no stopping Leon, and marched off to do important things. Becke talked a little, but he was cagey and he never for an instant stopped his work.

Later, in the office, Papa reemphasized the need for increased production. There was almost no markup between wholesale and retail, the retailer needed quantity for this expanding market. Leon's first concern would be to watch for inefficiency, suggest methods for speeding tempo, keep his eyes on the men.

"God, Becke is skillful," Leon said. And had Papa ever considered having someone read aloud? Eleven hours was a long stretch, they worked automatically, they'd work better if they had something to think about. They did too much thinking as it was, Papa said, they could be damned good and grateful, he didn't know what labor was coming to. What he needed was speed. And he'd get it more likely if the men weren't bored, replied Leon, Leon who had lived in the jungle where there were pink-headed doves and green peacocks. She was trembling, but Papa had actually begun to smile! Since Leon was responsible for increasing speed, he

109

was also responsible for the methods by which it would be achieved. Only, he mustn't put too much stock in their complaints and grumblings. He'd see for himself. Starting tomorrow. They shook hands on that, Leon smiling, not afraid of Papa at all.

9

Now they were really running down the hill, faster and faster toward their wedding day, toward church with its familiar yawning door, Mendelssohn sighing and singing of moist flowers, and all the bells. They were flying down into the stale, dainty, holy breath of church, the inexhaustible breath which stemmed from the minister himself—the Reverend Mr. Peabody whom Mr. Munzell would bring to London for the purpose, unwilling to take no for an answer, determined to have his part in this wedding, unto the very voice of God. Julie was glad to have the Reverend Mr. Peabody, remembering his Christmas-kindled face, his quiet wisdom, and the thin, piping words of Luke she had heard in his church at Croydon.

Even without a great wedding, there were a thousand details—the license with their two names legibly written in round letters, all vaguely like O's, the sizing of the ring. Ludwig had fashioned the golden band and sent it on ahead to be sure of the fit. At a pallid jeweler's in Piccadilly they had it cut down and engraved. It was a small shop, littered with scraps and strands of metal, gritty with dust, watch springs, rings with blind sockets, jewels on velvet trays, mourning brooches, and lumps of dull, pocked gold. Under a dusty glass bell stood a miniature duck, blood red and exquisitely carved. Carnelian, the jeweler said, from Chiney, and when she admired it, he lifted the bell and let her touch the round-beaked creature, trace with the tip of her finger the wings that

110

faded out from color to a smoky white. Then he brought out her shining wedding band and fitted it in place.

"Come out here, missus, see this fit," he called. The woman couldn't have been far away in the miniscule shop, she must have been hovering like a moth behind the curtain at the back and she came now, apologetically, to the counter.

"A-ha-ha," and he showed her how easily the ring slipped onto Julie's finger, how perfect, after all the bawling and scolding that he was getting it too small. "Too small, too small, eh?"

Well, she muttered, she was glad enough it was not too small, that he didn't have to make it good. A pale, meek woman with hair in limp strands across her skull; her face was an exact oval, and the colorless eyes gazed wistfully at Leon, at Julie, at the ring.

"So it's all right, missus, the old man's a neat goldsmith after all, eh?" He bid her show the ring he had made for *their* wedding; and the wife scrubbed her hand on her apron, then held out the swelled knuckles with the worn ring almost exactly like Phillip's! The ring that lay this minute folded in a handkerchief at the bottom of the linen drawer.

It was pretty enough in its time, the woman said, it had been and she had been, she tried to smile but the mouth wouldn't follow her. It was a gentled mouth, submissive, as if someone had hit her a blow across the shapeless, soft, coy lips. Afraid to open her face she was, the husband said, a shy one she was. He gave a final polish to the new circlet and peered in. "For Gypsy from Leon." The wife stared slyly, she squinted her eyes at Julie as if she knew all about her, the girl with two wedding rings, the bright shiny new one and that other like a discarded rind.

"You have fine plans, eh?" muttered the woman, squinting and staring after them. So she knew about the future, too. Julie could see her at the window when they'd gone, sad phantom or evil witch. And what did she see in the future that made her leer like that? Still at the window watching every step.

111

"Leon, nothing is wrong, is it? You're not sorry you went to work for Papa?" As if that might be the trouble, as if the jeweler's witch knew something she did not.

"What a strange little creature you are." Leon drew her arm through his. There were some good men at the shop, he said, old Becke, who had hands like a musician's, and Whitaker, the one who chewed tobacco. They'd been distant with him at first, his face colored, but they were coming around now, this morning he'd rolled a cigar Becke said could pass muster anywhere.

"But you didn't answer my question, Leon."

And he still didn't. He had to hurry now, get back to the shop, he'd come out on his dinnertime and there were no latecomers at the factory. That's as much as she could get him to say about business. Still, his enthusiasm for Becke and Whitaker knew no bounds, and when she caught him with the serious cleft between his brows, why, he was tired, that's all, getting to business at six o'clock was hard work "for a loafer like me." Then he'd turn the talk to suit himself, how was the little house today, what had she and Aunt Anna been up to?

For every afternoon was devoted to setting the new house to rights, the tiny chip of a house she and Leon had taken at Aldgate, a great bargain with its narrow windows and Gothic door, its brass knocker and wicket Julie had to mount a stool to see through. Emil always drove her and Aunt Anna and he was as big a fool as they were, stepping over the floor on the tips of his boots, polishing the door latch with his sleeve, fixing a faulty window shutter as delicately as a surgeon. When he had seen every last improvement, he'd drive away, leaving the two biddies to don aprons and bibs, stuff their hair up under thick caps, and start an endless round of brushing and whisking and scrubbing. Other folks who called themselves Christians might shut air and light out of their houses, but Aunt Anna was heathen in one thing, she liked plenty of good clean air to blow out other folks' dirt. She opened the windows to the winter wind and scrubbed with that as well as with soap and water. Not that she really needed to scrub. A charwoman had been found, a stout, grubby creature named Smicks whose numerous pockets bulged with the implements of her trade in such a way, that when she pulled forth a cloth for the furniture you weren't sure whether it was indeed a cloth or perhaps a petticoat still attached to her round person and merely called to emergency service. Like Pip's laundress, her head might have done for a mop, but unlike that stick of a woman, Mrs. Smicks seemed more likely to clean the stairs by rolling down them.

Julie and Leon had found this questionable domestic the day they signed for the lodgings. Women were hard to get with all the factory work. They had felt themselves lucky, until Aunt Anna was called for comment. Aunt Anna's eyes flew up and down in a hurry over Mrs. Smicks; she warranted the old hag wouldn't have sense to find the place three days running. But come one o'clock, came Mrs. Smicks, day in, day out, rocking from side to side on her shapeless shoes, carting her mop and pail and ruddy of flesh despite the thin shawl whose dusty texture suggested banisters and polished brass.

Aunt Anna sniffed at everything Mrs. Smicks did and as soon as she went rocking out of the house—and a good snootful in her, too—all the windows were flung open and Aunt Anna rescrubbed and repolished after her. The former occupants had been evicted and left the place dirty and the range crusted over; but it was a small house with only so many cracks and crannies to resist their armed might. Floors were sanded, cupboards scraped, every metal hinge polished until light glanced from it. Julie hung curtains and nailed a flowered flounce across the chimney piece, she unpacked boxes Leon had sent from Arnheim, leafed through his books, French, Dutch, German, and English, dusted and put them on the shelves beside her own pretty Browning and Keats, her Marlowe and Jonson and Dickens and the beautiful gilt leather Shakespeare that Phillip had given her. This she put away quickly as if it hurt to touch it, to one side, not nearly so conspicuous as Malthus and Saint Simon. She flung down the duster and ran to the scullery, to Aunt Anna who was cleaning silver, her soft dried-lavender hair the color of ash with the fire still under it.

"Well, speak up," Aunt Anna said. "Give a body the creeps."

She wanted it out, open and honest about Phillip and Leon. Aunt Anna heard her through. She burnished a pitcher until it melted to a blur of light and said Julie had nothing to answer to anyone. She'd gone on plenty mourning and grieving for Phillip; that choice had been made and there was no crying over what had been and done. Besides, she nodded briskly, she could just tell Julie good and plain, she was getting a better man. Not that she hadn't loved Phillip, he was a poet that boy, and God save him he had spunk! But Leon was something else again, a man you could depend on, he needn't go making a ruckus so you were happy one minute and crying your heart out the next, he made something out of life, she'd be switched if he didn't.

So it was said. One weak ray of light trickled into the little garden at the back, the bricks made an even line on the wall where Emil had mended them. Such a dear house, so compact and snug. The kitchen and scullery were below, the parlor above. She liked the way it went, in and out with window seats of good oak, a nook either side of the fireplace and the bookshelves above. The brass rods on the stair carpets had gone down only today and she leaned over, polished a dull spot here, a scratch there, as she went. Upstairs was the bedroom and that was best of all, for the beams were of rough wood, the eaves slanted outside the windows, and Aunt Anna had made heavy blue drapes that could be swung on their brass rings to cloak the glass. One starched ruffle of lace framed the small mirror.

This was the room where she would come with Leon, where they would be *together*. It was something to think of gravely, as you lined the drawers and hung summer frocks in the press. Not that she was afraid. She hadn't even been willing to talk of it with Emma and Ethelyn when they giggled and whispered, Ethelyn wheedling information from Emma who laughed a good deal and didn't Julie want to hear? She did not. She believed in Leon, she loved him, she was going to be his wife; and while she would have preferred to keep as they were now, except, of course, together and in the little house which smelled so beautifully of soap and silver and warm ironing, still . . . whatever the unknown, she'd be able to accept it. She knew that. She'd be able to lie rigid and ready to endure anything.

10

And almost before she knew it, there she was, in the little room, in the soft, deep bed, rigid and waiting. She could hear Leon whistle. Rain drizzled, wove about the house in a dense drape; and they were alone, completely alone with the good, thick walls about them.

Just then a board creaked and her heart flew, all the blood flew to her throat. Only a board in the parlor where he was waiting for her to call, only a board in the parlor! Back she lay against the pillows, weakened, trembling in her white linen gown. The curtains trembled, too. They had been drawn rich and blue across the glass, the brass rings glittered, candlelight waved over the duveteen, stroked the sinuous folds, shed a languorous, dreamy haze, around her finger bone the wide new golden ring flowed everlastingly. And suppose it had been that other, that hidden ring! Phillip would never have waited downstairs, he'd have— She scotched the shameful thought. Leon was whistling. It was one of the tunes he'd sung in Arnheim and he sounded so gay and steady, she breathed again. Rain flowed, streamed off the eaves sluicing and falling. It dabbled the pavement, thumped on the windows, sobbed and slushed and sealed her in. She was suspended in a cup at the very top of the house and had only to call, she would have loved to call Leon, have him come talk over the busy, happy day. Only. . . .

"Gypsy? May I?"

He loomed up big out of the stair well. His wild, curly hair brushed the low beams and his neck was bare. One little vein pulsed, Julie saw it when he bent above her, in his loose brown dressing gown.

"Hear the rain, darling? Know what it says?" His voice was husky, he whispered the words into her hair, he breathed against her ear and kissed her mouth and she lay rigid, shivering under the covers.

When Leon spoke again he had pulled his voice up. "It's a nice little house, isn't it, Julie? Not a leak anywhere." Rain had sounded differently out on maneuvers, out in the middle of nowhere drenching down, dripping from every leaf of every tree, dripping until it almost drove the soldiers crazy. He watched her while he talked. She never moved.

"You know what?" he said then. "I'm starved, darling. Let's go down and see what there is to eat." He found her pink quilted wrapper, brought it over and held it for her like a coat. She thrust her arms in hurriedly for it was miserable, naked, standing there without stays in her white linen night-dress. How could she have ever thought it would do? And she tried to catch back the lunatic frame of mind in which she had rippled blue ribbons through the flounces at wrist, throat, and hem and thought herself very well provided for in the matter of sleep. There, that was better. Fastening her wrapper snug, she hurried ahead of Leon, down the stairs, as if she didn't know who he was.

But it was different downstairs, it was her own dear house. Aunt Anna had left a pink roast beef and new bread wrapped in a cloth. Julie filled the kettle, hung it for the first time over the dying fire, while Leon poked at the embers until whole flames burst out, crackled and leapt so in no time the kettle was puffing away as merrily as Mrs. Peabody's.

"Oh, Mrs. Peabody," she murmured. "I don't think she liked our wedding, Leon."

"Well, I liked it. That was the pertest, prettiest bride." He forked another thin slice of roast beef and chewed with relish. He made a sandwich for Julie, but she couldn't eat, no, she certainly couldn't eat.

"Mrs. Peabody wouldn't even look at me. And she's such a nice person and I like her so." She smiled a little and blushed knowing why Mrs. Peabody. . . . Leon thought the Reverend had enjoyed it enough for both. Good Lord, he'd never heard a man make a longer to-do about anything! He'd given brother Munzell his money's worth and made it plain in heaven that they were married beyond a doubt. Besides, why wouldn't the old boy enjoy it—hadn't he taken occasion to kiss the bride, with more than clerical vigor, too?

"Leon!" But he made her laugh. "My, this is good bread, isn't it, Leon?" She chewed slowly. Grandma Stodel had baked that, you could taste the eggs and butter and the hard, tiny poppy seeds that peppered the crust. Grandma enjoyed their wedding more than anyone. Perhaps the older you grew, the more you did enjoy; Grandma might have thought it was the last wedding she would ever see, or she might have been thinking of her own wedding and of Grandpa. Only look what she'd given them, the handsome Stodel silver. Leon fetched the wooden chest so they could admire it again, dozens of lumpy bundles in dark red cotton flannel tied with ribbons. They unwrapped and brought into the firelight the dazzling silver spoons; tilt them as you would, the rounded bowls held light to the brim. They could use their Britannia metal for every day, but sterling silver Julie was not to be married without and Grandma had given them every piece, even the carved sugar tongs Julie had played with as a child. The room was as full of gifts as a bazaar: copper pieces from Emma and Lud, linens from Papa, a pewter jug from Aunt Mathilda's countess. Was Leon quite satisfied with the way she and Aunt Anna had stowed the furniture? They went over it for the thousandth time, the love seat and wing chair from Aunt Mathilda, the tables and carpet and sideboard from Leon's parents. Was he certain the sea chest was well

117

disposed in the hall? Then the small kerosene lamp must be carried about to try its effect, the roses in the carpet staring up bewildered in their own brightness.

Hadn't the Reverend Mr. Peabody's voice grown thin and quivery, though? She had feared it would break before he could finish. When he spoke of life and each thing in its own time, had Leon heard his mother crying? It must have been Mother Dekker, to the left behind them. Leon agreed; there was nothing his mama liked so much as a good cry. Lud, too, they were great ones for translating their joy into salt water.

They could talk of things like that now, intimate things. She could confide to Leon that once upon a time—yes, that's just how it was, almost as in a story—once upon a time she had not just loved her family, but had been of the same blood and bone, and how lonely it was when you didn't belong to anyone. Well, she had some blood and bone now, she had him, Leon said. He took her on his knee before the fire, unbraided the tight plaits and rumpled her hair with his hands. He drew her close to him, poked the fire so they kept warm while they talked. Did Leon really like her wedding dress and the small hat—which he most decidedly did— and wasn't she practical and thrifty to have had a daytime costume instead of white satin? Papa had been in such a hurry getting her down that aisle, keeping it all punctual. Oh, and Mr. Munzell. She hid her face against his brown dressing gown which didn't seem strange any more.

"Old Munzell carried it off very well. He wanted to win you, but he wanted just as much to make it all right when he didn't, and he certainly managed that."

"Poor Mrs. Peabody, I think she hates me."

"Don't laugh at Mrs. Peabody. She was only wishing you what you might have done better to wish yourself." His tone was so solemn, she looked up startled, and his face had changed.

"Something is wrong, Leon. Tell me."

He stood her on her feet in the small high box of a room. "Not exactly wrong, Julie, but different than we planned. I

118

wasn't going to trouble you at first, but I want you to know everything about us so you'll never be confused or frightened."

"It's Papa. What has he done?"

"Not exactly your papa. He offered the job as foreman fair and square. I just don't want it, Julie. I wouldn't be his foreman for five thousand pounds a year."

Then he told her why. He'd known from the first day that something was off key. In his life he'd never had trouble making friends, but the hands at the shop shut him out, they'd not say two words; when closing time came, he was glad enough to be leaving. He'd thought they would be, too, but instead of grabbing their coats and rushing out, the men lined up with their coats on and their dinner pails in their hands; they stood shuffling their feet and not looking. Julie's papa had come then, bade Leon stand to one side and observe one of the first duties of a foreman. Papa'd taken a place to the right of the door and Freddie to the left and as those poor, hard-working devils went through, they ran their hands expertly up and down each man's clothes to be sure he wasn't taking any cigars.

"No, Leon!"

"You see, dear, you understand." He resumed his chair before the fire and took her on his knees. What wonder that there was a deep antagonism between Papa and the hands? This was worse than the army, he'd never dreamed that in business, in modern England. . . . He was going to have to walk carefully to maintain an even keel between them, but against the men he could not be. They were good, honest fellows, wretchedly ill paid and poor. The job of foreman with its concomitants of petty policing her papa could give to someone with the stomach for it. He hadn't said it in so many words, but he had told Papa that until he learned the business and learned it well, he'd expect to be treated like the others. So, if it was all right with Julie, he'd just string along with Becke and the rest and they'd get by fair enough if they watched the pennies. Julie should just not expect others to understand, and she'd have been more of a lady if she'd taken Munzell.

She hugged her arms around his neck, she didn't want to be a lady. Leon said that eventually he might work into sales or some other capacity which would not put him over the men, then she could be a little of a lady after all.

And now they were very close indeed. The fire had burned to one fuming core of heat, it swung golden tongues on the walls, pressed the room so close Leon found it hard to breathe, she could hear the quick gasp each breath made in his chest. He held her clasped to him while rain rolled hard on the windows, beat and laved the panes, gushed in floods through the gutters. She felt the throb of it. When Leon lifted her she gave her mouth to him, hot for the first time and liquid as a lover's.

He carried her upstairs quickly, but it was different from anything one might have thought, confusing, the weight and drive and probing, pinioned flesh. Leon tried to be very kind, but the pain killed off her rich desire, bludgeoned and seared —there was no fighting it. Only dig the nails into your clenched hands.

Once in the tumult, his mouth lifted from hers. "It will all be different some day," he whispered. "You'll come to it with your blood singing like fire, dear."

11

Leon had to rise early, while it was still dark. The days started in a secret, confidential way as if they two were alone in the middle of the night world. He always had the fire blazing when she came down, the kettle singing on the hob; and Julie would toast the bread and her feet at the same time, spread the crusts over with butter, and they'd sip their tea

120

and eat their toast by firelight. Sandwiches must be made, too, thick roast beef or mutton sandwiches and tea which she poured scalding into the bottle, the heat dissipating, breathing itself away as she poured. She worried about his drinking cold tea but he said it wasn't bad, especially if she'd drop in a bit of treacle. There was never a moment to lose in the mornings; he was stanch for getting to work on time and when she couldn't prolong it another minute, when he had tilted his head for the last swallow of tea, wiped his mouth on the napkin and put the tray to one side, she helped him with his coat. It was something of importance to help him with his greatcoat, hand him the lunch pail, and be kissed good-by— his toast-and-butter kiss, she could catch the vanished golden crumbs on his clean breath. Then he was gone. Julie closed the pointed door, latched the fastenings against a drizzling day; with the final bolt drawn, this was indeed a fortress and she the queen of it. The keys to every cabinet clinked in a bunch at her waist.

Then there was shopping to do, she could buy and cook whatever she wished, concoct the most amazing dinners, not always too successfully. Often when Aunt Anna wasn't there, Leon's arrival would find her flying around the stove, her face hot from steam and even hotter from chagrin. She'd run to meet him ready to cry because dinner was spoiled. So what if it were, he didn't plan to beat her, and out he'd go to the cook's shop for a cold fowl and a jug of wine, maybe sixpenny-worth of Maids of Honor, so that in the long run, they'd have quite a feast. Then she did begin to get the hang of cooking. She'd lay the cloth with a flourish, turn out a fine batter pudding, and remember, when she heard the lamplighter, that it was time to fetch her brown bread from the baker and be back before Leon came whistling up the walk. Each dish was timed to that whistle. She scowled at the Dutch clock when he was late, ran to the window the minute she heard him, and while he unlatched the door was dishing up pork and greens or a leg of mutton that would have put cook's nose out of joint.

One night, it was not just Leon but Becke as well. That was the day she had bought a small-sized fish, worrying that it might not feed her and Leon and Aunt Anna. There was nothing to do but slice down her best brick cheese, thank heaven she had a pottle of strawberries, and bustle about making a hot punch of rum and water. Becke seemed to relish whatever he was served. He was a single man used to taking supper alone in his room, and not worth eating you could warrant, for he was lean as a lath. He limped upstairs and he limped down, approved their house from garret to cellar, and a deep crease came and went in his cheek at the spot intended for a dimple. He showed Leon how to fix the roasting jack, sat near the fire until very late, smoking his pipe and watching Aunt Anna's fingers dance the crochet hook.

He spoke quietly about matters at the shop, but the way he harped on collective bargaining! There were things that needed change. Ten hours it was in the cotton mills, even the cotton mills, ten hours, and here they were sweating out eleven, worse than eleven—hanged he'd be if that young one of the master's wasn't setting the clock forward of a morning and backward by night! Whitaker had been to the shop early, he'd seen Fred Corper climb down from the clock; he'd waited around at dinnertime, went back to the workroom sneaky like, and there was the lad climbing down from the clock again. He'd like to hear the answer to that. All the men wanted an answer. Leon thought Whitaker was mistaken, the boss was a hard man but not likely to be sly. Oh, he wasn't, wasn't he? said Becke. And even through her alarm, Julie smiled warmly at Aunt Anna because Becke had forgotten she belonged to Papa. He spoke out in front of her and Leon as if they were all together; and on the matter of the clock, why didn't Leon ask the boss, straight out, he said, go up for all of them and ask? Leon rocked back and forth on his tilted chair. He took another swallow of rum and water, reached for the pitcher and filled their guest's glass. Likely it was his own place to do it, Becke said, being oldest, but he wasn't much of a one with his lip and he'd think it kindly if Leon would confront the boss.

So Leon confronted Papa and the next night every man from the shop crowded into the little fortress, so many that Julie and Aunt Anna had to retreat to a high stair with their sewing. Leon had told Papa how the men felt, he'd asked point-blank about fixing the clock, and Papa had said to tell the men the clock was no concern of theirs; they'd put in that time and they'd be putting in five more hours before the month was out to make up for time lost on those hogsheads that had come watered down. It made the sewing drop right in Julie's lap! An angry murmur arose from below. They were making up the excise tax Papa had paid on a bad shipment. Too moist, not butted enough, and sand besides, Whitaker said; but it wasn't their fault, it was the fault of Papa or who-ever had inspected the shipment at customs. The men were restless; they rocked on their chairs.

"Your poor ma should hear this," Aunt Anna whispered, "after all the years she's bowed and scraped to that man like he was God Almighty." Then out loud, without stopping in her fast needlework, she said, instead of pacing around like helpless granny dears, why didn't they do something about it? They had a Cigar Makers' Society, didn't they? Well, what good was it if it didn't get them something one way or another, less hours or more pay?

Becke flung his head straight back to get a look at her. "Hear the woman," he said. "Makes more sense than the lot of you." He bowed to the staircase with such gallantry that Aunt Anna was hard pressed to clack her needles and look aloof. Aunt Anna was right, agreed Leon, what they needed was to put their amalgamation to use as the engineers had done, calm, reasonable action, collective bargaining. He would have liked to join their Cigar Makers' Society himself, she knew that, only how could he, with Papa? They wanted weekly in-stead of fortnightly pay, they wanted apprentices restricted one to five, they wanted more money and less hours and more air.

Gradually, as the months passed, Julie began to understand the passion they put into their talk. She went with Leon to visit at other homes, saw how poor they really were, poorer than you could guess by the worn clothes or haunted look. They lived in infested hovels, slept in stench from the foul alleyways, and saw their children drag off to work without sleep or enough food. Back in Aldgate with the door fast behind them, she would cling to Leon in the dark, peaked silence, sobbing against his coat for the poor people who had so little. He was to bring Becke as often as he could to dinner. She had seen his barren room and she wanted him here and Whitaker and the others too, as if, once inside her stronghold, she could keep them safe. She wanted to bring the whole world to her house.

12

What a joy to be ill this once; and not really ill, nothing to be alarmed about, Aunt Anna said, look at the trouble her own poor ma'd had when she was in a family way. Julie must follow the doctor, lie abed and not lift a finger. No cause for alarm.

"I'm not alarmed, Aunt Anna. I'm happy and lazy; you take such care of me."

The old eyes sharpened so they all but bored holes through their spectacles. Aunt Anna disappeared down the stairs which she said would be the death of her, reappeared immediately with a thick, creamy eggnog Julie could drink down for strength.

"How do you do it, Aunt Anna? Sit here, rest." She toyed with the glass, turning the spoon through the foam, trying not to smell the nutmeg or the port.

And who else was going to wait on Julie hand and foot? And since when was there any rest in the world for Anna

Perry? But she wouldn't let a soul in her place, marched in at five every morning, cooked a hot breakfast, joked and bullied Leon out of the house, and then came up to see, well, how was she today? Fine or no, Aunt Anna barely listened. The first glance set her off on a treadmill of cures and antidotes, pillows for the swollen feet, lotion for the brow, a hundred tempting trays carted in with sprigs of green to dress them up.

"I'm standing here to see you drink this eggnog."

The very sight of the sweet, cool glass turned her tongue to water. Aunt Anna snatched the glass as abruptly as if she planned to dump it out the window. "Well and good, don't eat, that's how to make a fat healthy baby, live on air," she muttered, and flung off down the stairs. She didn't mean it, she was patient and loyal and fretted herself a plenty, begging the Lord's pardon, there should be some easier way than this to manufacture human beings. Julie could hear her, bustling about below, while she lay in the deep bed, dreaming of her baby. It never had any definite form or shape, this baby, but it was a warm living bundle as Elsa had been, squirming and sucking and smelling of sweet oil. She could positively feel it within her from the first, listened intently to hear it breathe—which was stuff and nonsense to her nurse.

"But I can, Aunt Anna." She felt her stomach gently so as not to frighten it, the stomach still so small that the baby must be small, too. That was no surprise. Hadn't she been such a tiny thing they carried her on a pillow? Grandpa had cried like a woman when she was born, Grandma told her, because she looked so feeble. Food and care and love could change a baby, and hers would be stinted on none of the three. Only think what a father Leon would make, how many times he had rocked her as if she were a child! There'd be no frightening, no alone in the dark for this little one, it need never go with a hungry heart as she had, waiting for Grandpa to come. She was glad they could not afford a nursemaid, for how could you deliver over the little thing to anyone else to bathe and tend?

125

Often, to help pass the afternoons, Mother and Aunt Mathilda came, bringing needlework or netting apparatus and amazing accounts of previous pregnancies. This sort of thing had amused Julie when she'd listened with half an ear at Arnheim, but it was important and personal now. Ethelyn, too, did visit duty when she was in London; for she was Mrs. Potter, residing for the summer at Hampshire in what was evidently high style. Certainly she recounted brilliant episodes of chase and ball and innumerable family pedigrees which placed every member of the Hampshire set in palpitating acquaintance with the throne. Thin nosed as ever, Ethelyn, supremely conscious of what was right and what was wrong, and what could be more wrong than to live in London through the blatant summer heat, unless, appalling thought, it was to live in Aldgate?

Aunt Anna sniffed so hard her ears flattened. Ethelyn might be a Mrs. Potter with country house and shires and what-all, but if you asked *her*, she was nothing more than a bad-mannered, snippy little chit. Julie didn't mind what Ethelyn said. Nothing could penetrate her firm province, her house with its oak panels, the growing life which in no time would wave its fists in Ethelyn's face. Julie smiled mysteriously. Leon would be home soon, he'd carry her downstairs if she felt able, and later, through the long night, he would lie beside her warm and sheltering while she planned for the baby.

But after three months, it was all over. She heard herself scream, she screamed like a mad horse, turned and tossed until there was nothing left. The room was hot, she was bandaged tight, the sharp fumes of disinfectant put her into a doze. After that she cried when no one was there to see, when Aunt Anna was safely about her chores, she cried and cried without a sound for the sweet lively baby. It had been so real to her, so close to her and so real, sometimes a girl baby, sometimes a little boy with gray eyes like Leon's.

No one else understood that. They thought better this way than to have borne and lost it—look at Aunt Mathilda who had lost a child of three years, look at Mother who had lost three or four in the early months of their lives. She would not look. They didn't know a thing about it. She had loved her baby, been *in* love with it, for what a wonder when she never thought she could, never thought she'd be lucky or well enough to make a human life. Leon tried to soothe and gentle her, but sadness lay like stone between her breasts; and she might never be able to have another, that lay even colder.

She put herself down into the well of grief and stayed there. After a while, she was well enough to go to market, through air as empty as if she'd lost her nose and ears. The street teemed with babies; sometimes she stopped to give them a cooky or a bit of cake, but they had no substance, these live babies, like dolls of paper.

13

The family visitation had been long postponed, first by an illness of Mother's, then by her own; and when at last they were to come, she tried to summon up anticipation, tied on her dimity apron, and bade them welcome.

But Papa sat his chair as if the place disgraced him, no dining room, one box of a sitting room—he walked neither up nor down to see the added attractions. Tea itself did not please him, Mother had to brew a cup with her own hands while he delivered a lecture on the evils of the Cigar Makers' Society, the ingrates who were out to ruin England. Grandma and Aunt Mathilda alone admired things; even Mr. Munzell, who complimented her grace as hostess and the snugness of her ménage, said "snug" with certain satisfaction, contrasting it in his mind's eye with the halls-to-be of Munzell.

Maybe her house didn't have beads and tassels galore, maybe it wasn't as big as a barn, it was a dear house, and she wanted them out of it; but after they had gone, after the last rattle of wheels had died in the Sabbath quiet, some sharp new prescience lingered. Provoking sounds drifted in, the rude clatter of buckets as some lad ran down to Aldgate pump, a retching cough, a vulgar whacking spit. She closed the windows and latched them, but wasn't that a trace of damp mortar in the scullery passage? Didn't the walls want painting? Who ever heard of a room so small and cramped? She didn't look at Leon as he helped her pile the tea things. She scrubbed and polished every piece as if it had been exposed to tarnish which at any minute might insinuate a dull, corrupting stain. What she could not scrub out was the thin, perverse ridge of anger in herself.

It was a relief when the door knocker sounded and Becke and Whitaker dropped in. They had strolled over from Spitalfields for a dose of air, the drains "smelling so fine." But Becke and Whitaker weren't right either, they looked shabbier than ever, she saw them as if they were transparencies with bright, devastating light behind. Becke's greasy velveteen hung limp from his shoulders, heaven knew how many men had worn the same garment before they were slid from some obscure window and down the last black ladder to their graves. Whitaker's Sunday neckcloth glared raw and bulky as a bandage. Why, just once, couldn't they look like respectable people in decent linen and good cloth? She despised herself, knowing perfectly well why. It was as if the family visit had dropped a hard, nasty pebble on the water; each ripple sent a bitter, shocking thought into her ken.

Some of these thoughts concerned the cigar makers. The men were not lawless vandals the way Papa said, they weren't going to smash machinery or ruin Papa or run wild to break the economic woof of the empire. Certainly the men had more to fear from Papa than Papa from the men, Papa maintaining the same wages with prices rising steadily, only look at the sum she gave for butter! Barely a hundred pounds a year the hands were getting, how could they do anything

128

on that but perpetuate their own poverty, as Leon said, but why should he get involved with them? Maybe the law did say that operatives could combine to demand a change of wages and hours—Papa had told her the owners were going to smash amalgamation if needs be with their own fists. Who'd like to strike in his factory? Who'd like to say a word against wages that might not keep an establishment in Grovesnor Square but were well enough for beggars who hadn't the spunk to do better? But why did Leon have to be in it? Why couldn't he be friends with the men and friends with Papa, make as much as he could? Leon could be a big man in any business, but since he'd gone to work for Papa he seemed to hate money. Men could give too much for it, he said, some gave the honesty and blood right out of their veins. No danger he would, he was more interested in the men and their problems than in his own future!

Once she mentioned the matter to Leon, not in the wicked words she really thought, but in a sort of innocence. "Why do the cigar men have to be organized?" she asked sweetly. Leon answered first lightly, then in earnest. Where would any of the operatives in the realm be if they hadn't combined and hung together? Did Julie know how many were starving right now but for the little their societies gave them? He'd seen in the army that one man accomplished little in a fight, but he'd never thought about it until he went to the factory. Together they could present a front for negotiation, the only voice they could have since they'd none in government.

She wished they were back in Arnheim with nothing to do but be happy. Ludwig would be coming home with a bauble for his Em, Leon would take them driving, and there'd be no worry about factory hands with their vexing problems or the poor urchins who slept under the arches of Waterloo Bridge—and more of them every day, *those* women had no trouble bearing children, *they* didn't lose them after three months! Her eyes smarted with self-loathing and a bit of self-pity, too, and Aunt Anna left one night in a huff. "I swear

I don't know what's come over you, Julie Dekker, your husband ought to beat the nonsense out of you. I swear if he doesn't, I will."

She stirred a plum duff furiously. She'd show Aunt Anna, she'd show Leon, too! But when he came he pretended to ignore her mood, bidding her stow away the dinner for tomorrow, pin on her shawl, they were going to the Gompers'. She pouted all the way. Why couldn't they be going to the Music Hall where the daring trapeze men swung and dove, all boneless and supple as headstrong human birds, where music pounded and the claret was sweet and they shot Zazel from a cannon?

She pouted and pouted, but it was hard to stay glum, sitting beside Mrs. Gompers in the room strewn with white sand that took you straight to Grandma's kitchen in Gelderland. They were good Holland Dutch, these people, they cooked in stout iron pots on the hearth and the dinner of baked potatoes and rice had a savor to make the mouth water. How the boys ate! There were six of them, the five Gompers like stair steps and their Uncle Simon, still a boy, too. Mrs. Gompers told how well Sammy was doing at the trade. He was the oldest, twelve, and he'd been apprenticed now for two years to Schwab in Bishopsgate. Such a smart, quick boy that Sammy, he had done well at the free school, now he went when he could at night and what a pity he couldn't go straight through. Still, two shillings a week. . . . He didn't look much like a businessman, over in the corner playing with Simon while the grandfather gave stage directions. Theater, they were playing. Julie held the youngest boy, a robust child with sturdy legs. Leon talked with Mr. Gompers and a brother-in-law. A letter had come from a friend in America, an active abolitionist. They tilted their ale mugs and Mother Gompers filled them from the bucket with her long wooden dipper. The man in America worked in a shipyard, he was getting a good wage.

" 'To the west, to the west, to the land of the free,' " sang young Sammy, " 'Where mighty Missouri rolls down to the sea. . . .'" He'd learned that at the shop, his mother whispered above the din, for they were all singing. Rush lights fluttered the male faces with flame and shadow and the song resounded.

Where a man is a man if he's willing to toil
And the humblest may gather the fruits of the soil.

She heard Leon's strong voice above the others, and how proud she felt, a sure sudden pride in all he stood for. Of course he must be with the men, they needed him, and she should be right beside him. How selfish she'd been, thinking of nothing but her own disappointment, grieving and grieving for the lost baby, almost holding it against him! It had been his loss, too, and yet she'd built a wall, not let him come near her, denied him—as if that side of her marriage had been fulfilled.

"Leon," she whispered, the minute they were alone, "what a moaner and groaner I've been. Help me to do better. I'll have a baby yet, and next time I'll carry it through, you see if I don't!"

14

During that whole winter, whenever the men were together, the tantalizing, exciting prospect was with them. They spoke of America seriously, in practical terms, weighing the gamble against the certainty. They knew how it was here, and getting worse, factory after factory putting in machines, turning out fabulous quantities of cigars and turning away unneeded hands to tax the Society's funds until there was little left. This they knew fully. As for that other, they followed every word printed about the war, their browned fingers tracing down the columns, the bad turn the Eastern campaign had taken for the Union, Stonewall Jackson this and Lee that.

And how did they know they'd be any better off, supposing the Union won the war and they went, said Whitaker. That sort of talk be damned, cried Toole, they'd read the letters from his brother-in-law, hadn't they? You never knew what might happen in America, every man had a vote and every man had a chance, and what was to keep you from striking a gold mine? Becke had a special look he gave Toole. There was much head shaking, much puffing on pipes, they were not dreaming of Toole's gold mines, they wanted work and a decent wage and better living. Still it was true, as Whitaker said, they were not so bad off here as might be, they had places to live and they were working. Which didn't keep the Long Island coast line from rising up in Aldgate and Spitalfields like a mirage, a phantom panorama with clean blue sky and no smoke pall to hide it. The men began to lose their hangdog looks; when Leon laughed, they laughed with him like schoolboys. Like schoolboys up to mischief, if you asked Aunt Anna; they were drunk on America and that cautious way they talked didn't fool her.

Even old Becke had caught the undercurrent of excitement, slicked his hair and trimmed his mustache back so you could see his face. One night he brought a fine bottle of wine to dinner. It was such an extravagant vintage, Julie said they should put it away for some special occasion. But this was special enough for Becke. He pulled the cork himself, poured the glasses full with a flourish, and raised his as if to propose a toast. Then he changed his mind, closed his mouth, and didn't open it until Aunt Anna brought out the coffee cups. Right in the middle of a sentence about tariff he interrupted Leon.

"I've been a bachelor for fifty-three years," he suddenly announced, "and I'm not one for talk, but what would you say, ma'am, just what would you say to being Mrs. Becke?"

There was only one person to whom he could have been speaking, but Aunt Anna kept on pouring coffee until he said nervously, had she heard him, ma'am? Yes, she'd heard him. She cut off a good-sized piece of pie and slipped it to his plate. A fine one he was proposing marriage to a Christian woman when he was about to take off for hell and gone like some common sailor! She cut the rest of the pie while Julie and Leon laughed outright, and Becke drew his thin shoulders up in high good humor as if he'd known all along he could depend on Aunt Anna. Who said he was even going to America? If he did go, what was to keep her from joining right along? Aunt Anna took time out to savor a forkful of custard and look him sharp in the eye. Going to America he was, all right, she'd be switched if he wasn't, none of this shilly-shallying with her if you please, and as for her going, that was something'd have to be judged and judged quiet. She was getting along respectable enough in Bow Road.

"Aunt Anna, listen to Becke, go with him. It's high time you had a good, kind man to make a home for."

"You hear the girl, Mrs. Perry?"

"Hm. A good, kind man, is it? Some folks think a heap of themselves." But she was pleased, finished her pie, and had all she could do not to smile.

If she spoke gruffly to Becke, after that, scolded him more than ever about dressing too thin, smoking too much, and not minding his health, why, that fooled no one, Becke least of all. He continued in fine spirits all winter, came often and practiced the slyest, wittiest remarks imaginable to trap an inamorata who traded wit for wit, kept Julie and Leon and her suitor in perpetual glee, and wouldn't give her yes or no.

But she must, Aunt Anna must go, she deserved a life of her own.

"Seems you're mighty quick to be rid of me."

Julie flushed as if she were guilty. Didn't Aunt Anna think they were going, too? Maybe Leon hadn't said, but he was her husband, she knew what he was thinking. If she was any judge, he was just waiting for the end of the war.

And if she was any judge, they were riding teeter-totter, Aunt Anna said, took themselves up sky high and came down again quick.

Then in midwinter came two decisive events. President Lincoln issued his Emancipation Proclamation, and the Gompers' brother-in-law issued his. After the long talking about America, he went, despite winter storms, the dubious state of the war, or anything else. Both incidents lifted the dreams of the men, put them in action. Working people everywhere seized on Lincoln's move as a personal victory, sat down and wrote to Lincoln, got their societies to send messages, too. Leon wrote for the Cigar Makers' Society, though he wasn't a member. Liverpool and Manchester, hard hit as they'd been, went wild. It was the old fighting spirit of the Owenites, that's what Becke and Whitaker said. A promise of change, founded or unfounded, a promise of change! There were so many cigar makers out of work now that the Society was offering, in place of unemployment benefits, something between five and ten pounds to every member who wished to emigrate; and as spring came on, the New World phantom danced reckless and gay in the flames of every fire, through the stagnant morass of every street. The Gompers were going to try it in June. Leon wanted to go with them.

"Leon, we're really going! March, April, May, June, we've so much to do!"

"Julie, you'll not be going that soon. You're going to wait, dear, until I've found work and a suitable place to live."

"Leon!"

"Look how well you are. Three or four months give you that much more time. The ocean crossing's no easy matter, you'll need all the strength you can muster."

She teased and begged. What was there to fear, he'd get work quick enough and better than he had here. But he had seen her dwindle to nothing last summer, and he wasn't going to risk that again. The nights were long after that, she lay awake keeping close to Leon; the ocean was going to cut them off, she knew, she'd been left behind before. But when the passages were booked, the Gompers and Leon, Becke and Toole on the *City of London*, the rash, reckless daring of it infected all of them. Becke strutted like a rooster, although Aunt Anna hadn't said her yes or no; Becke could just run along, see how he'd make out in the new world, maybe he wouldn't want an old carrot top who could kick the hat off his head.

Their sailing date, the tenth of June. Days flew off the calendar, nights flew, and still Papa didn't know. No reason to rush toward trouble, Leon said, he wanted his tenure at the shop to remain as pleasant as possible. So they kept it secret, kept it in Aldgate while they packed up their precious possessions; Leon was not going to have her in the little house alone. He was packing everything, and it could sit in a warehouse until she was ready to sail.

"Leon, you love me? You really do love me?"

"Gypsy, this is my last Sunday. Instead of spending it beside my fire with my own friends, my own wife, and my pipe, I'm going to your papa's to dine, with the Potters thrown in for good measure. If that isn't love!"

He was most polite at dinner. He listened to Ethelyn as if she had sense, he tried to jest with Mr. Potter. When wine was poured, he bowed to her mother. "To you, dear, and to your home." Mother blushed, drank a swallow, and was about to put aside her glass when Leon stayed her. "And another swallow, dear, to the Dekkers and their new home across the sea." No one moved. Mother's hand trembled and dark wine spread into the cloth while Leon explained his interest in the democratic system, his belief that the climate would improve Julie's health. No, Mother's head said, no, no. He was sailing the tenth, if they would be so good as to keep Julie until he sent for her.

Papa heard him through. Forgive him his shortsightedness, he had been under the impression that the eager emigrant was in his employ, he had regarded the affiliation as of life duration, perhaps his son-in-law did not feel the offer duly magnanimous. Leon looked right into Papa's cold eyes. The offer had been kind and magnanimous, and he was grateful. The fault, if fault there were, lay in himself, he hadn't understood the setup of business, he'd thought of it in personal terms, you took employment, earned your way, became as successful as you could.

"Well?" Papa said.

Well, he had found it less simple. You were caught up with other men, it ceased to be just a matter of yourself but of the greatest good for all of you.

"Daydreams," Papa said. "Dog eats dog. You've let those beggars work your sympathies."

"If I had stayed, I'd have joined their society, sir. Your men are ill paid and overworked, neither years of service nor skill gives them any security. I'd have fought your policies tooth and nail." Then, before Papa could answer, Leon said, "It's a great deal better to go while we're still friends, isn't it? While there's no cause for bitterness."

Furious as Papa was, what could he say? He might cut them off without a shilling, but what could he do there at the dinner table except take the outstretched hand coldly, without comment.

15

In some ways it was most pleasant to be at home, a girl again, to lie in one's own bed, waken and find each object, the wash basin, the door latch, the nodding tree, so exactly as it had always been. How luxurious, how silken-safe to stretch, not have to struggle up because there was water to fetch from the barrel in back and breakfast to fix and lunch to pack. No need to shop or plan or cook or wash. All the grown-up, married responsibility lifted off like a ponderous blanket leaving you cool, idle, and young as when Grandpa used to sing, "Ride a Cock Horse." Her lean stomach was beginning to round out gently and she was proud and sleek as a basking

136

cat. She was *that way* again; and this time it was all right, this was going to be a good, healthy baby, an American!

"I swear you're getting to be the laziest crittur I ever set eyes on," Aunt Anna would say. "Perhaps you could have your maid hook you up, ma'am, and we might take us a walk, before you forget you have feet and get stuck like a fly in amber."

Indeed she wished to walk. No one knew yet of her interesting condition, so she was free to try out some new ideas. She'd talked with Mrs. Gompers and Mrs. Whitaker, and it didn't seem to her they had nearly so much trouble bearing children as the rich ladies did. Mrs. Smicks had toted her last under those dank rags until she was so swelled she could barely squeeze through the scullery way, and wasn't she back at work again ten days later?

Hm. Julie needn't mention that woman to Aunt Anna. The poor brat of hers would be drunk straight off from his ma's milk. The matter of exercise, however, was no bad idea. There'd been a girl in the days at Drury Lane, got into trouble, poor thing, and kept on dancing till it was a shame; but what a healthy baby she'd had and no more trouble bearing it than an Indian. The more Aunt Anna thought of how languid and weak Julie'd been last time in bed, the more she favored the new plan. Sometimes they strolled in Oxford Street, loitered before the shop windows. On occasion, they walked past the British Museum, laughing about the days when they went there for a purpose. My goodness, did Aunt Anna remember when they'd waded through the snow? She wanted to go in today and look up a book on American geography.

The old place was darker than ever. They faltered down the corridor, opened the door to the reading room, and Julie felt herself reel. Aunt Anna had to hold her. An attendant brought smelling salts, and they took a carriage home while Aunt Anna tried to figure how far they'd walked, why the customary exercise produced such an unexpected effect. But Julie knew, and the walking had nothing to do with it; she'd been stabbed to the heart by the sharp, cured-leather smell of the reading room, the pungent scent of floor covering that had been identified with Phillip's presence and which now, after the long time, had accidentally called up the old response. It was ridiculous. She went back to the Museum next day over Aunt Anna's protests. It was silly to tolerate such stupid weakness. This time she steeled herself so that the gap of pain came finger narrow, she could bear it almost with pleasure, such a separate far-off pain which had nothing to do with her now, so quiet and content and married, so filled with the coming life that this time was rooted sound and sure. After a day or so, Aunt Anna stopped worrying and they continued their regime of walks.

It was good to step out of the door into a neighborhood of fine houses, carriages rolling under the dull sun, and at the corner, the old crossing sweep, John Bolinggreen, raising his broom deferentially and bowing so low you half-expected him to martyr himself, throw himself prone in the muck so you might walk the bridge of him. "Good afternoon, m'lady," he said, because Papa paid him in gold coin once a year. Different indeed from the jostling, crowded streets in Aldgate where you fought your way across to the baker's and back across to the green grocer's. But she missed Leon. She missed not only his lively presence, but even talk about him; for he had been dropped from Corper conversation like a corpse. The only mention ever made was by courteous, ever attendant Mr. Munzell. Mother twitted that gentleman, he had not been so prompt at the Corpers' for a long time, must she entice him with Julie or Ethelyn? He enjoyed the fond reprimand. He attended Mother gallantly, talked business with Papa, and bless him, he asked for Leon as once he had asked. . . .

The difference was, she had news to tell. Leon never kept her in doubt or suspense, she never lost him. In New York, the Gompers had found rooms in Houston Street and Leon and Becke had taken lodgings nearby, across from Roach's shipyards. An extraordinary man, John Roach, he only let his hands work eight hours a day! Mr. Munzell listened attentively, his mouth worked, drew into a puckered ruffle of flesh about the tiny aperture which still wouldn't close together; for add weight as he would, fill out his great frame to handsome proportions, Mr. Munzell could not tenant that space.

"So," he would say, "you are really planning to go to America, to hazard that ocean by yourself?"

Julie nodded her curls in the affirmative.

But she was such a small girl, he insisted, no bigger than when he had first met her at the home of Emma Stodel, now Dekker. Why, he could circle her waist with his hands!

Julie felt so warm she fanned herself, for he certainly could not circle her waist any more, and she didn't wish to say so just yet. She was in her fifth month now. If Leon didn't hurry, there would be a brand-new someone to go with her, a sturdy youngster with legs like Leon's, she could tell the way they kicked. Right and left, and when she awoke in the night, she would poke gently at her side to encourage it, please kick, little baby, so she would know it was there. And she was beginning to show. Even with the great covering skirts, she thought everyone could tell. Strangely enough, they didn't. Mother only noticed when Aunt Anna was fitting the gray wool bodice for her traveling dress. It was a shame and a crime, Aunt Mathilda thought, for Frederic Corper not to outfit the child for her trip and she'd up and bought dress lengths herself, she had eyes in her head. They sat in the sewing room while Aunt Anna cut and fit the gray wool.

"Such a lovely color," Mother said. "It becomes you, Julie, although I must say, everything becomes you now, you look so. . . ." Her head began to turn from side to side as if saying no. "Julie, my dear child, are you sure you're not. . . ,"

"Oh, darling," laughed Julie, "I'm sure I *am*." Aunt Mathilda and Aunt Anna nodded gaily. "There was no sense telling you before, you'd have worried and I've been so well, if Leon doesn't hurry, I'll have the child in mid-Atlantic."

"You couldn't possibly, Julie. You couldn't go in that condition. Don't let your papa hear of it."

"Her young man'll have something to say," suggested Aunt Mathilda.

"I've told Leon, I wrote him two weeks ago, and whenever he says 'come'— Now, Mother, don't upset yourself. I'm so healthy, look at me, if you want you can put your hand here and feel it."

"Julie!" Mother edged back, blushing.

"Feel, Aunt Mathilda, feel the youngster!" Aunt Mathilda felt all right. Emma had kicked that way.

"Give me leave to tell your papa, Julie."

"Of course, Mother, tell everyone!"

"Be my sweet girl, Julie, stay until the child is delivered. You don't know what you're going through, a girl of your delicate health, you'll need all the care, all the nursing. . . . Any husband who asked you to come at such a time would be asking for your death." The gentle mouth quivered, the blond head turned in an endless no, no, no, it did no good to reaffirm one's health and vigor.

16

Where were the candles? Leon had especially warned her not to forget them, and a lantern in case of storms. Had Beatrice packed the lantern? She hurried across the room in her gray traveling dress, found the keys, reopened the deal chest, forced her hand down through the tight-packed . . . there it was, the cold handle of the lantern beneath the bedding and the saucepans. She dragged the poor arm up through all the stuff, marriage and baptismal records in the tin box, her extra hairpins and silver-headed comb and the packets of lavender; she crammed the lid down, flung herself against the top to force it, then when it was almost shut, she let it spring again while she went to the window for the hundredth time to see if that was Aunt Anna. There was a clatter in the driveway and unlikely as it was, Aunt Anna might have taken a cab so early in the morning. It was Aunt Mathilda's carriage instead; Ludwig and Emil stood below, helping Aunt Mathilda and Emma and Grandma; for the train to Liverpool left early, and they had decided to come to breakfast, invited themselves, Aunt Mathilda said, since Papa took no notice that this day was different from any other.

Julie leaned her warm cheek against the glass and watched Aunt Mathilda loaded with packages for which there certainly was no room, Emma in vibrant blue velvet, Ludwig trying to balance an enormous bottle of Sitzer water, and Grandma, Grandma Stodel, whom she'd never see again! A hot vacuous fist rose in Julie's throat. Grandma Stodel might not have been so important as Grandpa, but she was dearly loved all the same; and suddenly on the other side of the glass she was so feeble, so shaky and small, her fingers fumbled for Ludwig as he helped her out, not at all like the Grandma who bustled in the kitchen at Gelderland, baking nut and orange bread and walking straight as a stick. "Grandma. Oh, Grandma," sobbed Julie. Far away on the other side of the glass, the little old lady stepped uncertainly to the walk, beckoned Ludwig to mind the Sitzer, took hold of Emma's arm, and vanished slowly into the house. Julie sank to the edge of the bed, trying to forget what she had seen, trying to bring Grandma back to another day, quick and busy, with the black velvet band on her throat. It was no use. She'd never see her again, never. The loss was as keen as if Grandma were dead already out in the rain in some lonely grave with the leaves falling. She would see none of it again, not her room nor her bed nor the stand with its bowl that had always been, nor the pitcher she'd chipped once and Beatrice had been so mad she slapped her. No matter where she had been, Holland, Aldgate, this room had been there to come back to, her room and no one else's, her clothes-press where there must still be books hidden on the top shelf, stains on the floor from spilled medicine, the rocking chair where Grandpa used to sit, where Aunt Anna so often sat,

141

stitching at lengths of muslin and jabbering a mile a minute when Julie was unwell.

Aunt Anna had not come yet. She hadn't come yesterday, either. Surely Aunt Anna wasn't angry, surely she didn't think she made it easier to say good-by by not saying it, by staying away through most of these last trying weeks? Yes, she thought Aunt Anna should have gone, right with her, but Aunt Anna had evidently made up her own mind and there were personal matters where one could not prod another. Julie's head throbbed. There was furniture to be checked at the dock, the box of provisions Aunt Anna had packed and Emil had bound with iron hoops from the pantry, casks of flour and the stone jug of wine, the room she'd never see again, the window blinds with their tiny cracks running like blond hairs in the sun. It all mattered so much, and down below, they mattered, she must go down to them, spend every last minute.

It was not easy. Papa took his food that morning with particular relish, not only porridge with thick, hot cream, after which he wiped his mustache elaborately, but bacon and truffles too, and a choice side of bacon it was, Mrs. Corper, two inches of fat which was as bacon should be. Beatrice was passing the muffins as he spoke. Her tear-swelled face heaved and broke. Hard on the table came the plate of muffins, out ran Beatrice; after a moment in came the new maid, her face puffed, too, and her eyes all but closed. Papa took no notice.

Papa, she wanted to say, I know you've forbidden me to go, I know you won't forgive me, but please, Papa, we'll all not be together for so long. Don't send me away like this.

Aunt Mathilda spoke gaily of Elsa, what Elsa had said the day they left, how Elsa had looked. Grandma told of the night the ship came into port in America and the little boy who was Grandpa had crawled out on deck and called to an English sailor.

"As I was saying, Mrs. Corper, excellent bacon," remarked Papa; and her mother heard and did not hear, turning her head from side to side. The gesture had become chronic these last weeks, Mother's single answer to life and how could you

142

change it? Julie tried. She brought up anecdotes that had been good for a laugh in the family since time began, the way Grand-mère, trying to use elegant English, had said "bust" to the Prince Consort. It should have been enough to stop for just a moment the negative, pendular no. But I have to go. Leon says better even in my seventh month than to try it later with the baby and weakened . . . and he loves me and misses me and we'll have a good life in America. Don't send me away saying no, Mother, please, darling, don't send me that way.

Papa bit into the last morsel of bacon, sucked the savor from his teeth, and turned to a more responsive person, Mr. Munzell, who had come to breakfast tightly stocked, his face scraped pink and clean. Mr. Munzell was going to be there to the end, see her off at Liverpool, see her safely on the ship and wave from the dock until the ocean lay between them. The duty of England and Englishmen would be represented by him, whatever the absence on the part of others less fortunate in nationality; he left no doubt that neither wife nor sister of his would be abandoned to undertake such a passage under her own resources. Julie would have preferred Aunt Anna's company to Liverpool, but Mr. Munzell's was welcome; and Papa accepted the lawyer's presence at breakfast as most usual, addressing the pink and closely shaven one heatedly on affairs in Schleswig-Holstein where he hoped the new King Christian would have enough brains to sign the constitution.

Mr. Munzell swallowed his tea, the heat leaving his underlip inflated without a crinkle. If the protocol king signed the constitution, wouldn't it be violating the very terms of protocol which gave him title? An excellent point, but Papa felt this was no time for Britain to get involved in a war against the combined Germanic powers, Palmerston running over at the mouth with his "if Denmark has to fight, she won't fight alone!"

A clock chimed. Seven, eight, they'd leave in half an hour. Surely Aunt Anna would come to say good-by. If the omnibus were delayed, she could take a cab. Or had there been an accident? Soon anything could happen and she wouldn't know. Aunt Anna and Aunt Mathilda, Grandma, Mother would grow smaller and smaller while the train carried her to Liverpool and the ship. . . . They could fall ill. They could die! Papa kept on, denouncing Palmerston as if she were going no farther than Hyde Park. Even Emma and Ludwig said little, and what was there to say since they did things the right way and this wild exodus was something they could not understand, leaving family and security for what? They weren't with Papa, but they weren't against him, either. And his position was clear. If she went, she was cut off, no part of him, no part of Mother, whose finger had just traced falteringly the outline of hair against her cheek. Oop, the child kicked hard. Julie bit her lip to keep from crying. It was unfair of Papa, cruel, she was a grown woman following the life that she had chosen, that she had a right to choose. It was hard enough to leave all that had been without being ignored, or pitied, or punished, even by her oldest and dearest . . . but just then the front door banged open and there stood the oldest and dearest, muffled in tartan.

"Aunt Anna, I'd almost given you up," Julie cried. She hugged and kissed the old lady. "I thought you weren't even coming to say good-by."

"Good-by, fiddlesticks. What's wrong with you, Julie Dekker, did you think I was going to let you go kiting to glory by yourself? I've been wanting to set sail a lot longer than you have. *I* was all set to go once before."

"You're not?"

"Oh, yes, I am. All ready, packed up and sold out of Bow Road and going right along beside you, though I'm not sure but you'll drown us both, you're such a one for sniffling. Here, blow your nose."

Everyone had risen from the table, Aunt Mathilda, hugging and scolding Aunt Anna for "not telling me."

"Didn't tell anyone. Always did find you got more done

144

with less talk. Besides, I wanted to be certain this young one had made up her own mind." She looked meaningfully at Julie's mother. "You none of you can say I talked her into it or coddled her along."

"Dear, good Anna," Mother said.

Aunt Anna grimaced, wrinkled her nose, and wouldn't have it, but Emma said she was too dear and good, going off like this to look after Julie.

"And who says I'm going to look after or take care of anybody? I'll have you know, miss, I'm going to America on some little business of my own."

"Aunt Anna, have you told him, does he know?"

"Business, Mrs. Perry?" asked Mr. Potter, stroking his side whiskers.

"Business, Mr. Potter, I'm sashaying across that pond to marry!" She folded her arms on her bony front and gave them a chance to think about it.

But who was he? How could she have kept the secret? Anna! Anna! If Ethelyn raised her eyebrows, she was piqued with curiosity too, and condescended to ask the gentleman's name.

"Name's Becke and he's no gentleman." The bride-to-be wagged her bonnet gaily. "No shires and not a pound in the bank I'd warrant, your pa'll warrant, too, knowing his wages. But plenty of gentleman to our way of thinking, eh, Julie?"

"Oh, he's a fine man, Aunt Mathilda. You should have been there the night he—"

Papa interrupted. Since both ladies were so intent on getting away from England, perhaps they would be just as intent on catching the train that would enable them to do so. He consulted his watch. But Aunt Mathilda wouldn't hear of it. Train or no train, ship or no ship, they had to drink a toast to Anna Perry, God bless her, you were as young as you felt in this life. Mother managed to say yes to that. Beatrice was sent scurrying for champagne. They all stood up, glasses in hand, cook and Emil, too, and drank the health of the future Mrs.

Becke. The future Mrs. Becke stood and drank to herself. In her swirling tartan cape and disheveled bonnet she looked as gay, as flushed, and as happy as any bride Julie had ever seen.

17

They hurried along beside Mr. Munzell as he forced a way on the crowded dock, Aunt Anna and Julie giddy with the tumult, the bays and whistles, the noisy, milling throng. Wild, cold wind tore in off the sea, flinging gusts of spray. The Mersey teemed with boats. Tugs frisked in and out, big boats brooded like restless giants against the wharf. Whosh came the wind, the dock jarred heavily, a sail came unfurled, belted, smacked like a drum. Far down they could see one towering hull with the name *Calabria*. Three thousand tons, Julie told Mr. Munzell, a horsepower of seven hundred, they'd make it in two weeks.

Hm. Aunt Anna didn't know much about horsepower, one horse had plenty when he wanted to act ornery, but the floating monster was going to need whatever power to cart this crowd. The dock was jammed with people, bundles, bags, and boxes. Sailors ran, important in their lacquered hats and knotted kerchiefs, shouting at deck hands who stood guard over piles of rope thick as your arm. Animals were herded, wagons trundled out of the warehouses along the quay making a mighty clatter; Mr. Munzell strode along grimly, reproving, keeping his umbrella gripped under his arm, his eye on the fellow he'd hired to carry the luggage. He put sailors, passengers, dock hands, and vendors aside as to if to say, "Make way, you flotsam and jetsam."

"Looks to me as if the whole of Europe were trying to pack off," Aunt Anna said loudly. "I swan, you're not going to have a body left in England."

146

"Twenty-three millions, Mrs. Perry, last census. If we lose a few millions out of Scotland and Ireland, I doubt we'll worry."

"But did you ever," chattered Julie, "see so many people? They told us at the agent's counting house, ever since the news of Gettysburg. . . ." On she went, so frivolous and cheery that Mr. Munzell was about to reproach her when a knot of sailors jolted into their path. Two of them were trying to tow a third who was limp in the legs; hopelessly inebriated, he kept pulling the others down onto the dirty planks. "*Calabria*," he screamed, "puked he had for the last time, she was a she-devil."

"Sheer nonsense," Julie said, "she's a Cunarder, safe and steady," and she stepped right over the sailor's battered hat. Mr. Munzell said nothing, keeping close to shield her from the crowd; for the farther they advanced the more people there seemed to be, the more slowly they moved. Deep, throaty bellows rose from the funnels, chains rattled, so you were almost on your way. Julie kept one arm before her and smiled up at Mr. Munzell, but he seemed not to be enjoying it as she was. Cargo battered and banged as it was hoisted. "Taking all risks: Hudson's Household Removal" was written in red on some of the great crates. Those were her things! Julie shouted, certainly hers, the whole of the little house in Aldgate crammed in and swinging in the air.

They stood impatiently in the throng, vendors squeezing in and out waving shiny saucepans, pannikins and plates, foodstuffs of every kind and in every stage of decomposition. Here were the people already weighted with luggage and the vendors screaming were they prepared? Had they food? Provendor for their stock? Pans and cutlery to last the voyage? "Pannikins, pannikins!" "Ginger beer!" "Hot rolls!" The mush fakers, the men with extra bedding, the pan man.

"Those saucepans won't stand over a fire long enough to boil water," Aunt Anna said, but people bought all the same. One pretty, timid young wife clung to her husband's arm and made him select the pan. Something should be done by law,

Mr. Munzell said, to keep peddlers from cheating the poor gullible fools. He held Julie's hand in his, severely, as if that were a legitimate form of protection. Blast after blast. There was a nauseating whiff of strong, raw oil. The crowd surged slowly and came again to a halt.

"Oh, Aunt Anna, we're going!"

"And high time. There are two females I know of been caged birds long enough."

"Mr. Munzell, you must look after Mother, and give my love to the Peabodys, hear?" She had to shout, Mr. Munzell listening solemnly, his tongue as dry as cloth. The crowd took another step.

"You will understand," he articulated at last, "you, Julie, and you, Mrs. Perry. I speak as a friend of the family's, indeed almost as a relative. There is still time, Julie. I beg you, let me secure more comfortable passage on another ship, *The Great Eastern* or *The Persia*. You ladies could have a salon with privacy and comfort, your meals would be served. . . ." It did no good to interrupt, nothing could stanch the flow of eloquence issuing as from a caldron of hot lemonade. He and he alone would be responsible for the change of plan, he would purchase the passages, no one need ever know, or if they did what could possibly be misconstrued since he was as good as a brother to Julie Dekker?

"Better than a brother, my dear; but Aunt Anna and I are not afraid. I feel so well. See how stout I am!"

Mr. Munzell did not look. He looked into her face, perspiring miserably, his mustache coming away from the stiffening that held it. He feared for them, for them and for the expected child, and. . . .

"Why, this is the adventure of our lives!" exclaimed Aunt Anna. "We don't need coddling, neither one of us. . . ."

She never finished. A surge carried them forward, and Aunt Anna was up the gangplank. Julie had just time to seize Mr. Munzell's great thumbs, thank him for his love and loyalty —this was no time to mince matters—she felt the moist, fervid print of his mouth on her hand, then she was carried with the

148

flood, wedged tight with skirts, umbrellas, casks, and limbs, over the side into the swarming ship. Sailors ran, shouting, "Below decks!" But Julie and Aunt Anna pushed toward the rail. Aunt Anna used her elbows, and soon they had space to see the cables dragged on board. The big hulk shuddered, there was a cheer, one plump young lady sat down on her box, sobbing so there was much ado to comfort her.

"Captain's orders, below decks," cried a sailor.

Aunt Anna took firm hold. "He needn't think he can 'captain's order' me, we're staying here to have a look, we've paid enough." She shook her head, and all about, other people shook theirs.

"What's happened to Mr. Munzell? I can't see him."

Truth was, she had forgotten Mr. Munzell in the excitement, and now as the boat began to move, all the faces, the waving hands on shore fled together into a shapeless mass. She waved her hand timidly and a host of gulls waved back. They had been waiting at the breakwater and now as the boat slid past, they rose, sailed stiff down the sky with twitching wings.

The water swelled away in even lines, the black, inky Mersey water. Liverpool was almost gone, a child's city, its colors faded, a lavender haze absorbed them, fused the sharp spears of buildings, dwindled them to ghosts of a lost world. Still. Only the gull wings were quick to quiver in the gray air.

Part III

Those early years in New York folded up like the pleats of an accordion. This child ill, or that one coming, the flat to keep, the food to buy, clothes to make and wash and mend, cooking, cleaning, grubby faces, warm-ironed gingham, the pinch when one of them was ill, the scouring, the scrubbing, so much to do that Julie wished for ten more hours in every day and Aunt Anna said if there were, she'd like to know where they were going to get strength to stagger through them or the money to light 'em up with kerosene—those days and weeks and months and years of daily doing repeated themselves until they were as one tune folded swift into the pleats of an accordion, one was never sure what year it had been. There was the time little Ellen took her first step, let go of Leon's hand and tottered, her blue eyes wide with wonder, her hand still up in the air, three steps to Julie. There were all of Henry's colds and sniffles, he really scared them once with fever, and Julie's own abscessed ears, and the time the baby fell out of his battered perambulator in the middle of Avenue A; but dates melted beyond retrospect. Even holidays lacked definition, faded to much the same desperate effort to knit festivity without yarn; for winter was a hard, strained time in New York, it wore everyone thin. With all its heat, summer was welcome. Maybe you could fry an egg on the cobbles, but the street mire dried to dust at last, the days stayed light, and at night you could count on a spunky breeze to fly in from the Battery right up through the slats of the fire escape. That's where they'd sit when she was pregnant, up above the city, she and Leon and the heavy child. Stevie was the last. He'd weighed more than nine pounds, toward the end she could barely make it, over the window ledge to the fire escape. Leon helped her. He'd keep his arm between her and the hard rail, singing, humming, while the East River wind came fanning in, almost as clean, almost as moist as on shipboard years ago. The weather held warm through October, the children's heavy clothes could be spared, between tall buildings sun spilled into the air like quicksilver. That was when you felt the freedom and zest of the new world. Whatever of evil was in store saved itself for winter, held back and held back and came down with the bitter weather. Winter unemployment, it was called. Work slacked off, wages fell, tramp workers streamed into the city.

It wasn't just the cigar makers, it was every industry, Leon said, but the cigar makers were what she knew. Once quotas were filled, there'd be men out at Stachelberg's, then a few out at Orgler's, then a lockout at Straiton and Storm's where there'd been an attempted strike—and you never knew when it was going to be Leon, you never knew when it would be Becke. They had both been lucky, being skilled workers; old Becke was as expert as any hand in New York. They were steady at work, out of the house by six every morning, but they changed around, sixteen months at one shop, then somewhere else, and every winter, wherever they were, wages were cut and there was nothing to do but settle to the grim business of greater need and less money, the holidays to make and the threat of no work at all.

Not that Leon worried. Becke might, or their friend Stevens, but Leon kept exhilarated; he loved talking labor problems with the men, they talked all day as they worked. He went to meetings of their local, fifteen it was, up above Berlyn's saloon, but the locals meant little, they had no strength. The hope, the zeal that shot through Leon came from meetings of the

International at the Tenth Ward Hotel, from labor meetings at Cooper Union. He went with Sammy Gompers and they'd both come home drunk with trade unionism. They talked until you were dizzy. They joined the Eight Hour League. There had been too many radical, revolutionary ideas, Leon said, here was something practical, organize all labor for this! He couldn't convince Becke. Becke was interested in the cigar makers, let the other trades get along by themselves; and Becke was certainly right on one score, the Cigar Makers Union was not adequate. Too many workers were demoralized by the tenement system. They worked at home, buying supplies from the storehouses, and half the time couldn't find markets for their finished product. Too many were excluded from union membership by the prohibition against working with bunch breakers. The union represented only a small percentage, it needed reorganization and strength if they would arbitrate. Every time they tried, they took a licking. All they were good for was trying to help each other bear a mutual burden. That wasn't the meaning of unionism.

Talk, talk, talk, it was a wonder they had breath enough to get them to the shop and back. Much good it did Aunt Anna feeding Becke, she might as well throw the food to the poor starved cats, all the food she could put down him didn't make fuel enough for the hot air he talked in one day. The Cigar Makers Union, the labor movement, sometimes the talk grew to sound as vague and weary as winter itself, became part of the strain, had nothing to do with the fact that whenever they wished, employers forced wages down below endurance. Talk, talk, many times Julie and Aunt Anna shook their heads to hear it while they dealt with colic or with the plight of the Bagratunis downstairs, ten miserable Armenians crowded into two rooms with nothing but soup of flour and salt for weeks on end.

But a time finally came that was more than talking, something more than just isolated unrest or a shop strike. It was the drive for eight hours, and it had been gathering momentum a whole spring and summer. Every trade, every industry in the state was behind this, working together for the first time. Even Mrs. Stevens—who understood very little except the hunger of the numerous small Stevenses—agreed, well, it was something more than argument anyway, and God knew she had uses enough for Stevens should he be free from the shop somewhat more than just to eat and sleep. Mrs. Bagratuni's boy had got work finally; he was a carpenter and on the committee of his local to plan for the big eight-hour parade. When Julie met her at the butcher's, Mrs. Bagratuni laughed and joked, ordering scraps of lamb with confidence as if her boy Sirak was going to lift up not just the Bagratunis, but the whole of mankind. She was a dark, swarthy woman, with fierce eyebrows; dark shadows curved at the corners of her mouth as if God had almost decided to make a man of her. She stood up to the butcher for her wants, for Julie's, too, because Julie was such a little mite. And she needn't be minding about Julie, Aunt Anna said, Julie did all right, wheedled the butcher around smart enough with that young helpless look of hers.

"I do not look helpless and I couldn't look young. Goodness, see the size of Ellen." Aunt Anna ignored Ellen. If Julie didn't look better than she ever had in her life, more color to her and more like a flesh-and-blood human crittur, why, her name wasn't Anna Perry Becke. She was so positive that Julie, standing in the market, blushed hot down her throat and made an appointment to look in the mirror as soon as she got home. Of course, she forgot and remembered only much later after the mending was done and the plants watered and supper put to cook and the children washed and the baby down. Then, when Leon swung in the door, there she was standing on a chair by the window with the pocket mirror in hand, tilting her head for the last tiny bit of light which fell between their building and the roof of the one across. It was true, she looked . . . more like a gypsy than ever, Leon said. He lifted her from the chair, twirled her, and said it was too bad she was an old married lady with children, if she weren't she could march in the parade with Victoria Woodhull and

Tenny Claflin, waving flags and demanding not only an eight-hour day but women's suffrage and free love to boot.

"Leon Dekker, the children!"

He wouldn't be serious. He had just come from a meeting with Curran and Meyer. Curran was grand marshal of the parade, and they were going to have twenty-five thousand marching tomorrow. Twenty-five thousand! That was final, every organized man in the city. Maybe the cigar makers were too weak to fight in their own right, but they could march to get eight hours for everyone! He'd been sold on a shorter working day from the beginning, from the time he'd come to America. With shorter hours, men would have a chance to enlarge their lives, there would be less unemployment. His enthusiasm crackled out and set the children on fire. They romped. He tossed the baby and made him squeal; then, since it was a holiday dinner, he decided to go fetch some rum.

"Just quiet down," she told the children. "You can help me with the table, Ellen. You, too, Henry." She brought out the heavy white cloth Aunt Mathilda had hemmed and the gleaming silver, each piece to be polished first with a flannel cloth until it was blinding with light. She set Henry and Ellen to that. Everything else might change; the furniture was frayed, the dishes had a chip out here and there, but nothing could change Grandma Stodel's silver.

"My mama's mama." She stopped to wipe Henry's nose with a clean bit of cloth. "When I was your age, Ellen, Grandpa and Grandma used to come to London, my French grand-parents, too, and we had elegant dinners—my mother was very particular, I can tell you—every piece just so." Ellen placed a fork carefully, Henry tried to jerk it, he ran around the table. "And there was no monkey business, as there won't be tonight, Henry Dekker, or you'll find yourself in bed with-out so much as a dumpling." But she wasn't cross. She straightened his collar, ran her hand over Ellen's gleaming hair, and then hugged them both. They had such sweet skin, so firm and silken, the lobes of Ellen's ears were pink enough to bite. "Grandpa used to tell me stories, the way Papa tells

154

you, for he had been stolen away when he was a boy. You must never, never speak to people in the street, you hear, son?"

"Not to the peddler? Not Tony, the peddler?"

"But you know Tony."

"Yes," said Ellen in her most superior way, "you know Tony, silly."

Julie pulled down the lamp, turned it until the light flickered feebly. Why waste good oil this half hour when Leon wasn't home? Each spoon bowl filled with light, the knives lay dazzling daggers on the cloth. What a great length their table had been when her mother was alive, when the first cloth was lifted and the rose sateen damask lay naked under the candles. Knives were the gentlemen, forks were grand ladies, tall, elegant, with such narrow waists, and spoons were the young girls, gay and giddy, their heads round with light as hers and Emma's had been at that first ball.

"That is an 'S' for Stodel, Ellen, it's made like a fat lady, see, the round part in front and another behind. Will you please cut your dumplings gently tonight, my darlings, so as not to splash when Aunt Anna and Uncle Becke are here?" Then she had to tell them more, how Grandpa Stodel, yes the "S" was for Stodel, he was the great-grandpa for whom Henry had been named. Heinrich, Grandpa was, but now they were in America, it was Henry.

"Why, Mama?"

Well, Grandpa had been coming home from his tutor's, he didn't go to a real school like Ellen, but to the teacher's house, he and four other lads. After lessons they came walking home, a soft, smoky autumn night like this, darker every minute —Ellen moved closer—and suddenly out of the shadows stepped a strange lady all in black with a heavy veil. She carried three great sacks.

"Like you, Mama?"

"Like Aunt Anna and I carry from Washington Market, yes. And Grandpa and the other boys—"

"But Grandpa was an old man."

"Not then, Henry, he was a lad then, not much older than Ellen. But he was a gentleman, very polite, you hear? When the lady sighed in a fainting voice, would they help her, they said yes, they would, gladly, they said. It all came out much later. They carried the sacks and when they came to her door, the lady bade them come in. You understand, Henry, and you, Ellen, that Mama loves you and Papa loves you and you are never to speak to strangers and never, never enter anyone's house."

"Not Uncle Becke's?" said Henry.

"Oh-ho-ho!"

"Be quiet, Ellen. She was a foreign lady, she spoke with an accent."

"Like downstairs."

"Only she wasn't a nice, good person like Mrs. Bagratuni."

Just then footsteps sounded and she ran to turn the lamp, hoist it on its clanking chain while Ellen and Henry screamed a welcome to Aunt Anna and Uncle Becke, Aunt Anna in a funny turban she'd made from an artificial rose and an old sash. The baby woke up howling, and Leon came to take charge of him while she mixed the steaming pitcher of rum and water. It was so seldom they had leisure like this, just time to sit and drink with the children up. They lifted their glasses to each other, to tomorrow's parade, to eight hours for the workingmen of America.

2

They made the evening last as long as possible, threshing out prospects for tomorrow, what the newspapers would say, if they could say anything, hamstrung the way they were and always on the side of money; but tiredness caught them, the Beckes went home, and the children fell asleep in spite of themselves. After part-cooking gruel on the dying fire, washing the stockings and drawers and stretching them to dry, laying out clean clothes, and kneading fresh dough, Julie climbed into bed. Leon was warm in his sleep as if he had a self-stove glowing under his nightshirt. She lay carefully on her cold side of the bed not to disturb him. It was so lonely she almost wished he'd wake and take her, just to feel close to him. He seemed far away in sleep with all his busy dreams of public welfare. Which was nonsense. Those few seconds of merging proved nothing. Even in sleep Leon must know she loved him and said good night, such old solid married people as they were!

The next instant seemingly she jumped right up out of a dream, hearing her children and hearing above everything loud rain drilling the roof.

Not today, oh, not today. She ran to the other room, whacked hard at Henry as he raced past. "Ellen Dekker, Henry, aren't you ashamed? Your papa's sleeping. Look at this room!" She picked up the baby, thumped him on Ellen's bed and changed his diaper, hearing on the roof, on the glass, on the street, the steady drench and swill of rain.

"Mama, it's raining," wailed Ellen.

"Whining and whimpering's not going to help," she tucked the baby in coldly. "Climb into your clothes, Henry; Ellen, get away from the cold window. Look at this litter. You can help me clean and be quick about it." The poor men could never march in that, only hear the rain.

"I wanta see the parade," whined Henry. "I wanta. . . ." She whisked him up under one arm and scoured his face with water. She washed it so hard it grew ruddy and then faded out again white as milk.

"One more peep and you won't see the parade if the sun comes out strong as July."

She washed Ellen's face, too, brushed and braided her hair so briskly that Ellen stared her disapproval, without a murmur. Then Julie tried to waken Leon. Two big tears splashed onto the bedclothes as she leaned over. "Leon, Leon, it's *raining.*"

She was as bad as Henry, that was a fact; and of course the rain didn't last, it was over by noon. Sun came out, shyly at first, then with a smiling flood of light; and by one o'clock they were hurrying toward Broadway, the rose towering perilously on Aunt Anna's hat. All Avenue A was on the move; even Mrs. Wholbein's mother hobbled on her crutch. Henry and Ellen made a wide detour around her. Not a man to be seen. They had left early to join their contingents and by now were well on their way, down Fourteenth to Fourth, along the Bowery to Chatham, the City Hall and up Broadway, though how they were going to manage in that mud. . . . The children's boots were sodden already, a block from home. Mrs. Bagratuni stopped them, waving a crumpled bag of sweets. It was a sort of sweet gum, Ellen liked hers and sucked contentedly, Henry spit his out right in full sight of their good neighbor, and Stevie gradually smeared his over his face in a greenish mass, so Julie had to stop in Tompkins Square, sit for a moment on a bench, and clean his hands and face as best she could. He was heavy to carry, he was such an active child, squirming to see everything and almost ready to walk; but there was no use bringing the pram, since they'd see nothing that way. She tried to brace him, first on one hip, then on the other. This might have worked better if she'd had more hip, Aunt Anna said. Somewhere far off a drum was beating, that might be part of it, you couldn't tell. They passed one gala funeral with a white hearse and plumes, but no one stopped; they streamed on toward Broadway in their neat Sunday dresses, the children with bits of ribbon in their hair. Ellen and Henry ran with the Stevenses, in and out, Ellen's silk braids wagging. There was no hurry, but they rushed down crowded, narrow Eighth Street. Then suddenly there was light and room and broad clean pavement, the high spire of Trinity stabbed against the sky downtown and the spire of Grace Church uptown. Church bells tolled and rich carriages sauntered past, the horses hoof deep in mud.

"Where is the parade, Mama? Where?" yelled Henry.

"It will be right here, right opposite us in the street, son."

"But where is it now, Mama?"

"Ellen, don't stray off. It's down about City Hall, wouldn't you say, Aunt Anna?"

Twenty-five thousand they were supposed to be. Leon said the rain was a test of purpose, but would they prove themselves, would all those thousands march? "Henry, listen, you and Ellen may walk as far as the corner, but you are not to cross the streets, you hear? And don't jostle people, please, children."

"Just let me hold the baby," Aunt Anna said. "Everything on four wheels is out for hire. Wouldn't mind having a ride myself, eh, Julie?" They strolled along close together. Sun glanced on the shining horses, the gold threads in the livery; sides and tops of carriages quivered like water, and the shop windows! Gold and jewels and precious plate danced with light, so close, so personal behind the frail glass. If it had been any day but Sunday, one could walk in and buy. Certainly nothing displayed so casually could cost more than a few dollars, and didn't she have almost that much in the cracked china teapot, the one way back on the top shelf being saved, of course, for some unseen winter emergency, but for the moment, money that would buy any of those golden, silken things? Julie swung her aching arms. A bootblack called softly, "Black your boots?" and one well-dressed gentleman leaned against a lamppost and put his foot on the boy's box.

"Isn't Broadway beautiful? Isn't it!"

And Aunt Anna said she wouldn't have missed it, not an inch of Broadway nor an ounce of New York. Thank the Lord she'd had gumption to come and rub elbows with the whole world; for that had always fascinated them both, the conglomeration of people and language, so bawdy and free. There, that was the music, the rhythmic thump, the clang and beat. Some drifted to the curb to catch the sound. In an instant, there were throngs, more people every minute, laughing, eager, as if the parade had been arranged for them.

"No one can resist a parade," whispered Julie. "I can't. I'd have come from the other side of town."

"Like to get in the street myself. Wouldn't hurt the cause none were I to do a hornpipe."

The music had swelled now, you could see the band, it filled the street, drumming, blazoning, bursting every trumpet. Carriages scampered out of the way, the band passed, and behind it, marching fifty abreast, the men came singing. There were flags and banners—

EIGHT HOURS FOR LABOR, EIGHT HOURS FOR SLEEP, AND
EIGHT HOURS FOR NATURAL DEVELOPMENT
WE ARE DETERMINED TO HAVE THE EIGHT-HOUR LAW
ENFORCED, NO MORE PAPER LAWS
OUR STRENGTH LIES IN THE JUSTICE OF OUR DEMANDS
LET THE WORKING PEOPLE UNITE

So impressive! The faces of the men so serious, as if they knew the signs by heart.

"Dirty revolutionaries!" yelled a voice near Julie.

"Go back to Italy," screamed another. She stood rigid, grabbed Ellen's shoulder with her free hand, seeing the crazed face of the screamer, the elegant gentleman who'd had his boots blacked. "Go back to Italy, go back to France, you meddling communists!" he screamed hysterically. The people on the curb were frightened, they didn't move. A few more shouted insults. And it wasn't fair, it wasn't true! Leon was no radical, neither was Becke, nor Grunwald, nor the Gompers! They were hard-working men who believed in trade unions. The only revolutionary she knew was Etienne Clairevoissier, and he wasn't marching with the Cigar Makers, they didn't hold with Etienne, he was with the Internationals, who carried red flags and banners reading, "Liberty, Equality, Fraternity," and sang the *Marseillaise* at the tops of their lungs. The crowd murmured for Victoria Woodhull. She and her sister and a dozen other young women marched together gaily.

"Hi, Victoria, how's love?" yelled someone from the crowd. The slender young woman with the banner turned cordially and waved as if she weren't afraid.

The Cigar Makers, led by Hugo Meyer, passed soon after. There were all the familiar faces, Becke and Leon side by side, old Becke limping a little.

"Look, Julie, he's plumb tuckered, poor man. I said he'd do better to stay home and save those bones."

"Troublemakers! Bums!" There was a violent hiss.

"Papa," whispered Henry, too cowed to call aloud.

And there went Leon, handsomer than any man in the street, his fine, reckless head thrown back, carrying the big sign—

EIGHT HOURS FOR WORK, EIGHT HOURS FOR REST,
EIGHT HOURS FOR WHAT WE WILL

—as if it weighed nothing. He had a resolute look, and Julie's eyes filled with tears to see him, this man Leon had become. Somewhere in every life was a decisive turn—you lived along without direction and then suddenly, there it was in the road, a strong arrow you must follow no matter whether it said ten miles or ten thousand. All the dash, the verve of the man was harnessed to this mass of men, that's how he wanted it and bless him. How dared these people jeer, how dared they? Stevie, sound asleep, hung to her like dead weight. She watched Leon until he was lost in the march. Lost.

3

But the men weren't a bit discouraged. They marched their parade through the mud to Cooper Union and a fine demonstration to hear them tell it, with flaming speeches and the hall packed, then a meeting of their own local afterward. They came home victorious and drenched to the skin, Leon and Clairevoissier arm in arm and all of them, Grunwald, Stevens, Becke, swaggering through the downpour as if they'd won. When Julie suggested mildly that it might take a good while yet, Leon tweaked her apron strings. The hardest thing was to take the first step and they'd taken it, only a question of time now; management must give in, the building trades would likely have shorter hours by spring. By spring definitely, agreed Grunwald, usually conservative, the stonecutters would have their way by spring. The eight-hour movement would sweep the city, accomplish what all attempts at legislation never had, Becke said, pity was, they hadn't started it off in England years ago.

"Pity is taking your death in a damp shirt." Aunt Anna felt him mercilessly, his arms and back, he wasn't to complain to her of aches and pains. Becke enjoyed it. The woman would be the end of him, with her hard, bony hands. Worked to the bone taking care of him, Aunt Anna said, he should just get to the stove and she'd make him a hot cup.

Julie tried to remember the faces in the crowd on Broadway, the exact bitter, cold, mean looks. Why, she had seen the hateful way they flouted the signs and the marching men, their best trousers splattered over with mud—how she would ever get Leon's steamed out she didn't know. The potatoes were pared relentlessly as she thought of it, held like pale stones under the water, and dropped into the iron pot so drops of water flew hissing to the range.

If employers only realized how much better effort they'd get from men who weren't tired to death, Leon said. Look how successful Roach was with his shipyards. They repeated that like a litany. Young Clairevoissier paced back and forth tonguing his fast, labial speech. If you closed your eyes, it might have been Grand-père. Grand-père had a joke about Frenchmen, they were good only for love, was the joke. If a Frenchie sang a song, *cherchez la femme!* If he designed a beautiful gown, it was because he always saw the body for which the cloth was cut. But with Etienne, it was no woman, it was the proletariat. No lover could have known greater exaltation when the Commune had been set up in Paris in March, no Tristan could have been more oblivious to the disaster that must follow. Even when Blanqui was prisoner and the Commune had lost its genius, Clairevoissier would come running after work—he made it faster from Mulberry and Hester than Sirak Bagratuni from Clinton Street—to tell her that Thiers was bombarding Paris. He would sit up late with Leon, whispering not to wake the children, sometimes in English, sometimes in French; and he came to them the night the Commune was over, his face white as death. He had a soft, widely arched mouth, the web of the lips so sensitively grained, so darkly blooded.

The cigar makers were impatient with Etienne, they wanted no part in governmental theories and he talked too much and too fiercely; but they couldn't stay angry with him, and all the women, Mrs. Wholbein, Mrs. Grunwald, even Mrs. Stevens tried to help the boy who lived so miserably with a horde of people to support. His parents were deeply pious Jews; for Etienne they had been exiled from France and for his sake they endured it, but their lives were one long pedagogic lament. They knelt abjectly before Jehovah and put themselves and their dozen young children on His mercy, which was for all practical purposes Etienne's, since it was up to him to feed and keep them. But tonight none of that mattered, he was exhilarated by the parade, nervous and ecstatic, and filled with plans.

"Aunt Anna," Julie said. "You saw the faces in the crowd, the way they yelled."

"Should. I was there and still have my sense." She scattered flour over a stretch of dough and rolled it thin as a sheet. "You're in too much of a hurry, all of you. This world wasn't built in a day, not in seven, either, with God's grace I've always felt it was just for the story, the way it goes in Genesis. Took a lot more'n seven days with those oceans and trees, and the rest of it's going to take time, too. Don't you worry about them," she said, nodding brusquely toward the parlor. "They set as much store by the planning as you used to on going to a play with your young man." She tossed the dough over a pie plate, worked it down hard. "I'd a sight rather have 'em take it out in talk than in mischief, like plenty do in this up-to-date Babylon." Then she put a paper over her head and dashed out to empty the garbage. She was gone a good while, and when she came back, Etienne insisted she take his chair by the stove.

"Come, Ceetizen," he said.

"Don't you 'citizen' me," stormed Aunt Anna, waving a newspaper in his face. She'd picked up a *Herald* from the newsboy, kept it dry under her skirt, and she'd just like to read them the latest piece of tomfoolery from that Victoria Woodhull and her bunch. The whole circular was quoted in the *Herald,* alarming words advocating free love and anarchy and putting the authority of the International behind it. Which Victoria had no right to do, Leon said.

"The International! A fine lot you've got yourselves mixed up with. Read what the paper calls you. Decent, law-abiding workmen and they have you responsible now for that lawless, crazy outrage in France. That's what it was, Etienne, don't contradict me."

"I cannot see," the young man said, "why that word is so bad and angry, 'revolutionary.'"

"We aren't, that's why." Stevens talked as loud as he could, but Leon's steady voice won out.

"There is nothing wrong with the word, if that's what a man believes, Etienne, but 'revolutionary' applied to labor movements in America is ridiculous. We're trying to establish trade unions that have enough strength to bargain for better working conditions and a living wage. That's not revolutionary. You ought to talk with Sam Gompers at Hutchinson's, Etienne, he's smart and he's practical."

"The so-called intellectuals you hang around with, Etienne, will put a crimp in any constructive work we do," Becke said.

"They've already put the kibosh on your eight-hour parade," Aunt Anna shrugged. "Nobody saw anything except the red flags and that French song."

"All we do is talk," said Stevens.

"We'll do more. The International is going to the civic

164

authorities right after the first of the year. I'm on the committee. . . ."

"No, Leon!"

"Why not, dear? If things are as bad as usual this winter, we'll ask for the use of court halls to discuss public welfare."

"But, Leon, I saw those people at the parade. They hate us. There'll be trouble and you'll be hurt. Look what they did to those people in France."

Etienne flinched.

"Darling, this is America! And we're not trying to overthrow the government, we're asking the government to help us deal with mass undernourishment and need. That doesn't sound so awful, does it?"

But it did. Heads being broken or lockouts. Men had the excitement of doing, but women had to wait, and each small project took so long, and there was always something to worry about.

4

She ran all the way to Aunt Anna's, so fast the baby's head wobbled and he hung tight around her neck with both fat arms.

"Aunt Anna, Aunt Anna! A great big box, the biggest you ever saw, the freightman had trouble getting it up. Could it be the Christmas box already, or do you suppose . . . because it was late last time and missed Christmas altogether, that Emma . . . but it's bigger than last year or the year before!"

"It'd have to be, wouldn't it, seein' there's more of you? My stars, Julie, I wouldn't go busting stays till I saw what was inside." But she stabbed her hat on without looking at the glass, scurried about to lock windows, grabbed Stevie, and they were on their way, running as fast as Julie had run to her house.

"Only one thing to do, open it and have every scrap stowed before those youngsters get curious."

"Now, before Leon comes home?"

"Lock, stock, and barrel. Where's Henry?"

"Down the alley with Aram Bagratuni. Isn't it luck he was out of the house?" They exchanged Steve jerkily from one pair of arms to the other.

"Here comes that Stevens woman, why doesn't she peddle her papers, crossing so's not to miss us. Don't you gab with her, Julie." This last barely muttered, because Mrs. Stevens was upon them.

"How do you do, Mrs. Stevens, how's Deborah's cold?" Julie said cheerfully. "Hello, Agnes, hello Billy." The youngest Stevenses were shy, they hid their crusted noses in their mama's skirt.

"Deborah's cod's sobe bette, it's bide dad's sobethig sore." She dabbed her poor red beak like an injured cock.

"Stevie, stay still, dear, yes, that's Billy." She waved Stevie's hand.

"Here tell you god quide a parcel hour or so back," whined Mrs. Stevens through her kerchief. "Be it sobthing frob those rich folks of yours in the ode coudtry?"

"I think so, Mrs. Stevens. Our Christmas box, perhaps." You couldn't tell her to mind her own business, she was such a pathetic female, such a pale carbon copy of Mr. Stevens, the same bare frame, the same straight, angry mouth and red-rimmed eyes, as if Stevens had been stood before a mirror and given to have and to hold this pale blurred image of himself. Maybe that's why he hated her so.

"Have you oped it yed?"

"No, not yet. Aunt Anna's come to help me." The baby writhed and slid.

"I'll sed Deborah lateh to fetch the dews. Dot let her waste ady ob your tibe, Brs. Dekker. Good aterdood to you, Brs. Becke."

"Oh dot bide be," wheezed Aunt Anna, when the woman had passed. "Does rich redatives dot belog to be."

166

Mrs. Bagratuni was on the landing when they came. "I heard the man. What a commotion bumping up. From Holland? Maybe I should mind the baby?"

"Thank you, Mrs. Bagratuni, he won't bother us. I'll send you some ginger if there's any tucked away. Hello, Mrs. Wholbein, no, we haven't opened it yet. Hello, Etta, hello."

They didn't even take off their hats. They left the door open; Julie ran to close it just in time, or the baby—"Here, Stevie, play with the ladle like Mama's good boy. In a moment you shall have some stout string, hear?" Stevie stared solemnly and banged the ladle on the floor. Aunt Anna was at the box with knife and hammer.

"Now, then, if you'll stand to one side. I swear you're no more use than a chicken, Julie Dekker." She grunted, working her fingers under the gummed top until it burst. The first few stuffings sailed to the floor and the baby crawled after them. Julie and Aunt Anna felt for the precious lumps, all shapes and sizes secreted among crumpled news sheets. Ludwig had packed this, gauged the space, wedged in the shredded papers, and Aunt Anna smoothed each crinkled piece, just to make sure. A doll for Ellen, books and puzzles and a boat for Henry, doll clothes and dishes, rattles and games, tin boxes of comfits and tiffin cakes, two dear little casks of ginger, a plum pudding and marmalade and a tiny golden bracelet—look! —Ludwig had fashioned for Ellen. There were dresses Elsa had outgrown and boy's clothes from Emma's Pieter, and wasn't it a pity Emma's Pauline was a girl or Steve would have castoffs too, Aunt Anna said.

"Not castoffs, Aunt Anna, they're like new, look at the ruffles on that petticoat, you'd think it had never been worn. Emma's sewed fresh ribbons on everything."

"Don't know what makes you think she's took to the needle, that Dutchman spoiling her with diamonds big as bird eggs."

"Look at these handsome shirts for Leon, silk and hand tailored, see the edges." Julie leaned well into the box, came up with a heavy armful of tissue, not daring . . . yes it was, Aunt Anna, a dress! A brand-new dress, not one of Emma's

167

to be cut down, not something turned or bleached—which heaven knew one wouldn't complain of—but a new dress!

"I don't think I'd cry over it. Here, stand straight, I'll wager Mathilda guessed your waist to a quarter inch."

Such a lovely thing, the underskirt of blood-red velvet, almost as dark as mahogany, the overskirt of soft gray duveteen with a great bustle, and right up near the throat a ruffled jabot of the ruby color cascading like spilled wine. How long it had been since she'd had a new gown! She touched and smoothed it while Aunt Anna went on with the box.

"Aunt Anna, you wrote to Aunt Mathilda, you told her how to cut the waist—you even told her I needed a dress!"

"Not sayin' yes and not sayin' no." She had pulled a chair up and was stuffing the gifts, rewrapped against dust, into the top of the wardrobe. One package rattled and Stevie came crowing. "Not sayin' yes or no, but this I will say"—another package shot into the dark recess—"I'll say that if some folks weren't hardheaded as mules they'd say a word or two to them that could help 'em and never miss it. Why shouldn't you have a dress fit to wear or a pretty and the children, and him, too, working the way he does. They've more than plenty over there, wasting food left and right, not wearing out half their shoes, without the ghost of an idey how you have it."

"But Leon doesn't want—I don't know what he'll say." She put the dress aside and handed bundles up to Aunt Anna.

"Won't say anything if he has the brains I think. Believes in sharing, doesn't he? Believes in going out on strike, started the walkout himself when they tried to fire old McGinty, didn't he? Well, since he sets such store by being his brother's keeper, I can't see why he should rear up none when his brother keeps him!" In went the last of the booty, Aunt Anna's and Becke's, too, the wardrobe doors were locked, they lugged all the waste stuff, the cardboard and boxes and crumpled papers down the fire escape, the wind licking off a scrap here, a twisted fragment there, sailing them down into the cluttered areaway.

"Reuben, Reuben, I been thinkin'," sang Aunt Anna.

Once up in the flat, they remembered their hats, sadly battered and askew. They straightened their hair, gave the baby and themselves some lunch, and recounted the gifts, the voile for Aunt Anna and the socks for Becke, Good Lord, his old feet wouldn't know what to make of them, not likely to shrink to nothing, either, like the ones they bought in Stewart's basement. They hadn't done up the dishes when Deborah came.

"Yes, Deborah, it was our box from Holland. Tell your mama I'm saving the comfits and tiffin cakes, we'll have a holiday party."

Deborah stood trying to edge in, her big watery eyes so beseeching that Julie gave an inch.

"I'd be glad to ask you in, Debbie, but your mother wants you at home. Besides, dear, you have a bad cold; we don't want the baby to catch it, do we?"

Deborah edged her way another step. "I've a message from your mister. Oh, such a purty jug."

"It belonged to my grandmother. What was the message, Deborah?"

"If you used your head it'd be a wonder," put in Aunt Anna. "Speak up, child."

"Well, ma'am, I went to the shop noontime, ma'am, to take Pa somethin' to eat and the mister said I was to tell you . . ." she fingered the jug longingly.

"Yes, Deborah?"

". . . tell you he's two tickets and be ready."

"Tickets for what?" demanded Aunt Anna.

"Just tickets, I think."

"You and your fancy doin's," Aunt Anna said, when they'd shooed Deborah. "This at eleven o'clock, this at four, what'll it be at midnight, if you please?" She leaned out the window to watch for Ellen, no use the child running the stairs twice and she could just borrow a paper from the groceryman, so they could see what the tickets might mean. Up and down the column, her obdurate old pointer marked the place, squeaking over the bold black engravings. The children got

169

their heads right under Aunt Anna's nose. "Something with music, I'll wager, you don't think the opera?"

"Yes, I'm sure." Julie came to see. "I wanted to hear Nilsson that time Stevie was born. Then Aunt Anna spied the black dress swinging against the kitchen door and what was that?

"Why, my dress for tonight. I'm going to press it and. . . ."

"Would you tell me what ails you, wearing that sad excuse for a shroud when you know what's hanging in the wardrobe?"

So the rich dress was steamed and pressed and Julie hooked in tight. Aunt Anna parted her hair, combed it off from the center with curls dripping and drooping so "no one could tell her from Mrs. Astor." They fed the children early and tried to put them to bed. She was going to the theater!

"Julie, Gypsy, what a bustle!" Leon said. It was *Mignon* they were to hear, Christine Nilsson, he had two wonderful tickets almost in the center of next-to-the-top gallery, and where had she gotten that dress? She took him in the bedroom to tell, he was to wear one of the new shirts tonight, too, soft white silk, hardly like cloth. "Hurry, Leon." They walked uptown, the wind shipping in from the east, and when they got there, they stood before the Academy watching the carriages, watching the people stream into the light. Leon looked so handsome and she kept her shawl over her arm, so the dress would show, every bit of it. "Almost like old times, isn't it, Leon?" Carriage after carriage rolled up. Once she saw someone who frightened her, just the line of a back, but she trembled and said shouldn't they go in, the orchestra must be tuning. She had no desire to go downstairs at intermission either.

"What's come over you," teased Leon. "No one will see how beautiful you look." Down they went. Some strange falling away had taken hold of Julie, she looked straight ahead in the throng. Imagination, of course, you associated certain people with certain places and when you went to the theater. . . . She joined Leon in praise of Nilsson, her charm, the strength and clarity of her voice. She found the most unexpected things to say about the opera and said them faster and faster as if the greater the speed with which she spoke,

170

the more surely she held it back. Then someone touched her arm, frightened her so she could barely turn.

"Well, darling." Oh, yes, it was—Phillip! "I see you finally came to Broadway."

It could only have been a minute. Lights trembled, shook and swung, someone laughed piercingly and someone else, some timid girl said, "Leon, Phillip McManus. My husband, Mr. Dekker."

"Of course," Phillip said, and Leon shook hands cordially, shook and shook and she couldn't swallow. "I've had the advantage of you, McManus, I've heard so many fragments of the past."

"Not from Julie's estimable father, I hope." They both laughed. Leon told Phillip that Papa's enthusiasm would be hard put to it to find a favorite between them. They spoke of Papa without reticence, as if they were old friends. They spoke of Aunt Anna and Julie had time to breathe, deeply, look about, see the crowded lobby as it had been. The unreasonable panic began to ebb. Here was the moment she'd half-expected so long, every time they'd gone to a theater or walked past one. Here it was, and not bad. Phillip wasn't angry or vindictive as she'd thought. He didn't even look at her, and it wouldn't hurt if he did! Didn't she have on her new dress, wasn't Leon right beside her, talking to Phillip as easily as if it were Sirak or Etienne? The silly panic vanished, leaving her pulse hard and slow. Phillip's sideburns had grown long, his evening clothes were elegant, and, of course, in his lapel. . . .

"So you've stuck to the theater and it's paid off," Leon was saying.

Phillip protruded his lip in the old way. "Netta Davenport and I have a show opening soon, possibly at Niblo's. Nothing like it's ever hit the street." She had to smile, he was so nonchalant. "A great actress-manager, Lydia Thompson can't touch her." Netta, he meant. He drew out a silver case, sprang the clasp, and offered a cigarette to Leon, and to her, the very idea! Before she could say yes or no a warning bell sounded.

They'd meet after the last act, Phillip insisted, he was with superb people he wanted them to meet.

"Nice chap," Leon said. "Now aren't you glad you wore your fine dress?"

"Who is Netta, Leon?"

"Only one of the biggest names in the business. You don't read the papers, dear."

One of the biggest names in the business was a tall, radiant woman with hair almost the color of flame. Phillip ushered her across the lobby and everyone turned to stare while Netta bowed to either side. She wore a black velvet gown cut so low the swell of her breasts pulsed above it, her swath of white fur was scented, she came right up to Julie and Leon, close, with her powder and deep heliotrope, her blue-veined breasts and bright hair.

"Darling, this is Mrs. Dekker and Mr. Leon Dekker, very old, very dear friends of mine. They're going to be our guests opening night."

"How good to see you," Netta said kindly.

"And Mr. Phineas Barnum." A large, shaggy-headed man. There were others, four or five famous people, talking about Nilsson intimately, as if Julie and Leon *knew*. Someone had heard her sing in Paris and London and her voice was richer, fuller than ever he said. Mr. Barnum knew Rouzand, Nilsson's husband. Netta preferred Lucca in the role of Marguerite, Nilsson's voice might be better, but, ah, Lucca's dramatic ardor in the church scene! Then she mentioned Delmonico's—the Dekkers must join them. Yes, yes, by all means. But Julie said no, the children were at home. Netta's perfume made her dizzy, it made her feel fevered and flushed in the cool air.

"Phil, dear, we must go," Netta said. Phillip gave Leon his card, he took down their address with grave concern for he hoped to be allowed to call, he wanted to hear about the labor activities Leon had mentioned, see the children and Aunt Anna. That was his mistake, he should have married Aunt Anna himself, not left her for some Lothario of a cigar maker.

172

He shook hands solemnly with Leon, kissed Julie's wrist.

Then he was gone, off with the dazzling Netta and the pompous Barnum and, of course, as Julie told Leon, they would never see him again.

5

She said the same to Aunt Anna. "Of course, we'll never see him again."

"And why not? Glad enough he was to come to me in the old days, get his cup of coffee brewed black as paint, and glad he'll be to come again, to know it's an old friend looking him in the eye, none of your frilly-billies hanging around because he's in the chips. Don't you tell me about that business, I know all about it; I'll warrant he does, too, or he's forgotten the time he was ushering for Barnum." She held out the length of white sheet, yanked a clean raw tear down the center, and resumed her place at the machine.

"They are very fashionable," Julie said gently when she could be heard. "You should see Mr. Barnum arch out his frilled shirt, and, Aunt Anna, in your life, you've never seen . . . the way she was dressed!"

"I've seen. It's fancy enough while you have it. Pity is, you don't have it long. I could tell you plenty about Aggie Devereaux and Esther O'Rourke and some of the others when we were the big show at Drury Lane." She was pleased, though, for Phillip to have a taste of luck; he was a plucky lad and she'd never forget the way he'd stood up to Julie's pa.

"But wasn't it a wonder, meeting that way?"

"Only wonder is we didn't bump into him long ago, Netta Davenport packing them in next door the night we went to Steinway Hall."

"You mean you knew about Phillip? You never told me."

"Don't recall you asked." She bit off a thread, her head slant-

173

wise so light nestled in the soft, faded hair that had only a little of the ginger left, just a sprig here and there, a hint of the bright, naughty color that had been.

"But how did you know?" persisted Julie.

"By using the eyes God gave me, reading a newspaper now and then, the way you could if you weren't forever stewing over those children."

"I do read, the labor news and editorials. . . ."

"Everyone to his taste. I was in show business, and I'm not aimin' to lose touch." She stood again, flaunted the noisy sheet, folded it, and settled down to hem the rent sides.

"And what was in the papers about Phillip?"

"Not much about him. Mostly Netta, she's a headliner. Phillip's lucky to have teamed with her."

That, Julie had to think over. Teamed, Aunt Anna said. If he did come to call would Netta come, too? What in the world would the neighbors think? The flaming hair, the swollen breasts sweeping up past the Wholbeins and Bagratunis!

"Seein' as how you don't expect 'em, why worry? I'll wager if she does come, they'll break their necks to run after the carriage, touching her skirt and making real fools of themselves." She unpinned her spectacles and massaged each lens with vigor. "You know," she went on, sharper than ever, "it's no sin for a female to dye her hair. She can dye it purple if she's in the theater and has a mind."

The heat flew to Julie's scalp. "I didn't say . . . she's very beautiful, it's just. . . ."

"Just that she wants to make herself ravishing and if you saw her on a stage you'd think nothing of it. Your French grandpa didn't make love to Fidelio in his own gray hair, did he? You bet not. All rigged up in wig and paint to shame his grandson."

But about Netta, how old did Aunt Anna think she was —if she'd been in that play in London and in the music halls, how old did Aunt Anna think? And Aunt Anna guessed old enough but not wore out yet, look at Charlotte Cushman!

They chatted about the theater as if the subject had never

174

been closed. Phillip's name was free again, he added a welcome and colorful note to their conversational routine of cooking and cleaning, cigar makers' news, and the deplorable state of the Wholbeins, even if that were the end of it and they never saw him again.

Christmas came and went and still no word. Of course not. Aunt Anna should know that during a lifetime one lost many people, lost them more than in death, grandpa and grandpère were alive and living, compared with Ethelyn or Papa. You never thought of Ethelyn as she was now, Mrs. Potter in her fussy house at Hampshire, putting her Mr. Potter and her two young Master Potters in their place. You thought of her patronizing Aldgate or tiddling her fork at the Corper table as if that were the end of Ethelyn. With some people, your imagination ran along, as it did with Emma and Lud and Elsa, but others froze into time and space like figures in a tapestry—there was Ethelyn with square worsted corners, every stitch a lady, simpering over a cup of tea. To be sure, that was not true of Phillip, he had died rather more like Grandpa into part of a living past, but it was as impossible to imagine his walking into this room, into their lives again, as it was to imagine—well—Mr. Munzell. The name came easily since she held in her lap, half-read, that gentleman's annual copious communication with its holiday greetings and incongruous tidings of the tapestried figures—Papa and the boys, the Peabodys, full details of a week end he had spent with the Potters, every line, every syllable carefully transcribed with the bottoms of each letter blocked into line.

"Dear Mr. Munzell," she murmured.

"Hm. That one." Aunt Anna had seen many a dummy at the wax works, and if Julie was finished with his news, they'd best be getting to the fruit cookies, then tomorrow they could roast up chicken and steam puddings; for they were going to be in the swim this New Year's. They'd saved the goodies from the Christmas box, contented themselves with a meager Christmas, and Leon was inviting his friends and they'd set a table fit for a king, an actress, or anyone.

Their guests came early, almost as soon as the first pistol cracked. Etienne and Sirak helped Leon rearrange the furniture so the table could be laid in the living room, with Julie's best plates and Aunt Anna's coffeepot and sconces. The tankard of spiced rum filled the whole flat and drifted down the stairs with tantalizing gingered scent. Leon and Etienne, Sirak and Becke sampled it more than once. They flounced about like a quartet of jugglers in their white silk shirts; Leon had shared his gift, and a sight they were, for the shirt which had been measured to fit Leon did fairly well on Sirak, hung limp as a dishcloth on Clairevoissier, and as for Becke! The sleeves were so long they had to be held in place with bands of skinny black elastic, over which the silk bagged; his bony back asserted itself, and from the collar the old brown neck stuck up scrawny as a chicken's. Which didn't keep the four from being pleased with themselves, and how they were admired by their confederates—Stevens and Grunwald, Fatty Hoffenstein and old McGinty, all of them slicked spic and span, newly shaved so close that old McGinty was raw as a strawberry and Aunt Anna had to give him soda to dust under his chin.

The baby had been put down to nap now, the children were at play, it was still early, time to spare for any less intimate visitors who might come unexpectedly. Guns and pistols were firing all over town, such a frenzy of noise, and the flat packed. Barney Berlyn and others from the local, Sammy Gompers so grown you hardly knew him, and his father, and Shorty Hendricks from Stachelberg's, the whole crew from Orgler's where Leon had worked the year before, the Van Huesens, father, son, and grandson smoking long Dutch pipes in honor of the day. Leon knew what to say to everyone, to McGinty who was deaf, to Shorty Hendricks who'd lost two children with scarlet. There were New Year's stories from the old country, the Van Huesens puffed their pipes and told how old Van Huesen had emptied a barrel when he was young. There were jokes in Dutch and German, hushed over in the corner, then bellows of hearty mirth. Bagratuni came up and the head of the house of Wholbein, though how he had nerve to show his face, Julie and Aunt Anna didn't know. Why, it was only last week he'd stolen every cent out of his wife's household purse for drink, a fact known the length of Avenue A.

Which showed what a fool the woman was, not hiding her bounty. Men were hard-working creatures but fools with money, according to Aunt Anna, and it was up to a wife to put a trifle aside, button her lip, and hang onto it for when need be. Julie stirred the steaming pitcher, tasted, and held out the spoon for Aunt Anna.

"Whew, you need more sugar and less ginger. What are you trying to do, blow their heads off?" So more sugar it was, and they hurried in, the men gathered to fill their cups and the door opened and closed, opened and closed. In the excitement, she didn't see Phillip come, she didn't know he had come until the whiff of cool flowers touched her face. Blue-white hyacinths, two great mounds of them, and a pale gentleman. She could barely take the flowers, she fluttered so. Aunt Anna was hugging Phillip, holding him off at arm's length to see how the world had treated him, and she'd be switched if he wasn't as skinny as ever for all he'd gotten to be such a swell. How everyone roared!

"Mr. Fox, Julie," Phillip said. The tall man with the flowers begged forgiveness for intruding, helped Julie place the silvered pots—he and Phil usually made New Year's calls together and Phil had insisted. He had such a grave, kind face, his cheeks were so sunken, suddenly she knew who he was. "My children will be delighted, Mr. Fox. We took Ellen, she's our oldest, to see your Humpty Dumpty, and she's never forgotten. I've not forgotten, either." The punch she offered shook and quivered in its glass, but there was no need to be afraid, he was gentle and melancholy as a tired child. He listened gravely while she told of the first circus she had seen. Grandpa had come from Holland and taken her and Emma and Jack, a clown had popped out of a black box, thrown back the lid and popped right out—a memory at which, for some inexplicable reason, her heart filled with sadness on this merry New Year's Day.

Phillip was chatting rapidly with Leon and Aunt Anna. Leon dispatched Sirak to find the children and bring them home. It made one's stomach tighten into a fist of fear because Phillip was about to see her darling Ellen, and the boys, too, of course. Why was she frightened? Why?

"Children, your icy boots!" She forgot to excuse herself to Phillip's famous friend, running to save her carpet. In the bedroom, she straightened Ellen's hair and saw that Henry's face was clean, their Uncle Phillip had come, they were going to meet one of Mama's oldest friends. The baby was awake. She changed and dressed him and lugged him into the party, while Ellen and Henry hung to her skirts.

"My God, Fox, isn't this charming," laughed Phillip. "The Madonna of Avenue A!" He took no notice of her quick anger, shook hands with Henry, and questioned him flippantly about ice skating. Henry wouldn't talk.

"Come, son, you did pretty well last week when we went to the pond; your papa isn't a Dutchman for nothing," Leon said, but Henry eyed Phillip with suspicion. The more affable the one, the more retiring the other. Henry attached himself passionately to Mr. Fox; Ellen, who had been hiding behind the skirt, slid away to the safe shelter of Uncle Becke; Mr. Bagratuni took the baby downstairs; and the moment Julie had waited for was gone. The afternoon was gone. Behind the moist window film a deep blue spread and darkened, thin slits of wind sneaked under the sills. When she lit the tapers, they shivered unsteadily. Phillip should never have come. It was less than nothing. She wished he'd go. Other guests had begun to take their leave. Reluctantly, unsteady and somewhat rosy, they expressed their thanks and helped each other out the door. But not Phillip. He sat talking with Leon, not knowing how unwelcome he was. She didn't look at him, she looked at Mr. Fox who was putting on a show for Ellen and Henry. He flexed his shoulders, that was all, and there was Humpty Dumpty.

178

Since the ruckus was over, she and Julie would just warm them up a hot bowl of soup, eh? Aunt Anna led the way to the kitchen. What was wrong with Julie, anyhow, moping? She was not moping, she stomped about with the dull heat in her face. But when she came back to the living room with the big tureen, her anger faded—on the settee, as if the whole of the day's activities had been directed toward this end, sat Phillip and Ellen. He wasn't mocking now, he was speaking seriously, and Ellen had moved up until the folds of her holiday dress lay against his knee, staring with that candid, blue-eyed look of hers, the deep-eyed look with which another Ellen must have gone to summon the soldiers when there was war and Grandpa sent her with a lantern.

"Are you my uncle?"

Yes, he guessed he was.

"How, which way?" And Julie explained that Uncle Phillip was her uncle as Uncle Becke and Aunt Anna, because they had been part of the family for so many years, they really were family. Uncle Phillip could tell her wonderful stories about Grand-père, Uncle Phillip loved music, sometime he would like to hear her sing. Ellen promptly opened her mouth and sang one of the songs she knew from school. Not just because she was hers, Julie was sure it wasn't just that, but there was something so beautiful about the child's face, singing simply and sweetly. Phillip felt it, too. He marked Ellen as only Phillip could, so completely enthralled that one forgave him his flippancy, his mocking manner, and the way he had said, "Madonna of Avenue A."

He was the same Phillip; she saw the slight tremor of his hands, the eager expression he might have had in the old days looking at Herr Jan's woman with the crow. Yes, the same Phillip, except not the same for her. That had all changed as it must and should have, each of them growing into their own adult lives and away from each other, but the same *Phillip*. And he had made it back from the dead as Grandpa and Grand-père could not, back into this room, into their lives.

6

How many times in the old days she and Phillip had imagined his opening night, lived it through every step of the way to the theater, their seats second row on the aisle—right up to the awful, vibrant moment before the curtain. Leon held the program for her to read.

NETTA NETTA NETTA, DAVENPORT DAVENPORT DAVENPORT
in the musical extravaganza *By Jove,* produced, directed, and written by Miss Netta Davenport and Mr. Phil McManus, and starring none other as Juno than the same Miss NETTA NETTA. . . .

"Not going to be a stray seat in the house," Becke said. It was seldom the old man went to the theater, or as he said, "into sassiety," and he was making the most of it, white silk shirt and all. He leaned one pointed elbow on the arm of Aunt Anna's seat, talking under the shield of his hand so as not to make a noise. The effect didn't please Aunt Anna, who felt right at home in a theater, same as in her own kitchen, he was to go ahead, speak out if he had something worth the saying, not worry none about folks who were dolled up in new-fangled evening clothes the Lord never meant a human to wear in such weather. Becke pulled himself up at this reassurance, looked archly around, and right into the bosom of an opulent woman at his left, a *grande dame* whose low-cut gown afforded so unexpected a vista that Becke hid hastily behind his hand, edged as close as he could to Aunt Anna, mumbling incoherently about one time he'd gone to the Haymarket. Aunt Anna raised her sparse eyebrows, stared about undaunted, and gave her opinion that this was one house not too papered for profit. Looked to her as if Netta and Phillip knew what they were up to.

"You're a literary light, darling, what do they mean here, 'Scene One, battlefield before Latium'?"

But the program didn't make sense to Julie. "All Greek, eh?" Leon said.

"Leon!" She studied the program, the characters were mostly Greek gods; it certainly bore no relation to the old play she knew so well. And why should it? Tonight was something new, unfamiliar, written recently, a fact hard to keep straight in her mind; for the sense of fright, the nervous agitation merged in some way with the old play they had read aloud together, taking all the parts, every shred of voice she'd had—high, clear notes and soft, muted ones and the breathless notes which had been easy then because. . . .

"Good evening, Phil asked me to look after you," George Fox said, taking the seat next to Leon. Such a nice man, he was like a part of Phillip, the old, familiar, melancholy part. Julie shook hands warmly. "Isn't the curtain late?" she said. "Is everything. . . ."

There was a stir, Phillip came down the aisle with a bevy of fashionables to fill the first row. Barnum was on his left, a tall, catlike man on his right.

"Good of you to come, Aunt Anna, so good of you all. Hello, Leon." Phillip shook hands solemnly with each of them. His hands were cold. She would have liked to wish him luck.

"Let me present Thurlow Weed," Phillip said, loudly. People were making such a fuss over Barnum it was hard to hear. "Pay attention to my friend Dekker, you won't have any pauperism in the state, T.W."

Mr. Weed cringed his head to one side and took Leon's hand with interest, but there was a crash of music that shook the rafters, lights were dimmed, Phillip and his friends sank into silhouette against the widening, gaudy, brilliant span of space. Applause roared, drowned the music for the mass of people moving about in gorgeous costumes, bizarre and beautiful togas and chaplets. A few lay in lovely attitudes on the greensward, they were singing, when the roar died down, a dignified but catchy air. It was completely splendid. Then

181

surprisingly, Julie saw one man—no, two—vast, portly creatures, their stomachs hanging gross in the draperies. She was about to seize Leon's arm, they'd gotten in by mistake, when she spied another, thin as a stick, who now and again took a hopping step that didn't match the measured beat of the composition; his tunic fit no better than Becke's Christmas shirt, he was going to spoil the show! Now the ladies, the goddesses, were strolling by, languorous in their floating gowns, their eyes beautifully painted and glittering. Right among them tottered the awful fat men, she could have cried! She looked, terrified, to Phillip, but he was grinning; and at that moment the tempo leaped, jittered into ragtime, everyone on the stage began to sway and hop. They sang, "My, but it's fun to be close to the sun on Olympus, Olympus. Every god has his goddess, but if there is strife, he always can corner a mortal for wife. By Jove, oh, by Jove, we say, this is the life on Olympus!"

Julie flushed, although they sang well. There were baritones and fluty tenors, the ladies arching and flinging their limbs so the chiffon draperies flew. Phillip chuckled. A stream of laughter came trickling from the back of the house, another, another, like jets from a fountain, Leon was laughing. But it was vulgar, nothing funny about it, to start out seriously with the lovely scene and then change it, singing verse after verse so sly eyed and tantalizing that the words must mean something else, something outrageous. She was glad when Minerva came, a tall dark girl who knew everything and told what she knew. Jove might be a great king, she shrugged audaciously, and you could see to her knees! But he was no better than any other husband when it came to Juno, if he thought he would have his way about the war in Latium. . . . There was a storm of applause, a wild volley, a gasp ran through the house, not for Minerva, not for her, but for Juno, Netta Davenport Juno in a blouse cut square over the pellucid breasts and her skirt, one scant piece of gauze, caught up tight between the hips like a baby's . . . *well!* Nothing was left to imagination. Her whole rounded thigh, every inch of leg was revealed in a tight green stocking. The audience clapped to burst their gloves,

182

even Aunt Anna gasped; before there was time to catch your breath, all the other ladies on the stage had snatched away their skirts and stood in stockinged limbs, flirting drolly. Now the gauze legs went flying, capered through the air lithe as snakes. They had gloves on, these shameless women, gloves all the way to their shoulders, gray to match their lower extremities, only Netta wore the green, with her flaming hair and at the jogging breast, one blood-red rose.

"By God!" whispered Phillip to Leon, "did you ever see such a beauty?" And Leon, *her own Leon,* agreed, laughed and applauded. Poor Becke didn't know where to look; to the left was the threatening bosom, straight ahead the dancing, twirling legs, and to the right Aunt Anna, who wanted to know, if he looked her way, why he didn't keep his eyes on something worth the sight?

It grew worse every minute. When the dancers left the stage, the least savory of the men came forward. One fat monster spoke with a Dutch accent, the thin one shrugged his shoulders and said, "Whoops my deah!" in a way to make you shiver. The story of Jove and his roving Juno went right on. Netta parted her red lips, darted her tongue, and the audience clapped and called their bravos; she shook her head with its jaunty crown, singing in a voice as unctuous as ocher. And where was one flash of Phillip? In all the vulgarity, the syncopation, the burlesque—where was Phillip? Even the clever lines were slightly lewd, slightly gross, Netta was gross, any woman who would show her thighs! When it was over, Leon and Aunt Anna applauding, saying what a rip-roaring show, she was disgusted with them, too. She kept her opinion fiercely to herself.

7

Critics panned the show soundly, so there! She read the notices with mounting horror, finding her opinions given substance. Leon and Aunt Anna thought her nasty-nice, did they? Let them read William Winter in the *Tribune*. That eloquent man who could pour forth torrents of praise for Rehan or Terry or Booth had turned his full spigot of wrath on *By Jove*. Nothing original in it, he wrote, comparing the show with Thompson's *Ixion*, nothing subtle or smart except Netta Davenport herself, who was a great trouper and knew how to wheedle the maximum from every lyric. No mention as to who had written those lyrics. He called the show indecent, rare without being rarified, *illegitimate* vaudeville decked in the trappings of art. How could Phillip hold up his head!

But he did, and never in better spirits. He and George would breeze in on Sunday mornings, both immaculately shaved, immaculately whisked with lilac vegetal; the more acid the words of Winter, the more rakish and witty Phillip became. Money was rolling in at the box office. If the critical attack kept up another month, they'd outrun *The Black Crook*. He always brought something extravagant, a nosegay of heliotrope from Netta, Maillard's bonbons done up with pretty tongs from Netta, who sent her love, and the carriage would be by for them at eight. Julie found a thousand things to do on these Sunday mornings. Brisk, that's what she was, brisk and busy, while Phillip and George and Leon played with the children, talked about the show, or damned the Bohemians who were streaming into the cigar business with cheap labor. If Aunt Anna were there, they'd coax her into making the blackest, bitterest of coffee, and always, before they left, Phillip would have gained Leon's approval to some new outing, some-

184

thing beyond the tonight when the carriage would call at eight.

"Why, it's good for you, dear, to get out of this little world of ours into something gay and carefree," Leon would say when she'd protest. "You haven't had pleasure enough, these last years. I've been with the men, but you've been locked up in the house, you need a change." And she wasn't to worry if the party lasted late, he wasn't such a sober fellow as all that, he was enjoying himself. He liked Netta enormously, liked Phillip and Fox, even Barnum was jolly when he forgot how great he was. No, he didn't understand Julie's reluctance. How could he, when she didn't understand it herself?

Certainly it wasn't unpleasant to ride up Fifth Avenue in Netta's carriage, she should enjoy that as much as Leon, seeing the night city with its myriad lights winking as if a host of imps fanned and flashed the flames. Certainly it wasn't Netta. For once you got used to the burnished hair and carmined lips, you saw how good she was, warm and genuine; whatever she did on a stage, whatever she wore, she was no hypocrite. Anyone in the business could count on her, Julie'd seen them, the down-and-outs came with the favorites to the big brownstone house, they didn't go away empty handed, she saw that, too.

Annie usually met them at the door. She was Netta's secretary, a spare young woman with bright nun's eyes. Leon she would take to the parlor or to Phillip's rooms, but Julie must come up and she'd lead the way, open the door, as if it were a benediction. Netta usually reclined on a couch with a hand mirror, her velvet dressing gown rippled to the floor, Julie must come sit beside her. "How charming, how lovely, Julie; Annie, run down, get one of the white roses Mr. Weed sent, it's just what Julie wants in her hair." Perfumes were Netta's fancy, she would lift an atomizer, spray the scent lavishly, then spray Julie from another *flacon,* some gentler, flower fragrance, talking the while as if they were old friends, as if Julie knew the sisters, friends, and celebrities who wandered in and out of her conversation. No, the distaste could not be for Netta.

Nor for the house itself, which was richly done in tones of green to compliment the famous hair. Nor the guests. For what sense did it make to complain that they were too many, too clever, or too lively? Everyone came, the steady nucleus of show people, politicians, journalists, race-track sports, and those who didn't matter, the shabby tragedians and song-writers, pale comics in flashy clothes. They all accepted the Dekkers as Netta's intimates. Yet Julie didn't quite like them, not their wit nor their attitude toward Phillip, although she could not quite put her finger on that. Phillip was host of the house; Netta established that with every gesture. Holding court at the tea or the card table, tantalizing a dozen men with charming innuendoes, she still spoke for Phillip; any matter calling for decision she left unanswered until he could be summoned to join the group. Large as she was, taller than Phillip and full fleshed, she made it clear that he was motor and mainstay of their partnership. But did anyone believe it? Wasn't there a hint of patronage?

None of this Leon noticed. As in Arnheim or London, as anywhere, ten minutes after he entered a room, he was the core of it. With politicians he talked of labor and made what headway he could. With the show people he sang and danced until Netta swore he was wasting his time, let her introduce him to Tony Pastor. Oh, no, Leon laughed, he'd think twice if he were a glamorous lady who could wear tights, but . . . there was a friend of his cut out for the theater, and to the next Sunday "at home" he brought Etienne Clairevoissier, over whom Netta made a great fuss. Leon had worried about Etienne, he was afraid the boy might get into trouble, the theater was a place for that imagination and sense of drama. What Leon did not say was there were stage hands, musicians, none of them organized, all of then needing unions, Etienne would find more to do than dream. Julie sat beside the young man while Phillip sketched possibilities in stage building and stagecraft. He explained the sort of musicals they were planning for the future, more luxurious, more exorbitant than the theater had ever seen.

"Netta's discovered what the public wants and made an art of it!"

Art. The Phillip she had known had believed in art, he'd been brilliant and intense, and look how he'd cheapened the talent, made it a mockery. She wished she might slip away to George Fox, he of them all was least a clown. But Phillip stayed her. He was speaking of Barnum now.

"A genius, Etienne. Knows more about the theater than anyone since Shakespeare . . . wouldn't you say, darling?"

"I'd say nothing of the kind. He had a lucky break with Jenny Lind."

"But look what he's done since, the great strides in music."

"Phillip, that man's an opportunist and you know it. A great voice or a two-headed dog. The only thing big about Barnum's his vanity."

Etienne excused himself, embarrassed.

"And I wish you'd leave Etienne alone. He, at least, believes in something."

He looked at her stunned, his face suddenly naked, nothing of the knave or dandy in it. There was the face she knew, the face she'd loved, memorized, and owed a great debt. For how could she have ever been this Julie, if not for Phillip? He had been the beginning of seeing what there was in the world, he had opened the first doors, and down underneath this mask of his. . . .

"Phillip," she said impulsively, "I want to talk with you. Take me somewhere, we must talk."

He accepted that without surprise, guided her across the crowded room. Leon was playing cards, he thought it a fine idea that she and Phillip catch a breath of air. She must speak openly and honestly, she must not be afraid; but once in Phillip's gig, jolting slowly through the twilight streets, she didn't know where to start. Clusters of sunset cloud still scattered across the sky like garlands, bright pink deepening

187

to flame, casting bouquets of light to be caught in the endless mirrors of plate glass. Phillip flicked his whip, rolled a cigarette, and talked quietly to his impatient horse. He held the reins unconcernedly with one hand. Gouraud's Italian Soap, Coral Hair Restorative, Poor Man's Plasters, tattered men and boys paraded with the advertising placards. A lamplighter hauled his heavy ladder along the curb, he had work to manage with the crowds, pavement and street thronged with people out to catch the pageant or a whiff of spring. Phillip inched the horse through the mass of Brown's landaus, edged to the right and went slowly up Sixth. Finally they were free, free to gallop fast as the wind toward Bloomingdale.

"We could go somewhere for a bite to eat, but unless you'd rather, let's drive, dear."

"Yes," she said. "Yes."

The garlands had scattered, the sky was gray and darker by the minute. Phillip tucked a blanket over their knees, she had to help him as they went, almost flying, up to a rise of land, down, the wind tearing, the leather creaking, the hoofs clanging, as if time had flown ahead and they were racing it.

"Phillip, listen. I speak because we're friends, because I know you. Long ago you let me know you. What are you doing to yourself, Phillip? What have you done? Such talent and a mind like yours, wasted!" Wind took her breath away. Another dip, another rise, the buggy careened off, faster than ever on a narrow road. "Do you hear me . . . you were the one who told *me* there was no such thing as compromise." The low branch of a tree whipped her hair. The road grew rougher, the horse slowed, walked, picked its way.

"Phillip, I'm not trying to anger you. Tonight is the first time I've found you. You hide behind a barricade, behind a front. None of those people know who you are." Her heart pounded with the effort.

"Ho, boy." The buggy stopped under the drooping trees. He got down to tie the horse. She heard him rub the animal, "nice boy" and "fine boy," and the sweated beast stomped.

188

"Phillip, answer me. Tell me you know it's true." But she could barely speak, barely a sound.

He was beside her at once, fiercely, he held her sobbing against him and brushed her unsteady mouth with his own. Back and forth his lips brushed, and slowly, with caught breath, she turned her head to say no. That made it worse. He plied her mouth until she was wounded wild with desire. His lambent, supple tongue slipped sweet to hers. She couldn't stop him. Did she even try? She summoned up her children and Leon, she shook her head; but didn't that mean rather "we shouldn't," "we mustn't," "please, *please*, Phillip."

She was alive! She clung to him, to that dear familiar flesh, that face with its urgent, pungent scent. Nothing had been like this, ever, throbbing and swollen, stung to life. He stroked and cherished the silk of her dress until she could have torn off every barrier shred.

"Sweet, beloved." She had to lose his mouth to hear it, then he was back again. But now she seized his hands. She held them.

The task was to erase, bury the hour in Bloomingdale as if it hadn't been. She hadn't really betrayed Leon. Maybe she had acted like a lovesick girl, but it was not as if it were something new, it was something old, just a moment snatched back out of time, something that had been, as Leon knew, long before, and would never be again. Never. A few kisses—her face burned with guilt—a few kisses meant nothing compared with the years of understanding she and Leon. . . . But her body had come to some strange, palpable life of its own, fevered and craving and sad by turn. What was it Leon had said— "Someday you'll come to it with your blood singing"? She could have wept with anger.

189

And no word from Phillip. He must certainly know as she did that their moment had been snatched from time and best forgotten, but just a word to show she mattered, a message sent over by an usher from the theater, as he had once sent it when they were invited to an impromptu party, just a letter by post. As the days passed, she grew worn with waiting. What was to be said in those letters she didn't know, just a word to tell her . . . and if there was no word, then he'd never see her again, either, and it would be over. The bones of her knees wilted, she sank beside the table with her polishing cloth, resting her weary head against the wood. This was Phillip's revenge, his anger saved from long ago when Papa. . . . Or perhaps he was used to easy love affairs. He had Netta, didn't he, and who else, which of the shameless kicking girls?

Then she heard Phillip was in Boston, he'd gone to hire an Englishman to replace the current Jove. That was the night the pea soup wouldn't thicken and then thickened so fast it scorched and burned and Leon was so late the rest of the supper grew dry and stale and Henry cut his lip and lost two teeth in a fight. Then, of all times, she was suddenly pervaded with humor, bathed Henry's bruised face and amazed the children by sitting down on the floor and ignoring all misfortune. She sang them songs Grand-père had sung to her and told how once at the opera, Napoleon—"Napoleon was French like Etienne, he was the emperor, and if you'll hand me that newspaper, I'll make you each a hat."

"Now this is something like," Leon said when he came. He picked her and the baby up together from the floor. "Do you know how good it is to come home? What's got into you, little mother?"

"Everything's gone wrong," she laughed, hiding her hot face against his shirt.

"Women! I'll never understand 'em. One hour late and I'd expected to have my ears scorched. Do we eat? I'm starved." He ignored Henry's swollen face until the arrowroot pudding. Then he looked up, as if for the first time.

"Well, son, what happened to you?"

Henry said nothing.

"Fighting," offered Ellen, her mouth full.

"Henry will speak for himself. Talk up, son."

"Just a fight."

"He whipped Rudy Wholbein. He won." Ellen said.

"I'm sorry to hear it."

"But I *won!*"

"No one won. If you're stronger than Rudy, that proves nothing. In six months he may be stronger than you. Even if he isn't, he can become smarter than you. Suppose you fought one of the big fellows, Sirak, say. He could half-kill you with a punch. Would that make him right?"

"I'll fight if I want to."

"Henry!" Julie said.

"Now, dear, this is a man's affair. Best say you'll fight if you *have* to, son. There's a difference. I was a soldier. We fought, we had to, and we thought we won. We won nothing."

"Oh, all the kids. . . ."

"I'm not interested in all the kids, I'm interested in this family. If a family is not together in what they think, they're no family." He reached over and took Julie's hand. "I'm not always right, Henry, but until you're older, you'll have to take my word. You'll find being part of a family is good, you want to share with those you love best."

"I love you and Mama best," Ellen said.

"I'm speaking to Henry, Ellen. We all have quarrels in our lives, you know that. I could have fought the day we marched for eight hours and the crowd jeered us. But that would betray what your mother and I believe in. Unless I had her and you children to come home to, the rest would mean little. You won't enjoy your fights if you can't come home and have your face bathed and a good supper. Next time you'll have neither."

Henry sulked. He was stubborn, that was a fact; but before bed, he climbed shyly on Leon's lap and asked for a story. He got it, too, and not a word of reprimand, Leon winking at her

191

across the room. Once Henry interrupted. Softly, almost whispering, he put his cheek to Leon's.

"Papa, I'm sorry," he said.

He was sorry! Poor little lad, it was she who was sorry, who hated herself for the memory that went over and over like a monotonous music box. What a good man Leon was, what simplicity he brought to daily living. That's what she must get back to, that simplicity and honesty, and never, never lose it again.

9

He took to dropping by in the afternoons. The first time it was so unexpected she couldn't believe it. After that she believed it so implicitly that if two days passed and he did not, she walked through the hours dyed deep with anguish like some relentless purple stain. And it was all right now, he came as a friend, nothing clandestine, nothing perilous, not a gesture to negate her role as Leon's wife. She crammed her household chores into the mornings, the faster the better, washing, scrubbing, scouring, so that the afternoons might be tidy just in case. . . .

There was the midday meal and Henry and Steve could swallow it down, let her clean the kitchen, smooth her hair, change her collar and cuffs or her muslin tucker, and sit with Aunt Anna to sew. That's what she said, sit and sew, while some quick panic accumulated through the hours of rushing, mounted like madness. Aunt Anna's voice seemed far away with your senses tuned to the street, to a carriage, to the stairs. Let Aram come clumping up, even hearing his voice and knowing who it was, her breath quickened for someone else who might not stop at the second landing.

It was usually around two fifteen, two thirty, always a few

minutes later than she'd thought, just when she imagined him hopelessly bogged down with some new advertising stunt or other detail, in he'd saunter, as unconcerned about the show as if it were the hundredth smash hit he'd produced. What worried him, Phillip said, was that it could easily run all summer. He wanted a vacation, the troupe needed a rest, so did Netta. Imagine a place at Port Washington, go out by steamboat to Sands Point, or perhaps a place at Fishkill. Julie had to smile at the little air with which he said it.

He'd do a heap better sticking some of that easy money in the bank, according to Aunt Anna, he was getting pretty high and mighty, maybe he'd be wanting his own private boat next. She lashed thread around Becke's worn collar and bit it off hard. She'd been in this business longer than he'd been in britches, he'd show sense to pay closer attention to his box office, see that the thieves behind the grating didn't rob him blind. Phillip listened earnestly. Aunt Anna'd given him two capital ideas, he should have a boat of his own, a side-wheeler would be the thing, and she was undoubtedly right about the box office, Hammersmith was probably crooked as Pearl Street, he'd fire him tonight. Which threat completely upset Aunt Anna, who had no evidence of guilt and who now pleaded that Phillip use discretion, Hammersmith might be the world's one honest cashier and he had a family.

That being settled, they could proceed with the reading. Phillip usually brought the *Atlantic* or the *Nation,* and while they sewed, he would read aloud, pieces by Howells, Aldrich, Twain, and stories by a new young man named James. He brought her Whitman's *Leaves of Grass*, bound in leather the color of burned almonds. His hands were tender on the book. Sometimes they looked at each other through swimming eyes. They read Harte's *M'liss* and *The Outcasts of Poker Flat,* that was to Aunt Anna's taste. He brought Ellen books, too; when she came from school, she could listen while Phillip read, or she could explore her own books. Ellen loved listening, she sat quietly on the floor while Phillip's eyes glowed, his fingers

193

were nervous on the leaves, looking up, looking up to see what Julie thought. If Aunt Anna weren't there, if Ellen was still at school, he would touch Julie's hand, the response flowing through their fingers quicker than speech. Door after door into mysterious corridors of thought and feeling which had long been closed. It was she, Julie, restored from the anonymity of fetch and carry. And didn't she have the right? Didn't everyone have the right to be intensely themselves? Well, she hadn't, for eight years she'd not given a thought except to the children and Leon and the needs of the cigar makers. This was herself again, and nothing to be ashamed of. She and Phillip had put passion aside, without another word or hint. They were just sharing the intellectual things Phillip had taught her to love and which they were now giving back to each other.

At the big house, she'd wondered at the absence of books. None of Phillip's were in evidence, and the ornately bound volumes behind the diamond panes of the bookcase were just five dozen books in assorted gold stamping, please. The same with pictures. Phillip, who had taken her to galleries, who had complained of collections being mere samplings and criticized the hackneyed pieces in her papa's house, that same Phillip lived where every picture was an afterthought, a badly reproduced, garishly framed outrage. The only room in that house with a decent picture was Annie's, the brown, dull little cell with its two steel-engraved views of Ireland and the one rich Madonna. No evidence of Phillip anywhere in the big house.

It was a question she had saved to ask him, when she felt more sure. For she was only sure of Phillip when he was there, reading from the almond-brown book—

> Hark close and still what I now whisper to you
> I love you, O you entirely possess me,
> O that you and I escape from the rest and go
> utterly off, free and lawless

Two hawks in the air, two fishes swimming in
the sea, not more lawless than we.

In his absence, she sat with Aunt Anna sewing stupidly,
trying to hear what her old friend said, trying to avoid her
bright spectacles. The same old noises drifted up from the
street—"Glass put'een, glass put'een!" "Strawberries!" "Fresh
shad!" One long blast from the fishmonger's horn, then three
little short ones that pierced you to the core.

10

What days those were at Coney Island—to wake up smelling
the sea! Even half asleep, you knew where you were, the air,
moist and motile, lending sheets and pillow slips a cool, silken
feel. She could lie, hearing the waves run and ripple and under
it the children's breathing—if only Henry would breathe
through his nose. She awoke knowing everything, where she
was, where Phillip was. She couldn't lie but must slip out and
across to the window, kneeling there with her cheek to the
damp sill to watch the long ever running ribs of the tide. How
wonderful to be sharing the sea with Phillip, to know that he
was at a window watching. First it was gray, sea and skyscape
washed clear of color. Then came a tinge of opal, it seeped and
spread, stained the long horizon like a drop of paint on wet
water color. Gradually the sea backed off, relinquished the
beach gracefully and with noblesse as if it could easily claim
the whole of it, hotel, feeble shacks, and all the little people of
the shore. It chose to ebb, the long unbroken ribs leaving the
blue mirror of their touch to breath off, yield the sand pale and
newly molded. It was hard to remember any other world, the
world of Wholbeins and Bagratunis and the close cooking

smells. Leon was awake, he had already taken his dish of tea and was off toward the shop. She hoped he and Becke would come on Sunday, for Netta had invited them and they could all go exploring down the beach to the pavilion where Professor Bekins played the piano and they served such good Milwaukee beer.

She always thought of Leon in the morning before anything else should intrude, directing her thought so that wherever he was, just entering the shop now, sitting before his pile of crinkled leaves, Leon would know she was thinking. He was her husband, she was not forgetting that, nor his generosity, letting her and the children come away for the summer with Netta and Phillip. It was such a quiet time to think, the world so orderly, the youngsters not yet up and boisterous. She and Aunt Anna had their hands full then, for the pair of spinster ladies in the next suite did not take to children and had a sharp way of rapping on the wall that made one nervous, then annoyed. On occasion, she rapped just as sharply in return. The idea. What were you supposed to do with a two-year-old, strap and gag him?

Their rapping didn't perturb Aunt Anna. Do the old bats good to hear some healthy noise, take their minds off their sorrows, of which she doubted they had half as many as they thought, the two of them with plenty of money to dress in silk and travel fancy free. No need to hurry the children into clothes and through their breakfast. The first scars in the smooth new world were marks of their bare feet. Phillip had bought them hoops. Ellen chased hers along the hard sand, her cheeks glowing, her legs sturdy under the tucked-up skirt, and Stevie after her like perpetual motion. Henry sat at the water's edge in his soaking britches and built castles, dug moats and let them fill with water. His hair spiraled from a central core until it looked like blown wheat. They were hungry constantly, gobbled down the rich food; the baby must have eaten a peck of sand, he was crusted with it.

Phillip and Netta were never visible until afternoon. They were writing a new musical, there was much work to be done,

196

they took breakfast and boullion in their joint sitting room, the big rounded windows under the turret of the hotel. If Julie took the children back upstairs, they had to dodge waiters running with silver-hooded trays, Netta and Phillip's breakfast, you could smell the coffee and buttered fish. It would be served at the small table and Annie would be there, keeping to herself like a monk. It made Julie sick to see the sun on the rounded windows. And it was none of her business! She was lucky to be here. Phillip had his obligations, as she had. She'd rouse herself and take the children to watch the Coney catchers rake in their clams. Gradually, the morning would wear away. It grew warm. Sun fell like a living cloak, struck lines of fire in the cracks of your straw hat, set your blood to drumming. The beach would become busy, hotel guests splashing the scene with color, noise, and motion. Now, any minute now, Netta and Phillip would appear in bathing dress.

Aunt Anna said if she was as skinny a specimen as Phillip McManus, she'd be hung if she'd make a spectacle of herself. Phillip laughed. He was comedy relief, he said. Netta looked glorious. Her bathing dress was of navy blue cut in a modest V, but it was belted tight and she walked in ballet slippers, not even stockings; below the bloomer legs, the ribbons crossed and recrossed her white calves with their fell of blond hair. Annie followed, carrying towels and other gear, Annie in her bathing costume, identical with Netta's, save on her it was nondescript and shapeless. There was no pleading you didn't want to go bathing, Netta marshaled them like a commanding general and in they went. Then lunch was served out of hampers, their wet clothes withering in the wind. She'd catch Phillip watching her, watching her; and she wished for once he'd take over, not just let Netta decide now they'd ride to Norton's Point to watch the rabble at three-card monte, now they'd visit the beach pavilions.

Then one day a letter of importance came for Netta; and nothing would do, it seemed, but she return to New York. No, no one was to come with her except Annie. The seashore was doing Phil good. He'd closed the show so he could come, hadn't he? Well, stay then. If he wanted to please her, he could finish the new third act. And Julie was not to be a goose, she was to stay on with the children, make the most of the fine weather.

"I really want to go. It's such a long trip alone for you and Annie and I'm sure Leon. . . ." She was too confused to know what to say.

Leon was able to take care of himself, replied Netta, and since when would she rather travel with yelping youngsters than alone with Annie who had nothing to yelp about? So it was settled as Julie had known it would be. Netta went, leaving her and Phillip alone. Not numerically alone perhaps, but alone.

11

Against the moving panorama of sea and sky, they were together, hands and thoughts close enough to touch. Far as they could follow, north and south, one long, unbroken swell tented from the mass of water, arched, towered, yearned into a tall translucent wall, then crashed toward shore. It left the sand writhing and coiling like Medusa's locks. Eyes closed, she could hear the rush and whisper grow into a bursting race while the steady tenor of Phillip's voice read on. She opened her eyes, and there were the tiny dents and tunnels of sand, a miniature desert, each tuft of seaweed, each stick no larger than a match became a tree, one small ant scurrying across, a furry monster quick and nervous on his way through the world, and the breeze whisked this mighty animal with his many legs back under her shawl in one puff, less than a gust.

The sand was still mildly warm at night. Phillip spread the buggy robe, made a sandpile for them to lean on while the moon rose and water rushed toward them, sank away. Their thin strip of sand was sheltered by rocks, curved toward the water like an outstretched arm. The arm held them close to the sea, every breaker might claim them.

"It's hypnotic, darling, it's eternity," Phillip said. "Think of the men and women who have stood on this same shore—old Professor Bekins's father used to fish off that cove before the hotel was built—think of those who'll come here long after we're dead."

She thought.

"It just goes on and on, washing away the footprints, beating out the rhythm like a mighty clock."

"You should have known Stephen, the sailor on the boat when Aunt Anna and I came to America. How he loved the sea!" And she told Phillip how Stephen had tried, but not all the strong roots, not his wife nor children, could save Stephen.

"What an idea for a play!" Phillip got to his feet and started pacing. He was shaken. He ran his hands through the soft tuft of his beard.

"Phillip, write it! Why not write what you believe in, a play with beauty and meaning?"

He had turned away.

"Anyone could produce it. Frohman could. Writing honestly is what's important. To you, I mean."

"It *was* important."

But why? Certainly the basic values didn't change. Certainly Netta would understand. She persisted, until he turned on her, lashing out bitterly.

"It was our life, Julie, art and love, you and I, what could it possibly mean without you? Maybe I should have been able to go on alone. I didn't! I wanted you, without you there was nothing. Without you there is nothing."

The wild staccato beat was drilling, like music, the ocean echoed it, purled, surged, mightier every instant. Phillip caught her, sank with her onto the sand.

"Tell me to write for *you*," he whispered. "Tell me, darling, *tell* me."

199

"Phillip! Oh, Phillip, Phillip, Phillip."

It plunged ravishing, inflamed as a pent tide, this longing, his warm breath on her eyes, her hair, evocative, fervid at her ear. Mist flew. She felt the spray on one bared breast. Phillip had loosened, freed, captured it in his cupped hand, he laved it lip and tongue and she held his head, with both hands held him hard to the source, to the fount. She had nursed children, three of them, but never had sap so risen as this love fluid for Phillip's thirst. She pitched and throbbed under his kisses, sensing through all their clothes the sure shaft of his maleness. He could have claimed her, yes, right there beside the shrieking sea. But that he saved her. He wanted her as no one's wife but his own.

12

She must go to Indianapolis, Phillip said. As soon as they returned home, she must go to Indianapolis and get a divorce. It would take eighteen months. He'd send a maid with her and the children, he'd come down as often as he could, they'd be married the very minute. . . .

"Phillip! How could I ask Leon to give up his children? How?"

They went over and over the same ground. Phillip understood and suffered with her but they had no choice, he said, every fiber of their being was rooted to each other. Hadn't he tried not to love her? When she failed him years ago hadn't he tried to eradicate everything that bore her image? Even that night at the opera . . . she seemed so poised and safe he merely thought to see her again, see what kind of woman she had become. And how could you watch your beautiful Julie struggle in that dismal flat without trying to add a hint of gaiety? For Leon, too. He liked Leon sincerely, admired him, it was torture to know he worshiped the woman who was Leon's wife. After the unexpected night in Bloomingdale, he'd tried to stanch it, bury love as he had before and settle for being a friend of the family, privileged to come and go in the house, be near her. There was no choice. She was his soul and he must claim her, how resist when her eyes, her mouth were suppliant for love?

"You're a virgin, darling, you're untouched."

That she could not answer. It sounded ridiculous, a mother and married so long . . . but why lie to herself, why push down or corrupt the truth? Leon, bless him, was a good man, she loved him dearly, but it was another thing from this ecstasy of sharing. He was affectionate rather than impassioned. Phillip's kiss was a whole love story compared with the quick, businesslike coupling which had given her her children. Let it be shameful, for once be honest. Hadn't she longed—not for Phillip, actually—but for the sense of profound feeling he had long ago begun to awake in her? Hadn't she longed for something more than the crowded life she and Leon lived, the life filled with cigar makers and neighbors and labor men, in the old country, in the new. When had they ever been alone? Even in the beginning, it had been Emma and Ludwig, all of them congenial together, and had it ever been enough? Hadn't she longed to find the elusive core of self in fierce encounter?

"There is only one road, dearest. We turned our backs on truth, you and I, we must return to it."

"But Leon, Phillip. And Netta."

"Yes, I know. If only they were villains." He told her about Netta at some length, how they had met years ago, how candid and generous she had been. He and Netta were working together now, that was all. He'd dropped all the rest months ago. "After I saw you again, Julie. There could be no other woman for me. Anything else, anyone else would be unthinkable."

"You live in the same house," she said, ready to cry.

"Darling, darling. Netta knows, believe me. She's not a

201

child, Julie, she's a woman of the world and a great trouper. What makes this situation poignant is that we are adults with obligations. You're a trouper too, dear. I'm proud of you, the way you raise the children and bolster Leon, you do a magnificent job. But you were made for me, Julie, I want to love and cherish you until the end of time."

It was fulfillment. The graven texture of his lower lip, his voice, the fingers graining sand raised a persistent drumming pulse in her. There were flowers on her tray at breakfast, sheaves of notepaper covered with his impatient scrawl and to what he wrote, to what he said, she found a swift response. Nothing like the days on Gower Street. He had been avid then, but he had been cruel, warring toward some dream perfection. This was a wiser Phillip, he was suffering, he gripped her hand with such need that one thumbprint stayed for days like a brand. She watched it secretly, certain that it was the exact spot, when it had already disappeared. No need to hammer for significance as the young Phillip had, significance was there; it had achieved a continuity that made time malleable. One morning on the beach became a vast stretch of space, one evening, a thousand nights. What would she not have given in the long time past for one hour like this, her pilgrim senses wooed to pliancy? At night, exhausted and overwrought, she would lie in bed, careful not to disturb Ellen, groping over the twisted lanes of past and future. What a woman she might be if she were free to give herself wholly to Phillip, what it could mean to his writing, all those wasted years writing nothing and it was her fault.

"Your fault, my grandfather's mule," Aunt Anna said, when she mentioned it to her. "We've been through a lot, Julie Dekker. I nursed and babied you and followed along to America like an old nanny goat; but if you're set on making a fool of yourself, you'll do it without help from me."

Aunt Anna was unjust, denying them this brief time of beauty, for it couldn't last, summer was almost over, almost gone. Perhaps she and Phillip were just loaned to each other so he could get back to the artist he essentially was. She'd plait her hair, cross the braids, and be his gentle, friendly Julie, sit beside him while he worked; for he was working.

But there was no middle ground with Phillip. Loaned to each other, nonsense! He made that clear long before they stood at last against the rail of the boat watching waves widen and race away to Gravesend taking the summer with them. The band played, boat whistles bayed out of tune, the other passengers had just come up for the excursion, day up, day back, and they were in a loud holiday mood; but it was different if you had spent the whole summer. Clerks and butcher boys rocked along arm in arm, three pert young girls flounced by, milliners perhaps, they giggled, pouted their lips at Phillip and never looked toward shore. It was different if you had seen the first gleam of light stroke the sea, slept and wakened to the sound of it and walked on the dark beach. The children tried to identify moving, dwindling objects on the shore, Aunt Anna tried, but it went. . . . The thick grass stubble behind Norton's Point was rusted and coarse, then nothing but a blotch of brown.

"Ask me, every last one on this crate's three sheets to the wind," muttered Aunt Anna, glaring at the raucous crowd. She kept to the rail, herded the children in around her skirts, and grabbed onto Phillip's arm.

"See out there at the point?" he lowered his voice. "That's where they found the bodies, Aunt Anna, tossed off a boat like this."

Aunt Anna sucked in her breath.

"Don't you worry, sweetheart. The steamboat company has a whole regiment of fellows with blackjacks on board. If there's any rough stuff. . . ."

"Ellen, boys, you come here, I'll tan your backsides!" Off raced Aunt Anna through the throng, one hand clamped to her big straw hat; for she'd taken a fancy to the thing and limp and faded as it was, would wear it home. The big beach hat bounced, flopped, and disappeared.

Julie and Phillip clung together. As long as they could, they watched a tree wave its blood-bright leaves, then there was

203

just the long curve of Gravesend Beach and the restless canvas of the horsecar terminal.

"Hold fast, my darling," Phillip said.

But how could she ask Leon to give up his children? The geyser of hot tears rose. Perhaps she could keep Ellen and he . . . a fine mother, ready to give up her own boys! Think, she told herself, think—while the strong tendon bound her. Phillip was so different from Leon, who could love and lend you, grant you a freedom outside himself. There was no *outside* Phillip. He took and bound you so there was not a bone without his flesh.

The shore came close again, no beach but bleached fields flowing with drab autumn light. Leaves sailed out like skiffs, the wind trying to flex them. For a moment they had pliancy and grace, then down like dead chips on the water, like stones. Phillip's skin was so brown, he had never looked better, tanned and with his beard clipped close. She must tell Leon the truth, that she loved Phillip, she must tell him tonight before it was time for bed. She leaned against her lover while the wind rushed past.

And of a sudden, the melancholy began lifting up and out of her, up and out of the cuff and flow. There was the water that had always been and always would be, the shore skimming along beside it, autumn, winter, spring, and summer, the trees yielding up their luxury, crumpling and growing old while she herself had such a flare for life. Down, down, the prow cut its way into the vast depths, sample of all hidden things, the crevices, the yawning spaces only half comprehended. The world never changed, you changed, you had your seasons but more slowly; and long after it was over, after the wild sweet spring and hot summer, you were swept along like jaunty leaves, the little soul and the world soul in touching cycles. Why not love, why not fill your heart to bursting while there was still time? Leon was an honest man, he'd understand honesty, he merited it. She would tell him at once.

13

The sound of angry voices grew, threatening, all the way upstairs, louder and louder. They hurried, alarmed, and found
the flat packed with men, dense with tension, thick with
smoke. Not like her house at all, the house of a stranger. The
arguments were furious.

"Papa!" "Papa!" Ellen and Henry seized their papa, shrieking to be heard. Stevie screamed, Leon came and took him
from Phillip. Sirak struggled out of the group, shame-faced
and formal, to help with baggage. Once they became aware
of intrusion, the men quieted down, some of them nodded.
They looked haggard and surly, veins stood on their temples
like crimped rope. Becke, hemmed in behind the table, stood
and bowed.

"Woman, I'd plumb gave you up," he said, his face breaking into dry cracks of relief.

"I'll tend to you later," retorted Aunt Anna. She stood, jerk-
ing her head at him, smiling beautifully.

The men fidgeted, impatient. Leon thanked Phillip for taking such care of his family. His. Phillip's face tightened under
the tan. He hated to leave her, she knew that. Still, the sooner
he went, the sooner. . . . He left quickly, not looking back.
She and Aunt Anna dragged the children to the bedroom, the
growling voices broke out anew.

"Stop shaking, Ellen, don't cry, Henry. Here, put your arms
around Mama, we're all safe together and there's no harm."
They pressed against her, buried their heads, Stevie too, half-
asleep already, and she smoothed their hair, lulled them,
kneaded their tight little backs with a knowing touch. "There,
now to bed with you." She helped with shoelaces and buttons,
turned back the big bed, and gave them to sleep with a full

heart. Had she ever loved them more than now, dilated with feeling, sharing her womanhood with them.

Aunt Anna had taken Stevie down the back way to the water closet, the child so tired he couldn't walk. Julie picked up the empty clothes, sorted and hung. . . .

"Gypsy, I'm glad you're home. I couldn't face another day without you." Leon startled her. He took her in his arms quickly, stroking her face as if she were Ellen.

"Oh, but Leon. . . ."

"Don't say a word. It was I who said go to Coney in the first place, and I who said stay. I'm glad you missed this miserable summer, but I've missed you, worse than waiting for you to cross the sea. There've been layoffs all through the heat. Straiton and Storm've cut, so has Pohlaski and Upmann and Stachelberg. Stevens is out and old Bagratuni and the Van Huesens. We've had our hands full, and worse coming."

"Leon, you should have written."

"And spoiled the holiday? Look at those youngsters, they're pictures. And you, little mother, you look radiant!"

"I . . . I feel well." She edged away from him just slightly, as if not meaning to. "You should have seen the children eat, Leon."

He drew her back to where she'd been. "I'm glad we have them, I wish we had more. In this crazy world, those children make sense." The noise grew louder. Aunt Anna herded Stevie in and straight to bed.

"What is it, a strike?" Aunt Anna said.

"I don't know, dear. We can't take any more cuts, that's a cinch. We took another this week, that's twice since you went away. And the men out of work, there's never been anything like this, in every industry." He sounded tired, he looked tired. This had been going on all summer.

"What's behind it?" Aunt Anna wanted to know. "What started it?" If he knew, he'd be the smartest Joe in the country, Leon said, but it looked like a national catastrophe. There'd been rumors—hadn't Netta told them? That's why she'd come

206

back, to scurry around investing money, getting everything out of Wall Street and into gold, where she could. Precious little she was able to lay hands on, even with the Tammany crowd to help her. The goldbugs had a strangle hold, that's why manufacturers were dropping wages and firing. Didn't they read the newspapers out there at Coney? The talk about railroads?

"And might well be," exclaimed Aunt Anna, "those thieving Congressmen lining their pockets and safeguarding their bosses. Corrupt as Sodom."

Leon managed a smile. He didn't know how the country had gotten by with these two suffragettes away all summer. He kissed the sleeping children. "Why don't you girls make yourselves a cup of tea?" he said. "You must be tired."

"We *girls* don't seem as tired as you *boys*," sniffed Aunt Anna. "You, just skeddadle, we'll brew you up a good strong mess."

They put on water, hauled out saucers, cups, and spoons. Every least thing in the kitchen had to be washed for dust, those two had been living on grit if you asked Aunt Anna. Leaving two helpless men! It was dog foolish, now she was home to see it. Julie could do as she pleased with Leon, this with a canny look, but she was going to dose Becke good and proper with calomel. She attacked pots and skillets as if the nation depended on it, while Julie automatically made tea. She felt mute.

"And how much longer will our funds hold out?" yelled Eric Stevens. "And when they're gone, what good's the union? Not powder to blow it to pieces!" He yelled so loud, Julie and Aunt Anna stepped quick to see. He'd stretched one arm across the table, his eyes like a madman's. So they paid their dues, stuck together, spilled out a lot of tripe. The union could go hang for all of him!

Grunwald spoke, slowly and sternly. Strike funds had been dissipated, he said, by all the small, spontaneous, unplanned strikes. The most powerful weapon they had, and what did labor do with it? One man got up, walked out, and told the

207

others if they stayed they were scabs. At which remark Stevens grew more frenzied than ever, for he had done just that, started it at Hutchinson's.

Etienne jumped to his feet. "Capitalism treats the unions like conspiracies! We need politics, a cooperative commonwealth!"

"Leave radicalism to the intellectuals," said Becke.

"Socialism won't work, Etienne." This was a new voice, abrupt and bare, it belonged to a well-dressed man who had just raised the globe of the lamp to draw on a cigar. "I tried it, that's where I began," the man said. He was probably Strasser. "But stop and figure. We don't want to control industry, we want to control the labor of industry. Unify your wage earners through a strong trade-union movement, not locals, *nationals,* we're just beginning—what we've done this year with the Cigar Makers, getting in everybody, the poor devils who were excluded. It's a beginning."

"And we'll rot in our graves before there's an end!" screamed Stevens, and someone else shouted he was right. Etienne tried to stand, and someone yelled "radical," grabbed his coat, and tried to pull him down. Stevens flung across the table, both arms flying. Leon put Stevens back hard, then tackled the fellow on Etienne's arm. Julie and Aunt Anna stood together, paralyzed.

"Every cent Etienne earns over the old ten a week goes into union benefits," yelled Leon. "Keep your hands to yourselves! It takes all kinds to make a world, the thing is—stick together. Why be afraid of socialists? I'm a union man myself, no socialist, but they want the same things I do, a dollar an hour and fewer hours!"

Aunt Anna hoisted the kettle and went charging through bedlam. "Hush up, the lot of you, and drink some tea," she snapped. "The idea, turning on each other like Bowery toughs. If it's so serious, you'd better sharpen your wits and spare your tongues."

The men sniffed the boiling tea and stopped shouting. They were dog tired, no wonder they were irritable and gruff. What would happen to the Stevenses, all of them coughing in that drafty back flat? What would happen if Leon. . . . Julie climbed on a kitchen chair, fingered, reached, and brought down the old sugar bowl with its cracked top, wiped it on her apron, and lifted the lid. All there, silver coins and a bill and the gold piece Aunt Mathilda had sent two years ago, every cent.

"Poor Gypsy, counting your pennies?" Leon surprised her again.

"You're not supposed to know they're there," she said weakly, her lips too tremulous to form the words.

"Julie, I want to ask you something. Do I make sense? Am I telling them right? They put stock in me and suppose I'm wrong?"

"You tell them what you believe," she whispered. "That's all you can do."

It seemed to comfort him. He went back to the men. They were talking sensibly now. Plain to see they were going to keep it up all night, Aunt Anna said. Whatever their interest in mankind, they certainly weren't giving two pins for where a couple of worn-out women laid their bones.

"Aunt Anna, you must be exhausted, forgive me, I hadn't thought. . . ."

"No tireder than anyone else up since five and the liver jolted out of 'em on that rattletrap boat."

Julie wouldn't let her go home. They undressed by candle-light, took down their hair, sponged their faces and arms and lay across the bed where the children were already deep in sleep. Julie rolled Ellen toward the center, tucked Aunt Anna in with a sheet, and lay herself at the foot with a shawl over her. It was good to be free of stays. The room was stuffy. In the crowded, humid dark she had a rush of longing for the sea, not as if she had sailed on it this very day, but as for something out of childhood, a fringe of memory. Phillip!

14

And life went on, not her own life, not she, Julie, but a succession of days and nights while fear rose, shooing all the bright dreams into a heap. Everywhere in the streets were piles of brown crumbles, the small blaze and surge of smoke. The sweeps made their rounds calling, "Sweepho!" The glass put'een man changed from his linen coat to his frieze, and little business he or the sweeps did, each house hoarding against a day when no more would come in. They knew. A third of the tenants on that block hadn't paid the month's rent, or the month's before. Everyone knew and wondered what stand landlords would take.

At night, waiting for the men to come from their endless meetings, Julie could hear the tense hush, tightly scored with nerves as if no one in the city slept but lay, tightening their girth against hunger, an entire population separated by doors and walls but not separate, edged and naked together with waiting. Leon and Becke were still on, but the streets were crowded with men who were not. Materials were at hand, Leon said, so were mechanical means of production, but factory doors were shut and barred because the men who could give the work were waiting, too, frightened and holding onto what they had. Why wouldn't they be frightened with the collapse of the Northern Pacific, the ruin of the firm of Jay Cooke? Leon's logic and strength were tonic. They cut their own table to the bone and shared every week with those they could. He was worried, too, but he kept the worry inside their four walls, no need to parade that. A dubious enough buzz filled the streets, men standing in huddles moving their anxious mouths.

Julie and Aunt Anna walked arm in arm for greater warmth. "I swan, you're shivering," Aunt Anna would say; and she was, wind perforated her clothing, swift, stealthy as through a sieve. Only a little while ago she had been walking by the sea, only a little while. No use to think of that, just keep going, as Leon did, day by day, hoping for the best.

One morning as they turned the corner into Eighth, they bumped abruptly into a crowd jamming the pavement. Two policemen walked up and down telling the people to stand back. Julie grasped Stevie from behind. Men and women were leaning from windows, they came rushing in shirt sleeves and aprons. It looked like—oh, but it couldn't be an eviction, if one landlord started it, only think! In this damp weather! They hurried around until they stood facing the house, facing the lane the police kept open. There on the pavement was the Stevens' big dresser, the round table, the chair Mrs. Stevens was so particular about, looking worn and wretched.

"Stand back, young woman, stand back here," a policeman said, thrusting out his arm. Julie and Aunt Anna retreated into the throng, but in front, where they could see. Two burly workmen came through the door with a stove, a bowl, and a water pitcher. As they came, the pitcher fell, cracked, and smashed on down the stairs. Out ran a woman, half demented, to catch the fragments. She pounced on the handle which was still whole but which belonged now to nothing, she waved it frantically, trying to stop the thick-shouldered man as he went back to the building. "You can't do it, you can't!" she shrilled in a nasal voice. Mrs. Stevens! The torn hair and crazed face were totally unfamiliar, but the voice was there. "You can't, you can't!" She hung to his arm. As he plowed up the steps, she was dragged along.

Worse than a nightmare. Aunt Anna was breathing hard. All around them people were breathing hard. Then the big shoulders reappeared and the man backed down, carrying one end of the bed. Deborah was in it, you could hear her crying and coughing even before you saw. . . . Mrs. Stevens rushed from behind, threw herself on the man carrying the head of the bed, the Stevens children were screaming, Deborah shook with cold and with her cries, and the oldest

Stevens boy grabbed the arm of the moving man and bit it. Only an instant! Before the blood came, a policeman collared the boy and started clubbing him over the head. His knees promptly buckled. Stiff with terror, Julie shoved Stevie at Aunt Anna and ran straight out of the crowd. She yanked the limp Stevens boy away from the policeman's club, whirled him behind her back.

"He's a child. Aren't you ashamed, hitting a child!" There was a murmur rising. The policeman's chin was on a level with her eyes, red and angry and thick fleshed as beef. "Putting people on the street with rain coming. The girl is ill, she can die!"

"You dirty bastards, why don't you see justice done?" hollered someone. The big chin was wobbling with rage. His uniform swung and lunged into the crowd. People yelled and surged on the pavement, there were screams and a sickening thud. Not knowing what she did, Julie ran to the moving man who still stood leaning against the bed, nursing his arm.

"For God's sake, take her back. Don't leave that girl in the damp," she said. He rubbed his arm where the boy had bitten it.

"Don't like this job no better'n you," he said. "Mine have to eat, too."

"Stop crying, Deborah, it makes you cough."

"Now, look here, lady!" The same chin. The policeman shook her roughly by the arm. "This ain't your business and I'd advise you not to disturb the peace."

Aunt Anna was there in a flash. "Take your hands off her! She's breaking no law and if there's talk of disturbing the peace, I'd say you've taken care of that good and proper! You, Deborah, keep still before you work into a fit."

The policeman stared down at them. Aunt Anna's hat was over one ear and she waved the dumfounded Stevie like a club. Mrs. Stevens threw herself on all of them, on the policeman, on Aunt Anna, on Julie, sobbing and wailing. The men carried the last of the furniture to the edge of the street, dumped it down, and left.

"Now break it up," yelled the other officer, and the one with the chin barked yes, break it up in one damned hurry or he'd run them in.

Julie tugged at his coat, she tugged hard before he felt it. "Listen. You don't want these people left here on the street. You don't want that girl to die of pneumonia and have it your fault. Give us a few minutes, just a few, we'll get them cleared away. You'll all help, won't you?" She walked back and forth in the lane between the crowd. She and Aunt Anna would take the Stevenses until they could find a place. Some of the men could carry Deborah and the furniture. Certainly they knew they were going to have to help each other.

One man worked his way forward, picked up a table. Several followed him. Finally there was a parade, pots and pans, the stove, the bed with Debbie, slow down Eighth into Avenue A. When they passed Aunt Anna's, she gave the oldest boy the key, he was to take his brothers, go on up and soak his head in cold water. She directed the men with the dresser, the chairs, and china bowl. The rest of the parade marched on. The female Stevenses were going to Julie's. No use thinking where she'd put them or how they'd manage, just try to keep them and their sniffles away from her own children. And Mrs. Stevens with her wailing. She needed some strong tea and physic. They all needed tea and physic. Julie marched them up past the Bagratunis', unlocked her door with a firm twist of the key.

15

"Where's my wife? Where's that suffragist menace to law and order?" shouted Leon. He had to shout, the place was deranged with noise and she came hurrying from the kitchen, her face flushed, her sleeves rolled above the elbow, for

Grandma Stodel's old preserving kettle was the only thing big enough to cook that stew.

"How did you know?" she cried, trying to wade across the room.

"Why, girl, the whole East Side knows." Shaking the children off, stepping right over them, Leon caught her about the waist and swung her up.

"I was frightened. If you could have seen him hit the boy, and Deborah screaming."

"She was frightened," roared Leon. "You hear her, Becke? You weren't half as frightened as the policeman. Ollie van Huesen told me."

"Ollie and the rest are worse than a pack of old women," sniffed Aunt Anna. "No wonder they're starving and getting thrown in the street. Not an ounce of spunk."

Becke and Leon nudged each other. "They'll call it hidin' behind a female's skirt," said Becke wryly, "but I can't think of a skirt I'd rather hide behind than Annie's, skimpy as she makes 'em." His eyes fairly flickered with fun. He gave Aunt Anna a whack across her bustle, and then stepped smartly out of reach.

If only he'd been there, Stevens kept saying, if only he'd been there; and Becke said if he had, he'd most likely have opened that fool mouth of his and gotten a policeman's billy smack in the middle of it.

Out in the bedroom, Deborah started to cough, the hard hack pumped through the other noises, there was a strangle and a choke, and Julie ran. Leon was there already, holding the girl's arms and Deborah hung, head forward, the stringy hair shaking like a mop. Aunt Anna had smelling salts Netta had given her for the boat ride; she held the bottle while Julie heated a towel for the girl's chest. Then back to stir the stew, not let a particle stick to the bottom, it was the first decent meal they'd had in a month and it had cost, Lordy, it had cost! She dampened a cloth for Deborah's face, what they needed was camphorated oil and hot lard. Leon said they'd have to try to get the doctor from the Hand in Hand Society. Better

214

off treating her for pneumony themselves, declared Aunt Anna, she'd have it certain before that doctor ever came. Julie glared. Deborah was not going to have pneumonia, all she needed was nourishment and sleep—and air, she added irritably, yanking Ellen away from the bed where she hung, fascinated, breathing in the air Debbie had just breathed out. She hurried Ellen out of the room.

"I want you to keep away from that sickbed," she hissed, her mouth close to the blond braids. "Deborah is ill. If you stay around her, you will be, too."

"Why?" wailed Ellen, and Henry followed, whining. "I don't have to let Stanley play with my boat, do I?" he whined, edging his way between her and whatever she was doing, the stove, the sink, the pantry shelves. "I don't have to let Stanley, do I, Mama?" Until she cuffed him across the back, grabbed the boat Phillip had bought at Coney, and dumped it in the clothespress.

"If I hear one more whine out of you or Stanley, you can both go without dinner. Go down to the water closet this minute, scrub your filthy hands, tuck in your shirt, and be ready." She ground the pepper mill hard over the kettle, but only a few specks flew out. There weren't turnips either, but it would have to do. Deborah and the other Stevens children with fever stayed in the bed drinking hot stew juice without meat in it, but the others crowded around the table, gorged and stuffed the juicy, soft-cooked meat and wilted carrots. They ate like starved ones, the big kettle went down alarmingly; and after all the money she'd spent, hers and Aunt Anna's for the whole week, the stew wouldn't last three nights, not even two!

"Deborah add Alice Bay wadt bore," wailed Mrs. Stevens from the bedroom.

"You hear the lady," Aunt Anna said.

The nerve of it! Mrs. Stevens sitting in the rocker like a dishrag, taking it all for granted, stuffing down her stew without so much as a thank you; what was she to feed them tomorrow, and the day after? She sliced more bread, took it with the soup so the children would have something to sop up with. She tried to smile at Mrs. Stevens, but the woman had no spine to her, she had only that nose like a leaky faucet.

What she couldn't understand, she told Leon, was the police right there watching respectable people being thrown out. That's why they were going to the Mayor, Leon said, to ask him to prevent evictions of the unemployed, put those men to work on public projects. Aunt Anna could see that in her mind's eye, Hall and Hoffman digging down in their jeans for public projects. Stevens began to grow rash again. He had eaten ravenously, more than Leon or Becke, now he tossed his arms and yelled they should march on the City Hall with clubs! Futile, crazy talk, Leon said, they'd do it right, the Mayor and the Governor couldn't turn them away. Julie looked at her fork and put it down. Not a bite, she couldn't eat a bite.

Just then someone rapped. George and Phillip, lugging heavy brown-paper parcels. Such excitement, even Mrs. Stevens came to see the beef and pork and sausage, pounds and pounds and pounds. Everyone talked at once, telling the story, how the Stevenses had been put out and how Julie. . . .

"I've always said you should be an actress, darling, can't you imagine the scene, George, when she walked up to the bully and shook her fist?" Phillip's tone was light, but he touched her with a look so palpate that every drop of blood drained to a quick sensual core. He and George drank Aunt Anna's coffee, chatted with the Stevenses as if their cluttered presence were most natural and welcome. Mrs. Stevens smiled in her silly way and apologized for looking dowdy. Who'd have expected such fine company, she said.

How Julie longed to talk with Phillip! She saw him watching every move, waiting for the moment, gauging it. When she excused herself to take a piece of the beef to Mrs. Bagratuni, he insisted on carrying the platter. His hands were nervous. Out through the swarm of children into the dank hall, she descended the stairs, sensing him behind her every step. She heard the platter set down, the next instant Phillip took her and turned her to him. He found her mouth and held her, the two of them bone to bone, warm and wedded. Phillip so fused her to him, she had no need for her own feet. He cradled her head tenderly and the tears started, without a sob they rushed over her face like hot blood.

"Darling, for God's sake, let me get you out of this. Let me take you and the children to Indianapolis, tonight."

She let him kiss her, she answered him again and again before whispering, "Not now, Phillip. How could I, now?"

"You're killing yourself, Julie. For what, for a miserable existence, when the whole world lies before us. Beauty. . . ."

"Oh, Phillip," she sobbed, "this *is* the world. Look what's happening to it."

"You have to think of yourself, darling."

"I'm one of a million selves with children who are hungry." She held him off. "There's work to be done. We should pool everything, we ought to sink the last cent the union has for food, feed everyone in the neighborhood, at least bread and soup before they're dead."

"Julie, Julie." He touched her, he tried to change her with his hands.

16

To cook for any number, they needed a place—empty store or flat or basement—and that wasn't easy. Landlords had troubles of their own, with rents not coming in. People were starving. Winter moved in cruelly before they finally did get a basement on Eighth. Julie and Aunt Anna and Mrs. Wholbein, holding back skirts and petticoats, felt their way down the dark, smelly steps with the precious key. The stairs were slimy, but no matter about that, the door all but rusted shut. When they forced it with their combined weight, out rushed an overwhelming draft of sewer gas and rot. They kept the door open. Aunt Anna had brought matches and a candle. She lit it gingerly, and they stood aghast, staring at the filth. Mrs. Stevens trailed in, holding her nose.

"Soub kitched! Oh, by God, a soub kitched," she shrilled, breaking into silly streams of laughter. It struck her so funny, she had to bend over and pound the floor with her foot.

"Poppycock," Julie said, brushing past her. Hadn't she walked all the way to Madison Square in the bitter cold to beg the landlady for this very place? Hadn't the men scoured the neighborhood for weeks before that, seeking out landlord after landlord while they collected their census on unemployment, the frightening ciphers that spelled hunger and need? Unemployment had grown by the day, men were too weak for food to seek work. The city did nothing. The International, which might have represented all working people, was divided by warring factions. Leon's report to the Mayor would take time and the whole East Side could starve. Let Mrs. Stevens laugh! She went for Mr. Bagratuni and Ollie van Huesen, brought them and half a dozen more, and got them to work unboarding windows.

The men brought strong soap, what they thought was an ample supply and then twice as much. They brought lye, and four or five women at a time got to their knees on the foul floor. Women left their work, left their children with some old grandma, and rolled up their sleeves. Mr. Wholbein came, shame-faced and meek, to ask if he might help. He lifted a tentative eye toward Julie, "Missy," he called her, and Missy put him with two men she'd never seen before whitewashing walls with lime and water. Mr. Bagratuni was in charge of traps. He got poison somewhere and killed off the rats. Aram and Henry climbed up to clean the windows, so that by the third day, the place was fit to be seen. Everyone volunteered. Men out of work were glad to handle scrub brushes and lye, carry stoves on their backs, stagger downstairs with kettles and wash tubs and lamps. What they were to use for kerosene and fuel was another matter. Phillip would have to take care of that.

218

The shopping she did at Washington Market, dried peas by the sack, onions, flour, and meat bones to season the soup. The glass put'een man loaned his cart, he went along with her and Mr. Bagratuni, both men standing back while she bargained with the money from the Council. They made fun of her haggling, were ashamed, then awed, but every penny had to stretch. Salt, yeast, lard, it was all they could do to pile the load on the glass man's cart and trundle it back through the streets. At Broadway one of the squad helped them, walked out into the traffic with raised arm, and said Julie must have some family.

Then came the cooking. The women could work in crews, six to ten, ten to one, and on until eight at night. There was no lack of volunteers here either, those you'd never have expected—Mrs. Grunwald's crippled sister, Etienne's mother who had spent her life complaining. "You've got 'em buffaloed," laughed Aunt Anna. Old Mrs. van Huesen brought her iron pots, her prized possessions, others brought theirs, some of them none too clean; but they were boiled out with lye, the dish towels, too. Even Mrs. Stevens worked. Julie hadn't wanted her sneezing around the food, but within a few weeks everyone had colds so what did it matter?

It was partly the lack of clothes, everything substantial disappearing, heavy overcoats, mantles; old-clothes hawks hovered like vultures. The women huddled into the steamy basement in their thin shawls, faces flushed with fever, to serve the other fevered people who came flocking the minute they heard. . . . It was unbelievable how fast they heard and how many were hungry. They were standing in line before the first batch was cooked up, and from then on they kept pressing together on the basement stairs and out for a block at mealtimes. Wonder was they didn't lose their appetites, for not lime nor even charcoal quenched the damp, strong kidney smell on those stairs. They didn't mind. They stood patiently with bowls, cups, and pots. Some took the soup home, others ate it at once, now and again a person would snatch at the bowl while soup was being ladled, get his fingers

219

in the thick stream, cry out, and suck his filthy, scalded hands. Some few gagged and vomited at the first swallow. The mess must be cleaned while others stood about, eating without pause.

Julie had to keep reminding herself that these were unfortunate, hungry people, no different from her own. Leon helped her. He told how hard it had been for him at first in the labor movement to accept men whose manners were gross. He'd been used to spruceness in habit and thought, but you couldn't make people over, you had to look down through the coarse outside and see the basic humanity each one had. Christ hadn't let a man's table manners divert Him, had He? Well, she was doing a great job. While the rest talked, she'd shown the whole of New York how to feed its poor. A dozen soup kitchens were under way, that was her doing, she'd done the work of ten men, was still doing it, he begged her to work shorter hours. But she couldn't, how could she when the hungry crowd increased as it did every day? No, it wasn't their fault if they spilled and dribbled and dragged slop in from the wet streets. Their hands and feet were numb, the weather was against them. When the freeze thawed, there was snow, fluffed and white for a day, then an obscene, sodden mass, blotted with rank orange spittle and manure. It thawed, froze over, and the streets were dangerous. Once, in his hurry, a man slipped and came sprawling into the basement, his head at a deformed angle on the nasty floor. Sirak and Ollie had work finding a blanket to carry him away. He'd have to hurry, Ollie said, his wife's pains had started and he was afraid to leave her.

Julie and Aunt Anna pursed their lips. It was too early for Ollie's wife, a buxom girl with hair like Emma's but with flaccid, unhealthy flesh. She'd been unwell the whole time. Right after Ollie lost his work, she had fallen a flight of stairs, fallen on purpose if you asked Aunt Anna, and a piece of tom foolishness, for it did no good and might have killed the child. Julie shifted from one weary foot to the other, stirring the iron pot. If Ollie's wife could feed the baby, well and good, but what if she had no milk? And by the size of her it might be twins!

As soon as Mrs. Grunwald and her sister came, Julie and Aunt Anna hung their aprons, put shawls over their heads, and worked their way through the choked doorway, up the stairs into the harsh air, a weird yellow twilight fuming with unshed snow. The swollen sky pressed on roof tops and spires, advertising placards changed color in the jaundiced light. One's bones ached after the long hours on the concrete floor. It was an effort to walk straight and nod to the line of waiting people bunched together for warmth. A policeman was on hand to keep order, but there was no order to keep. No one talked, the breath had been frozen out of them, you could see it, suspended and colorless as smoke. It was the policeman with the meaty jaw, his face exploded with color that raced out to the ends of his whiskers, but Julie wasn't afraid of him any more.

"What is it today?" he said. "Peas, beans, or old shoes?" He always said the same, and some days the soup was pretty thin. They thickened it with flour and put in salt until more money could be scraped together and they could buy peas again; but thick or thin, the policeman always shoved down the steps for a bowl of it.

The Van Huesens lived two doors away. Julie and Aunt Anna hadn't climbed to the landing when they heard a brutal scream. The door was open, the place swelled with steam. On the bed, Ollie's wife twisted so it was all he and Dyke's wife and old Mrs. van Huesen could do to hold her. She threw herself from side to side, her plump face caved in like dough, her blatant shrieks pierced the ears. Julie held cold compresses to the woman's head. She sent Ollie to the street with buckets for more water, while old Mrs. van Huesen and Aunt Anna said, "Bear down, push." Julie knotted stockings, tied them to the bed, making a rope to pull on, but the poor thing rolled so they couldn't hold her. She'd free her hands and beat her stomach with both fists. Dyke's wife collapsed, crying.

Julie ran back to the street, seized the policeman, and pulled him toward the house. He kept saying he couldn't, he had to walk his beat, but he'd eaten their soup and he could just help them when need be. Once there, he took off his coat and held the woman down strongly, his face redder than ever under his bowler hat. He didn't like the look of it: Ollie's wife was sweating heavily, the room soured with the heft of it, she had lost all semblance of sanity, and no trace of the baby. Julie went for the doctor. He lived on Ninth near Avenue C, and the streets were slippery. When she got there, he wasn't home. His wife said he was run to death, she was sorry he had ever signed on with the Hand in Hand; as for Ollie's wife, plenty of women gave birth without doctors. She didn't wait to hear the end of that, she was hurrying toward Broadway, to Dr. Wentworth, clumping and sliding over the cobbles. Block after block, so cold her ears and nose first tingled, then disappeared, her feet were like things of wood, hurting relentlessly. A stiff-faced man marched toward her, carrying this wisdom on a stick, "Do you love your baby? Then give it Moggs' Mixture." Do you love . . . she was sobbing for breath.

It looked as though she needed attention herself, Dr. Wentworth said when he opened the door. He took hold of her wrist but she flung him off, he was to come this minute, Mrs. van Huesen was dying! He narrowed his skinny mouth. Had they money? He'd get his money, she retorted, they had union benefits and he'd get paid. Still the man wouldn't budge, he'd have to be paid in advance, he knew all about union benefits, he'd delivered union babies before, and he smiled like a fawning undertaker. Julie clenched her teeth. "Get your coat! You'll be paid. I'll pay you myself, same as for Stevie, but come this instant!" She drove the man into his coat and back over the slippery streets. You could hear Ollie's wife a block off.

"Mrs. Dekker," yelled Aram. He came running drunkenly, and clutched her skirt. "Ma says come. Debbie's took bad."

She sent the doctor on to the Van Huesens, turned and made

her way home with Aram. She kept her hand on his shoulder, moving as fast as her numbed feet would go.

"She's bloody," Aram whispered. "Bloody."

"You stay here at your own house, Aram. Play with the children and keep them quiet." She took the last stairs shivering worse than she had on the street. Mrs. Bagratuni was trying to stop the blood that gushed like a fountain, soaking everything, dyeing the cloths she held to Debbie's mouth with a sickening, bright-red splash.

"Hello, Debbie, don't be frightened," Julie said. "Come, we'll sit you up a little higher." They raised and kept her as cool as they could while the hemorrhage poured and welled and soaked them. They worked together quickly, knowing it was useless. Julie could hear her own voice talking and talking, she held the child with her own blood-slippery hands and tried to give her strength. She hung on as long as she could, she tried to help Mrs. Bagratuni clean up; when she fell, it must have been right across the dead girl's bed.

17

She lay in the dusk of a strange room, fevered and weak, so lost to life she thought she was a child again. There were thin gold hairs on the window blind, the days quavered, eased together in an endless surge of heaviness and lightness, nausea and dreams. There was the cold spoon, the oily, thick, medicinal smell, she even scolded Beatrice, pushed her hand away, raving in the fashion Papa called unruly. But it was always Annie, not Beatrice, Netta's Annie with her patient nun's face, hovering about the bed, bodiless as a moth. Let Julie shove her off and rave when she tied a hot onion to her ear, or, thinking it was Mother, cling to her and plead that she stay, never leave her—it was always Annie. She begged for Grandpa. Certainly if she were sick, if she were going to die as Dr. Potter thought, Grandpa would come from Holland.

Then the pressure began to sheer off. She was alone, light, aerial, and free as one of the fairies swinging from a wire in the Punch and Judy. She could open her eyes and keep them open, recognizing the panels of Annie's room, fine-combed as molten honey, the sewing box, the two engravings of Ireland, the gold-handled comb and brush which seemed obscene in this chaste cell. They made one smile, these brazen crested gifts from Netta on the boards of Annie's dresser, they never belonged. This was a selfless room. Perhaps the very anonymity, the four monastic walls without a garment, made it possible for one's self to move back into its normal place, only stronger, with more determination and grit. There was daylight again and the rigid, carefully pronounced scales of the piano player next door. There was Phillip.

She didn't even wonder how he could be away from the theater, how he could be so constantly beside her, stroking her temples, touching the hollowed pulse in her bent arm so she might fall asleep. He read from his books and she watched minutely to memorize, having almost lost him, the sharp nose, the crisp, fine hair that lengthened out his chin. There was a fresh look in Phillip's face, he laughed sometimes like a boy; his flesh was tuned to hers, he knew when to turn the pillow, when to smooth her hair. Half-asleep, she'd catch the soft, liquid entrance of his mouth.

How precious life was after illness, the bits of vivacity, each small, bright, animate thing—Annie polishing her garish hairbrush, Netta sweeping in like a burst of trumpets, her plumes teasing the bare walls, the flash of her striped hosiery. The children came, Henry thinned like a string bean and shy, all of them shy as if they didn't recognize Mama without her black dress. Leon came. She understood him better now than she ever had since he'd become a part of the labor movement. He wasn't impersonal, he wasn't invincible, he was a live man trying to live in the world where he found himself; she knew, she'd had her brush with reality, too. The self was effaced in

224

times of crisis but not obliterated, it was still there underneath the day's necessity, clamoring for warmth and love. Far from knowing nothing about Phillip, as she had thought before, she now felt he knew all about Phillip and was watching her with a questioning, pleading look as if to say, "Are you ever coming back to me, Julie? To be my *wife?*" That she was not quite ready to discuss. She plied him with questions, rather, about the outside world. How was the soup kitchen going? Was Mrs. Stevens doing her part? In one of the journals, there'd been a reference to rioting in Tompkins Square. Well, Leon?

He tried to pass it off lightly. Just a mass meeting which the police had decided to attend and Etienne was still in jail; but then, you knew Etienne, he was enjoying the "Bastille," the city'd be lucky if he didn't convert the warden. But how had it started? She wormed out the details, how first a permit had been granted, then reneged, how Laurrell had gone from house to house warning the people. Even Laurrell couldn't stop a move with such momentum behind it. The Safety Committee simply dispersed so the authorities couldn't find them to revoke the permit, and workers crowded the drill ground. Their group had carried the old banner—*Tenth Ward Union Labor.* The police charged them as they entered the square. Men, women, and children. Mounted police sent night sticks flying, and they didn't stop at the square, either. They rode down Avenue A and over the whole neighborhood bashing skulls; another force charged from St. Mark's. Mrs. Grunwald's sister and Becke and Sirak—Leon caught himself—they weren't badly hurt, and Sammy Gompers missed a clubbing when he jumped down the cellarway into the soup stand.

All so wrong, so unnecessary and cruel that long after Leon had left, she started crying and couldn't stop. Phillip tried to calm her while Annie sent for the doctor, the one with brown whiskers. He wasn't sympathetic when he came. This patient was to be kept quiet, not inflamed by anarchist propaganda. You could tell what newspapers he read! She stopped crying abruptly, told him how her friends had been clubbed for nothing, for holding a meeting to ask for help—poor, half-starved people. Becke still couldn't straighten up from a blow across the back, and Sirak was trying to support eight people with a broken arm. She couldn't trust herself to mention Mrs. Grunwald's crippled sister. It was not revolutionary agitation, people were out of work, they were turned into the street, and something must be done! The doctor listened impatiently, wrote out a prescription for sleeping powders, and went away with his ugly, arrogant beard. He'd check the facts about Tompkins Square for himself.

"Phillip, I want to go out. I've been in too long. Please, Phillip, don't say we'll ask the doctor. I've seen enough of him."

So Phillip carried her, the next day, down to the carriage. Annie tucked her in with a thin shawl and a bottle of smelling salts and waved cheerily from the curb.

"Smell it," Phillip said. "Smell the summer, darling." How much time she had lost! Part of winter, all of spring, every awning was flaunting its red or blue or green against a piercing sun. Phillip took Broadway, turned off at City Hall and across to South Street into the warm, redolent day beside the sea. Big ships rode lazily up and down, their bowsprits pointing into the countinghouse windows. Phillip drew up at the bottom of Beekman, jumped down with a jaunty air, and came around for her. Slowly they walked, close together, along the waterfront, completely attuned, catching the idle, lazy motion of the ships, smelling the sweet pine shavings and the gummy, penetrating scents of tar and turpentine. Even the wagons trundled slowly, spray flew, the air barely stirred, flags hung. Under their little umbrellas, street vendors wrapped sandwiches and called their wares. "Ravioli, ravioli!" One dark man fished meat up out of the smoking pot, rolled it deftly in the damp dough. As fast as he could make them, his small sons stuffed the sandwiches into their mouths. "You're never going to get rich," Phillip laughed, and the brown man laughed, too, showing his coarse, even teeth. It made one's mouth water to smell the spice. They stood beside the pot while the man rolled two more and handed them over wrapped in bits of paper. Aunt Anna would have fainted to see her eat such a thing, but with Phillip she could eat anything. They walked along munching the hot meat and dough as if they were famished. "God, darling, to see you eat!" Phillip said.

Near the Fulton Ferry, a neat fellow in bowler hat was standing with a handful of cards. He bowed elaborately, presenting his gaudy announcement—the *Dreadnought* was now loading for San Francisco and would leave in about three weeks. Phillip asked what the passenger facilities were, what accommodations for those traveling with children? Then they wandered on, found an empty loading platform and sat on the warm rail, Phillip still studying the multicolor notice for the *Dreadnought*.

"We'll go to San Francisco, as soon as you come back from Indianapolis, Julie. We'll take the children and start out like explorers. Just look at the coast line beckoning! I want to take you by the hand and follow that without regard for time or space. I want to go where we can have a simple, clean life. I want to make love to you out of doors under the sun." He took her hand and pulled the glove off, pressed the fingers to his lips. It was so good to have Phillip touch her, so moving. If only it could be the first time, all the rest lying ahead. She had all she could do not to turn and put her mouth to his.

"And what a chance to write my play," he said. "On shipboard, rounding the Cape. Think of it!" He was serious, completely serious, and carried away as if he were already nine days out on the voyage. Still dreaming of that play. The day was growing foggy now. First a thin mist, then great rolls of it drowned out the sun. Rain hung in the air unshed, afraid to spend itself, the pale gray sky stretched tenderly to gather up the sea. Flies buzzed.

There was so much to tell Phillip, so much he should know, now. She wanted to say how she loved him, deeply, with every sense, how hard it was to tear herself away from him. But there was something else. . . . He had shocked her out of the daily doing, the over and over without thought or dimension, he had shocked her into the need for living with a purpose. You knew what you must do, you couldn't run from the

227

life you'd made with its grave obligations, the life she and Leon and the children were part of. What happiness could you achieve with all that guilt? If you did your best with each day, those days could add up to a real significance, there was no other way. Her heart hung heavy as the rain burden, heavy as the surge of the sea. The time had come to tell Phillip.

Part IV

The great hands of the depot clock pointed toward four. The long top spear shuddered upward, jerked, enunciating seconds so you could see time skitter by without a stop; and almost before it found the twelve, a mighty *bong* hurtled from the tower, rolled the whole fifteen stories, drowned out the wagons and din of traffic, shook the hot air to the very cobbles underfoot. Julie and Ellen hurried across Harrison Street. Bong, again and again and again.

"You're running. It's only four, Mother!"

"You, miss, are laced too tight." And of course she was running—to meet Emma and Ludwig after all these years. The echo of the gong eddied like dead thunder, drifted off southwest toward the stockyards. Thank heaven the wind was in the right direction; Emma and Lud wouldn't get the stench full face.

"Mother, my hat!"

"I'm sorry, dear." Now they had gained the curb, she stopped to let the child straighten the little hat Aunt Anna had finished whipping together this morning by candlelight. "What did they say at the store, Ellen, did they like it?"

"Mr. St. Elmo did." Ellen's ears grew pink as the plume. "I happened to pass the accounting office. . . ."

Mr. St. Elmo—and how did you like that for a name? "I suppose he was standing there stroking his whiskers." Julie drew down her mouth and stroked her own cheek until Ellen laughed aloud and they had to hurry to make the door the Parmalee man held open. A mighty breeze caught their bustles, rushed them into the dark, busy caverns of the depot, into a commotion of coming and going, uniformed men shouting, "Chicago Great Western leaving track four, Dubuque, St. Paul, and Minneapolis," like the voice of doom.

"Maud Watkins, at the lace counter, calls it Duba-q," laughed Ellen. They linked arms tightly while a wild rumble descended, bags were trundled by in carts, people rushed in and out. Your heart beat as if Emma and Lud and the young ones were here already, a family again, a whole, great family!

"I don't remember it like this. When we came from New York I mean, Mother."

"Well, you weren't exactly a young lady. You and Henry were worn out. Henry managed to stay on his feet, but Papa carried you, and Aunt Anna and I took turns with Steve."

"We're lucky we didn't have Richard then."

"We're lucky to have him at all." She could feel the blush, the heat rushing just when she wanted to appear neat and cool, every pleat in her starched lace bosom so immaculately pressed against the summer day, and here she was flustering over Richard who had been such a surprise, her surprise baby born Christmas before last when she never thought. . . . Hadn't she dosed with Arend's Kumyss and paregoric thinking it was indigestion? Not knowing, as Leon put it, that she was still "quite a wench." Oh, she'd taken a good deal of joshing with Richard. Aunt Anna said if she was going to keep on counting her blessings, she'd better find a nurse to match, some gamp with young bones who didn't mind racing down Wabash or through the alley. And Leon! He was likely to march in tonight with the baby on his shoulder, saying, "Why, Lud, Gypsy says she wants another dozen before she's through, eh, Gypsy?" He adored that child, as if Richard was proof of how strong and whole they had grown together.

She tugged at the man's arm. He wore a cap with a celluloid badge. When, if he pleased, did the Baltimore and Ohio ar-

230

rive from New York, was it on time, and were the Pullman Palace sleeping cars to front or rear? He paid more heed when he heard how her people were coming, studied his leaden watch, and compared it with the blackboard where a Negro porter was lettering in chalk. On the dot, he said, he'd know which track in ten minutes, madam should keep an eye on him.

That brought it closer. She must ask Emma right off about Fred and Ethelyn. It was plain they were at each other's throats over the way Papa'd left his money, but why should Ethelyn care? Potter had left her rich as royalty. She herself might be the one to care, but if Papa had never mentioned her name or Leon's in all that time, so be it, they didn't want his money. As she had told Aunt Anna time and again, the good and bad braided together, better not to have too much, the ones with money quibbled and hated each other to boot, like Fred and Ethelyn. There was such a lot to talk over with Emma. Letters never said enough. There were things you could *not* say, like the matter of Mr. St. Elmo's intentions, how he sat strumming his mandolin in the summer dark, stroking his sideburns in a way that made you wish Ellen were ten, that she still wore her hair in braids and had never gone to work at Marshall Field's. Nothing was really told in letters, how could you explain about Leon's union with the Amalgamated Assembly this and the Knights of Labor that and the tenement-house cigar makers breaking away to go with the anarchists? How could you even describe Chicago, the raw, teeming look of it, to people who had lived where every stone was aged and old before they were born?

Ellen whispered she would like to visit the rest room, Cissy Lindquist said the wash basins were of genuine marble! Into thick, perfumed disinfectant—Julie sat absently on a settee while Ellen removed her gloves before a marble stand. Emma and Ludwig's house did have a bathroom, that was one thing, and better plumbing then any in Arnheim, but would Emma think Wabash Avenue fine enough, wouldn't she be sick not living on Prairie or up along the north shore, no matter if Lud-

231

wig did say he wanted to live right next to them, no farther than across the street? The new house was ready down to the last starched curtain, the wrought-steel range was the best in town. Still, Emma had been one for elegance; that didn't change, fourteen or forty, and when she didn't get what she wanted, she'd pout. That was Emma, and right now in the glass, Ellen's face was so exactly the same! Ellen had removed her hat and couldn't get it back on. The blond chignon bounced precariously, and Ellen frowned into the glass with Emma's old pout.

"Here, dear, let me help." There wasn't a girl to compare with Ellen, Emma would see, and it was going to mean so much for Ellen—theaters and concerts they could never have afforded, girl cousins to whisper with, and parties, and young men who would put Mr. St. Elmo and his sideburns to shame.

"Baltimore and Ohio!" The shocking news bellowed and snored as through a tunnel.

"Mama, hurry! Don't you hear?"

But she had caught sight of herself in the mirror, and how would she look to Emma? There had been that other mirror, Emma with blue flowers and herself with pink. . . .

"Yes, yes, Ellen." They hurried into the churning crowd, hearing "Baltimore and Ohio, track three," the rumble and distant drum of the train. Her hands were the sad thing, but they were safe inside her gloves. Her hands were so hardened and cracked, and no keeping smooth nails with housework and all the extra sewing they took in. She and Emma used to wear gloves to bed, cotton gloves, with glycerin inside. Beatrice cooked it up especially, and Emma would never tell the secret of how their hands kept so white.

Out in the train shed, a thick chug of smoke rose, volcanic, and there was the glowering yellow eye. "Pullman Palace sleeping cars to the end, ma'am." The conductor bustled by importantly and they toddled after as fast as their high heels would go. The strident monster came rushing, cinders flew, smoke swooped in clouds, then vanished, there were gold-incrusted carriages shuttling by, the glass vestibules where passengers stood, waiting for the train to halt. Was that Emma? No. Nor there. The train ground to a stop. Steam hissed. Passengers were handed out into the nitrogen-exhausted air. Where was Emma?

"You don't think we missed—"

No, no, far down at the end, no doubt of it, they had just stepped out. She broke from Ellen, picked up her skirts, and ran. "Emma, Emma!" Far off Emma heard, picked up her skirts, and started. Julie ran like a wild thing, crying, flung both arms about Emma's neck, and they kissed each other, hugged each other, Emma's arms so strong and real they made your hat slide off. Ludwig had her now, fast against his whiskers. How was that scoundrel Leon? And behind Lud, the children—tall, handsome blond boys and girls, embracing her own Ellen, who blushed under the little plume and who was, yes, even if her clothes weren't so fashionable, prettiest of them all.

"Auntie!" The one who should have been Elsa was Pauline. Elsa was the shorter, plumper one in blue taffeta, with, now you came to notice, the same violet baby eyes, but an unexpectedly broad mouth and firm chin, Elsa who had been like her own baby. What a time they had, what a chaos of questions no one had a chance to answer, the children rattling away in Dutch, catching themselves and trying again in very English English. "Couldn't Uncle Leon come?" "How is Uncle Leon?" "Where are the little lads?" Pauline was like Emma in the old days. Tilda was different—small, dark, a miniature Aunt Mathilda with bird-bright eyes.

"You're like your pictures, Aunt Emma, I'd have known you anywhere," Ellen said, as they stood in the sun waiting for carriages. It made you narrow your eyes and wish Leon were here for confirmation. Certainly the Stodel hair was still bright, only darker, richer, like ripe corn, and the teeth were white and hard as ever with their tiny ridges; but some shyness confused the issue, as if, at close range these were not her people but strangers embraced by mistake. The accent was strange. Emma seemed limp and listless now the meeting

233

was over, she leaned on Pieter; and let them say what they wanted, it wasn't so bad to be thin, not skinny, either, the way she'd filled out with Richard. Emma's skin had changed, too, but whose wouldn't in so many. . . .

"You haven't changed, Julie. How do you keep such a small bundle of bones together?" Ludwig hugged her as if she were a child.

"She never walks, she runs," said Ellen.

"Not me, Julie, not when you're with me," drawled Emma. "Tell me, how is Aunt Anna?"

"Wonderful, isn't she Ellen? Full of spunk."

"She must be seventy-five. Maybe more. And the drinking water, Julie. On the train I met a doctor's wife. . . ."

The young man with slender hands, the one talking to Ellen, would be Dirk, Jack Stodel's oldest boy who was going up as a doctor. "There's so much to tell you, Emma, about the house."

"Don't worry about the house," Lud said. "We just need four walls and plenty to eat!"

How the children laughed. They stopped talking and burst into a big Dekker laugh, even Tilda, even young Louis Stodel who hid like an imp behind tall Dirk. So familiar, so reassuring, that laugh, just like Leon's. How good it would be for Ellen, for Henry, Steve, and the baby to have a family as she had had when she was little. What holidays there'd be, with Christmas trees in both houses and food for an army.

"How about help, Julie? We'll want a cook and one servant, anyhow." There was the old Emma pout, the pink mouth under the elegant satin hat, the blue eyes that held yours hard, then shifted one iota to the side and back.

"We'll find you help, Aunt Em. Irish girls strong enough to lift up a dining-room table." Pieter nudged Dirk. Who'd be strong enough to lift the Irish girls?

"Ellen's to sit beside me," declared Elsa. "And beside me," Pauline said. Dirk handed them in and got up next himself. "Out of my way, son," Pieter told Louis, and Louis said who cared, he was going with the baggage. Tilda accompanied the

234

grownups, much more sober and sedate than Julie and Emma, who kept turning to watch the young people, the flaxen-haired, blue-eyed lot in the second carriage.

"The Stodel boys are so like your own children, I'd not be able to tell them apart."

"Not so much alike," said Emma with a knowing look.

"All right, Em, let it be," said Ludwig quickly.

But he couldn't stop Emma. "Nothing's been said yet, but that Dirk is crazy for my Elsa."

In the other carriage, Dirk was leaning forward and Ellen was answering delightedly, one deep dimple showing in her cheek. Julie flushed, she looked away quickly, right into Tilda's sharp eyes. Images of Aunt Mathilda blinked on and off like magic-lantern slides, leaving a soft, wounded place in Julie's heart. It was having her own people again, that's what it was.

2

They slipped quickly and easily into each other's lives—almost as one had dreamed. The children surged back and forth across Wabash from house to house, kicking up volcanoes of summer dust and wading, when autumn came, through muddy ruts so there was never a shoelace among them free from the gummy mass. Henry, Steve, and Louis Stodel skated and found odd jobs and carted each other off to school. Tilda attached herself to Aunt Anna, following the old lady so close she all but trod her heels.

"I swear, Aunt Anna's bewitched Tilly," Emma would say. "I don't know how. I never could make head or tail of the child, like a chicken with a duck egg."

At night the youngsters worked their sums, pestering Pieter for help while Dirk pored over his medical books and the girls chattered, pricked at embroidery frames, and fixed each

235

other's hair. They had made a little queen of Ellen. Elsa was teaching her to play the piano, Emma took charge of her clothes, the boys showed her every gallantry. She was helping Dirk with his English, she had the brains of the family, Lud said; but Ellen scarcely heard, sitting beside Dirk in a pool of lamplight, helping to translate the long sentences about vaccine. There were concerts and plays. Lud did business with prosperous merchants, and Ellen was invited to parties on the north shore with the rest. When her friends came from Field's, when Mr. St. Elmo came, there were marshmallow roasts and corn popping and such singing the Beerenbroecks and the O'Reillys opened their windows to hear.

Leon was in his glory. "This is something like, eh, girl?" Full of life! He and Ludwig would sit at the head of the table, their chairs touching, while the nights flowed backward, linking onto suppers of the past. Grandpa had once sat where Pieter sat, and Grand-mère there, and she herself next to Grandpa where Tilda sat, her little claws on the table ledge.

"May first, you'll see it, Lud, every union man in the country will walk out for eight hours," Leon would say. "For the first time, all union men working together."

"And they'd have had their eight hours way back if they'd let us women folks in on it. Old Becke used to say there wasn't a copper in New York could stand up to Julie or me, no, nor a Pinkerton man, either." Aunt Anna wagged her old dandelion head while they laughed and Tilda sat, scrutinizing the crinkled profile in a way to have driven anyone else out of countenance.

Ludwig smacked his lips over Julie's quince jam and potato pudding. Em used to cook like that; he doubted she could boil water now. This talk of the robbed class. He was a capitalist, and he'd never robbed anyone. Then he'd grin. Maybe he had overcharged on a diamond, but always to people able to pay and always perfect stones. Men had a right to build their business and take their profit, that's how the world went.

But how about the unemployed? Leon said. This was a time of cutthroat competition, low prices, low profits, a steady pressure on wages. Jobbers played the manufacturers one against the other, workers came streaming in from the old country, and new machines every minute. Unemployment was inevitable, but those out of work were regarded as no-good bums.

"The same Leon," Lud said, "fighting the same as when you came from Java. Always Utopia."

"What a handsome one you were, Leon, coming home in your uniform," Emma sighed.

"I was there," laughed Elsa. "I remember."

"The fanciest christening *I* ever saw. We spoiled you from the first," declared Aunt Anna.

"No Utopia to it," insisted Leon, "just common sense— strengthen the workers' bargaining power, get shorter hours, put more men to work."

"Papa held Elsa at the church, children, or we'd never have gotten her baptized."

"Julie, that's not true, she was a lamb." Emma said it her way, and Leon and Lud, the same memory but varied as through a tipped glass. Now they had been here a while, it was difficult to remember Emma and Ludwig any different, any younger. Emma was wild for Richard. Why her ungrateful girls didn't hurry up, marry, and give her some grandbabies, she didn't know. That was her pet topic, matchmaking. Leon talked his talk, Dirk talked bacteriology.

"Don't let Dirk get started with his bugs," Elsa would say. She never spoke sharply, but Dirk would flinch and Tilda lean forward quick and eager as if there might be a fight. But why? It was interesting to hear how they planned to immunize against disease, the work at Northwestern Medical School and at the hospital where Dirk interned. He believed in his work as Leon believed, that was something good. Most men started well enough, but they curled like touchy leaves at the first blow, you had to have faith and fight in you, and Dirk did, she'd watched him.

"Oh, and Julie, you heartless wretch, you haven't mentioned the man whose life you blighted!" An agony of pause, then Emma said, "You haven't asked for Mr. Munzell."

Blood burst back into her throat and arms, "Oh, Mr. Munzell!"

"He carried us about London, practically on a silver platter, didn't he, Lud? Still pining after twenty years. You needn't color so, Julie, he is. With his success in Parliament, he's had chances galore to marry, and I don't mean your sister Ethelyn."

"Emma, hush." For the children had ceased talking and were licking the gossip up with their apricot rolypoly. Ludwig roared.

"Is it true about Aunt Ethelyn?" whispered Ellen. She looked so lovely, so confused and merry, Dirk must have taken her hand.

"Of course not."

"Ha!" shouted Emma. "Ethelyn married her Potter because she couldn't get your mama's Munzell, and the minute old Potter lay down and died, she started off on the old chase. She'll probably land him this time. Why, she's rigged herself out in St. James and even has Lord Salisbury to tea."

"Minx." Aunt Anna slapped her napkin down. Julie fixed her with a stern eye. This was dangerous ground, it bordered on too many grievances Aunt Anna had stored up against the Dekkers and Corpers, living sassy as kings in the old country, Ethelyn parading in sable and letting her own sister. . . .

"Scheming, selfish minx," muttered Aunt Anna, not to be ruled completely.

"It's wicked to make sport of a good, upright man like Mr. Munzell," murmured Julie, remembering like yesterday how he had taken them to Liverpool, begging to book them passage on another ship. Like yesterday? Sharper and clearer—every word, and the galloping, briny wind—while what happened yesterday was likely to flirt by without a shadow.

"And what about the other, the half-starved genius, McManus?"

"Uncle Phillip!" cried Ellen.

"Phil's done well," Leon said evenly. "He's an important playwright in New York, a sort of American Ibsen."

Emma looked sharp at Julie.

"Why not?" snapped Aunt Anna. "Always had the gift."

The blue eyes twitched sharp now to Aunt Anna, for no mention had been made, never a word in the letters.

"We owe Phil a great deal," Leon said. "Those were tough years in New York. He and Netta Davenport were wonderful to us Dekkers." And he told of the opening of *By Jove,* how they'd gone in style and Aunt Anna made eyes at Barnum, as if that's all there had been to it. Her good Leon.

"So," Emma said later, when they were in the kitchen cleaning up, "you ran into that Irishman again in New York. Hm. Lucky he was tied up with another woman, that one I wouldn't trust."

"Grandpa brought all that silver home from America," Julie told Pauline and Elsa, who were polishing. "See how it came out and balanced? He was stolen away with nothing and came back both hands full."

"You ought to use skin balm, Julie, it's a shame how you ruin yourself. That knife could show more elbow grease, Pauline. Learn now, and you'll know how to care for your own. Elsa's picked her pattern already and you two shall have yours as soon as you find young men. I don't know what ails girls nowadays, no get up or push to 'em. Believe me, I didn't need any coaxing when I met Ludwig Dekker. Did I, Julie?"

Emma's favorite topic again. That was the only thing, the only flaw in all the happiness of being together. Emma kept right on planning a trousseau for Dirk and Elsa when it was plain to see . . . she'd known from the first day when they rode from the station and Emma had said. . . .

"If Dirk and Elsa are so stuck on each other, when are they gonna do something about it?" Aunt Anna asked finally.

"No rushing Elsa," sighed Emma. "I don't see how the boy puts up with it. He's used worse than Julie's Munzell."

"Well, she'd better get him while the gettin's good. He'd not be the first man in history to switch horses."

"Not Dirk," laughed Emma. "I know him through and through. Not that Elsa couldn't do better, a girl with her looks and Lud's money. But, Julie, I set my mind to this. Lud used to say I was forcing nature, like as not, Elsa'd run off with the boatman and Dirk would have our Tilda, when they all grew up." She raised her blue eyes. "I doubt anyone'll have our Tilda."

Emma believed in keeping families together, blood was thicker than water. She said it over and over. Julie would smile at Aunt Anna, for look how close they'd been and no blood between them. Some fountain of recognition picked up two people and held them, everything open and understood. There was nothing that could make it happen, it was there, love instant and cleaved or not at all.

If Emma would only open her eyes, glance this minute into the dining room, she could see for herself, Ellen and Dirk, steeped in love. You caught it the minute they walked into a room, heard their hushed voices, both the same cadence, saw their tender heads bowed together over a book. Dirk called for Ellen every evening at Field's, you even knew when Mr. St. Elmo had walked along to the carline. Sometimes you thought, "It serves Dirk right, let him speak up and put St. Elmo out of it," but that was lost in a flood of gentleness; she was half in love with Dirk herself, frightened and tremulous for Ellen. No one could understand that, not even Aunt Anna, the sense of identification which could make a child separate and yet not separate, a self you loved beyond self. It wasn't at birth, only later, your own heart beating inside the little thing, maybe because Ellen was first. You felt the child looking at Dirk, saw her hand rest on his shoulder or brush his hair in passing. No mistaking this need to touch.

"Dirk will be a great doctor, don't you think, Mother? He's so earnest and skillful. I even like the smell of disinfectant, don't you, Mother?" But *like* was not the word, one grew faint with recognition at the whiff of it.

"Leon, if anything should happen, it would break the

child's heart," she would whisper, grieving at night, in the dark.

"There, there, little mother, it's probably girl-and-boy nonsense," he'd say. But he was worried, too, she knew. Emma and Lud had come a long way to be with them, and Emma counted on Dirk and Elsa. Except for this, it was all as one had dreamed.

3

On hands and knees through the clean, stale smell of starch. The parlor floor was covered with lace curtains pinned down to stretch. Aunt Anna came right behind, and as the pins came from each point of lace, she gathered the stiff rectangle and marched it off to hang. Julie pushed the mean, hard, little pins into the emery ball at her waist and crawled on, the baby crawling after, crowing to be heard a mile.

"Having a party?" Emma said, rustling in from a trip to town. "Didn't invite me."

"Hello, Emma, it's no party. Leon's bringing union men from out of town." She got up from her knees with the last curtain. It was lumpy from mending, but it hung behind the sofa.

"Julie, sit a minute. I swear, you never rest."

But the chandelier had to be done, and Aunt Anna was dragging in the ladder. Julie climbed up, steadied herself, and disengaged the first small dangler. Down it went to Aunt Anna to be dipped in suds, breathed on, and polished. Then she herself breathed on each again, polished it with a chamois, and rehung until the whole cascade of points shimmered and danced. She and Aunt Anna had paid for that by making curtains for every room at the Kuypers'.

"My maid Sheilah should take lessons from you. A lick and a promise, that's her style, and an Irish brogue you can cut with a knife. I got a box for the children for the Thomas concert. Ellen will need another dress. Don't argue, Julie. I know you think I'm extravagant, but when in Rome . . . and these rich Chicago people *dress*. I've got some handsome brocade Aunt Anna can—"

"Aunt Anna, Aunt Anna," mimicked the old lady. "Don't know as she sews elegant enough."

"You do fine when you have a decent pattern. I'll get you one from Mademoiselle Thalia. Now, Julie, when I was at the ticket broker's—the Armours send in their driver, but believe me, I get better by going myself—well, there's a play opens next week, Terry's in it, and guess who wrote . . . you needn't look so surprised, you told me yourself he's a genius. *Many Mansions*, he calls it. What kind of a title is that?"

" 'In my Father's house are many mansions,' maybe you've heard," Aunt Anna said.

Julie climbed down from the ladder and shook her skirt. "Emma, dear, I can't stop and talk right now. May the children bring their books to your house tonight? Mr. Strasser is coming."

"Wouldn't hurt you none to give 'em dinner, too," Aunt Anna said. "Tilda and Louis all but live *here*."

"Aunt Anna!" She hurried to the kitchen to baste her meat. *Many Mansions*, she would have liked to sit down quietly and think about that, but not now, there was much to do, it was an honor to have Mr. Strasser and Mr. Paul Grottkau from Milwaukee. Grottkau had been on a tour east for the eight-hour movement and had seen Sam Gompers at the Federation convention in Washington. Sam was a big man now, organizing all unions into one federation.

"There's no question," Grottkau said, when he came, "the Federation is not yet what we want it to be. The Knights have cut in on us, and how they're growing!"

"Because they take in anyone," Strasser said hotly. She knew why he was angry. He'd been president when the radical cigar makers withdrew to form their own union, and he'd been fighting ever since to get the Progressives, as they called themselves, back into the fold. The trade-union element was coming back, but the anarchists and tenement-house scum would go their own way, why not, he said, with the K of L to back them?

"We have to build the national Federation," Grottkau said in his eloquent voice. "The eight-hour strike will do it!"

"As it stands today, the Federation isn't strong enough to make that strike work," Leon said. "We have five months. I'm for Eight Hour Associations in every city. Get everyone in on it, the Knights, the Socialists, everyone. So far, it's been up to the locals. The Cigar Makers are the only national union to tackle the issue. Locals will get nowhere."

"Right," Grottkau said.

"I've asked George Schillings to come tonight," Leon said. "We've worked together in the city assembly, we've fought the radical Council for a year and a half. He can tell you—the strike won't come off in Chicago unless the Council will come in, too. They're dangerous and they're powerful."

Strasser wanted to know more. They had the same problem in New York, two city union councils and no cooperation. Leon told how his assembly organized a Labor Day parade with Mayor Harrison and Congressman Foran to speak, and what did the Council do but stage a grand march to show them up. Same last week on Thanksgiving. The Council had five thousand marching, a lot of unemployed, a lot more tramps, and in an ugly, threatening mood to rouse the city. "This town has the best brains of the Black International," Leon said. "Men of Parsons' caliber are to be reckoned with. I wish he'd stayed with trade unions, but he's got class struggle like religion, and there's no stopping that. I only hope they come along on the eight-hour deal. We need them even if they do talk too much about homemade bombs."

Strasser and Grottkau had faith in Leon, it made you proud to see. Julie poured more coffee.

"Ask me," Aunt Anna said, "every time you get mixed up with those red-flag wavers or the like, you're in trouble. Those anarchists cry out to Pinkerton clubs like bait to fish, and the next thing, there're broken heads."

243

They didn't laugh at Aunt Anna. They drank their coffee and passed their cups for more. Mr. Schillings came, and they went over plans for an Eight Hour Association for Chicago. The trade unions from the Assembly were in, they'd pledged, and the Socialist Labor party. Schillings had the word of the K of L—for what it was worth, Strasser said. There would have to be careful planning with each group—the carpenters, the furniture makers—to see that the walkout was absolute at every plant. All unions must be circularized. All employers must be given the same agreement to sign, come May first.

There was a commotion outside and boys from the typographical union came thronging in with something they had just printed. The radical Council had had a meeting. Strasser read what they had to say: ". . . notwithstanding that we expect very little from the introduction of the eight-hour day, we firmly promise to assist our more backward brethren in this class struggle, with all means and power at our disposal so long as they will continue to show an open and resolute front to our common oppressors, the aristocratic vagabonds and exploiters. Our war cry is, 'Death to the foes of the human race.'"

"'Our more backward brethren,' they call us!" Everyone talked at once.

"'Death to the foes of the human race'—the capitalist press can pick that up and make a holler."

"Just talk," Leon said. "I know Parsons and Spies and Fielden. They use hot words that give the unemployed a sense of power. It's up to us to see that the May first strike is orderly and peaceful. We can't give the police a chance even to look for trouble, and we won't. But at least they're with us. We have a chance for unanimous action."

Grottkau agreed. The eight-hour move had captured the mass of workingmen; this situation in Chicago proved it. No matter what the rival affiliations, everyone was in it now, even the radicals who set no store by strikes.

"We should have forty thousand out by May first" . . . "if we can trust the Knights" . . . "the more the merrier." The room was filled with smoke, dense murky gauze flowing from wall to wall, hanging from the ceiling like cobweb.

"Always trouble and big times brewing," whispered Aunt Anna. "Old Becke likely eats his heart out in heaven."

Many Mansions. Well, this was hers—Aldgate, New York, Chicago, always the earnest, planning men trying to get some dignity into the work world. It never changed. And you were proud and frightened, that didn't change either.

4

The lighted square held you as a magnet, you alone, completely compelled out of the darkness that is never dark but lighted like dreams in the dark of sleep. Down below in the lighted square, a woman named Juliet fought for love. She had started out poised and ready, but it wasn't easy once she stepped from the room she knew, the room where her mother ruled and swayed her. She had gone seeking a security of her own making, a modern woman like Victoria Woodhull or Frances Willard, no Juliet of Shakespeare's but a new kind of heroine, without a nurse, with a driving, maturing mind and no Romeo strong enough. There was Jacques, young revolutionary who buried his weakness in causes, and Henry, the businessman, who loved but not enough, only with his outside senses, and Stephen, who loved her not as she was but as he wanted her to be. The four people struggled and fought without fighting and you knew what they meant, and beyond that, what they thought and didn't say, could not say because they were caught and webbed, the day-to-day necessity blinding them to that ultimate which in their hearts they yearned for. You knew these people as if you'd known them all your life, not one of them without promise and only one, only Juliet, with the courage to live or die.

The curtain fell finally, cutting off the square of sun, leaving you filled with these people and bereft of them as if they had died. Julie sat, hearing the applause, seeing the excited faces, the young men and women, students mostly, who leaned with her against the gallery rail. When she sat back, her ribs ached. It was a shock for the lights to come up, to find herself standing, inching slowly toward the exit in the crowd, out and down the iron stairs which hung to the side of the building in the raw wind.

It was the first play of Phillip's she had seen in many years. Not that she didn't care—he'd understand that—but tickets were dear and you couldn't go to the theater knowing the boys' boots were worn through. That you couldn't do. It had to suffice to walk past the theater, see the illustrations, read the notices. Something had happened in that lapse of time, something had grown in Phillip so it shook your heart and sent the thoughts cascading, as you went slowly down the iron steps. No wonder he was famous now, and they wrote long columns about him in the newspapers. What he was doing was different. The stage set didn't matter. No one cared whether the doors opened and closed or windows went up and down or if water ran when you turned a faucet. There were no tricks. After all the realism and melodrama, here was something truly real, characters you could not forget. Doors would open in your mind into a thousand rooms, because of Jacques and Henry, Stephen and Juliet. He had used the name with that extra T not to embarrass her, made the woman tall and blond and a different person. He had created situations out of his talent, and yet . . . there was some essence that caught up a strand of her very self. She'd have to think about that, think it out and put it all together before she saw the play again; for of course, they were all coming to see it, Emma and Lud and Leon and the children. It was merely that she had to see it alone first. That wasn't too much to ask, was it?

Warmer now, nearing the bottom, slower, too, with the added throng from the balcony. Back down the alley was the stage door and people waiting in line to catch sight of the players. She turned up the alley slowly, avoiding the horse droppings, just to walk past the gaudy bills, not expecting, not even hoping, just to pass the stage door. Almost at once she saw someone—a dark gentleman in a gray derby hat and fine coat, talking with friends. He saw her, too, threw away his cigar, and stood transfixed. They walked toward each other slowly, the tears running cold on their faces. Etienne Clairevoissier! He took her in his arms right there in the alley and kissed her wet face.

"Julie, Julie, Julie." He whispered the name against her cheek and she knew without seeing how the fine nostrils quivered. The next instant, she was inside the stage door, past the milling people, and into a small office. Etienne held both her hands.

"I cry like a child, after all the years. How beautiful you are, Julie, how I wish Phillip were here to see you."

"You haven't changed, Etienne, only stouter. You still use big adjectives." Then she held him tightly by the arm. "I'm glad you're with Phillip, so glad, Etienne, and he has done it, hasn't he? Such a deep play, I'm thrilled to see it. As if all he suffered. . . ."

He knew. She had a right to be proud, he said, everything Phillip had written—for every play, he said it himself, she was the spring board. He had told it all to some fine writer in New York who was doing a biography, not Julie's name, of course, but how she had ridiculed the gaudy shows and told him . . . how even when he was a young boy, the only good things he had written were for her. Then he showed Phillip's picture, a face like a woodcarving for the newspapers. The hair had thinned on top and he parted it far over on the side and brushed it across. She saw the face through a blur of feeling, as if this were a secret she alone knew, the dear, thin face with its searching eyes, the left lid drooping a trifle in that way Phillip had that made his glance the keener.

Etienne spoke of a new play now in progress, and how Phillip had lectured at Harvard on playwriting, while she sat at the desk studying the picture, knowing the texture of the facial flesh and how the beard grew quick and rough. Etienne begged her to write to Phillip, let him know she had seen the play. She shook her head, let the past stay. It was enough for her to have seen it come out well, as if all the disappointments of Phillip's life were absorbed now, had become part of him and turned to good. A man could not have written *Many Mansions* if he had not felt and suffered and learned to part his hair deep on the side. Etienne was to take him her love and say how happy she was in his triumph.

5

She almost thought she heard voices, that's how frayed and worn she was, voices whispering "Auntie" outside the kitchen window at that hour of night! She packed the last of the fruit cookies in the jar, screwed the lid tight, and tried to breathe, but there was something else she could not pack down. An unwieldy wedge of sorrow kept rising, like leaven. Christmas was over. Not a merry Christmas but a tense, disappointing one. She filled the small kettle, blew out the lamp, and took her way in darkness through the windy hall. Even the kettle was a burden. Water lurched, slipped through the spout, and she had to go back for a cloth and stoop down, while stiff slivers of cold shot in under the door, sharp as glass. Julie made short work of that. She felt cold through, stopped only to see the front door bolted and the snow flying thick as birds against the glass. Across the way, the big house was dark. It had moved off in the night, back into an avalanche of flying birds, not one smiling light. She gripped her cold kettle and hurried into the parlor feeling the first thin warmth, closed the door quickly to hold it. The fire might well have gone out with wind shuddering and groaning down the flue; but one luminous branch still breathed fire, the flame throbbed and flickered, she put the kettle to boil and sank down herself, close, so she could rest her head on the screen and let the warm air blow and bathe her. Then it happened again, the voice calling "Auntie," and now a tapping—why it *was*—she ran to unbolt the door. Blown snow caught in Dirk's eyebrows and his hair and lay like fur on the shoulders of his coat. There was a gaunt line to his face, his mouth was chapped, Dirk for the first time bare with agony and love so that she knew him.

"Just for a minute, Auntie."

She helped him with his coat, brushed the snow, and hung it on the hall tree while he kicked off his overshoes—all as casually as if she were used to entertaining at two hours past midnight and the kettle boiling for tea. She was trembling, the whole of that strained Christmas Day came trembling back, Leon distributing the gifts, Elsa opening her chest of silver, the linens marked with the Stodel S and the deed to the house on Prairie that Ludwig had given Dirk. And the quiet. And Ellen's face. And Dirk's, as if he had come into Christmas a boy, years ago, and had grown old before the plum pudding.

He went to the fire, squatted to his heels, took the tongs and spun the log over so its glowing underside came full face and radiant as a heart. He took the heat to his bones as she had, forgetting to put the tongs down. When the tea was brewed strong, she poured in a flash of brandy from the decanter, stirred and handed him a cup. Dirk didn't move, he kept his eyes to the fire while she brought a sofa cushion, tucked her skirts up, and tried to wait. It was open and honest between her and Dirk and they both knew it—although there had never been a word.

"Look here, Auntie," he said putting the cup down. "I think I should go away."

"Go where, Dirk?"

"There are plenty of hospitals. It won't matter."

"I thought it did. I thought the experiments you were doing with Dr. Billings meant so much."

The muscles of Dirk's jaw moved, and this time he faced her. "Thank you, Aunt Julie. I'll try to talk sense. You don't know how hard. . . ." He only faltered for a moment. "Our work with disease bacteria means a great deal. But, you know, I want to marry Ellen. If I go away now and stay for two years until I'm ready to practice, this family matter may work itself out. The rest of you can go on together. In two years I can send for Ellen; if they've forgiven me, I can even come back."

"Have you told Elsa—you needn't answer that, Dirk."

"I've said nothing to Elsa, now or ever. She doesn't care for me, Auntie, I simply was there and Elsa loves taking people over. In the old country, we went to parties and flirted, you know how it is when you're growing up. But I talked with Uncle Lud tonight. He and Aunt Emma have been like parents to us. I hate to hurt them. I always thought someone would come along, someone really good for Elsa, and this would right itself. Can you imagine her a doctor's wife? Putting up with the hours and all the rest I believe in?"

He was so right.

"But you saw today, the deed to that house and the silver. I told Uncle Lud about Ellen. Lord, I thought everyone could see that. I gave back the deed and told him I'd go away."

The log crackled, writhed, and sent up a spray of sparks.

"You see that's right, Auntie?"

"That would solve everything," she said crisply. "Run far and fast enough and problems settle themselves."

"Don't make fun of me, Aunt Julie."

"Running has solved nothing since the world began." She put her cup on the floor and her fist down behind it so soundly the china jumped. "You have to decide what's important and fight for it. That's how to live. The minute you stop fighting, you're through, buried or upright makes no difference. If love is important, you fight for it. If research is important. . . ."

"But the family, the rest of you—"

"Are old enough to work out our problems. If what we've built through the years is genuine and real, it'll take some battering. If it isn't, we'd be fools to keep on. I'm not telling you what to do, son, but two years is a long time, even a day is, when you consider you can't live it again. You may not

250

have the same opportunities anywhere you have interning at County, or the chance to experiment you have with Dr. Billings. And as for obligation to us, you have one supreme obligation, Dirk, to yourself. Whoever shirks that is worth a whit to no one. Ask your Uncle Leon."

"Aunt Julie!" At least she thought he spoke. The chapped lips, darker now and sealed smooth with heat, moved; but he turned his face so she couldn't see.

"There, now," standing up and shaking her skirts. "You put another piece of wood to that fire and I'll send Ellen down. You two haven't had a word alone the whole day. You'll rest better." Out in the dark, drafty hall, she took a shawl from the clothes tree, and the small round mirror jumped out in flames from the parlor fire. Up the stairs gently through the sleeping house, the rise and fall of sleep. The minute she touched the knob, Ellen called, "What is it, what is it, Mother?" She was sitting in the bed, her face puffed and shiny with crying.

"Dirk is here. Get on your pink flannel wrapper, Ellen, and go down for a minute. Here, bathe your face, dear, no more of that." She held Ellen close. "There, now, let's have a touch of toilet water." She found the brush and stroked Ellen's hair. "Take the candle, dear, don't be afraid." The sweet face had begun to burn now, it was flushed in the candlelight.

"You're coming too, Mother."

"No such thing. I'm going to bed. Your papa never rests until I'm there, and he has to be up at five, love or no love."

She watched while Ellen slipped down the stairs, the parlor door closed, cutting off the flickering light, then Julie went quickly into her own room, into her nightdress, into her bed. She drew up close to Leon and shared his warmth, put her arms around the good, solid bulk of him. He murmured in his sleep and moved slightly so that they were both comfortable and one together, as they always were, not a scar between them. She was warm all night, warm and brightly awake, thinking it out, how one was to act tomorrow when Lud and Emma would stiffen and stand off. It was not going to be easy, she hoped she hadn't given Dirk that impression. It wasn't going to be easy at all. But there were many things not easy, and they came out right in the long run. She kissed Leon's neck, buried her head against his sleeping flesh.

6

No sign came from the big house next day. The snow had left off abruptly in the night, but the house across kept to itself wrapped in dry white silence, not even the walks swept free. Steve and Henry were all for fetching Louis Stodel to play in the snow, but if they were so wild for snow, they could just get at it with shovel and broom. She had them out early, to sweep the walk clean and not just a skinny trail, either. She kept them at it until they'd cleared a way past the Beeren-broecks', you couldn't expect old Mr. Beerenbroeck to shovel at his age, he'd neither the strength nor the wit, and the walk must be cleared for Ellen and for their papa after work, poor man, he'd had trouble enough wading through. A path was needed to the shed, wood must be cut, so many chores it was lucky there was no school. Then the Kuyper boys came by, dragging their sled, and Steve and Henry went off with them. No sign from the other house, not even Tilda.

"Without Miss Busybody under foot, maybe I can get some-thing done," declared Aunt Anna. But she spent most of the morning at the window, peering through the peephole she blew and then rubbed hard with her apron. Maybe Aunt Anna shouldn't have been worried with what was going on. But that wouldn't have been fair; she was one of them and loved being in on things. Julie brought piles of darning, put their two chairs beside the stove, and suggested that this was a good time to take Richard in hand. The way he'd acted on Christmas! Whining for this and not letting a body say two words uninterrupted. They'd been too lax with Richard, Emma and Ludwig and Leon all spoiled him, but Christmas brought it to the fore, showed in a flash how bad he was. "S-t-u-b-b-o-r-n a-s a m-u-l-e," spelled Julie while the subject under discussion scuttled from under a table to pull at her skirt. She gave him a ball of yarn to play with, sat him down hard on a blanket, he was to sit and not interrupt her again, hear? They concentrated on the baby, so stern eyed he didn't know what had struck him. First he screamed. Aunt Anna and Julie darned without notice. After a while, he played with the yarn, but that didn't last long. By afternoon, he was pitching about the house, drunk with admonitions and glad to be carried off for his nap. Having given him not one smile, Julie relented when she put him down. The child wasn't half as ornery as some grownups she knew, who made up their minds and wouldn't change no matter what. She rocked him and sang his favorite *"Trip a trop a traunches,"* softly so Aunt Anna shouldn't hear.

Down in the parlor, Aunt Anna was back at the window. You couldn't expect visitors in this weather, she said. But they had come on worse days. Emma liked a cup of tea and a chance to tell the most recent caprices of Sheilah, the maid, whose career was approaching one of those mad, gyrating climaxes which always marked the end of Emma's "jewels." No sign. Nor the next day, nor the next. Maybe there would never be. They'd live across for the rest of their lives without a word.

Julie could have cried. She ransacked closets, scoured cupboards, dug into corners and aired clothes, there wasn't to be a speck of dust to greet the new year. Hmpf, wasn't going to be a whole curtain or a shred of carpet left to greet it, either, Aunt Anna said, scrubbing everything thin. They stood out in the snowy yard beating at carpets with wire weapons as if that would do some good, baked pies and cakes and sent them with Dirk when he brought Ellen from Field's. Still no sign.

The first one to come was Tilda. She stole in the back way, slipped out of her coat and overshoes and shawl, tied on an apron, and started polishing lamp chimneys at Aunt Anna's side as if she'd never been away. Julie saw it from high up, from the top rung of the ladder in the pantry.

"Well, look who's here," exclaimed Aunt Anna. "Thought you'd moved away."

"No," Tilda said.

"Maybe you went visiting some of those fine, elegant friends on Prairie?"

Tilda stooped to pick up Richard, her face dark with the effort.

"Mama's mad," she blurted.

"Oh, she is, is she? What about, miss?"

"That will do," Julie called down. "Let's have no more."

"She's mad at you, Aunt Julie, you. She says you're a schemer and planned every bit of it, bought the house and got us to America just to swipe Dirk."

Julie hurried down the ladder. "Mathilda, button your lip and button it quick!" She clapped her hand over the child's mouth. "I didn't hear one word."

Tight as she held, one more phrase mumbled out. "I don't care, I'm glad. Elsa's a witch!" she screamed.

"You shut your mouth or I'll wash it with yellow soap."

Tilda went back to her place at the table, Julie to the pantry. The minute she thought herself unobserved, Aunt Anna patted her small helper's hand and gave her a good, pleased nod. There was a petulant look to Aunt Anna, as if there was more to hear and she for one would like to hear it. A little later, Louis came, stuck his head in just long enough to find out where Steve and Henry were.

At least the children had come. Perhaps by afternoon, Emma. But before afternoon, the storm came, sealing them off more effectively than anger. It started before noon with a gale from the lake. There was one hesitant half hour lit with eerie orange light, then the scowling sky cracked open and dense motile white came massing down, thronged, packed, drifted like dunes. Over in the whiteness were Emma and Elsa, and the anger still to be faced. Well, you couldn't hurry life, you couldn't force it, every time you tried it went wrong like a balky horse. There was nothing to do but plod through the hours, just as outside the mail carrier forced a way, foot by foot.

"He's stopped across!" yelled Aunt Anna from the front. "He's having hard going, I can tell you. Just rapped at Emma's door." He'd had to get as far south as Sixteenth, if he could make it, then cross over and come back on their side. Hot fat sizzled in the pot. Julie dropped in the floured beef, let it brown until it all but stuck. The next thing, the old lady was in the kitchen.

"She's coming, don't you hear?" yelled Aunt Anna. "Emma's coming." Julie ran without even turning the meat. Emma was wading through the white swamp of Wabash, through the driving snow, her face flushed and laughing. She looked. . . .

"I'll be switched if she isn't wearing Ludwig's pants!" Aunt Anna was right. Ludwig's enormous trousers were belted in at Emma's waist; she came plunging across, her head tied in a woolen muffler. Julie ran back to turn her beef, put on a shawl, and went to meet the voyager who had just clambered to the sidewalk, breathless and half dead from laughing. One whole side was snow to the shoulder where she'd fallen. They had to take the broom to Emma, brush her, and help with her overshoes.

"I couldn't wait, has the carrier been here? Well, he's been to us!" and Emma collapsed on the couch. "Guess who's coming, who's almost here." She waved the envelopes. "Munzell!" She howled, shaking so with merriment the tears ran. Julie had to read aloud the letters which had been sent at intervals over a period of three weeks but had been delayed by storms so they arrived at once. The gentleman from Parliament had landed in North Carolina early in December. He had made an extensive tour of the South, been most cordially received, learned the meaning of blood and family which characterized that portion of the country, and was now veering north, toward Chicago, where they might expect him on New Year's Day.

"What a lark!" sighed Emma. "What a jolly lark we'll have with Julie's Munzell."

"Emma, a joke's a joke but he isn't mine, he's forgotten me completely."

Just then the mail carrier arrived with another sheaf of letters, painfully inscribed to Mrs. Leon Dekker, matching Emma's letters date for date and conveying similar information. He remembered that their Dutch tradition concerned itself with the observance of the New Year, and they were to deviate from none of their plans. No, indeed. He would be residing at the Palmer House, he had much of a business nature to transact in the city and letters of introduction to numerous dignitaries. Still, his heart warmed at the thought of seeing old friends whom he regarded as only a degree less than kin.

Emma leaped up in Ludwig's trousers to give a hilarious imitation of Mr. Munzell being received by the fair flower of the South—as he put it. She had not been in such spirits since they came to Chicago, as if no other matter of importance had ever occurred. No mention of Dirk and Ellen. She must give a ball. It was high time she entertained Ludwig's choice customers. A visiting member of Parliament was not to be sneezed at. Julie, she said, should write a letter to the Palmer House, since it was to her he had confided his whereabouts.

By nightfall, the families were reunited. Whatever might happen afterward, they were all together once again in Emma's living room planning for their first visitor from home.

7

Forty hooks, and every one elusive in the soft velvet nap. How warm it was! She missed one and had to unfasten a dozen, and he was here already, waiting downstairs. Pieter and the other children had fetched their visitor, made an expedition of it in two sleighs and delivered him on the dot; but they hadn't stayed, they'd given him over to Aunt Anna and hurried across the street, not to miss a minute of the party. Julie sucked in her waist, feeling for the wire hoops. Such a day! Leon had his hands full helping Lud, and there were the pies she'd promised Emma, the kettle of toddy, Ellen to lace, and Richard had spilled his whole bowl of gruel on the parlor carpet. There, the last small eye eased into place, probably into the good cloth, but at least she could take a breath. She rubbed her fingers, yanked at a drawer, found a handkerchief, but not her pearls. They weren't in the box and they weren't . . . she'd lent them to Ellen nights ago, goodness, goodness, there they finally were in Ellen's box, and she ran down the stairs, holding the soft velvet folds, trembling and shy at being late. She had planned to be dressed and ready, open the door herself calmly, say . . . but there suddenly below was Mr. Munzell in the middle of her parlor, big, smooth, the very same. He had grown, perhaps, but in the identical mold, the wax had hardened, that was all, her thumb would probably not leave a dent.

He thought himself quite alone, certainly there was no sign of Aunt Anna or of Richard. He tapped one pointed patent toe, studying the carpet, and fingered his smooth, legal face. Slowly, taking his time, he wheeled, sizing up the worn upholstery, boot marks on the table legs, the damp stain from spilled gruel, estimating it all down to a farthing. Poor man, what would he have thought if he had come to visit them in New York?

"Happy New Year. Forgive my tardiness, dear Mr. Munzell."

But he was so pleased, so delighted, so overwhelmed! Waves of pleasure toppled up his brow while he beheld—for behold her he certainly did, from top to toe, from toe to top. How lucky she had worn the lovely dress, the soft, supple velvet cut down from one of Emma's and good as new; bless the fortitude that had kept at the ornery hooks when she'd almost given up, torn the whole thing off, and worn the black silk. It was easy now to see how right this was, every fold fitting and clinging, freshly steamed and verdant as grass. She smiled at Mr. Munzell, shook Grand-mère's earrings, and held out both her hands while he advanced stiff-legged.

"Twenty years, ta-weh-henty years, little Julie!" He bent gallantly to kiss her hands, enunciating the words so he might have spelled them. The great pomaded head came down to eye level, the humble, flushed neck leaned quite out of its Parliamentary pomp. It was such an unexpected view of the gentleman, so intimate, she could see where he shaved his neck—and how badly she had used him in the old days, flirting under the mistletoe. She put her face quickly against his tallow one, meaning to kiss his cheek, but he moved so it was his sideburn she kissed. "There, we're such old friends, do sit down, Herbert Munzell, tell me all the news about our friends at home."

He was still dry and unwieldy. He trusted Leon was well, how greatly he admired her children, the three he had met this morning; and there was a look to him mentioning the children that threatened gravity; she had gone up a notch, the substantiated fact of motherhood had promoted her to that hallowed sphere to which Mr. Munzell relegated the best of womankind.

"Let me give you a glass of wine. You must be chilled through," she murmured wickedly.

Mr. Munzell, mopping his brow, would have detained her. He had by no means finished eulogizing the beauty of Ellen, the manners of Henry and of Steve. It was incredible that those strapping youngsters could belong to such a slight little thing, no larger than the girl he had first escorted through the waltz.

She hurried away for the wine. The kitchen door was open, and Richard leaning over the cellar steps, just far enough . . . she grabbed him by the seat of his pants. Aunt Anna came toiling up. Well, Julie had finally gotten herself fixed, had she, a fine how-de-do, primping like a chit of twenty and leaving these old bones to trot the cellar steps. And what, if you pleased, was Julie so lit up about, she'd almost swear she'd painted her face! Julie snatched the dish towel, scrubbed her cheek, and held it out for inspection. Aunt Anna repossessed herself of the towel, dusted the bottle of sherry, and twisted in her corkscrew. She'd be hanged if she could see anything in that tame parlor duck to whip up color. Hadn't been much twenty years ago for her money, didn't have the pep old Becke, rest him, carried in a finger; ask her, the only change time had made was to embalm him so like a store dummy you couldn't tell the one from the other.

Julie would not laugh. She put three glasses on a tray, trying to walk primly before Aunt Anna, but some obstinate, spiced edge furled and preened in her as she approached the parlor, and she *did* look . . . well, much better than he had expected. Mr. Munzell had regained some composure. He sat in the big chair with his color down to pink, every crease running straight in his excellent clothes. When he had moistened and remoistened his plump lips with wine, he drank to both their healths and so far forgot himself as to clink glasses and wink one watery eye at Aunt Anna.

"I know not what this tiny mite of a person does to me, Mrs. Becke, she has the knack of making me feel young again, venturesome. How about it, young fellow?" He turned abruptly to Richard who had just entered and was standing, spread-legged, gazing up. "How about it, young fellow?" and out went one great white finger which Richard promptly seized. Mr. Munzell was gratified. He sat down, careful not to move the finger; he gave the child his full attention. "Now then, who am I, since you're getting so friendly. Who do you think I am?"

"Uncle Herbert," replied Richard monotonously. But he had a crafty look; he wasn't sure whether he was being made sport of. The Lord knew what he'd come out with next, there had been family conversations in which this Uncle Herbert's name. . . .

259

"Richard, you're not to pester our visitor. Aunt Anna, let him have the new blocks."

Mr. Munzell said he did not mind being pestered. He worked his mustache as if it itched and confided his boundless pleasure at the warmth and familiarity of her children and Emma's. It was by far the most—should he say "personal," yes, that was quite the word—the most personal experience he had had since the death of his sister. Not that the Peabody children lacked affection. They were devoted to him. Still, success had its price. It built one up and kept the world, even one's niece and nephew, at arm's length. The fact was that pleasant as his life had become—and one's political career did not go unattended by its social component—there had never again been the intimacy he had known in the days when he was a member of the inner circle at the Corpers' and the Stodels'. It was a long sentence, he took a long swallow to punctuate it, allowing Julie to refill his glass, almost making a point of it, as if he wanted her to see he had become a man of the world, able to take his portion without notice. He lifted his glass to her.

"I have never forgotten or ceased to value the kindness shown me by your mother and your aunt, or the trust of your fine father which continued undiminished to the end." He raised his brows that she might savor that. "Above all, I've valued that sincere confidence *you*, Julie, had in my future."

It was bewildering.

"Slightly too formal, I dare say you found that young Munzell, but your faith in his ability to carve a niche in the heights did much to brighten the long road." Julie was more bewildered than ever. She would have looked to Aunt Anna, but that one had taken as much of Mr. Munzell's success story as she could stomach and at the allusion to Papa had withdrawn to fetch their wraps. She was pushing Richard into leggings now and mumbling noisily about Emma who had a hundred visitors, to judge from the traffic, and could use some help.

"Tucked deep among the things one cherishes, lies a letter

penned by none other than yourself, dear little Julie, a missive more charged with inspiration. . . ."

"*I* wrote?"

"When we were engaged in controversy on the value of women's rights."

"Oh," she said, "did I?"

"Perhaps the passage of years has persuaded you. . . ."

"Not a bit," and oh, how she laughed. He was so reliable. "The one solid, unchanging thing in the universe."

That he did not know how to take. He contemplated the last of his wine and decided to take it sportingly, helped them to their wraps, and escorted them across to Emma's New Year's reception, as if he were out to set the Thames on fire.

Whatever had brought Mr. Munzell to Chicago kept him and kept him. He had constant recourse to city fathers, to the best legal brains at the new court house, visited the court, factories, and hospitals, went with Leon to Cigar Makers meetings and gave him advice (unofficial, of course, and always discouraging) over the latest setback. For United Manufacturers had ordered a wage cut on January second. There had been immediate lockouts, ten thousand out of work in New York and the Knights backing the radical Progressive Cigar Makers to make a deal of their own with the manufacturers. If they did, it would mean the breakdown of the International Cigar Makers Union—you didn't need Munzell to tell you that—it would cut the profession to tenement level for all time. Now there were two cigar labels, the regular blue and the new white label, endorsed by the Knights and boycotted by legitimate union men. Mr. Munzell listened to it all with grave and immobile face, and thought that, with bitter feeling and scabbing on both sides, the two opposing union elements would ruin each other. Which, he probably also thought, was well and good.

But at least his presence was an interlude of peace in the family, both houses united as a regiment, no mention of Dirk and Ellen, poor earnest lovers—what would happen to them when he was gone? It made one nervous and quick to worry. Julie held a lemon hard and rubbed it over the grater to make tarnished shavings for pudding.

"Just smell that, Aunt Anna. Smell that, Tilda." She crossed from the sink to hold the naked pulp under their noses. Tilda wrinkled hers, but Aunt Anna whipped out a paring knife, split the fruit through, then in fourths, and popped one quarter into her mouth with relish. Julie picked up another lemon and rubbed it against the prongs. How much of that stuff was she making? Aunt Anna wanted to know, there'd be eggs to match and no one leaving 'em free at the door. She had borrowed a dozen eggs from Emma, and they'd skimped plenty the last few weeks to have this dinner. Sixteen to feed. Well, it would take a gallon, Emma and Lud and theirs and hers and Mr. Munzell.

"Elsa's stuck on him," Tilda said.

"Mathilda, that's silly. Mr. Munzell's like an uncle."

"I don't care, Elsa's stuck on him."

Julie cracked one of the precious eggs to separate the white. Her hand wasn't steady, and the round yellow blob of yolk fell into the rind.

"I don't mind stories, so long's they aren't made up," Aunt Anna said. "Seems to me you're making this straight out of your head."

"I am not," cried Tilda. "Richard and I are going out to play. He's *not* like Uncle Leon. He's stuck up and stingy and Elsa treats him like a goose." She slammed the back door going out.

"That child! Aunt Anna, it's frightening the way she . . . we shouldn't let her talk, it's not right."

It wasn't as if they were prying and snooping, Aunt Anna

said, the youngster couldn't keep her mouth shut, that was a fact, and she wasn't so far off the track, either, the way Elsa was turning the rope and the big fool mincing and skipping to her turn.

"But Elsa's so young, it doesn't seem. . . ."

"Old enough to know what she wants. And he's a sight better for her than Dirk. She's got a hard hand, that Elsa. A young man'd break or bend, but old Munzell's tough. He'll hold his own, and a fine battle they'll have of it."

"You mean you think. . . ."

"No more'n you've been thinking and wouldn't open your head about. I never saw such a close mouth, miss. It's lucky we have Tilda for all your trying to shut her up. Sometimes I think you've gone righteous as your pa."

But she had been afraid to say, for fear she had just imagined. Did Aunt Anna remember New Year's Day how Elsa had shown him off like a prime minister, making him tell everyone at the party what he thought of India and Home Rule? And it was true, she never called him "Uncle Herbert" as the other children did, and she certainly had been busy enough driving out with him.

"Curling him around her wrist's more to the point. Him staying on when it was supposed to be three weeks at the outside and so many mighty things to do in Washington."

"Yes, yes, I thought of that. And Elsa looks better, too. She isn't a bit downhearted and flounces her bustle. . . ."

"I've seen the bustle," said Aunt Anna dryly. "Here, let me whisk those eggs." She took the paddle, whipped until the foam shook, creamed, quivered to a peak. "There's no love lost, never was, between me and your old beau. Stingy's only half what I'd say, never spending a penny he hasn't pinched big, but I'd dance at his wedding in tight shoes to help our Ellen."

"What about Emma? Would it please Emma?"

"He's a member of Parliament, isn't he? She'll be putting Ethelyn's nose out of joint, won't she?"

Julie filled a pail with warm water, shaved in yellow soap,

and got to her knees. Strange what people wanted out of life. A swift little chill went down her back and she plunged one arm into the hot suds. Some craved love and others pounds sterling. The good life was with a man you honored, a man sound and strong with a sense of humor like Leon's. She must study Mr. Munzell well tonight and see what it was Elsa saw.

The potential bridegroom arrived earlier than she had expected, well before twilight, polished down to the last gleaming hair caught and congealed within his sharp mustache. He had come in the hope that she would honor him on a short drive, he had a matter of importance. . . . A matter of importance! Aunt Anna might accompany them if she preferred, he said, this with an arch look as he held her shawl. "How prudent and old-fashioned you are," Julie countered. "Phillip McManus and I used to run off unchaperoned when we were children, and I've never improved. I'm a very advanced woman, Herbert Munzell!" He was embarrassed and enchanted, tucked her into the carriage, and closed the window which communicated with the driver. Then a pause. Whatever he had to say was long in preparation, and so much depended on it, so much happiness for Ellen, for them all.

"I trust you will not misconstrue, little Julie, when I say that admirable as large families are, they sometimes prove inconvenient. I have had scant opportunity to speak with you, and I can wait no longer."

The lake seemed to break into a thousand pieces, glistening flashes of water cracked the ice to catch the purple light. God, let him love Elsa, let him. . . .

"I went with Leon last night to the eight-hour meeting. I came away thoroughly alarmed. There has been secret word sent out by Grand Master Powderly of the Knights of Labor discouraging that mighty organization from participating. He's withdrawn support. . . ."

"The men won't listen to Powderly. He's a traitor. The majority *will* strike!" she turned quickly, facing him.

"Come, don't be angry. Hear me out, Julie. I cannot influence Leon, but I would be less than friend if I didn't try to accomplish the same good through you. Powderly's missive can cut the strike to nothing. The Knights are more than six hundred thousand now, more than two hundred locals in this state alone. And employers are ready to fight. Look how McCormick handled the situation at the Harvester works. Those men will never get back. McCormick and other big employers have money for detectives and police protection. They won't be forced to reduce the working day. It's like trying to outlaw war by refusing to fight—the plans of dreamers and we live in a real world. Ah, ah, ah, *ah!* Julie, be sensible. You know the only legitimate means of controlling human destiny is via legislation. That's why I wouldn't be anything but a pawn in the great legal game."

"And Leon would be nothing but a trade unionist! He believes in legal procedure as much as you do. Let me tell you something, Herbert Munzell, there'd be no need for strikes if lawmakers were less often tools and pawns!"

"Julie, Julie." His mouth was so dry he had to pause for moisture. "I turned to you in hope that as a mother you would sense the danger, the inevitable defeat. A man is ruthless, but a wife, nobler natured and with little children, can sometimes swerve and stay. . . ."

"Then she's a poor wife!"

That stopped him. He breathed with feeling. "We will say no more, Julie. Only this—yesterday I spoke with Mayor Harrison. He needs ward organizers, and any time Leon. . . ." He presented a card from his notecase. "Mayor Harrison feels no animosity for Leon's past union work. This card would suffice to procure a paid job in the Democratic party."

Offering Leon a job as ward heeler! Talking as if the fight were lost! And if it were, some fights were worth the cost if they did lose. Look at Christ and the dreams He lived by, that some men still lived by, even if the main tenets were forgotten and muddied down to ritual. Wan pinks and blues left over from sunset dragged their frayed shreds across the sky into the night. She wished to turn home.

"Your statement as to the duty of a wife I cannot abandon,

little Julie. You will forgive my repeating it." And he did. "It is of special interest to me since I have always put a high premium on marriage and on the benign influence of a fine, womanly nature." She scarcely listened. "I admire you for putting the aims of the husband above all else. It is as if my own sister had spoken from the grave." Dead or alive, there was evidently to be no escaping Sister Peabody. "I tell you frankly, Julie, I have much regretted the fate that isolated me to the bachelor's rank."

"You're young! You ought to be ashamed of yourself, when happiness lies right under your nose."

He took this so coyly, she was at once alert. He turned pink, and the old familiar lemon stabbed the dark. "In the old days, Julie, I'd have given a great deal to make a declaration to a certain young lady, yes." He pressed her hand and drew one finger waggishly down the center of her glove. "My prospects were not sufficient then, and with the years I never did find another creature who so appealed to me."

"Oh, nonsense, Herbert, you sentimentalize like a dodo."

He roared at that, laughed so hard that he had to clear his throat many times. "The fact of the matter is, my dear, that your earlier statement of a wife's duty has convinced me of a step on which I have been hesitant; for I *have* found another young lady, and while I weighed the matter, you, Julie, have tipped the scales. Yes, the die is cast, your old friend contemplates matrimony!"

9

He spoke to Emma and Ludwig without delay. He spoke with Pieter, sought sanction from Leon, conveyed the honor of his intentions to Pauline, to everyone except Elsa, until that young lady took him to task. He'd better stop asking her papa and mama and ask her. Suppose everyone else said yes and she said no? This merrily, her violet baby eyes blazing with fun; having flustered and surprised her suitor, she discomposed him utterly by sitting on his knee before them all. Heat flooded to Mr. Munzell's anointed hair. Awkwardly, playfully, not unlike some twenty years ago, his big knee jounced up and down with its load of perky satin.

From that instant of his acceptance, he advanced his suit with method and efficiency—a hamper of oranges, a pound of mints, dates bound in a cask of silver foil. No flowers, he apologized for that, but florists' prices were exorbitant, it would be vain outlay while candies and fruit could be enjoyed by all—*were* enjoyed, with such quick relish that their donor must watch in some surprise as if he had never noticed how hearty the Dekker appetites were. Then came the ring, purchased under the aegis of the future father-in-law, with a fat discount, Aunt Anna could bet her boots. And within a fortnight, faster than one thought it might be arranged, a photograph of himself in full parliamentary regalia, solemn, exact, the lips slightly puckered as the gentleman gazed toward the camera for posterity, for Elsa, too, of course. Nor were his tokens of chivalry withheld from the house across the street. He took them to his broadcloth bosom *in toto*, a less ornate frame, silvered instead of gilt, but just as true to life. And what fun the boys made of that picture, Henry, Steve, and Louis Stodel running to the broom closet to explode with glee, while Julie explained that it was a silly game, boys that age, you know. Mr. Munzell twitched his mustache; he even brought long licorice whips as a bribe to boys that age.

No time was lost in these pleasantries, and he expected the Dekkers to lose as little in wedding preparations. He had a duty to his constituents, and that included marrying Elsa with all speed, transporting her and his findings diplomatic over the sea for the disposal of the Empire. No one tried to retard him. Emma was for tying up this match before unpredictable Elsa could change her mind; and from another point of view, from across the street, the faster it went for Mr. Munzell and Elsa, the faster for Dirk and Ellen.

That was the big thing he had done without knowing. He had given full sanction to Dirk and Ellen, proclaimed and legalized their love so the whole family could rejoice in it. Now everyone was in love! Emma insisted on a joint betrothal. She was in her element of trousseau plans, wedding gowns, and furniture, for both couples impartially, since she could now regard Dirk as a sort of disappointed suitor. She came running across the street a dozen times a day to confide the latest details, the sport naughty Elsa made of Munzell and how nobly, with what dignity, he carried it off. Listen to this letter she had written Ethelyn! Would pink roses be right for the engagement party or mixed bouquets? The house must be properly dressed, not just a few sprigs on the buffet table, but handsome floor vases for parlor, staircase, and library.

Pity she didn't have a daughter to marry off every day, made her stir her stumps, Aunt Anna said, stirring her own stumps vigorously; for fancy dressmakers suited her no better than they had years ago. She was hand-drawing and scalloping lingerie for Ellen as fast as her gnarled hands would go. Let 'em order Elsa's at Marshall Field's or from that Frenchy woman who made drawers. Ellen should have homemade petticoats like her ma and grandma'd had, and nightdresses with seams that'd hold. This last Julie pondered; there was more to marriage than these pretty preliminaries.

She had given Ellen a book, *Eve's Daughters*, with its "common sense for wife, maid and mother." Elsa was reading it, too, although Emma scoffed and believed in letting nature take its course, why put bees in their bonnets? But Julie worried less for what the girls knew than for what they did not know. The book was wholesome so far as it went, but crucial matters were still left up in the air and there was the detail of nightdresses with seams that would hold. Thinking such thoughts of one's own daughter! Trying to shift from that, she thought of Elsa and Mr. Munzell, and that was such a picture she had much control to keep from sharing it with Aunt Anna who had already expressed herself dryly and coolly on Munzell's possibilities. Which wasn't true—Mr. Munzell would prove neither cool nor dry, it was simply a matter of Elsa's never, never being able to look a lemon in the face. "Julie Dekker, enough of that!" She grabbed some fine muslin and began to cut, so fast the scissors ground and scrawled across the table top, leaving, when she pulled away the scraps, the limp image of a female skirt.

The reception was set for the third week in April and with all they had to do, the weather did nothing to favor them. It thawed and turned warm as if July had insinuated itself into the end of winter. State Street was sloppy with mud, the stores were damp and hot, stockyard stench hung over the city, suffocating as a hood. This was bad weather for Henry; she tiptoed down the hall at night to hear him breathe. The boys came from school drenched with sweat under their heavy coats; but she couldn't chance changing them. Dirk agreed. There were hundreds of pneumonia cases at the hospital, they hadn't beds enough, a cold snap was needed to kill off the germs; but when cold came, it brought loose, wet snow with it and more sickness. Dirk was sometimes very late, but he came, he came, and the look on Ellen's face!

It was all one could have asked. It equalized and validated the past so Julie could see the *why*—why she had married Leon and clung to him and lived through the difficult years, all so that Ellen could wander through these enchanted days with Dirk, and not just Ellen, either, one's own self shimmering with joy. "Mr. Kuyper, have you met my fiancé, Dr. Dirk Stodel?" The sound of her voice saying it, the importance of that word, *doctor*, the way she touched his arm, stroked the soft web of hair on the backs of his hands. There was going to be no lying rigid under the eaves at Aldgate, Julie could see that. She answered many a question for Ellen, and there was no fear in the girl, just eagerness, love, and desire, rising like a plume. As Julie told Leon, young girls were different these days, they knew so much and made no bones about it, he'd be surprised to hear what Ellen had talked over with Cissy Lindquist. Leon laughed. It wouldn't hurt Ellen to know more than her mother had, remember how he had rocked her to sleep beside the waving blue curtains? What a funny, untutored little wife!

The words brought them very close. The change that was coming for Ellen brought them all three close. On the last nights before the betrothal party, Dirk had late duty at the hospital; he was on constant duty with pneumonia spreading. Long after the boys and Aunt Anna had retired, they three would sit before the fire, Leon reading from the new Blue Label paper, Ellen on the floor with her head against him, as if she were a child again. It was a drawing together before the irrevocable—not that any of them was losing anything, but it was change as life had to change, adding a new quantity, shifting the balance and adding another roof; and although they'd have had it no other way, they instinctively united to cherish what they had.

You could see how deeply Leon loved Ellen, how carefully he explained about the coming strike so she might judge him correctly. Ellen heard the other side at the store. Men like Mr. St. Elmo and her superior, Mr. Bucaine, gave service to the views of Mr. Field and ate up the morning headlines that instilled terror. The city was being threatened by hostile forces, according to this view. Come the first of May an army of anarchists would seize the city; Mr. St. Elmo said that armed sections of savage men would march out of the halls near Haymarket Square, they'd be armed with hand grenades . . . they'd kill the police . . . and Mr. Bucaine said. . . . Leon's brow creased deeply. It wasn't strange that the newspapers should be opposed to the strike, it was going to cost their big advertisers money to put men to work for eight hours, it would mean employing more men, that was the whole point of the strike. But this talk of violence was a needless beating of drums. There'd been strikes before, and this one especially, with all unions cooperating, would be orderly. Written demands would be presented to each employer on Saturday, the first of May. It many cases, there would be no need to strike, or they might negotiate for nine hours or ten (not the Cigar Makers, they were standing pat). Mr. St. Elmo should have no worry. Ellen could tell him to come out of his house bravely and go to work as usual. Field's would not be over-thrown nor a whisker molested in his sideburns.

Ellen smiled, stitching away at her betrothal petticoat, and Julie added piece after piece to the basket of mending she did for the Bucaines. So the hours lingered for a night or two, then flew away to the party, the musical-comedy finale when the orchestra zooms out and the ensemble sways together, beautiful and gay and fraught with tenderness. You forgot for a moment there was any other world, forgot the tension mounting like an overcharged powder keg over the May first strike. Here again was the stanch Emma, the generous Lud-wig, everyone at his best as if love and family feeling were of just the temperature to bring out the truest colors. None of them would ever look as they looked that night—Ellen and Dirk with clasped hands, Elsa leaving a jingle of excitement wherever she went, and Emma with every line and pore melted out of her skin. As hero of the show, Mr. Munzell flirted outrageously, not just with his plump, bustled bride-to-be, but with his first love in her old velvet gown, with his future mother-in-law, even with Aunt Anna.

"Someone had better tell Lothario to mind his p's and q's. He'll make goo-goo eyes at the parlor maid next," grumbled Aunt Anna, but she danced when he asked her, held up her taffeta skirt spry as you please. After several turns, she panted and had work to catch her breath, but a sip of spiced wine fixed that and she was off again, this time with Leon who was more to her liking and had some swing to him. And how Leon looked! Handsomer than when he'd first come from Java and electrified them with his views on mankind. Life might not have been good *to* Leon, he'd worked hard and fought for what he believed, but it had been good *for* him, brought out the honesty and power of the man so that his children could be proud of him. It would be easier now, he'd have more time with the eight hours to do the other things he'd always wanted, be with the children, and with Ellen's children when she. . . . Ellen was a woman, in love!

"What goes on in that gypsy head of yours, darling?" He caught her around the waist and waltzed away. "Why so pensive?"

But she couldn't say. It was all so good and going so fast and she held tightly as they glided, tight to Leon to keep time from galloping away.

10

It was like a holiday, riding out to the Reaper works with Leon and Mr. Munzell. The Blue Island car was almost empty, almost their own hired vehicle, with thin sunlight falling over the straw-backed seats. It went at a rapid clip, skipping and flying at the rails, and the motorman clanked his bell smartly as if he knew Leon was an important man on his way to make a speech to the strikers. There was no weight to the trolley with its light load, just themselves and the two old men who sat across, one with a basket of groceries, the other leaning forward to rest his weight on his cane while he studied a spread-out newspaper. He had a big head, very red, with a misshapen nose and a cap that rested tight on top his furrowed skull. Pop, Leon called him. He had dropped his cane just as they entered, and Leon had bent to retrieve it in the lurching car. "Here's your cane, Pop."

"Are you nervous, Leon, about your speech?"

No, he laughed. No, he wasn't nervous.

The old men across were in high spirits. They muttered together and shook their heads. The one with groceries repeated snatches of what the other read aloud from the paper.

"My son's at the packinghouse. Armour's," Pop announced suddenly to the motorman's back. "Got his eight hours without a walkout." He had to say it loudly over the racket of the car.

"Machinists and carpenters, too," shouted back the motor-man. "No reason why not, if you stick together. We did all right last year. Didn't we? A bad time for strikes, they told us. But we won and the Mayor himself said it—nine out of ten were with us, even if they did have to learn to use their feet." He thumped the bell with his own foot, maintaining his balance like a sailor while the car rocked from side to side.

Mr. Munzell listened intently.

"I'm a cigar maker," Leon said. "We got ours Saturday, and not an hour lost."

The old men nodded and smiled as if they were proud of Leon. "It goes good," said the one with the groceries. "I'm glad to see it. I lost out last year at the Reaper works, never did get back. The damned, lousy strikebreakers got plenty of our jobs—beg your pardon, ma'am."

"We had rough times on the Black Road, let me tell you," remarked the motorman. "Wouldn't surprise me none to see more."

"Not now. We got past Saturday, it'll be peaceful," Leon said. "For all the newspapers crying, you saw, eighty thousand struck, half of 'em got what they asked for, there wasn't an excuse for the police to move in. That's the big thing—the quieter, the better."

"I note," said Mr. Munzell stiffly, "that Bradstreet's esti-mates a total of three hundred and forty thousand on strike across the nation. I must admit surprise at that. I thought Powderly's withdrawal would have destroyed anything like such participation."

Julie was amused at Mr. Munzell, finally entering the con-versation, as if he had been introduced. She wagered that Powderly's circular would cause the Knights of Labor plenty. The rank and file of the workers would see that trade unions were best. Leon thought so, too. When this strike was over, they'd really be able to build a national federation. Pop pounded on the floor with his cane, and both old men beamed.

It made one feel spirited and free—the sunlight, the good humor, and the way they went, careening through the country. That fateful May first had come and gone, thank God. It had stood so long on the kitchen calendar, an ominous red exclamation point, and in the end nothing had happened, at least nothing violent or ill. Chief of Police Ebersold had kept his forces on duty, but the strike had been peaceful and strong, "bloody May first" had merely seen strikers and their families promenading the city while moist spring air raced overhead like a benediction.

Yes, Mr. Munzell admitted, events had gone differently than he had expected. It amazed him to find such unanimity among the working class after the bitter controversies, something to bear in mind in the future, in England. Still, it was well to be on guard. Half the strikers had received their terms, but not the other half. Hadn't the planing-mill bosses and other adjuncts of the lumber industry met this morning and agreed on no concessions? Down near the Exchange, he'd heard that some three hundred vessels, loaded with lumber, were blocking the river. Building interests would not take this sitting down, if he might say so. Metal foundries and freight yards would be tied up, and that could mean serious trouble. A squad of police was on the docks with clubs ready to quell the slightest sign of disorder. That's what he'd heard.

And they'd be fooled, Leon said, there would be no disorder. Take this afternoon's meeting of the Lumber Shovers. They had asked for a speaker and the Eight Hour Association and decided on Spies; but hadn't the workers themselves protested that Spies talked too much like an anarchist and they wanted someone on the trade-union side as well? They weren't looking for trouble; that's why he had gotten the afternoon off to speak. The Lumber Shovers would be giving the bosses no chance for cracking skulls. Even Spies was not to talk in incendiary fashion, but to keep the men strong for their part in the strike. Munzell would see.

Yes, it was like a holiday. By the time they reached their destination, they were old friends with their fellow travelers.

274

"Make a fine speech now," the motorman said. "Make the boys stick to their guns. Like as not I'll be picking you up this evening to take you home."

Mr. Munzell and Leon stepped down. They each took an arm and lifted her high from the top step across the muddy gutter to the sidewalk. Air swept in from the dank river and scattered the coiled black smoke that rose from the funnels of a dozen boats. Hundreds of other craft, the lumber boats, lay jammed idly in the slips as far west as you could see. Off to the east the Reaper works spread like a city. A freight train came by, and they had to wait in the dirty path. Leon put his handkerchief over her nose so she wouldn't breathe cinders.

There was a mass of men in the distance. First it looked like hundreds, then like thousands. Leon strode along toward them holding her arm. Mr. Munzell was on her other side, so it was almost as if her feet didn't move, they carried her so fast. Mr. Munzell consulted his watch. Four o'clock on the head, he said. The sun had come out strongly.

Several men came to meet them. They were very serious but they joked with Leon. "You cigar makers," they said, "you lucky devils." August Spies hadn't arrived, so Leon should speak first, better anyhow, they said, since so many didn't hold with the anarchists. Spies would speak as a member of the Eight Hour Association, Leon reminded them. Then he handed Julie his overcoat and got up on the wagon where there were a couple of rickety chairs. The heads of the Lumber Shovers got up with him, and the men moved in tight. Mr. Munzell would have kept her toward the rear, but she wanted to be at the front to hear Leon. The men made way for them close beside the wagon, and they stood packed in, warmed and part of the crowd. At least six thousand, Mr. Munzell said approvingly, as if he wouldn't want Leon to speak to a man less.

Oh, and Leon was wonderful. He looked like a giant up there on the wagon. He stood, spread-legged, talking about the eight-hour movement, how weak and undirected their efforts had been when he came to America twenty-three years

275

ago, how now for the first time, working men of all trades had united for a joint objective. The men nodded and followed every word. There was no doubt they were going to have a hard fight in the lumber trades, he said, but there was no doubt that they would win. The bosses weren't going to sit forever and watch those loaded vessels jam the river. With building trades booming, they'd cut their own throats to call a lockout; he doubted that they could find enough skilled scabs to replace them. Someone yelled, "McCormick did!" Leon nodded. It was easier for one company boss to hold stubborn than when there was a big group of them trying to hold stubborn together. The individual construction men, the individual furniture men would crack. The Lumber Shovers must get a committee organized at once to meet with the owners and see what could be done by arbitration. This was the third day of the strike, they might have to compromise on the number of hours, settle for ten, but at least hold out for improvement. Spies had come now and was sitting on a chair behind Leon. He listened attentively, they all did, while Leon listed the objectives of this strike, which would make the union position strong for the first time, and beyond that, outlined possibilities of a federation that could override interunion squabbles. The men applauded. Leon looked down into their faces, talking simply, as if he knew them.

Then Spies got up. It was growing late now, the sun exploding into fire behind the Reaper works. For a minute you couldn't hear the speech for a shrill whistle that rose like steam from a splitting valve. Then Spies was talking again. Mr. Munzell had taken a firm grip of her arm. She looked up to smile at him, but his face was serious. Following his glance, she saw that edges of the crowd were fraying. Men were drifting toward the cinder path to jeer at homeward-bound workers coming from the Reaper works. These were men who had not gone out on strike and no wonder, many of them were strikebreakers who had taken these jobs a year ago. It was too far to hear what the strikers were saying, but she knew, she'd heard strikers and scabs go at it.

Suddenly, there was a great detachment of police. Probably they'd been stationed on the docks. They seemed to fill the road with their solid ranks; at once, she felt herself moving. There was a murmur, and the massed listeners began to move curiously, eager to see what would happen. Mr. Munzell couldn't resist them. He grabbed her arms firmly and tried to hold ground, but they moved slowly, then faster with the mass. And why not? She wanted to see what was going on herself. She held tightly to Leon's overcoat, she certainly didn't want to lose that. Spies still talked, but Leon leaped off the wagon. She saw him drop into the crowd not ten feet away. He couldn't reach her, of course. They moved rapidly, and if you were tall, you might see something. Envy Mr. Munzell, whose head was in the air while she was buried in cloth backs. "Well, well, our old friends the cops," one said. Another muttered, "Take it easy, give 'em no excuses." He was right, she hadn't forgotten New York or the way the squad had been quick to swing those clubs. You could get hurt the way Becke had; better to take it easy. And they did, moving slowly, steadily forward. They were on the cinders now. "Takin' care of the scabs," shrilled the man ahead, "takin' 'em home from school!"

Just then there was a frenzied yelling, you could see helmets gleaming close in the bronze sun. The next instant—a burst of gunfire. Out of nowhere! For nothing! Sharper than thunder the pistols cracked. You stood paralyzed, the whole' crowd tight in an agony of fright. Then they broke, they ran, demented, she too not knowing that she ran, until she was seized and jerked up and realized Leon had her. He went, bumping and lurching over the crazy field with her, he pitched forward, he fell, abruptly, hard and heavy on the ground. Mr. Munzell was yelling, yelling like a madman, and something left her. Leon left her. Munzell was dragging him away, and she crawled after them stupidly, not able to stand, dragging herself and some other rough, heavy weight—Leon's coat, Leon's coat. They were pulling him under the wagon, his legs dangled behind limp and boneless. It was blurred after that. They grasped her hands and hauled her over the brutal earth until she was under, too, kneeling on wet, sticky ground with the broken people.

"It's all right, Leon. It's all right," she kept saying. But she saw how he breathed, how the light left his skin. Screams and gasps all about them, Leon looking at her without a word. He breathed in the sickening stench of blood and tried to breathe it out. "Leon, Leon!" She was suddenly screaming, as if he were deaf. "Leon!" Without any sense to it, rocking in agony, still clutching his empty coat.

11

It was cold and wet for the funeral. Leon's friends stood like a regiment with their bared heads, but she didn't look at them, she didn't meet their eyes. They had tried to dissuade her from this hasty burial, but she wanted it over and done with. The longer the body stayed above ground, the more bitter the men would be. She knew. She'd seen what Spies had written in the paper: "*Revenge*. They killed six of your brothers. . . . To arms!" Much good that would do. Whip up violence and there'd be riots and slaughter, lose all the hard-won gains. Leon's body should have no part in it.

The clergyman talked on. Union benefits took care of him, and he was seeing to it they got their money's worth. She stood stubbornly to herself hearing the empty words, letting no one touch her or take her arm. Let them look to Aunt Anna, poor soul, sobbing like a weak baby. Let Lud and Emma and the girls have their tears. They had loved Leon, yes, but they thought him a fool throwing his life away, hadn't they always said? Well, he'd thrown it. And hers, too. They'd fallen together and let that be the end of it, the end of feeling, the end of a world. Let the rest of them go on living, you heard their wailing as through a wall.

The clergyman raised his voice to whine of the circle of birth and death like seasons. But Leon's was no season. He had been vital as a boy, full of strength and humor. If he had a breath left in him he'd put that minister to shame, milking every nasal note for cadence like a street vendor, like the old glass put'een man. "God's will," he intoned, "God's inscrutable will." She'd like to know what will God had had yesterday, the police shooting off their guns because, they said, they saw the crowd coming and were afraid. Afraid! They might have stopped, armed to the hilt as they were, to be certain they had something to be afraid of.

It was raining now. Rain sifted down, fouling the headstones. Her clammy cloth skirts hung like dead weight. She'd had enough, all of them out there paying homage to a lifeless thing, no better than refuse now with the man gone from it. She turned and walked stubbornly through the ooze, toward the buggy. Ollie and Dyke saw and would have helped her, but she didn't want them, she despised them for being alive and Leon might have been, too, if in the old days he hadn't gotten mixed up with Becke and Whitaker and the others. How cheap life was and how dirty, to work through the years as he had and what for? To get a bullet in his back! And how could she think that way? Betray Leon that way?

Ellen came running and slipping through the mud and tried to stop her. "Mother, Mother dearest," but Julie put her aside and walked alone. Ellen had her own young man, and lucky, he was in a profession, they could have a life without always a threat over it. That, too, was far away. The driver helped her up and she sat, every bone aching, the scuffed flesh of elbows and knees smarted raw against the black cloth. They'd dragged the skin off her, pulling her under the wagon. At least there was an outside pain to make up for the numb bitterness inside. But even the outside pain was dulled; it might belong to someone else.

"Julie, let us help you." Ludwig hoisted his great bulk and sat beside her while Pieter half-carried the weeping Emma. He put his arm on her shoulders, she could feel the great sobs that rose in him, but she sat stiff, not answering Ludwig, who had grown fat and comfortable while Leon worked and strove, for nothing. When they returned home, she marched up to her room and closed the door. No, she didn't wish to see the baby, he was well enough.

Her room and Leon's, the room where they had slept night after night through the many years, everything easy between them, everything forgiven. You could say that but you couldn't feel it. The strange sight of him on the ground without a word negated every living image. It was her room, her lonely room as barred from the rest as if she were in jail. No use in walking up and down, the carpet was thin enough. She opened closet and drawers and took out his things, the Sunday shoes scarred where he'd fallen, his nightshirt and drawers and the good shirts Ludwig had given him. These and the overcoat she rolled into a neat bundle and tied with twine. Her mouth curled bitterly over the overcoat. What a hero she had been, saving that. Well, the Stevenses could use it, their boys were grown now and none of them had anything. She went through his papers, the Eight Hour Association notes, endless, empty words, bundled them into a box, and wrote out a label. At the bottom of his bureau drawer lay an old envelope soft as cloth. It was addressed to Mr. Leon Dekker in a familiar hand—her own! The letter she had written from London to tell him she was pregnant and when should she come to America? The beginning of Ellen. She read the letter through as if it were a foreign script. How quickly life went, how the years blotted out and the hope and the promise and what did it matter? She sat on the bed weary to death, clogged and remote from sense as if she had a cold. Nothingness, to close your eyes and not see, not hear.

She awoke in the dark and in fright. She ran into the hall, shivering as if the stairs had creaked, as if someone were in the house. One sharp twist of light leaped blinding from the wall and almost stopped her. A picture glass magnifying a scrap of moon. Nothing. She lit a candle and went in to the

280

boys. Once she had wakened like this in the old life to find Henry with bronchitis, but he was huddled now with Steve, breathing quietly. Richard hung to himself like a lump on the edge of the bed. She tucked the covers to hold him. Strange, the children seemed strange to her, as if she hadn't seen them in a long time, as if she'd been away. Down the stairs to Aunt Anna, turning the knob carefully to make no noise.

"Julie Dekker, I declare, you don't give those feet a minute's rest. What are you snooping for?" She mumbled vacantly, the way she did without her teeth. "Yes, I'm just fine, and no, I don't think there's burglars. It'd take a real fool to break in here with pickings galore across the way."

She went upstairs slowly, not even recognizing the feel of the banister. And suddenly she heard it—a harsh, shallow breath, coming fast. Ellen! She knew, before she touched her, how dry and fevered the skin would be, such parched, withering heat, so soft and urgent and corrupting. This didn't look like Ellen, the gentle coloring flushed dark, the great blank glass eyes. Poor child, poor little bride, she'd stood out in that wet cemetery and gotten chilled. And if she had had any sense, she would have noticed, she would have thought how hot the cheek was that Ellen had put to hers on the way to the buggy. Some pain made Ellen's knees jerk up. Julie ran for quinine. She worked the spoon between the clenched teeth and gave her water, but the bitter taste gagged and retched the child and made her vomit. She whimpered piteously against Julie's arm, and said, very softly, a few words that made no sense.

"Henry, Henry." She had to shake that one. "You run across the street for Dirk, Henry. Tell him Ellen's running a high fever. He'll know what to do." She told Aunt Anna, who had heard the noise and come up. She moistened a cloth with alcohol and water and put it to Ellen's forehead, to take it away, the next moment, wilted hot. Fever heated the whole room, but why should it be frightening? The children had all had fevers at one time or another. She moistened a handkerchief and put it to Ellen's mouth, and the girl gazed out at her with eyes like two blue marbles. Aunt Anna brought extra quilts. When Ellen coughed, her face was distorted.

"Time it's taking Henry, you'd think he'd gone to China."

"Why don't you get a basin of fresh water, Aunt Anna? Dirk will be here in a minute." She said it calmly, as if she weren't raging inside at the whole great house of them sleeping and well while Ellen burned with fever.

"It's all right, Ellen. Dirk is coming. You hear Mother? Dirk will know what to do." *It's all right.* She had said that to him, and he had slipped away from life the next instant. She felt the fear start, but there was no time for fear. She went for toilet water, touched the bottle to her fingers, then to the sheet, then to Ellen's hair, and the girl understood. Her face moved sweetly under the damp handkerchief. The pulse beat out strong and fast. Julie counted it, about three beats to one of her own. She wrung out another alcohol cloth, covered the sewing table with white linen, put out a bowl of water so all would be ready for Dirk.

"Don't worry, Ellen. We'll have you well in no time." Then Aunt Anna came with another basin, mumbling in her fallen face, and that was not to be endured! "Let me get your teeth, for heaven's sake." She hurried off, found the teeth in their glass, picked up the old lady's shawl and brought that. "You'll want to fix your hair before Dirk comes," she said crisply. Aunt Anna glared. Maybe she should take a bath and polish her nails! Then she shoved her teeth in, clicked them to one side, and became Aunt Anna. Ellen almost smiled.

"You see, you're better already." But she was shaking. Let Dirk hurry, let him *know*.

He ran in, out of breath from the stairs, and took Ellen's wrist with his thumb and first finger, on his face the intent, listening look doctors have.

"Spent enough time getting here," Aunt Anna said.

Ellen coughed, buckled in bed, coughing and gasping and choking for air.

"Take her arm, Aunt Julie." Dirk took the other, and they

raised her gently. When it finally stopped, Dirk lay her back against the pillows, loosened her gown at the top, and brought out his stethoscope. It was hard to remember who he was, Doctor Dirk, holding the hard black pellet against her chest. To the right, to the left, over the breast, under, not noticing the rounded little hill with its pink tip. His chest still pounded from running. He listened a long while, moving the rubber pellet, hearing what? Then he buttoned her gown gently, the lover-doctor, moistened her mouth and slid in the thermometer, touching the lips with his fingers to close them.

"This will only take a few minutes, dear. It's mean to trouble you, but we want to know everything, don't we? Now where in your side does it hurt?" It took a long while for the temperature. His face never changed when he read it. He rinsed and dried the thermometer and brought out a small flask of brandy, raising Ellen so she could drink.

"Now, darling, I want to take you to the hospital, right away, don't you agree, Aunt Julie? I'll get Uncle Lud's carriage and we'll wrap you in blankets. We could wait until morning, but we're awake now, so why put it off? Don't you agree, darling?" That's what he said to Ellen. For Julie he had one other word. "Pneumonia," he said.

12

Sometimes it was day. Light filtered from the noisy ward into the small white tent where she and Ellen floated, just the two of them in air heavy with flannel and camphor. They needed no clock. The beat of time was the rasped breath. So immaculate the scene, so sharp, it etched on the mind like stamping on a coin—the narrow bed on its high crane legs; Ellen, her pink face in the pillows like some great drowsing doll; the small stand with its water bottle, its glass, and its bent tube.

There was a basin and a cloth, always damp, hanging to the rod on the side. There was a door in the front of the stand and inside, lost in the old-wood smell, their papier-mâché valise and all the small, useless things from home—the toothbrush they never used, the comb and brush, and a worn, dry bar of soap. There was the narrow chair Julie sat on and the unsteady canvas curtains separating them from the rest. Dirk was in and out, in and out, other doctors came in a phalanx to surround the bed, then they were alone again. When Ellen moaned, she rose, sponged the warm face, carried the glass and the tube, from which the child turned fretfully, not knowing what to make of it. After a while, Julie found that if she held her finger over the submerged tube, the water stayed; then if she carried it intact to Ellen's mouth and removed the finger, the water slipped in and was swallowed. Time after time until you knew just how much to hold in the glass straw. Occasionally, a nurse entered to give a salt enema or renew the ice in the poultice. It was never the same nurse, or perhaps you forgot. They were terribly busy, they told her, if she didn't mind, she'd find a bedpan under the cabinet, she could just slide it under the patient when needed. They showed her the bell pull that would summon them, but the bathroom was near and she carried it herself. If she didn't mind! This was her child, she'd nursed and bathed her and knew every inch of her flesh. Out in the ward patients groaned and coughed and vomited, but back in the tent, just she and Ellen, there was only the breathing.

Sometimes it was dusk. Powdery, soft, it flew through the white walls until the tent was dense with it. Ellen's coughing came in violent spasms. Julie braced the girl against her and held a cloth to catch the foaming, rusty phlegm. When she put her back on the pillow, Ellen was exhausted. Then there was the sweet face to bathe, the damp hair to smooth. Under the bedclothes she would find Ellen's hand and hold it.

"There, darling, isn't that better? You sleep and get your strength, they'll be bringing dinner." Or was it lunch? And when it did come, Ellen wasn't to be roused. Julie would catch up broth in the glass tube and slip it into her mouth, talking to keep her awake. Ellen didn't want to be skin and bone, did she? She had to keep her figure so they could start fitting that wedding gown. They didn't want Dirk shaking the sheets to find her. Ellen smiled at times and tried to swallow. Again, the broth would ooze from her lax-lips, and Julie would need to be quick to catch it.

Sometimes it was night. It was dark then. She sat close to the bed to feel any motion; when the coughing started, she would waken, startled, her head bursting from where it had come to rest against the mattress. The first night they had told her to go home. One of the white-dressed women came. Visitors were not permitted after eight. The sharp way her mouth fit, you knew it was after eight already. Julie brushed off her skirt. The child had high fever, she needed her lips moistened, and if she did wake, she'd be frightened alone, not knowing where she was. The nurse vanished. Julie warmed the bedpan with her own hands, slid it under Ellen's night-dress. "Come, dear, it's all right." Then she carried it to the bathroom, rinsed it, and came back. So did the superintend-ent. She understood Mrs. Dekker's concern—very professional and smooth she talked—but Mrs. Dekker needn't worry, her daughter would be well cared for, and Mrs. Dekker herself would be refreshed if she went home for a night's rest. Julie thanked her and sat up straight so as not to tremble. They were busy at the hospital, and she would not leave Ellen; she had had experience with pneumonia, with Debbie Stevens. That's what she said, to woman after woman. From then on, she had her way. Dirk approved. He came in toward morning each day so she could go home. He watched over Ellen for four hours. He was the only one in the world she would have left with her child. She went, haunted by the look, the sad, infinitely longing look Ellen had when she opened her eyes to gaze at her lover.

Out into the pale dirty morning, the street lamps still lit and ineffectual. Their yellow, fluttering hands were obscene against the rising day. Lud lent her the carriage, and she drove herself, standing straight up holding the reins, through the smoky streets. "Ellen's better," she'd tell them at home. "She doesn't moan the way she did."

"March into the kitchen, Julie, and drink some hot tea," Aunt Anna would say. "Unhook that dress. Let me press it for you."

"The temperature," Emma would ask, "that's gone down?"

But who ever heard of pneumonia running its course in less than a week? She answered them angrily, with pneumonia you *ran* a fever. She couldn't bear being home, in this house without Leon, couldn't bear Emma's tears or the children's grief or Mr. Munzell's solicitude. He expected her to collapse under the double disaster. Well, she wasn't going to. She hurried away, back where she belonged, to the hospital.

Ellen had small blisters about her mouth. Julie put salve to them, talking about the wedding. Uncle Lud was going to buy her parlor rugs from a shipment of Persians that had just come in. Ellen followed every word, her eyes never wavering. Once she spoke right out, clearly. "Mother . . . do you know . . . you're wonderful? Did . . . we . . . ever . . . tell . . . you?" There was an expression, a flash of love and radiance and trust that was like the real Ellen, but she fell into a stupor after that. Dirk sent for Dr. Billings and he came to listen to the hard, irregular pulse.

"You've a sick girl there, Mother. We've had hundreds just like this."

"That's no way to talk," she whispered, smiling toward Ellen in case she should open her eyes. "Ellen's a good strong girl. She'll be well in no time."

Dr. Billings touched her arm. "We're trying, Mother."

But Ellen was strong, the legs on her rolling her hoop along the beach at Coney Island, never a sore throat and working those hours at Field's with not a day off. She didn't ask Dirk what he thought. He loved Ellen, too, and there was only one way to think. She felt under the covers, found the hot small hand which closed on hers at once, confidingly. She held hard, giving Ellen her strength, letting it flow from hand to hand,

286

forcing her will on the relaxed flesh. Nothing could take Ellen from her! This was what she and Leon had done in life, and it was not to be lost.

She spoke to him, quietly, in the dark night tent. She forgave him for dying. He had died wrong, but that was not his fault, and he had lived right. It was continuity you wanted, and his was in the big movement of the workingmen. Hers was different; her continuity was in specific love. You couldn't blame a person for his way. Leon's was big, so be it; but her love was hard, it clove to this child unequivocally. Maybe for a day or two she had been bitter, maybe there had been hate and the thought that life was ended—she could only ask that Leon, wherever he was, understand and forgive that. Nothing was ever ended. They both lived again in Ellen. From far off came a rough, friendly string of sound, a cable car moaning and crawling up Van Buren, the life of the night letting her know. The metal rails leaped like cymbals, the car roared, screamed, lengthened away to a thin drone. They would ride that car someday, right past this hospital. They'd look up and find the window and recall how sick she had been.

"Why, you're awake, Ellen! Do you want water? Hear the cars, dear. Someday you and Dirk and I are going to take a ride, right past this hospital."

Ellen worked her parched little mouth. "Are I?" she said.

"Yes, you are." Oh, and much more than that. She was going to live to marry her doctor and have her children and go through all the worry and the sickness and the fuss. The thought kept Julie on her feet, morning, noon, and night. Everyone pitied her. The doctors, Dr. Billings himself, tried to make her stop. She was killing herself, he said. But she was strong and she knew—life had to come around full circle somehow. You couldn't lose, love couldn't always slip your heart. Someday there'd be another Ellen and all she, Julie, had ever been would walk with that one like a new beginning.

She would not give up. She did not.